Barefoot with a STRANGER

Barefoot Bay Undercover #2

roxanne st. claire

Barefoot with a Stranger

Copyright © 2015 South Street Publishing

This novel is a work of fiction. Any references to historical events, real people, or real locales are used fictitiously. Other names, characters, places, and incidents are the product of the author's imagination, and any resemblance to actual events or locales or persons, living or dead, is coincidental.

All rights to reproduction of this work are reserved. No part of this publication may be reproduced, stored in or introduced into a retrieval system, or transmitted, in any form, or by any means (electronic, mechanical, photocopying, recording, or otherwise) without prior written permission from the copyright owner. Thank you for respecting the copyright. For permission or information on foreign, audio, or other rights, contact the author, roxanne@roxannestclaire.com

COVER ART: The Killion Group, Inc.
DIGITAL FORMATTING: Author E.M.S.
Seashell graphic used with permission under Creative Commons CC0 public domain.

ISBN-13: 978-0-9908607-5-4

Published in the United States of America.

DISCARD

Critical Reviews of Roxanne St. Claire Novels

"St. Claire, as always, brings a scorching tear-up-the-sheets romance combined with a great story: dealing with real issues starring memorable characters in vivid scenes."

— *Romantic Times Magazine*

"Non-stop action, sweet and sexy romance, lively characters, and a celebration of family and forgiveness."

— *Publishers Weekly*

"Plenty of heat, humor, and heart!"

— *USA Today's Happy Ever After blog*

"It's safe to say I will try any novel with St. Claire's name on it."

— *www.smartbitchestrashybooks.com*

"The writing was perfectly on point as always and the pace of the story was flawless. But be forewarned that you will laugh, cry, and sigh with happiness. I sure did."

— *www.harlequinjunkies.com*

"The Barefoot Bay series is an all-around knockout, soul-satisfying read. Roxanne St. Claire writes with warmth and heart and the community she's built at Barefoot Bay is one I want to visit again and again."

— *Mariah Stewart, New York Times bestselling author*

"This book stayed with me long after I put it down."

— *All About Romance*

Dear Reader,

Welcome to Barefoot Bay Undercover...where love is in the air and suspense will heat up the sand. Like every book set in Barefoot Bay, this novel stands entirely alone, but why stop at just one? Kick off your shoes and fall in love in Barefoot Bay!

The Barefoot Bay Billionaires
Secrets on the Sand
Seduction on the Sand
Scandal on the Sand

The Barefoot Bay Brides
Barefoot in White
Barefoot in Lace
Barefoot in Pearls

Barefoot Bay Undercover
Barefoot Bound (prequel)
Barefoot with a Bodyguard
Barefoot with a Stranger
Barefoot with a Bad Boy (Gabe's book!)

Want to know the day the next Barefoot Bay book is released? Sign up for the newsletter! You'll get brief monthly e-mails about new releases and book sales.

http://www.roxannestclaire.com/newsletter.html

Acknowledgments

I received some special help on this fictional side trip to Cuba! *Muchas gracias* to Michel Mendez (and his beautiful wife, Eileen) who assisted me with first-hand knowledge of Cuba, including the geography and layout of Cairabién and the *municipal*. And huge writer-sister hugs to Maria Geraci, who patiently vetted every word of Spanish. (Read her books—they are fantastic!!)

As always, major props to the whole team of professionals who work with me on every book. In addition to my amazing editor, Kristi Yanta, I'm corrected by a brilliant copyeditor, Joyce Lamb; dressed by a talented cover artist, Kim Killion; perfected by a detail-oriented formatter, Amy Atwell; and supported by a tireless assistant, Maria Connor. And, of course, I'm loved by a street team beyond compare. (Join the Rocki Roadies on Facebook if you enjoy my books! We have a blast and they get secret scenes and book info!)

Lastly, love and gratitude to my family, most especially my dear husband, Rich, who helps with the details on cooking and airplanes and guns because he's my personal Renaissance Man.

Barefoot with a STRANGER

roxanne st. claire

Dedication

This one is for Kristi Yanta, the Picky Editor without equal,
whose delicate touch magically transforms my lifeless
first draft into living, breathing color.

I would crumble and cry (even more)
over every book without her.

Chapter One

Chessie squinted at the departures screen and adjusted her glasses, certain she had to be reading the numbers wrong. Her connection was delayed for *three* hours?

Sheesh. This was not in Francesca Rossi's carefully laid-out plan for tonight.

She turned away, spinning through her options like they were hypothetical computer bugs she needed to identify and eliminate. But this was not a tech issue she could solve with a few smart keystrokes. This was Atlanta Hartsfield Airport, full of grumbling travelers trapped by the stormy night skies and widespread delays for many flights, not just her commuter hop to southwest Florida where her brother waited.

The jammed gate area practically vibrated with frustration and inconvenience. Behind her, the concourse bustled with impatient people rolling their bags, and the airport restaurant teemed with captive customers. Leaning against a sliver of space on the wall, Chessie pulled out her phone and texted her brother Gabe to deliver news she knew would elicit enough cursing to stroke out a nun.

Gabe had been breathing fire down her neck for weeks,

desperate to get Chessie to Barefoot Bay to help accomplish what he called "the plan."

The plan. Chessie loved a plan as much—probably more—than the next person and appreciated a clever and succinct title to sit on top of a well-ordered list. But this plan?

There were no fancy covert names, like *Operation BabyLift* or *Mission: Munchkin* for this project. Locating a child that could be Gabe's son was too serious and too major for cutesy code words.

Weeks earlier, Gabe had flown Chessie down to Florida and enlisted her help in hacking an encrypted website to search for a woman supposedly living in Cuba. She didn't know who Isadora Winter was or why Gabe wanted to find her, but when Chessie discovered the woman was dead, Gabe's response told Chessie plenty. Isadora *mattered* to him. A lot. So Chessie had dug deeper into the layers of code to discover that Isadora had a child…named Gabriel.

And that news had stunned them both.

Her phone buzzed with Gabe's reply. *WTF? Get your ass on another flight!*

She looked at the board again, which flashed with even more cancellations. She *still* didn't know why she couldn't do her computer research from Boston, where she worked as a tech specialist for the Guardian Angelinos, their family's security firm. But Gabe had insisted she return to the Gulf Coast island where he was running his own security-type of business, and he also insisted she tell no one about the child or their plans to find him.

That last bit wasn't a surprise. Like the rest of her siblings and cousins, ex-spook Gabe was always up to something adventurous and dangerous and secretive, saving lives and taking names.

But not Chessie. The youngest in a long line of bodyguards, investigators, cops, agents, and spies, she was convinced that the Rossi and Angelino gene pool must have run out of the Badass DNA by the time she emerged. She was happiest in front of a computer monitor. Her idea of a brush with danger was refuctoring a line of code to make it irreversible. And maybe, when she felt wild, kicking her Mustang into fourth gear and doing doughnuts in an empty parking lot.

Her phone flashed with another text from her brother.

Fly to Orlando or Tampa, rent a car and drive. Or rent one in Atlanta and drive all night. You can be here in time for Nino's peppers and eggs.

There weren't going to be flights to Orlando or Tampa, and while the idea of her grandfather's signature breakfast sounded heavenly, Gabe was smoking something if he thought she was going to drive eight or nine hours at night in this weather.

Not in the plan, bro.

She texted back a sisterly "shut your pie hole" and peered over the gate crowd again, catching sight of a woman getting up to free a seat near the back. Shouldering the oversized handbag that carried her laptop and grateful she'd checked her suitcase, Chessie headed straight to the vacancy. She was two feet away when a middle-age man with a shiny dome and mustache beat her, practically throwing his backside into the chair to make sure he got it before she did.

Chessie slammed on her brakes with a soft grunt, a little taken aback at his audacity. The man whipped out an iPad and ignored her, leaving Chessie feeling awkward as a few people stared at her. She glanced around on the off chance there was another open seat.

Not happening. Her gaze landed on the man in the chair

directly across from the one she'd almost snagged, meeting dark eyes that glinted with a mix of dismay and humor. Instantly, he stood.

"Here, take mine."

"Oh, no, I…" Damn, he was big. Not just tall, but solid and broad. "That's not necessary."

"I insist."

She started to reply but got a little lost while looking at his face, which was pretty much a straight-up dime. A rugged blend of chiseled and rough, a strong nose, soft lips, and a shadow of whiskers that didn't quite hide a cleft in his chin that was downright *lickable*.

She shook her head. "I…I…can't." Can't think or talk, apparently.

Slowly becoming aware of her surroundings again, she realized most everyone in earshot observed the exchange—but not the tacky seat-thief.

"Please. It would be rude of me to let you stand there." He put the slightest emphasis on *rude*, more of a deep rumble from that impressive chest, and a few onlookers shifted their attention to the *truly* rude guy. Who didn't look up from a riveting game of Words With Friends.

"Nope, you had it first." Chessie smiled up at him. "Giving your seat away would be a breach of airport protocol."

"What about gentleman's protocol?"

Oh, a gentleman. A big, hot, sexy, *lickable* gentleman. "You would set dangerous precedent," she agreed. "Every man in this place would have to get up and let the ladies sit."

"It could start a riot." He added a smile that was purely unfair.

"But you'd be a national hero."

The smile faded, and he shrugged a little, as if hero status held no appeal for him. Well, he certainly held appeal for her.

Easy, girl. You're nursing a heartbreak, remember? But one look at thick black hair that curled over his collar and framed chiseled features and a slash of black brows…and she pretty much forgot good ol' Matt Whatshisname.

The seat-stealer cleared his throat without looking up from his iPad. "Do us all a favor and go flirt with each other in the bar."

The man standing in front of her flinched ever so slightly, his eyes flicking to the right but not actually shooting the chair hog a proper dirty look. Instead, he gave Chessie a slow, conspiratorial grin that took him straight to an eleven. And a half.

For one, two, maybe the span of three insane heartbeats, they looked at each other, and at least one X in every female chromosome in her body climbed out of their breakup funk to momentarily consider what else was out there.

He openly checked her out for a few seconds, his gaze practically feasting on her face, then the faintest shrug gave her the impression he'd lost some kind of inner battle.

He nodded toward the concourse. "Can I buy you a drink?"

Chessie opened her mouth to say no. She hadn't planned on a drink. But she hadn't planned on a three-hour delay between Boston and Barefoot Bay, either. Gabe hadn't said she couldn't talk to anyone, just not share why she was on her way to Florida.

For once, she should go with the flow because this particular flow was so fine. "Sure, thanks."

The man leaned over to grab a duffel bag, then turned and got in the seat-stealer's face. "I owe you one, dickhead," he whispered.

As they walked away, a woman watching the whole exchange gave a loud, slow clap, and a few others joined her.

Well, what do you know? A drink with a smokin' hot stranger. That was an interesting change in plan.

Mal knew they'd be watching him from the minute he walked out of Allenwood Federal Correctional Institution and started his journey. But he honestly didn't think they'd be so damn obvious about it, throwing a tag team at him, using the tired cliché of a sexy woman being mistreated by a smartass stranger.

They must truly believe he didn't know how to spot or shake a tail. Maybe they'd forgotten who he really was. Maybe they figured four years on the wrong side of a cell door had destroyed his finely trained skills along with his spirit. Maybe they were all a pack of idiots with no imagination.

For his part, Mal had taken and dumped two different cars, then boarded a train, followed by a Greyhound to Atlanta, and now he just wanted to fly to his final destination, for God's sake. But he mustn't have been clever or deceptive enough, because the babe and her buddy nailed him like a wanted poster on a tree.

Mal hung back as the hostess led them to a table, taking the opportunity to check out the woman they'd sent to soften him up.

Well, nothing about him would be soft around this woman, and they'd know that. She had that thick, inky black hair he'd always liked, though sloppily braided and hanging down to the middle of her back. It wasn't her hair that got his attention, though. Or her ass, though it was perfection, round and high and youthful in faded jeans. It swayed side to side, powered by boots with just enough heel to tap a drumbeat on his stretched-to-the-limits libido.

All very nice. But it was her smile that drew him closer, and proved the CIA knew him all too well. Somewhere in a file in Langley, it probably said "sucker for a smile that lights up a face." And hers looked like someone had struck a match in her heart.

So he followed and played their game. Because he wanted to know how far they'd go. And he wanted to look at that smile. Shit, he wanted to eat it.

When they sat down, she ordered an Amstel Light but said no to a frosty mug. Beer from the bottle. Okay, that was hot.

Of course, he was a man six days out of federal prison, and she was the first female he'd talked to in three and a half years who wasn't washing his clothes or shoveling chow onto a plate. So she could have ordered piss in a bucket and he'd have probably sprung a boner.

"Thanks for the rescue," she said after the waitress left, crossing her arms to settle her elbows on the table and lean in enough to treat him to a glimpse of skin thanks to the open top button of an expensive-looking sweater. "I think we shamed him effectively."

Yeah, sweet thing. Like you two didn't plan that since you followed my ass to the gate.

"He should be ashamed," Mal agreed. And so should Mal if he let a little cleavage make him forget how *not* unplanned this meeting was.

He'd noticed this woman on the tram, then spotted her again in a bookstore. Hartsfield was a big airport, and a double sighting of anyone was unusual, but when she just missed the empty seat five feet from his face and looked right at him for help? They might as well have put it on the loudspeaker.

Attention, Malcolm Harris. You are currently under surveillance.

And now he was going to let her believe he was duped by her ruse and awestruck by her baby blues, which got even babier and bluer when she pushed her black-rimmed glasses to rest on top of her head.

Which meant she didn't need them and they were just part of her disguise. Amateurs.

Mal inched just a little bit closer to inspect all the pretty she was showing him. And to be sure her mic could pick up whatever he was saying, so his half-truths would have all her colleagues scratching their heads instead of their balls.

"What's your name?" he asked.

She actually took a little breath before answering, as if she had to think about it. Field rookie, no doubt. "Chessie."

"Jessie?" *C'mon, girl, get your fake name right.*

She shook her head. "No, Chessie. Short for Francesca."

Wasn't like spooks to use unusual names. "You don't look like a Francesca."

"No kidding." And there was that smile again, showing perfect teeth and softening her features. "That's my mother. *Frann-ie.*" She said it in a nasal, whiny voice and rolled her eyes. "And you?"

Why lie? She knew damn well what his name was, along with his Social, his former agency rank, his famous fall from grace, and his stellar prison record. Shit, his whole miserable childhood was probably downloaded on her phone and filed under E for Embezzler.

"I'm Mal." He added a sly smile and extended his hand over the table. "Pleasure to meet you, Francesca."

She slid silken and slender fingers into his grip, and her mouth quirked with a tease. "I think we're even in the weird-name department. Mal?"

As if she didn't know. "Malcolm," he explained. "Not so weird."

"Traveling on business?" she asked, letting go of his hand after an extra second of contact.

Oh yeah, let's get right down to what the hell their man was doing crisscrossing the country and headed south. *Headed to the Caymans, by any chance? Tapping into an offshore account?*

"More or less," he replied. "You?"

"Um…I'm going to see my brother down in Florida."

Someone at Langley needed to teach the rookies to lie without hesitation. But he just nodded as the waitress arrived and placed two beers on paper cocktail napkins, and rushed to get the next order.

Chessie lifted her bottle. "To chivalry. Long may it live in the heart of a perfect stranger."

He tapped her amber bottle with his bright green Heineken. "I'm not perfect." *As you well know.*

She locked on him a few seconds too long over the bottle. "Pretty close," she whispered, and damn it, his body instantly betrayed his head with a low, deep, primal stir. No surprise there. He hadn't gotten laid in so long, his balls had formed their own picket line to protest.

He took a long pull on the beer, still snagged by her mesmerizing crystal blue rimmed in navy eyes, knowing he had a challenge in his own gaze. Part of him wanted her to know he was not ignorant of her ploy, and part of him—the protesting-balls part—wanted to see just how far she'd go with this honey trap of an operation.

"You're staring," she observed with a pointed look.

"You're gorgeous." And that was no lie. With the little bit of beer moisture clinging to lips darkened by now-faded lipstick, her mouth was luscious. When she looked down, long lashes lay dark and thick against creamy skin. She brushed an escaped lock of ebony hair off her cheek, just the right blend of self-conscious and flirtatious.

Man, those pricks had pulled out all the stops today.

"Thanks." She glanced up, all wide-eyed and womanly. "I haven't felt very gorgeous lately."

And now we get the made-up sob story meant to get him to open up and share. He'd stood guard in prison cells when lesser men than he were brought to their knees and made to vomit state secrets. And his training certainly taught him just how effectively the right woman could pull tales, and the truth, from loose lips.

But he could play, right? Watch this sassy doll work for her paycheck, at least.

"You haven't felt gorgeous?" He snorted softly. "Are all the mirrors broken in…where are you from?"

"New England," she said, sounding obviously vague. Maybe they hadn't worked out her cover that thoroughly.

Time to needle her a little. Time to let her know he wasn't as dumb as they thought. "Something you're not telling me, Chessie?"

A slow burn started down by the pretty cleavage, the blush working its way up to the hollows of her sculpted cheeks. Maybe it was her obvious embarrassment at being so transparent, or maybe four years in prison hadn't turned him into enough of a dick, because that little flush caused an unexpected twist of pity in his gut. Poor kid would be on the receiving end of a shit storm if they thought she wasn't ready for field work.

She picked up her beer and worked hard for nonchalance. "Why would you ask that?"

He reached for her left hand and thought of a way to save her from herself. "Because I don't flirt with married women, so if you're hiding a husband, let me know."

Her ring finger was bare—he'd already noted that—but she gave his hand a squeeze. "Not married," she assured him. "And so nice to meet a solid citizen."

He almost snorted at the irony. "Define solid," he said, shifting his gaze away but still holding her hand because it felt so damn good to touch the smooth palm of a pretty girl, even if she worked for the enemy.

"'Solid' is a guy who offered his seat, bought me a drink, and doesn't flirt with married women." Slipping out of his touch, she searched his face, no doubt comparing the real thing to the pictures in her file. He hadn't shaved in a week and had let his hair grow since he'd known he'd be getting out of Allenwood, but surely they knew that.

"So, what about you?" she asked, her voice just the right amount of tentative and hopeful. "Are you…unattached?"

"I'm a free man," he said, for the benefit of any bastards listening who would like to change that status. He might be out of prison and not even on house arrest, like he thought he'd be, but he'd never be *free*. Never. He'd be hunted and watched and followed and pestered until they got what they thought he was hiding. And if they couldn't, then they'd be happy to dream up a way to put his ass back in the slammer, just for spite.

They stared at each other for a few seconds, and this time neither looked away. "And you're from Texas," she said. At his raised eyebrows, she laughed. "Very subtle, but I hear…Houston?"

You should know, honey. "Dallas. And San Antonio. And…" Where the hell had he lived after that? Some trailer park in some dump. "Yeah, around Texas."

"What do you do?"

Time. He did lots and lots of time for crime. He stalled with a long, slow sip of beer. "I'm between jobs now."

"Ahh." She gave a knowing nod.

"What about you?" he asked.

"I'm in, uh, well, I guess the best way to describe it is computer research."

He almost laughed out loud. Is that what the kids were calling spy work today? "You must be smart," he said, adding a smile for the sheer pleasure of getting one back.

"Well, I work for my family, so I get away with a lot."

Family. How sweet. He gulped some beer.

"Are you looking for work in Florida?" she asked.

This was getting tiresome. Not looking at this lovely woman—he actually could do that for hours. But the volley of lies was wearing him down. He wasn't going to lose her now, that much was certain. She'd end up next to him on the flight, then follow him after they landed. He'd be wearing her.

Which didn't exactly suck. Because if she wasn't one of them, this wouldn't end here. Not a chance. And that wasn't just his poor, lonely, unloved, semi-hard-twenty-three-hours-a-day dick talking. That was just him, starved for an easy smile, a quick wit, and that sweet something in her eyes that made him think of…hope.

He shifted in his seat, mentally repacking the ice that had slipped from his heart. Well, *hell.* Maybe he'd underestimated this woman's talent in the field.

He leaned much closer and ran a light finger over her knuckles, daring himself not to react to the feel of her. He lost that dare. "I'm boring, Francesca. Let's talk about you."

She let her gaze drop to where he touched her hand. "No one calls me Francesca."

'Cause it's not your name. And he couldn't forget that. "It suits you. It's a graceful name, with depth and class. It's sexy."

She frowned as if she wasn't buying it. "It's old school and sounds like I should be kneading pizza dough in an apron."

"You'd look hot in an apron." And nothing else.

She pointed to him, giving a throaty laugh. "You're good, you know that?"

And so was she. Because, damn, this was some real electricity, and if he wasn't careful, he'd be fried. He leaned back and assessed her, wondering what they gave her as a backstory. "So who was this bonehead who made you feel like you weren't pretty? I might have to make him eat my fist."

"Wow. You really do take this knight-in-shining-armor thing seriously. His name was Matt."

"Like in 'door'?"

She gave a genuine laugh, tilting her head back with gusto. "Exactly. He was my boyfriend for the past year. And two months. And ten days." She gave a self-deprecating eye roll. "Oh, I'm pathetic, right?"

He scanned her face for a tell, but couldn't find one. No color rising, no averted glance, and her hand was utterly still under his. Okay, he'd jumped the gun assuming she was a rookie.

"He's the one who's pathetic," he said, dying to hear the tale she'd spin. There might even be some truth in it, as he recalled from his training. "What happened?"

She took a drink and squinted back across the concourse

at their gate, then lowered her glasses back to her nose as if they weren't a disguise at all and she really was nearsighted. "Oh crap. We have trouble."

He followed her gaze, wondering if her buddy had blown their cover. But as he watched the flock of people milling about and caught a glimpse of the departure board, he knew exactly what trouble they had.

"The flight's canceled," she said, standing up. "Son of a…"

He threw money on the table and grabbed his bag, following her out to the gate. "Come on, let's go see what the deal is."

Except he knew the deal. They'd canceled the flight to give this woman time to worm her way into his head. Yes, damn it, they had that much power.

"There are no more flights tonight," a man informed them, sounding disgusted as he walked by.

"I have to find an airport hotel," another woman said into her phone. "I am not sleeping in the terminal."

Chessie looked up at him, her eyes wide, as if this news actually surprised her.

He put his hand on her shoulder. "A hotel might be a good idea, Francesca."

He felt her shudder under his touch. A shudder that felt damn real, and damn…interested.

Just how far would this talented little spy take her mission tonight?

Chapter Two

There was a low-grade panic humming through the tight squeeze of humanity packed into the Marriott hotel's airport shuttle. Or maybe that was just Chessie's fried nerve endings vibrating with a bad case of *now what?*

As if she didn't know *what.*

The other dozen or so stranded travelers were griping about inconvenience, worried about room availability, questioning where they'd get a toothbrush or clean underwear. Chessie, with nothing but a handbag, laptop, wallet, cell phone, and an e-reader, was in the same boat.

But she could handle the possibility of wearing the same clothes for twenty-four hours. Her tension was caused by a whole different unexpected problem—namely, taking *off* those clothes with a perfect stranger.

Damn near perfect, and getting to be less of a stranger with each passing minute. Right this second, he was the intense, sexy, attentive, and *oh so* ridiculously hot guy who made her laugh and whose muscles tensed against her every time the van hit a bump.

By unspoken agreement, they'd stuck close to each other in the airport, getting information on possible solutions, the shared travel glitch intensifying, and justifying, the connection. They'd finally walked with a small group of weary travelers to the transportation area and stayed close while waiting for the shuttle to an airport hotel reported to have vacancies.

He hadn't texted or called anyone, she noticed, and he didn't seem overly put out by the delay. She'd sent a text to Gabe that she'd be on the first flight to Fort Myers, leaving at ten thirty a.m., and then she did the unthinkable and shut off her phone.

Just that little act of defiance sent a shiver of anticipation through her, a little frisson of tension that made her feel like *anything* could happen. Anything and everything.

She glanced up at the man on her right and caught him eyeing her as well. Silent in their secret companionship with only the background sounds of unhappy phone calls and explanations still going on inside the overly warm van, it was like they were magnetically pulled to each other.

"You need anything to make it through the night?" he asked.

Um...sex. Lots of it. "I'll buy a toothbrush and can sleep in my clothes." Or naked. She swallowed, her throat dry.

"You can borrow a T-shirt, if you want."

His voice, with just enough of a timbre of implication, rolled over her, warming her so much that she turned to the rain-streaked windows, tempted to press her cheek against the cool glass. Instead, she let the blur of the Atlanta airport pass by.

Chessie had never had a one-night stand, didn't do the hookup thing that was considered the norm among many thirty-year-olds. The whole idea was just too damn spontaneous for a planner like her. But this situation was different. Weird. Electrified. Off anything that resembled a plan.

Screw a plan.

No, no. She fought a secret smile and a tingling in her lower half. A plan was not what she wanted to screw tonight.

"Here we are," Mal said, shifting slightly in his seat, making her unable to think about anything except how his leg felt pressed against her. It was hard, thick, and strong. She'd never really thought about a man's leg before. She was a shoulder and biceps kind of girl. But his leg…

Lust had clearly fried her motherboard.

He met her look with the slightest hint of amusement in his dark eyes. Like he knew something about her that even she didn't know. That was part of his appeal, she noticed. Always a very subtle, tacit hint that he knew what she was thinking.

And she was thinking about legs. And…other parts.

She let out a sigh as the van pulled under the hotel overhang, the lights of the lobby looking warm and inviting on the cool, December night.

"You okay?" Mal asked, leaning close to her ear so his breath fluttered some of her hair and launched a landslide of goose bumps.

"Yeah, sure. I mean…" She wet her lips and looked up at him. "Are you?"

They were dancing around the obvious. *Are we doing this or not?*

He broke into a slow grin that made her stomach feel like a butterfly garden during a windstorm. "Define okay, Francesca."

And did he have to say her much-hated name in a way that sounded like a warm breeze over flower petals? She wanted him to say it again and again, in her ear, against her mouth, as he got on top of her and—

"Out to the right, please," the driver barked as he stopped the van and silenced her thoughts.

Blood thrummed in her head as she waited her turn to climb out from the corner at the way back, but Mal was on her right, so he had to go first, giving her a bird's-eye view of his ass in jeans.

A gorgeous ass. A strong ass. An ass custom-made for a woman's first one-night stand. She couldn't wait to get a handful of that ass.

And why the hell shouldn't she? No one even knew where she was, not a brother, cousin, or overprotective grandfather to put the brakes on this hairpin turn the night was about to take.

He stood on the sidewalk, giving her a hand as she hopped out of the van. And then he kept holding it as they walked into the lobby. His palm was rough and masculine, his fingers strong and protective.

Her heart flipped around helplessly, like that of a teenage girl about to get felt up for the first time. The whole thing was so sexy and illicit, so blissfully impromptu.

The registration line was long, and they ended up separated for a bit while they each checked in. Yes, it was nice not to be forced into an awkward discussion over sharing a room in front of the hotel staff, but the brief separation also left her uncertain if hot sex with a stranger was in her immediate future.

With her key in hand, she met him across the lobby, where he stood holding his own key and his brown duffel bag. Oh shit, moment of truth. Didn't these things usually happen after too much booze? At least enough to fend off some kind of anxiety attack in which she would blab on about how she'd never done this before?

But he just stared at her, a challenge in his eyes. No smile, now, but the corner of his mouth turned up with an unspoken question.

"I, um, need to go in here," she said, hating the bout of nerves that clutched her. She turned to the tiny convenience store, already full of several of their vanmates. "To get…stuff."

"All right." He didn't move, but didn't offer to wait, clearly leaving the next step up to her. That was another thing she liked; he wasn't aggressive. He was letting her call the shots, but all along, there was that secret suggestion that he was the one in control.

It made her dizzy.

She headed into the little store, rounding a rack of books to get to the toiletries in the back. She picked up a toothbrush, travel-size toothpaste, and skimmed the rest of the items, imagining what she'd need for one night.

Trojans.

She stared at the box.

"Francesca." A hand landed on her shoulder, making her startle and turn to see an unexpected fierceness in his narrowed eyes. "You can call this thing quits any time you want."

This thing? Quits? Her heart dipped. "What if I don't want to…call it quits?"

He didn't move his hand or make any effort to step away. Instead, he studied her face to the point of uncomfortable scrutiny. "I mean you don't have to."

She gave an awkward laugh. "I know I don't have to. I…want to. I mean, not if you don't, but I like you, and I'm…" She closed her eyes and let out a ragged sigh. "You're not making this whole seduction thing very easy."

His eyes flashed for a second, and he inched back, almost as if this news surprised him. He didn't know where this was headed.

"Francesca." He added some pressure to her shoulders. "You're not who I think you are…are you?"

What the hell? Who did he think she was? An easy lay, of course. She'd practically thrown her panties at him. She wasn't, normally. But nothing was normal about tonight. "Is that some kind of trick question?"

He stared so hard it felt as if he were trying to see right through her. And from the look on his face, he did. At least, his expression changed in some immeasurable way. That challenge disappeared from his eyes, and he almost looked…like he was seeing her for the first time.

"I thought…" Her voice caught. "I misread you…this." She shook her head and tried to step away. "Sorry."

"No, no. I'm the one who misread you." Very slowly, he skimmed his hand down the length of her arm, burning every centimeter he touched with promise.

She didn't answer—*couldn't* trust her shaky voice—but held his gaze, his face so close she could kiss him by moving one, maybe two, inches closer. And, good God, she wanted to.

She took a slow breath and closed her eyes, steadying herself. Before she opened them, he brushed her lips with the softest kiss. "I'm in 318," he whispered before slipping away, disappearing into the lobby, and rounding the corner to the elevators.

She stood there for a good thirty seconds, trying to find her balance. There was nothing balanced about this, but…

She bought the condoms.

Holy shit, he was off his game. A *spy*? She was no more

a spy than his grandmother. How could he have been so wrong?

She couldn't fake that reaction to his question. Her eyes were pure and honest, and she wasn't trailing him or trying to get information. She was a damned beautiful computer tech traveling to Florida, stuck in a hotel on a rainy night…as hungry for the pure release of sex as he was.

What a fucking idiot you are, Mal Harris.

He stood over the sink, his hands under cold water, trying to wash away the frustration. He *wanted* her. Sure, it had been a long time since he'd been with a woman, but it was more than that. He liked her.

And, damn it, she wanted him, based on every physical response he'd been trained to read in a woman. Hell, it didn't take CIA schooling to see the way her eyes devoured him or hear the quick intake of breath when they not-so-accidentally touched.

He bent over and splashed his face. All that time he spent analyzing her and surmising her motives when he should have been—

A soft knock on the door made him stand up straight.

He smiled like he had the day they unlocked his cell. Hell yeah. Second chance.

He looked through the peephole, catching her looking from side to side. Before, he would have assumed she was looking for her partner, or even sending a signal. She self-consciously touched the button of her sweater, which paranoid Mal would have thought meant she was adjusting a mic.

And he'd have been wrong.

His hand trembled just a little as he fumbled with the lock, a sign of just how badly he wanted this woman.

He took a slow breath and opened the door, letting her speak first.

Uncertainty played at the edges of her features as she held up two bottles of beer. "We didn't get to finish our drink."

He took one and let her in and closed the door, snapping the security bar.

She took a few steps into the room and put her beer, handbag, and a plastic bag on the desk.

"You seem—"

"I don't usually—"

They talked right over each other, and she gave a self-conscious laugh. "You first."

"You don't usually what?" he asked.

She crossed her arms and leaned against the dresser. "It doesn't matter. I'm here."

He took a few steps closer, noticing the slightest quiver in her chin and a wariness behind her glasses. How could he have missed that?

"Yes, you are." He slipped off the specs and set them on the dresser, not surprised to confirm she was nearsighted, not *fake*-sighted. "And you want a T-shirt."

"Or something to sleep in." She took a slow, uneven breath, staring up at him as he placed his hands on her cheeks and jaw, easily feeling the thump of her pulse.

"Sleep with me," he whispered. "And don't wear anything."

She angled her head, biting her lower lip as she studied him. "I'm not, you know, the most experienced traveler in this airport hotel, but I'm pretty sure that's why I came here."

That made him smile. Okay, so the only thing she was a rookie at might be casual sex. Good thing for her, he wasn't feeling *casual* at all.

"You have no idea how glad I am that you did." He slid

his hands down her throat, and that pulse jacked up even more. She breathed again, her chest rising and falling, her lips parted, her pupils wide with arousal.

"Did you think I wouldn't?"

He stroked her jaw and lower lip, reveling in their smoothness, and the absolute rare moment of trusting someone. Someone beautiful and sexy and willing to take his pain away tonight.

"I think that from the moment I met you, I wasn't thinking straight, Francesca."

She leaned into him, offering her full body. "I love the way you say my name."

He lowered his head and almost kissed her, wanting to delay the gratification of the first taste, wanting to make every move of this dance last as long as possible. But she wanted no part of waiting, closing the space like she demanded to be kissed, molding into him, wrapping her arms around him, taking ownership like…like, well, no rookie.

"Francesca," he murmured against her mouth.

"The apron-wearing pizza maker."

He laughed and slid his hands to the first button of a thin sweater. "Let's get you out of that apron."

She answered with a soft mew from her throat, lifting her chin to give him access to the source of the sound, a sweet, soft column of skin that tasted like pure heaven.

She spread her hands over the back of his head, guiding his kisses where she wanted them. He got stuck on the second button, distracted by the sight of more cleavage, so he spread his hands over her breasts. Budded nipples popped against the thin sweater material. He caressed and thumbed them, eliciting another moan and a slight rock of her hips into his erection. The below-the-belt contact shot fire through him, the ache squeezing need from his balls to his brain.

It had been so long...and she was perfect. Absolutely *perfect*.

"Let me help you." She unbuttoned the flimsy sweater with slow hands, as sexy as any striptease he'd ever seen. His mouth went bone dry, and his hands itched to touch *everything*.

She let the black material fall open to reveal a lacy bra in the same color, looking up at him with nothing but raw and genuine desire. How the hell could he have ever doubted her?

He closed his eyes and shut out the question with another kiss, reckless and hungry, opening his mouth, meeting her tongue, and thoroughly palming one tender breast. He nearly cried at how good she felt, so warm and feminine and round.

She groaned and bowed her back, all permission and agreement and compliance.

He tossed the sweater somewhere behind him, turning her to walk her backward toward the bed. She paused long enough to grab the small plastic bag from the desk.

She plucked out a box of Trojans and gave him a smile. "You knew I was going to buy these."

"I swear to God, I didn't know anything." And that was the whole truth.

As he backed her to the bed, she flicked off her bra, wetting her lips while she slid the straps down her arms to reveal perfect, sweet perky tits with rosy nipples that he wanted to suck to precious points. "Holy shit," he murmured, making her laugh softly.

"I'm going to take that as a compliment."

He lifted his gaze, holding hers while he reached to the collar of his T-shirt and snapped it over his head, tossing it to the floor next to her bra. She stared at his body, her jaw going slack, hunger flashing in her eyes.

"Holy shit is right." She lifted her hands and spread them over his chest the way he wanted to spread his. "I'm so glad you thanked that guy at the airport who stole my seat."

He stilled for a moment, remembering the guy and how one hundred percent certain he'd been that that had been a ruse. A tendril of doubt tugged at his chest. Was she really who she—

"What's the matter?" she asked.

He lifted his head and looked at her, and the doubt disappeared. He was going to have to live that way, but not tonight. Tonight was him, her, a hotel, and hot sex.

"Nothing's the matter," he said. "I'm just…happy."

"Oh. Happy." She smiled and slowly slid her hand lower, pressing against his hard-on. "Is that what you call this?"

"Among other things." His laugh got lost in the next kiss and a thorough inspection of her breasts, and getting her completely underneath him. He worked his way down her curves and skin, licking and sucking while she writhed with pleasure, letting him taste and touch everything.

He unsnapped her jeans and felt her toeing off her boots, the sound of them hitting the floor like little grenades in his balls. He couldn't remember wanting to be inside a woman this bad. Just to get lost, buried, and satisfied.

He licked her belly, letting his tongue trail the contours of smooth, taut flesh. He kissed her thighs, parted her legs, and tasted the sweetest thing to touch his tongue in…shit, forever.

Her breath was nothing but raw desperation, her hands as manic as his, exploring his body with the same thoroughness he took hers, until he couldn't stand it one more second.

In silent agreement, he sheathed himself and positioned himself on top of her, forcing himself to wait when all he wanted to do was thrust and plunge and fill her up.

Time suspended just long enough for them to have eye contact, two complete strangers doing the most intimate, personal, real act two people could do.

"Please, Mal." She grabbed his ass and guided him all the way in, making him let out a loud groan of pleasure.

Sensations ripped through him, tearing at every cell, yanking sanity and sense from his brain. He pumped hard, and she met every stroke, her nails digging into his back, her mouth pressed against his shoulder, her body so willing and wet and warm he couldn't stand it one more second.

He came so hard it was like he'd fired a bullet into her, an explosion of everything he'd held pent up for forty-two months. Fury and frustration, loneliness and pain, truth and lies and secrets and raw desperation.

Giving into it all with blind need for comfort and release, he finished his climax with multiple thrusts, vaguely aware that she was pulsing and coming with him.

He finally collapsed against her, listening to her agonizing effort to catch her breath as it found a rhythm that matched his own.

She loosened her death grip, relaxing enough to stroke his shoulders and thread her fingers in his hair.

"I don't even know your last name," she whispered into his ear.

For good reason. He wouldn't go around telling people his last name, despite how common it was. She was a computer tech, for crying out loud. Ten seconds on Google and she'd know she just nailed an ex-con who'd served time for stealing money from the federal government when he was a prison guard at Gitmo. 'Cause that's what his record said…what it would always say.

She inched him up a little when he didn't answer. "Will you tell me?"

He searched her face. He shouldn't. He really should let this be the one-night stand it had to be. "It doesn't matter," he said.

He saw the flicker of disappointment in her eyes, the millisecond flash of hurt. "Yeah, I know, of course. Doesn't matter." And, then, shame.

Damn it. He might have been wrong about her being a spy, but he wasn't wrong about her lack of experience at casual sex. "No, no, Chessie," he assured her. "It's not like that."

She gave a smile that didn't reach her eyes. "And now I'm Chessie. No more Francesca."

He'd hurt her. Son of a bitch, he'd hurt her five seconds after she opened her body and gave herself to him. What a douche. "I'm sorry," he murmured.

"Don't be." She reached up and pressed her mouth against his ear, kissing softly. "Rossi." The word, like air on his ear, tickled and shocked him.

He jerked back. "What?"

"I don't care about what's right or wrong in this situation, I want you to know my last name."

"Rossi?" He only mouthed it, because actually saying it would make it too, too real.

She smiled and lifted a brow, as if to say, *I told you mine, now tell me yours.*

"My name is Francesca Rossi."

But…but… *Rossi*? The real, the impossibly real, truth hit, and now he knew exactly who she was.

Not a spy. Not someone trying to follow and trap him. And not a stranger, either.

No, she was Gabe Rossi's sister, and she was on her way to see her brother. Good Lord, that was so much worse than anything he could have imagined.

Chapter Three

Something pulled Chessie from a deep sleep, but everything was black when she opened her eyes. She blinked, fighting brain fog and exhaustion and disorientation. And bone-deep contentment.

The hotel. She was in a hotel room with…the best lover she'd ever experienced in her life. The *best*. Yes, he'd gotten a little weird after she'd told him her last name, confirming her suspicion that he really wanted this to start and end tonight.

That was fine, but tonight wasn't over yet. Instantly aching for more of him, she turned, but everything was still completely dark. She pressed the empty pillow next to her and slid her leg over the sheets, bumping into no one.

Sitting up, she peered into the utter blackness, listening for a sound and vaguely impressed by just how effective the Marriott's light-blocking curtains were.

"Are you there?" she whispered, tentative for some reason.

"Uh, yeah." His voice, as low and sexy as it had been in her ear when they'd…well, you couldn't exactly call it *making love*. What they'd done was flat-out fu—

"You can go back to sleep."

Her heart dropped. Weirdly, quickly, and for no good reason. It wasn't like she ever expected to see him again after this. It was just that...she didn't want to go back to sleep. She wanted more. More of those hands and that mouth and, holy, holy hell, that massive hard-on that'd been the best ride of her life. And more of his dry humor and blend of rough and sweet.

She liked him, damn it. Was that against the rules?

"Come back to bed," she said, only a little surprised by the sultriness in her voice.

"No, I'm leaving."

What? She tamped down what might have come out as the sound of begging, staying silent while she waited for an explanation or something. Something that didn't sound so much like ugly rejection. She'd put herself on the line, damn it, and when they'd—

The door clicked open, and finally some light spilled into the room, highlighting the man she'd just given her body to. She could see that, standing in the doorway with the hall light silhouetting him, he wore the same clothes she'd taken off him, and carried his duffel bag.

"You really are leaving." Like, *leaving the building* leaving. Wow.

He turned to look back at her, and even though his face was in shadow, something about his demeanor had changed. The challenge was gone from his broad-shouldered stance, along with the sense that he was doing something on a dare.

Guess that was 'cause he'd *done* something, and now he was out.

Prick.

He cut a glance into the hallway, then back to her. "I left you a T-shirt," he said, nodding toward something white hanging on the back of a chair.

"Oh, thanks," she said, not hiding the dry sarcasm. "Should I consider it payment for services rendered?"

Even in the shadows, she could see his eyes close like he'd been hit by her shot. *Good. Hope it hurt as much as the punch to her gut.*

"More like an explanation for why I'm leaving." With that, he stepped into the hall and shut the door, leaving her bathed in black again.

And stupidly sad.

Throwing back the covers, she stood and yanked the drapes back to let in the suddenly sordid ambience of an airport hotel in the middle of the night. It was enough light to find the chair, pick up the plain white T-shirt, and turn it over as if expecting some kind of handwritten note.

Nothing, just a tiny imprint over the space that would cover the bastard's cold heart. She stepped to the nightstand and found the switch, frowning at the brightness and sliding her hand under the T-shirt so she could read what it said.

Allenwood Federal Correctional Institution

Chessie stared at the words, a chill slipping up her spine and blossoming over her whole body.

He was an ex-con?

Oh hell, maybe he was an escapee? No, Chessie might not do the field investigations that her cousins and brothers did, but she'd worked in the security business long enough to know he hadn't had the aura of a man on the run.

How was this an explanation for why he left?

Something about him had been strange, she thought as their brief exchanges in the last few hours flitted through her memory. Like he'd thought she knew who he was, or should have. Was she supposed to smell prison on him or something?

She sat on the bed, sighing softly. Okay. This was why a

person with a brain and self-control didn't just veer off into spontaneity without a good reason.

He was a good reason, a voice in her head whispered. Good and sexy and sweet and…oh, that thing he did with his tongue?

She shook out the sex-charged memory.

Still not the smartest choice she'd ever made, tongue notwithstanding. And something in the back of her mind told her Allenwood wasn't exactly hard time. Minimum security? She'd have to do some digging into the prison databases.

No. Not smart. She'd have to forget this. Forget *him*.

She lifted the shirt and sniffed, hating herself only a little bit for wanting one more scent of the man. Detergent, the strong institutional variety, filled her nose. She fell back on the pillow with a moan of pure agony. She'd just pretend it never happened, her one-night stand with an inmate who tried to escape the hotel without even saying good-bye.

"Way to pick 'em, Chess," she whispered into the empty room.

Although she *had* picked pretty well for the purposes of mind-blowing, body-quaking, orgasm-making sex.

"Damn it." She thwacked the bed with the T-shirt, pushing herself up again and looking around the barren hotel room. There was no way she was staying here alone tonight, smelling the memory of the two of them on the sheets, and feeling sorry for her stupid self. She had her own room, and that's where she belonged.

She washed up, used the new toothbrush, and slipped her panties and jeans back on in less than five minutes. She hooked her bra and looked around the floor for her favorite black cardigan that her cousin had given her last Christmas. Vivi probably hadn't planned on the designer sweater becoming part of a sexy one-button-at-a-time striptease for a lover fresh from federal prison.

But there was no sign of her top. Maybe he took it so she'd be forced to walk around in an Allenwood prison T-shirt. A convict with a mocking sense of humor, then.

She yanked up the spread that had fallen to the floor.

There it was. She reached for the sweater, but the edge of the sleeve had become wedged into the iron rail of the bedframe. She didn't even remember him getting the sweater off her, she thought as she bent lower to free the fabric without tearing it. No, she'd been too busy stripping him down, too, and getting her hands on all those freaking muscles.

That he built in the *prison gym*.

"Ugh," she grunted, still attempting to loosen the sweater without putting a hole in the delicate knit.

The sucker wouldn't budge. "Oh, come on." She got on her knees, slipping her fingers behind the bedframe to carefully slide out the sweater sleeve. Under the material, she felt a little bump, like a screw trapping the fabric. She pulled a little more, but any harder and she'd ruin the cardigan. Of course, she had a nice, clean Allenwood federal prison T-shirt to wear. Wouldn't Gabe and their grandfather have a field day with that when she showed up in Barefoot Bay?

If he found out… No, Gabe would freaking kill her for this, and then he'd call in their brothers to hunt the guy down—Marc would do that. JP would threaten him with more jail time. And then, for good measure, he'd tell their cousin Zach, who'd put his fist through the guy's–

Something popped into the air, breaking away from the bedframe as her top snapped free.

"What the—" She looked down at the spread on the floor.

A black disc lay against the cream color, making her jerk back at the possibility it was a roach.

But then a tiny red light flashed once right in the middle of it.

“Holy shit,” she whispered, reaching her hand closer but not actually touching it.

It flashed again. This was a bug, all right. But not the creepy-crawly kind.

Though every bit as creepy. Very slowly, Chessie backed away, covering her mouth as the horrific reality of this settled over her.

The room was *bugged*—and the light said the bug was active—and all that mind-blowing, body-quaking, orgasm-making sex she had enjoyed so boisterously?

She sucked in a slow breath as the implications piled up one by one. This could be used against her. This could be sent to her family. This could turn up on the Internet.

But this was *his* room. Someone could be after him. Holy hell, he *could* be an escaped convict! And she’d inadvertently aided and abetted him. Or had just unknowingly become an alibi in a murder.

Holy God, the list of possibilities were endless, and not one of them any good.

She stood, suddenly aware of how very vulnerable she was, uneasily looking around for the camera that might be in the room, too.

“Son of a...” She stopped herself from saying another word, silently slipping into her cardigan and buttoning it with trembling hands. She had to get out of there. She had to get out of Atlanta. And not by way of the airport, either.

A plan started to form, point by point. Check out. Take cab to car rental. Leave for Barefoot Bay tonight. She’d already checked the driving time in the airport after the flight was canceled. Eight and a half hours for regular people. Chessie could make it in seven. And a quarter. So she'd be there by eight thirty or nine at the latest.

Shit, her luggage. Plan snag.

No, no. Her bag would make it to Fort Myers because she was booked on that plane, and she could get it from the airport that afternoon.

Okay, a plan. She loved a plan. A calming, direct plan to counteract the raw stupidity of casual sex with an escaped prisoner in a bugged room.

Her hands shook as she tried to pull on her ankle-high boots.

"You are so not cut out for field work," she mumbled, then remembered the bug and slammed her mouth shut. Shit. She had to get out of here.

Snagging her handbag, she looked around for anything else she might have left, besides her dignity and sanity.

Oh, his Allenwood federal prison T-shirt.

Should she take it? Or leave it? Instinct and self-preservation made her grab the T-shirt and stuff it into her bag.

But then there was the bug, still on the floor, still flashing a slender red beam of light. She took a step, then another, and let her boot heel *accidentally* crush the small device.

"That bug's dead." Then she scooped the pieces up, stuffed them in her jeans pocket, and hustled out the door, already reviewing her steps and loving her new plan. This could be good. Gabe would think she was heroic for driving all night. And she'd make it in time for peppers and eggs, and some good old Italian food love from her grandfather.

It was all good. Her big mistake was nothing but a bad memory.

Define bad. She could still hear his baritone voice and his clever little expressions. *Define okay, Francesca. Define solid.*

Here's how she'd define bad: going off plan. And she would never, ever do that again.

Chapter Four

Ninety-eight…ninety-nine…one mothereffing hundred.

Gabe bounced to his feet after the last one-armed push-up and shook out his burning tricep, stomping around the fifteen-square-foot back porch he'd turned into his simple home gym, complete with a punching bag and set of weights under the awning, and one bench. No matter where he lived, or what hellacious country he woke up in, Gabe figured out a way to take care of his temple.

He squinted into the sun, already nearly in the middle of the sky over Bareass Bay, as he'd taken to calling his prison in paradise. He used to get up early, but these days? He didn't even sleep, so he'd start working out at dawn just to get the hell out of his misery.

He wiped his face with a T-shirt and looked around the tropical cul-de-sac. Palm trees swayed against achingly blue skies, the breeze heavy with the ever-present salt smell of the bay just on the other side of a lush garden. Beyond that, the high-end villas and expansive private beach of Casa Blanca Resort & Spa sat like a jewel in the Gulf of Mexico.

It was still a prison for him now that his only reason for choosing to live in this out-of-the-way playground was…*deceased.* Well, technically, his reason was proximity to Cuba, but the reason he wanted that proximity was...*dead.*

Unless the child she'd left behind really was his. Then he had another reason to be here. Another reason to live at all.

In the days that'd passed since he learned that he'd never see Isadora Winter again, the pain still burned a hole in his heart, infusing every breath he took with the unfamiliar blackness of mourning.

But he refused to let it break him.

Not until he found out if her four-year-old son was his. The name Gabriel was only one clue. And the age, of course. Now came the hard part, and if his team would just get here, he could get them briefed and started.

He had to know. Had to. If he had a son, well, he'd move heaven, earth, and the whole fucking island of Cuba to get that kid. If he didn't, then it was time to accept the loss of Isa forever. Until then, he lived in limbo, which felt a lot like hell, despite the postcard surroundings.

He pushed open the back door into the bungalow's kitchen and sucked in a noisy breath. And got nothing but the lingering aroma of last night's veal Marsala.

At the sound in the hall, Gabe turned to find his grandfather lumbering toward him, his white hair brushed as neatly as the mop could get, his crisp shirt—Pepto pink today—buttoned like he was on his way to the Oval Office for a press conference.

"Do you want some breakfast, Gabriel?"

"You look too dolled up to cook, old man. I'll wing it."

"Pffft!" Nino yanked an apron from a hook and waved one of his massive, gnarled hands. "I dress for my job, Gabriel. And part of my job is feeding you."

Gabe stifled a smile, not bothering to tell the octogenarian that no one expected him to show up in his office dressed for a funeral. Gabe rarely wore anything but board shorts and an old T-shirt, but then he was only a "consultant" to McBain Security. And by consultant, he meant that Luke McBain gave him free office space in exchange for the occasional bit of advice on how to run the resort's security firm.

That way, Gabe had a safe cover for his *real* work of helping people who needed to stay off the radar and turn up with new lives. The US Marshals might think they owned that space with wit-sec, but Gabe knew shit that put those jokers to shame. And, based on the number of clients ready to throw money at him for private-sector witness protection, his idea was freaking genius.

But he couldn't do the job alone. He'd brought his grandfather into the fold for a number of reasons, not the least of which was the old man was possibly his favorite person on earth. Well, his favorite person still living on earth.

So Nino Rossi, commonly known as Uncle Nino to the family, became Gabe's personal assistant, a job the eightysomething-year-old man did with surprising vigor.

But only for a half day. The rest of the time he puttered in a corner of the farmette that belonged to the resort and he cooked. Like a god. And he was Gabe's only sounding board on most days, which meant...he should know what was about to happen.

When Chessie showed up, he couldn't hide the truth from Nino, and he honestly didn't want to. He just wasn't sure how the old guy would respond to a great-grandchild currently locked in Cuba. But it was time to find out. He loved Nino too much to keep him in the dark, and his grandfather had proven himself to be beyond trustworthy with the secrets of their undercover business. If he could just get Nino to get along with the one other woman on the resort staff, a housekeeper, who was "in the know" about the business, then they might have a good thing going here.

But first, the news.

"I have a surprise for you today," Gabe said, walking to the refrigerator. "Since you're hitting the stove to do your thing, I'll dish up good news."

Nino put his hand on the refrigerator door, holding it closed. "If you gulp down milk from the bottle, I'll…" He made a fist. "You'll eat this instead of eggs." The words rolled out with an Italian accent as faint as the threat itself.

Gabe easily yanked the door open, reaching for a plastic container. "Fuck it, Nino, we got separate bottles for this."

"It's not healthy, that habit of yours."

Gabe shot him a look. "I know, bacteria. You told me. Bring on the botulism, baby. I just sweat out every little bugger in my body, and I need my milk, old man."

Nino gave the apron tie a good pull, making sure it protected Brooks Brothers' finest.

He pushed Gabe out of the way of the open fridge to get eggs from the carton. "Gimme the good news, Gabriel. A new client? Another make-believe honeymoon couple like the last two?"

"Hey, that was sheer genius," Gabe replied. "The MMA trainer on the run from the mob pretending to be married to the hot lawyer who had a stalker? Dude, that kind of undercover gig was exactly why I started this business. They're not complaining that the fake honeymoon turned real, by the way."

Nino made a classic Italian mug and shrugged. "I give you that, grandson. It worked out. So who's our next undercover client? I'm getting really good at that fake paperwork. Can I make up the names again?"

Gabe stifled a proud grin. The Marshals would be lucky

to have such an assistant for wit-sec. Plus, Gabe got paid obscene money, and even though Nino didn't want a dime, the old man's bank account would have a tidy sum before long. He might not want to spend it, but someday he could leave it to all those Rossi and Angelino kids who loved his cranky old ass.

"Sorry to say I'm not taking any clients for a few weeks, but we are getting a guest, and she's your second-favorite grandchild."

Nino turned, his eyes wide and, to his credit, unsure. He loved the whole brood equally, though everyone was convinced they were his favorite. Didn't matter; Gabe *was* his favorite.

"Chessie's on her way," Gabe said, saving him from making the wrong guess.

"She is?" He beamed. "I liked it when she was here before, but she left so quickly. More computer work for you?"

Not exactly. "She's helping me find someone," Gabe explained, mentally pumping up for the big news.

Nino chuckled as he chopped peppers and onions like a cooking ninja. "That's what Chessie does. She finds people with those busy fingers on the keyboard. Who are you looking for?"

"A boy."

Nino didn't answer, but a frown formed as he moved on to the eggs. When Gabe didn't offer more, the other man looked up with a question on his weathered expression. "For a client?"

"For me." Gabe took a slow breath and poured a giant bacteria-free glass of milk into a real glass, since that might make Nino predisposed to be happy about this. "He's my boy."

Nino's whole body stilled, the whisk dripping with raw eggs. "*Scusi*?"

"Maybe my boy. We don't know yet."

The old man's jaw loosened, and a sound came out, not quite a word, not really a grunt, completely a demand for more information.

"Look," Gabe said, putting the glass on the counter with too much force. "I had a…" What could he call it? A thing? A romance? An affair with the love of his life? "A *friend* on that last assignment at Gitmo."

Nino still stared.

"And I've been trying to find her for years." Five years. Five *long* years. "I had a good lead, but the files were encrypted, and that's why I flew Chessie down here a couple of weeks ago. Turns out she—my friend—had a kid."

"Your kid?" Nino asked.

He tried to imagine Isadora with another man and couldn't. Not then. Not ever. "Possibly. Probably. I don't know."

"A woman had your baby and didn't tell you?" Nino's voice lifted sky-high.

"Maybe had my baby. We haven't confirmed it."

"*Cavolo*!" Nino choked, the Italian curse cracking his voice. "Why wouldn't she tell you?"

Most likely because it would put the kid in danger. Or maybe it would put Gabe in danger. Or her. There were plenty of reasons she'd make the choice, but he'd never know unless Junior came with his mother's diary.

"I don't know," he admitted. "And I may never know because she…" Fuck the world, he hated to say the word. It made it so real. "She died."

"Oh, Gabriel." Nino took a step closer, but Gabe held up his hand.

"It's fine." Of course, it wasn't fine, and Nino could see

that. "It's nothing." Now there was a whopper of an understatement.

Nino searched his face, his old features processing the news. "You have a son?" For a normally loud Italian, Nino barely whispered the question.

"I might. She had a kid, and all we know about him is his first name, but birth records are questionable because it's Cuba, and up to about five minutes ago, everything was questionable about that dung heap, but he's four, so about the right age."

"A four-year-old boy." Nino's eyes filled. "What's his name?"

Gabe looked down at the milk and took a shallow breath. "Gabriel. Which means nothing, of course—"

"Nothing?" Nino shot into Gabe's face, the whisk still in hand. "*Nothing*? Family is everything!"

"Do you think I don't know that?" Gabe fired back. "Do you think I don't wake up in a cold sweat with bile in my throat at the thought of a child, *my child*, living on this earth for four years *and I didn't even know he existed*?"

Nino didn't flinch but met Gabe's anger with tapered black eyes. "Then why the hell are you here and not in Cuba?"

Gabe swallowed. "I can't go there."

"But that's changing! They've opened an embassy. We're all good with Cuba now!" Nino shook his head, vehement, as if Gabe didn't read the damn newspaper. "We can both go, Gabriel. We'll go find him and—"

"No." Gabe put his hands on Nino's shoulders. "I cannot go to that country no matter what happens between Cuba and the US. It doesn't really have anything to do with politics, really."

"Why?"

Gabe shot him a *get real* look, which he knew Nino

instantly understood. Certain things—most things—about Gabe's previous life as a consultant for the CIA were closed topics. "Let's just say I pissed off the wrong people."

"Then what are you going to do?" Nino asked.

"I'm not going to do anything. Chessie is—"

"Here!" The female voice rang through the living area as the screen door banged. "Don't you two lock this door?"

Nino's eyes popped wide as he tossed his whisk back into the egg mix and opened his arms for a hug. "Francesca!"

Coming into the kitchen, Chessie slowed for a split second. "Don't call me that, Nino." She fell into her grandfather's arms and looked over his shoulder at Gabe, whose own jaw dropped.

"How the hell did you get here so fast?" he asked.

"Because I'm amazing." She stuck her tongue out at him. "And you're welcome."

He shook his head, shocked that his sister had veered from an agenda. It was so rare and…a good sign. A very good sign. Maybe it wouldn't take as much convincing as he thought to get her to lose her field status virginity.

"Well, you were supposed to be here last night," he said. "So not that early, technically."

The faintest shadow crossed her eyes just before she closed them. "Even I can't make Southwest fly planes if they don't want to. But Avis had a Mustang, so I blew down here almost as fast as a 747."

Nino pushed back and frowned at her. "You drive too fast, Chess."

"Only Fords. And my bag is on the plane that I wasn't, so one of us will have to make a run to the airport." She batted her eyelashes at Nino.

"After I feed you," Nino agreed easily, his priorities always in order.

Chessie pecked the old cheek and tucked a lock of hair behind her ear, her usually bright and perfectly made-up face looking pretty worn from the overnight drive. That she'd made for him because, like Nino said, family is everything.

Instantly, Gabe's heart softened as he took his own brotherly hug. She cared so much that she'd rushed down here and didn't even worry about not having luggage. So not like her, and such a testament to the fact that he picked the right person for the job.

"Thanks, kid." He gave her a squeeze. "I appreciate you dropping everything for this."

She eased back. "Anything to, um, fix your computer system." She winked.

Nino nudged into both of them. "Stop the lying, Francesca Rossi. I know why you're here."

"You do?" She looked from one to the other. "He does?"

Gabe nodded. "Welcome Nino to the vault, Chess. I just told him."

She broke into a wide smile. "Pretty cool, isn't it? A new little baby Rossi."

"Not exactly a baby," Nino replied. "Gabe says he's four."

Guilt punched, along with a numb ache that Gabe couldn't get used to. "We don't even know if he's mine," he said quickly, taking his fallback rationalization every time he allowed himself to believe the boy was indeed his and he'd missed four years of his life.

"Then let's find out!" Chessie gave his shoulder a solid punch. "I brought my laptop, but if this on-site security company you work for has better systems, let's use them. Or maybe you've stolen more files from that Cuban TV station like you did a few weeks ago. Whatever, dear brother, I am on it like a bonnet." She grinned. "And I've been working up some algorithms that might let me crack those Cuba files even deeper. Also, I've found a few more databases—"

"You're not going to need a computer, Chess."

She laughed and looked at Nino. "That's like you saying you don't need your perfectly seasoned cast-iron skillet."

Nino lifted his brows, clearly pleased with the fact that he knew something Chessie didn't. "Listen to your brother," he said.

Chessie turned back to Gabe. "Why wouldn't I need a computer?"

"Oh, you can take it, but the Internet is notoriously bad to nonexistent in Cuba." He could actually see his words hit her brain like little bullets, making her lips part in shock.

"*What*?" she managed to choke out the word.

"You're going in the field."

She lifted her glasses and peered at him like that might help her make sense of what he was saying. "I know you've been away from the Guardian Angelino offices for a while, Gabe, but I'm the computer girl, remember? If it's digital, it's my domain. I don't go in the…"

Her voice faded as she realized he was serious. She looked at Nino for help, and Nino gave her his infamous one-shoulder shrug that had a million interpretations. This one said, *Tough shit, kid. You're going to Cuba.*

"Nino!" she exclaimed.

"Chessie, it's a *new member of the family*," he said, as if that covered all things holy.

"We *think*," Gabe added. "I have to find out for certain, and that has to be done on the ground."

"By me?" Chessie's voice rose, not exactly in fear, but with the tension that thrummed through her when a curve ball came her way. "How can I go to Cuba?"

"Easily. It's all arranged. I even have a great cover for you."

"I'm going *undercover*?"

"That's kind of what we do here, Chess."

She let out a breath. Or maybe hyperventilated. "Am I going alone?"

"No, no. God no, I wouldn't do that to you."

He could see visible relief on her face. "Thank God. So you're able to get into Cuba now?"

"I wish, but no. Never." Or he would have blown out of here a few weeks ago, minutes after Chessie discovered the existence of a four-year-old Gabriel listed as the child of Isadora Winter.

Chessie canted her head with a questioning look. "Nino's going?"

Their grandfather puffed up. "I'd love that!"

"And come back with a recipe for *arroz con pollo* and no word on the kid?" Gabe shook his head. "No, sorry. I have someone assigned to go with you, Chessie, and—"

A solid rap on the screen door silenced him. "Gabe?"

At the sound of his friend's voice from the front door, Gabe grinned. "And there he is. Come on in, Mal," he called.

Chessie startled. "*Mal*?"

"No worries, kid," he whispered. "Malcolm Harris is the perfect partner for you on this job."

All the color in her face drained, leaving her pale and wide-eyed.

"It's going to be okay, Chess." He gave his sister a hug. "I promise you'll love this plan. You don't have to be afraid of the field."

"It's not the field I'm afraid of," she whispered.

Just then, Mal Harris came into the kitchen, looking bigger and tougher than before he went to Allenwood. He started to smile at Gabe, but his gaze snagged on Chessie, and suddenly he looked as shocked as she did.

For one long second, they stared at each other, and Gabe could have sworn the lights flickered with the power charge that surged through the room.

What the fuck?

Chapter Five

How the hell had she beat him here? Why wasn't she boarding that morning flight right now, still hours away? That's what Mal had been counting on, giving him plenty of time to get here, get briefed, and get going without ever having to bump into *Gabe's little sister*.

But here she was, just as pretty and desirable as before he knew who she was and why screwing her was such a bad idea. He'd likely lose his balls and a few teeth when Gabe found out what they'd done. He might even lose a valued friend, which was worse.

Mal managed to tear his gaze from the woman whose scent still clung to him and reached out to shake Gabe's hand, copping a look of complete innocence that he hoped the other spook couldn't see right through. "Good to see you, Gabe."

"Is it?" Gabe returned the shake, but then added the quick man-hug that their friendship—and Mal's four years in the house—demanded.

Mal gave Gabe's back an easy punch, guilt tamping his enthusiasm. "Of course it's good to see you."

Gabe backed away, still giving Mal the stink eye. "You look like you just pissed on an electric fence."

Mal didn't laugh or even steal an uncertain glance at Chessie. If she was as smart as he thought she was, she'd pick up the cue and stay silent. "Just shell-shocked by a long trip."

"This is my sister Chessie," Gabe said. "She'll be your mission partner."

Holy sweet mother of Jesus. The slightest flash of horror crossed her expression, which probably matched his.

Mission partner.

Mal extended his hand to Chessie and finally made direct eye contact, long enough to see the infinitesimal flicker of surprise and, shit, hurt. Maybe some really pissed-offness, too.

"Nice to meet you, Chessie."

It certainly pained her to take his hand and offer the most lackluster shake in history, pulling away before he even had his fingers around hers. "Hello, Malcolm."

He could have sworn Gabe looked from one to the other with the crooked frown that meant he smelled something. And in this case? He'd smell sex. On both of them.

So Mal seized on the other person in the room, reaching his hand to the older man's shoulder. "And this must be the famous grandfather who goes by Uncle Nino."

"Nino Rossi," the older man confirmed, banging his gnarled hand over Mal's arm and adding an impressive squeeze. "It's always a surprise and honor that my grandson talks about me."

"Are you kidding?" Mal asked. "Gabe talked about his whole family." He glanced at Chessie and couldn't help adding, "Which is big, so I might not have remembered everyone's names."

Truth was, Gabe *had* mentioned a "baby sister"—not a thirty-year-old beauty with a hot bod and a killer mouth. No, he'd said nothing at all about that in the Rossi family line.

"I'm sure I told you about our family nerd." Gabe patted Chessie's back, a joke in his voice, but his gaze a little too inquisitive. Of course, the super spy didn't miss a beat, and, shit, if they weren't careful, Gabe would know exactly what beat was pounding in this room.

Chessie inched out of Gabe's brotherly touch. "Well, you certainly never mentioned anyone named Mal, which I would remember, because that name means *bad* in so many languages."

Ouch.

"I met Mal at Gitmo," Gabe said. "He was a guard there."

"A *prison* guard?" Chessie asked, her brows lifting, a subtle expression of hope or relief in her eyes.

Because of the T-shirt, of course. Which he'd left as a way of saying, *You made a bad choice*, and prayed that would keep her from confiding in her big brother about a stranger named Malcolm Harris.

"He'll make a great partner for you," Gabe said to his sister, and to her credit, she didn't even flinch.

But Mal had had no idea Gabe wanted him to partner on this job. Gabe had called in the middle of the night a few days after Mal got out of Allenwood. He'd agreed to help instantly, even if it meant going back to Cuba undercover.

"But you know I can handle alone whatever you have, Gabe," Mal said, on the off chance they could get out of this awkward mess.

"It's going to take a team, and you two are it." Gabe looked from one to the other, frowning slightly, and Mal braced for the inevitable. *Have you two already met? Did you, by any chance, fuck each other's brains out? Excuse me while I kick the living shit out of Mal.* "I think the cover will work perfectly," Gabe finally said.

And Mal and Chessie exhaled in perfect unison.

"I'm sure it will," Mal said quietly.

"As long as there's a good, clear game plan to follow," Chessie added.

Gabe laughed. "Well, it is Cuba, so plans are, what would you say, Mal?"

"Subject to change," he replied.

"Then blown to shit," Gabe added.

Chessie made a face like she didn't like the sound of that. "Why do you need us both?"

"Mal can't go into Cuba solo, even with the new ID I cooked up. With a woman, he'll fly more under the radar."

"Why not a different woman?" Chessie asked, her tone telling Mal just how much she didn't want to go.

"Chessie's new to field work," Gabe explained to Mal.

"And he's a prison guard," she fired back. "So neither one of us is exactly trained for a mission."

Gabe got right in her face. "He's not your run-of-the-mill prison guard, okay, Chess? He speaks decent Spanish and knows the entire island like you know a computer."

"Then let me use one."

Gabe's eyes narrowed. "And you're the only person on earth besides the people in this room who knows about this kid."

"Which is probably the real reason I got the job," she said, no small amount of sarcasm in her voice.

"Maybe it is," Gabe agreed. "But whatever my reasons, you're going to do this for me because…" He swallowed hard. "Because that child could be your nephew, and I think you are incredibly qualified to find him."

Chessie softened visibly. The fight went out of her as her shoulders sank and her eyes shuttered closed. "Of course," she whispered. "I would do anything for you and for…your son." She glanced at Mal and gave him a look he couldn't quite interpret. "And I'm sure Mal and I can *work* together."

She put enough emphasis on *work* that he could figure that message: work and only work.

"Good." Gabe gestured toward the table nestled near sliding glass doors. "Nino," he yelled over his shoulder. "Feed us, old man."

"You got it, Gabriel!"

"And you two…" He draped one arm around Chessie and one arm around Mal and pushed them a little closer. "You are going to love each other."

Six inches apart, they could barely look at each other, let alone manage a reply that wouldn't be loaded with irony.

Chessie was the first to slip away, narrowing her eyes at her brother. "I swear to God, if you say we pretend to be married—"

"Married?" The word caught in Mal's throat.

"What do I look like?" Gabe scoffed. "A man with no imagination? You think I'd pull that same stunt twice?" He scooped Chessie back under his arm and led them both to waiting chairs at a table covered with papers, fake passports, airline tickets, and an open map of a country Mal would prefer never to step foot in again.

"You are traveling to Cuba as a production duo to make a documentary on how the new political climate is changing life for the common man and children," Gabe said, urging Mal into the chair next to Chessie.

They were so close, Mal had to make an effort not to touch her. Which was damn hard as her scent—a sexy, feminine, peppery scent that reminded him of last night—teased his nose.

He stole a look, close enough to see traces of makeup

under her eyes, smudged during her overnight drive here. His gaze dropped to the top button of a black sweater he had stripped off her about twelve hours ago and landed right on a tiny hickey under her collarbone.

Holy shit. Talk about a dead giveaway. He tried to give her a look, to tell her to cover it, but she refused to look directly at him.

"All right, then," Gabe said, taking the other seat and picking up some papers.

Under the table, Mal bumped her with his leg, forcing Chessie to look at him. He surreptitiously flicked his T-shirt collar, trying to silently tell her to button the sweater and cover the evidence.

She just gave him an incredulous look. And he gave her one back. It was only a matter of time before Gabe—

"Is that a fucking hickey on your neck, Chess?"

Instantly, Chessie yanked her sweater over the mark that Mal would have bet a grand she hadn't even known she had. Mal gave the slightest *I tried to warn you* side-eye.

"I thought you broke up with Matt the Asswipe," Gabe said.

So there really was a Door-Matt who broke her heart. Of course there was. Because when he was busy assuming she was a lying spy making shit up, she was a perfectly innocent woman sharing her personal history.

And he took her to bed.

And she…didn't hate it.

"Shut it, Gabe," she said, finally closing the top two buttons. "I…it was…" She looked anywhere but at Mal. "It was…*nothing*." She put too much emphasis on the last word. Way too much.

But Gabe wasn't letting it go. "He's not good enough for you, Chess. You deserve better."

"He's not *that* bad." She lifted one judgmental eyebrow in Mal's direction. "I mean, he's never been in jail or anything."

Damn, the woman had a mean underhand zing.

Gabe pushed a paper to the side. "No, but I will be for killing him if he puts his turd-eating mouth on your neck again."

She puffed out a breath. "Do you mind?" she demanded.

"I mind like hell," Gabe continued. "I hate that little scum-sucker and—"

"It wasn't him!" she exclaimed.

For a long moment, no one said a word. To Mal, the only sound was the sizzle of eggs in a pan, and the steady beat of his pulse as he waited for her to make the call. Gabe would go bat-shit crazy, no doubt about it. But if she wanted the truth out there, Mal would own up to what happened.

Gabe lifted one brow. "You're seeing someone already? You just dumped that douche."

She threw up her hands in exasperation. "Can you please stop? Either you get off my case and stop treating me like I'm thirteen, or I'm back in my rental driving to Boston. Which is it, Gabe?"

They both stared at each other, sibling sparks crackling. So the whole clan could hold their own in a fight, Mal mused.

Finally, Gabe looked down at the map. "You'll fly into Havana," he said.

Chessie leaned back, crossed her arms, and shot Mal a warning look, and this one he could read like a billboard. *Don't mess with me.*

And all that did was make him want to.

Breakfast had been finished and cleared, and Nino had gone off to work. Gabe had reviewed the plan multiple times, and Mal seemed to fully understand it.

But Chessie was having an impossible time focusing, her brain still stalled on the fact that she was going into the field—something she'd never wanted to do—with a man she stupidly had a one-night stand with the night before.

"You get this, right, Chess?" Gabe demanded, no doubt sensing her lack of concentration on the maps and paperwork in front of them.

"Yeah, I get it." *Don't like it, but I get it.* "We're flying into José Martí International from New York, with press passes and these passports, posing as two independent producers filming a spec documentary about how the new relations with the US are affecting the everyday man in Cuba with a focus on the children and their future." She looked up, kind of proud of herself. "I get it. But how do we stay in contact with you?"

"Satellite phones will work, maybe outdoors in the more rural areas. I'll give you two. You can take your computer, but Internet is unreliable."

"Unless you're on Gitmo or you know how to access a Canadian server," Mal added.

"I can do that," she said brightly, thrilled that someone was finally speaking her language. Even if it was *him*.

"You have all the clearances lined up, Gabe?" Mal asked, his deep, sensual voice a constant reminder of the things he'd whispered to her last night.

Kiss me, Francesca. Do you like that, Francesca? I want to taste you, Francesca.

"Francesca!"

Her head popped up at the sound of the very word she'd been thinking, but it wasn't Mal's sexy use of her full name. It was Gabe, looking dark and angry.

"What the hell is wrong with you?" he demanded.

"I was just thinking…wondering…um…"

Mal put his hand up. "Give her a break, man. She's probably exhausted from driving all night and it's legit to wonder how and why we can get in and get around Cuba so easily."

She resisted the urge to smile at him, though she was begrudgingly grateful for the backup. And she seized on the excuse.

"Of course I am," she said. "I know relations are normalizing and we've reopened an embassy and Americans can essentially travel there with ease, but of all countries to slip into undercover, it seems like a challenging one."

"It's really not," Mal assured her. "Even before all this happened, Americans could get in for the right reasons. It's Cubans they don't want to let out."

"And certain Americans they really don't want to let in," Chessie added, eyeing her brother.

"Obviously, I'd go if I could," Gabe said. "But I trust Mal." At her look, he added, "And you."

Chessie could feel the blood drain from her head and pool in her stomach, the image of that flashing black listening device she'd found in the hotel room burned in her memory. Could he trust either of them?

"Clearances," Mal repeated, bringing the subject back on topic. "Do you have them all lined up?"

Gabe tapped his sizable chest and puffed a breath. "*I* arranged this. Of course I have clearances. I have everything you need, but it is Cuba, so you will step into shit now and again. You'll have to be nimble and ready to rock some new plans if things get dicey."

Dicey. New plans. *Nimble.*

Not a single thing that felt comfortable to Chessie. She didn't like dicey. New plans meant something had gone wrong with the old ones. And the only place she was nimble was on a keyboard.

"So, let me get this straight, Gabe," she said, gathering her wits, because it appeared she needed every single one. "We're going to a Communist country under false pretenses with fake names and a plan that's written on toilet paper blowing in the wind."

Gabe grinned. "Pretty much how I roll."

She stared at her brother. "You know I don't work like that. I need steps, dates, times, maps, codes, and detailed information. Preferably on a screen in front of me. In an office. In a country I'm welcome to visit. That's pretty much how *I* roll."

She could feel Mal's ebony eyes again. "You've never done anything spontaneous, Chessie?" he asked.

She might kill him. Was that an option in this plan?

Was he trying to make her writhe in misery? The flashing-neon hickey on her neck wasn't agonizing enough? "Spontaneity rarely works out well for me. Especially recently."

They stared at each other for a second, just long enough for Chessie's mouth to go bone dry and her heart rate to kick back up again. Did he have to be so freaking gorgeous? Did he have to undress her with his eyes and give just enough of a smile that she could remember everything that mouth did to her?

"Chessie, I know," Gabe asked, making them both whip around to give him their attention. Here it comes, Chessie thought. Here it comes. *We are so busted.*

"What?" she asked, mustering innocence.

"I *know* you don't want to do this. I know it's not in your wheelhouse, Chess." Gabe put his hand over hers. "But I need blood on the ground."

"That's what I'm afraid of."

"You won't shed any," he assured her. "But you're family. And this boy could be, too. I need to find out."

She felt her eyes shutter in disgust at his use of the ultimate F-word, and the fact that he was essentially misreading her hesitation as fear. She wasn't afraid of the field. She was just afraid of complications in the field.

On a sigh, she reached into her bag for the laptop sleeve like a baby grabbing a blankie.

"Family," she muttered, thinking back to a few weeks ago when she'd last been here, helping Gabe hack a jump drive he'd stolen from the TV and radio station that broadcasted news from the States to Cuba.

The moment was still crystal clear in her memory: She'd located in the encrypted database a woman Gabe had been asking her to find, only to discover the word "deceased" next to her name.

Overcome by his emotions and unwilling to explain anything to Chessie, Gabe had left her the room, and Chessie had done what she always did in a crisis—look for more information to make sense of it. What she'd found didn't make sense at all, except that it did. A boy named Gabriel left behind by a dead woman.

"So, we're in Cuba," she said, opening the computer. "We have our cover. We get past customs, security, and clearances. Then what?"

"You'll start in a town about a three-and-a-half-hour drive from Havana. My best contact in Cuba told me to look for a Ramos family on a farm in Caibarién."

While she typed the name into Google Earth, Mal snorted. “Caibarién? The town that time forgot.”

“You’ve been there?” Chessie asked.

“I’ve been all over Cuba,” he said.

“Which is why he’s the perfect person to be your partner for this job,” Gabe reminded her. “But he’s right. It might be waterfront, but Caibarién is a pretty sad place. Don’t expect palm trees, sunshine, or umbrella drinks. Just go to this farm and find out what you can. Get in and get out.”

Frustration zinged through her, as it always did when directions were vague and…squishy. “Be specific, Gabe. What do we do before we get out?”

“Find Gabriel Winter,” Gabe said.

“And I absolutely can’t do that online?” Couldn’t she just use her computer to start digging? Not get on a plane with some sexy guy who gave her one crazy night of toe-curling sex and then took off like a thief in the night when he found out her name.

“Maybe you *could* do it online, Chess,” Gabe said, exasperation clipping his words. “But. I need proof. I need DNA. I need a…piece of this kid. Hair, skin, a toothbrush. Something.”

“We go in and get this kid’s toothbrush?” she asked, her voice rising. “Like the witch’s broomstick?”

“We can do it,” Mal said. “We’ll find the child, ascertain his situation, get some DNA, and come back.”

His confidence was…attractive. And a little scary. “But how do you just waltz onto a farm and steal a four-year-old’s toothbrush?” she asked.

Gabe looked skyward in disgust, but Mal took over, touching her arm. “We’ll be creative,” he said. “We’ll interview the family, take a little footage.”

“Yes, video, please,” Gabe said, his voice more

emotional than Chessie could ever remember hearing it.

"And while we're filming," Mal said, "you can slip into the bathroom and find his toothbrush. Or comb his hair for the camera and get some strands on a brush."

She finally stared at him, hating the fact that she was dying to put her hand over his and lean closer. That mouth was like a freaking magnet. "You make it sound easy."

"It will be, Francesca."

The name slid off his tongue and heated her like he'd just dripped liquid mercury through her veins.

"It will be?" she managed.

"If we are together, in concert, as a team."

Her heart rolled around and knocked on a few ribs during a free fall to her stomach. "Together…" she whispered the word.

There was no way—no way in heaven or hell—she could travel with this man and not end up back in bed with him.

"Can you do that?" Gabe asked.

"Can I not?" she replied to a different worry.

Gabe grinned. "I knew you were the right person for the job, little sister."

She finally found the power to pull her hand out from under Mal's hot touch, focusing on Gabe. "Yeah, well…if we can't get the DNA, surely I'll know if he's your child when I see him."

Gabe shook his head vehemently. "That won't help me when I kick down doors and shoot fuckers dead for the right to get him."

"Gabe," Mal said sharply. "You can't go there."

Gabe looked away and outside at the expansive resort gardens beyond what looked like a home gym he'd built on the back deck.

Chessie suddenly realized this was why he was in

Barefoot Bay. This woman had caused Gabe to turn his life upside down, come to this resort, start a business that was really a cover, and seek his past.

Which turned up a child.

She had to remember what was at stake here. This child was her *nephew*. And if she didn't go with Mal to Cuba, she knew Gabe would, which obviously was not a good thing.

"Can you tell us anything at all about him, Gabe?" she asked. "Anything at all?"

He exhaled silently, as if he'd been holding that breath for the whole time it took Chessie to finally realize what truly mattered.

"I can tell you when I think he might have been born, if my math is correct. I know when I last saw…his mother. If the child is mine, he would have to have been conceived before I left"—he glanced at Mal—"that last time."

Gabe had been in Miami for a while, then off the radar, then, boom, he'd shown up in Boston a few months after their cousins had opened the Guardian Angelinos. All he said was he'd quit working as a consultant for the CIA, and he'd picked up assignments for the family company. No mention of a woman in his life, ever.

"So what's the math?" Mal asked. "Sometime in 2011?"

"Summer," Gabe said. "Would have been born in summer of 2011. Much after that, and he can't…be mine."

The twist of pain in his voice cut right through Chessie. "I can do this," she reassured him.

Mal's eyes flickered with a hint of admiration. "*We* can do it," he corrected.

Gabe flopped back in his chair. "Which is why I picked you two."

Maybe, maybe not. She knew her brother well enough to know that if someone else had opened that file, someone else would go because Gabe would involve as few people as possible.

And that thought only reminded her of the bugged hotel room.

Yes, she'd destroyed the device, and on the ride down, she'd gone over everything she and Mal had said. Anyone listening would know they had sex—good, loud, lively sex—but she'd whispered her last name to him, and they'd barely talked after that.

But she had to tell Mal about it, and soon.

"Hey, I'm really tired," she said, the lie rolling easily off her lips. Truth was, she felt fiery and alert. And burning with the need to tell Mal about the bug, without telling Gabe. "Can I go to that beachfront villa you promised me?"

"Yeah, sure," Gabe agreed. "You drove all night, and you two have a long travel day ahead. You'll stay here, Mal. I need to finalize some details anyway. Nino can take you on the golf cart, Chess."

Chessie pushed back from the table. "Nino really ought to get my bag at the airport. Can't Mal drive me?"

Mal looked up, visibly surprised at the suggestion.

"He doesn't know where the villa is," Gabe said.

She looked hard at Mal, and he returned the stare, just enough silent communication in his nearly black eyes to give her hope that he'd go along with this emergency plan.

"That's okay." He stood. "I can figure it out and take her there."

Gabe shook his head. "For crying out loud, you can drive a golf cart yourself, Chessie. I need to talk to Mal."

No matter what they decided or who might have planted that listening device, she had to tell Mal first, alone and fast. Then they could decide what to tell Gabe, if anything.

"When you're done, then," she said, putting a light hand

on Mal's arm, trying not to think about the dusting of hair on his corded forearm and how it made her body quiver. "I'd like to get to know you better if we're going to be on this assignment together."

Mal's brow lifted slightly. He definitely took that suggestion the wrong way. Well, let him. If it got him alone with her, she'd have accomplished her goal.

"If that's what you want," he said, making no move to get out of her touch.

Gabe muttered a curse. "Go to dinner tonight if you want to play twenty questions with your life histories. I need Mal all day for some other stuff. Come on, Chess. Golf cart's outside, and I'll tell you how to get to the villa."

If she pushed any harder, it would just be weird. She'd have to wait until they were alone, if Gabe ever let them be alone before they landed in Cuba. For all she knew, he was going to fly to New York with them.

That's how overprotective her brothers were. And that's why she followed his orders for now, because if he found out the truth…no, Chessie didn't even want to think about it.

Chapter Six

Mal watched Chessie drive off in a golf cart, still trying to discern the unspoken signals she'd been sending him. She was mad? She had every right to be after he skulked out in the middle of the night. She was scared? He got that she didn't do field work and might think she was in over her head, but she didn't strike him as a woman who cowered easily.

Most likely, she wanted to cook up a story in case Gabe somehow figured out they'd met. The former CIA consultant was whip-smart and could easily spot discrepancies if he interrogated them apart from each other. He didn't think they'd done a bang-up job of pretending they'd never seen each other before, but then, he was trained in nuances of spying and she wasn't.

"She's gone," Gabe said, giving him a nudge.

"I see that." Mal kept his gaze on the asphalt trail that Chessie had taken to the resort.

"Then stop staring after my sister."

Mal turned and blinked at Gabe, bracing for the shakedown. He was totally ready to man up to what happened, but not without Chessie's permission. This was her family relationship at stake, and he had no right to kiss and tell. Even under some torture from Gabe, he wouldn't crack. He'd stay silent until they agreed otherwise. "I just wanted to be sure she followed your directions," he said.

Gabe looked skyward.

"How else would I know if she's going to be a good partner on this assignment?" Mal demanded.

Gabe tipped his head, no doubt loading up two barrels of sarcasm and accusations.

"She seems reluctant," Mal added. "Are you sure she's the right person for the job?"

Blue eyes the same deep Wedgwood blue as Chessie's—why the hell hadn't he noticed that when he met her?—narrowed like a pitcher about to wind up and throw a hundred-mile-an-hour fastball. Mal braced for the assault.

"For one thing, she's lovesick over this dick-brain bozo who's been stringing her along like she was fishing line on the end of his pencil-sized pole." Gabe put his hand on Mal's shoulder and guided him toward the road that joined all the bungalows on the cul-de-sac. "Maybe you can help in that regard."

Mal's steps slowed. Help? Gabe was giving him *permission*?

"I mean, you could be like a father figure, but not one of her brothers or her cousin."

Mal choked. "A *father* figure?" Oh hell no.

"She might look up to you."

Or up *at* him, from flat on her back. Like she did last night. "Hate to break it to you, big bro, but I'm not *that* much older than she is. She's thirty, right? That's what you put on the passport."

"Yeah, but..." Gabe shook his head and led Mal to another one of the Spanish-style bungalows. "Shit. I keep forgetting she's not sixteen."

"She is certainly not sixteen," Mal said, keeping all irony out of his voice. "And I'm thirty-eight. Definitely not old enough to be her father."

"But you are wise," Gabe shot back. "One of the best spooks I know."

"Used to be," he said, this time not able to keep anything out of his voice. Not the longing for his old life, not the bitterness for how it had been taken away from him.

Even if it was by his own doing.

"The main thing is that you're not her brother or cousin, so maybe she'll listen to you," Gabe continued, his brain obviously on his sister's past and not Mal's.

"Define listen," he muttered. 'Cause he was pretty sure Gabe didn't mean Mal should be teaching her the things they covered in the sack.

"She's a planner, our Chess," Gabe said. "She's obsessed with things being done in order and by an agreed-upon agenda. Must be the computer programmer nerd in her. She's never made an impulsive move in her life."

Yeah? She was pretty fucking impulsive last night. "That so? Why is that?"

"Who knows? She's the baby of the family, so maybe we've overprotected her a little bit."

"A little bit?" Mal joked.

"Fine, a lot. And I'm the worst, probably, so I guess that's why I should be the one to encourage her to get out of her, you know, comfort zone."

Oh, he knew her comfort zone. He remembered exactly how it tasted. "I'm sure she can get out of it when she really wants to."

"But she's never been interested in the family business beyond computer shit and claims she's not an adventure and danger junkie like the rest of us."

He considered that. If true, she sure acted out of character last night, or maybe Gabe didn't know his little sister at all.

"In my opinion, I'm doing her a favor with this gig," Gabe continued. "She needs to get out and see the world and stop obsessing about settling down and having kids. She hears that clock ticking."

Well, that took Mal out of the running. Not that he wanted to run with her, but it was good to know what she was about. Although, last night? There was no settling down going on.

Mal glanced in the general direction she'd gone, trying to reset his understanding of Chessie. "Maybe you see her one way, but she acts another when she's out in the world?"

Gabe shot him a look. "She's my sister, man. I know her better than anyone."

Maybe. Maybe not.

"Chess needs to get out more, so this job is perfect. Especially if you can make her forget that fuckwad she's been with for a year."

And two months. And ten days. "How do you think I'm going to do that?"

"Make her love life in the field, bro." He elbowed Mal. "I want her to move here and work for me, so help me sell this shit."

Not exactly how he was thinking about making her forget her ex. But, if Gabe was right about her life goals, Mal was all wrong for her. Hell, with his life, he was all wrong for any woman who wanted more than one night of a good time. That's all he could offer.

Gabe walked to the door of the last bungalow on the cul-de-sac, but stopped a few yards away. "Now let's talk about what I really want from you down there."

"Not to guide her through Caibarién and act as the

producer of a fake documentary while she snags some DNA?" He'd had a sneaking suspicion it was more than that when Gabe briefed him on the phone a few days ago.

"Well, yes, that, and..." Gabe turned to Mal, a world of hurt in his eyes. "I gotta know what happened to Isadora, Mal."

He stared at his friend, completely understanding the request. Except... "You know I'm banned from ever entering Gitmo, right? They think I'd have some kind of access to secret files, so denied access is part of my punishment."

"Punishment?" Gabe snorted. "That part's a blessing. But, you don't have anywhere near the prison. She left our...her...kid in Caibarién, so there must be a clue there. Someone must know something. Maybe why...she stayed there after I had to leave."

Mal eyed Gabe closely. "Are you pissed at her for not telling you?"

He didn't answer right away, looking off with uncertainty in his eyes. "She couldn't leave Cuba if she had a baby, because he would have been a Cuban citizen and you know they wouldn't let him go easily. And she knew as well as I did the consequences of me returning to the island."

Death. That was the consequence. The pricks who wanted him dead would never touch Gabe on US soil, or anywhere else, but if he tried to enter Cuba? He wouldn't make it through José Martí airport without a bullet in his back. Even Gabe. Especially Gabe.

"I just have to be sure no one knew that she and I were...." He closed his eyes. "If someone took her out as vengeance against me, that someone's gonna die."

He didn't bother to argue or suggest that the someone dying might be Gabe if he made the mistake of trying to go to Cuba. Why state the obvious? "Investigating her death is not a two-day job, Gabe. You need a spy on the ground, a professional who can infiltrate and dig. You know I can't do that for very long without getting on the CIA radar. Drummand still has spies in the country and a staff up in DC that does what he wants them to do."

Gabe looked skyward at the mention of the CIA supervisor they'd both worked for when they were at Guantanamo Bay prison on assignment.

"Whose dick does Roger Drummand suck to keep his job anyway?" Gabe mused. "He can't still be getting a paycheck based on the power of his father's reputation."

"Like hell he couldn't be. William Drummand's face is practically etched in marble in the entry of Langley, still the most-revered Cold War spy ever to come through the agency."

"I met him once," Gabe said.

"Don't tell me. He has an ego the size of Russia, lives on his past glories and expects his son to do the same?"

"Actually, he was a cool old dude. Powerful as shit, yeah. And he really cares about the agency."

Mal snorted. "Then that apple fell far because Roger's not even fit to tie Dad's shoes. Every assignment and promotion he ever got was because of his last name. When William Drummand kicks, Roger will be shuffled to an even less important job than whatever he has now."

"But in the meantime…" Gabe reminded him.

"In the meantime, I have to remember that uncovering an embezzler in his organization was probably Roger Drummand's greatest career achievement. And if he thinks I got the money they never found and he could lock me up again, it would be another feather in his almost bald cap."

"You mean to tell me they never located the half mill?" Gabe blew out a whistle as he reached the door.

"I guess someone found it, but not the US government."

"Think your old pal the motherly secretary has it?"

Mal shook his head. "Don't know, don't care. And I won't let Alana Cevallos take the blame now any more than I would then."

"My pal, the fucking hero."

Mal ignored the comment. "Did what I had to do."

"Taking the fall for Drummand's secretary and spending four years in prison wouldn't have been idiotic at all, Mal, if she'd been a hot piece of ass you were boning instead of a middle-aged single mother of three."

"Three kids eight and under," Mal said. "All of whom would have been orphans and trapped in a wretched Communist country if Alana had gone to prison. They had everything to lose, and I had nothing."

"Just a hot-shit undercover career that some people would kill to have."

He still didn't care. Those kids would have been lost, or worse, if he hadn't taken the blame when Roger Drummand discovered that someone had stolen five hundred grand from the government coffers at Gitmo. And when Alana came to him and told him she was going to be blamed for it, he did the only thing he could do for the single mother.

Gabe headed up the stairs to a sunny-yellow bungalow with a small brass sign that said McBain Security, pausing for a second. "Don't you *want* to know where that money is?"

He hoped it was in four healthy accounts, accruing a future for those kids and their mother. "Don't know, don't care."

"Think she has it?" Gabe asked, clearly still a master at reading people's thoughts.

"Then she wouldn't still work at Gitmo," Mal said, purposely not answering the question. "Or stay in that crappy Cuban town." At Gabe's look, Mal added, "I know people, too."

"The only person you need to know is me," Gabe said.

Mal laughed. "Still the most arrogant dickhead around."

"Usually. And I'm also the only arrogant dickhead around who can help you."

"I thought I was here to help you," Mal said.

"How do you think I'm going to pay you for this favor?"

"I don't want to be paid, Gabe."

Gabe put his hand on the door and nodded to the sign. "You do realize I don't really work for a resort bodyguard company, right? You *do* know what I do here, right? Private witness protection. People who don't want to be found, ever, by anyone, come to me. You could be a client. No charge. I can get you everything you need, every single piece of paper and ID, to set you up somewhere else. Not a federal agent in sight watching your every move."

It wasn't the first time he'd considered putting Gabe's talent to work. But it never felt right. Why should he run when he was an innocent man? Still, the possibility intrigued. "Where would I live?"

"I got people all over the world, my friend. Fiji, Hong Kong, Tokelau. You could be the fucking King of Micronesia. Name a country that appeals."

"The United States of America. You know, the country where I was born and the one I fought for as a Marine, then worked for as a spy on the side of the red, white, and blue. That country."

"Sorry." The single word held so much punch, it made Mal swallow hard. "That country thinks you stole half a million dollars from the Guantanamo till. Pick another one."

"I'm not interested in another one."

Gabe looked genuinely disgusted. "Instead, you'll spend your life looking over your shoulder knowing that no matter what you do someone is always watching, waiting for you to slip up."

"At least I'm not looking over my shoulder at Micronesia."

"Have you seen those islands? The place is a damn paradise."

"Would you live there?" Mal challenged.

"Dude. I'm living *here*." He swept his hand. "Bareass Bay. Where lost spies come to die. You'll fit right in, my man."

Mal followed Gabe into a small office, the front area desks peppered with a few muscular guys who probably worked as freelance bodyguards or resort security, two women on computers, and, tucked in the back, Uncle Nino in his bright pink shirt, a phone to his ear.

"My office is back there," Gabe said. "Don't pinch my sexy assistant, or he'll sauté you in hot garlic oil."

Mal smiled as he nodded to the old man and followed Gabe into an unremarkable space that consisted of little more than a desk and chair, a bookshelf, and a straight-backed and rather uninviting guest chair. The only thing of visual interest in the room was a glass jar stuffed with cash on top of the shelves.

"Speaking of what's wrong with this picture…" Mal said, a little stunned at the sparse surroundings. "Is that how you pay people?"

Gabe threw a dirty look at the money jar. "I got a woman on staff who charges me every time I swear."

Mal let out a hoot. "Bet she's rich."

Gabe fell into the chair behind his desk, no humor on his

face. “I don’t want to be here in this particular hellhole, and yet, here I am. My own private Micronesia.”

Mal frowned. “The private wit-sec program isn’t going well?”

“It’s fine. It’s actually a brilliant idea, and I could stay busy and rich, but…” He huffed out a breath and looked out a small window that faced a building similar to this one, probably housing another service for the resort. “I came here to be close to where I hoped Isadora would be.”

Mal’s gut tightened at the admission. “Cuba.”

Gabe nodded slowly. “And now she’s…”

Dead. Fuck. “I’m really sorry, Gabe,” he said, not for the first time. “I know…I know what she meant to you.”

“You better than anyone,” Gabe said.

“The glory days at Gitmo…” Mal could still smell the back room at Abbey Road where they’d worked together. Mal, armed to the nines, pretending to be a guard but really trying to get the detainees to trust him so he could get inside information. Meanwhile, Gabe used his extraordinary skills to persuade the “borderline terrorists,” as they used to call the ones who weren’t totally hard-core, to help the United States. And Isadora, the talented and beautiful CIA translator who managed to take Gabe’s mostly off-color words and make them work in Pakistani, Arabic, and Kurdish.

“They weren’t exactly glory days,” Gabe said. “But I was really happy. Proving you can be happy in any shithole if you’re with the right person.”

Mal couldn’t help smiling, just remembering how good Gabe and Isa were together. “She brought out a side in you I don’t think many people see. Tender Gabe.”

“Shut the fuck up.”

Mal leaned forward. “Love-Note-Leaving Gabe.”

His friend laughed, shaking his head. “Stuck them in our

secret cubbyhole in the Country Club like a couple of teenagers."

"In the benches along the wall." Mal remembered everything about where they'd done their best work. Dubbed the Country Club, it was more like a lounge, a spacious area where a few particularly talented CIA consultants worked under the relentless watch of Roger Drummand on his pet project of turning detainees into US spies in their own countries. "We used to stash porn in there for when you really needed to make one of those scum-suckers switch sides. Yeah, I remember."

"That's not all I stashed," Gabe said, laughing at a memory. "There's a beauty of a Beretta Nano in there."

"What?" Mal choked a laugh. "How the hell did you do that and I didn't know?"

"I did a lot of things you didn't know. I was scared something could happen. A riot or uprising. Something that would trap Isadora in that room with a detainee, so I used our note cubby to hide the pistol."

Mal shook his head. "Ballsy."

"Those morons couldn't find a gun if it was stuck up their ass. That pistol is probably still there." He shifted his gaze to the small window, his smile fading. "And so's Isadora's kid, Mal. Somewhere on that fucking rock. And I *know* he's mine."

He'd never heard Gabe sound so…beaten.

"I'll help you," Mal promised. "I won't be able to bring him back myself, but we'll find him. We'll make sure he's yours. And then we'll come up with a way to get him to you."

Gabe gave a tight smile. "And find out what happened to Isadora."

"Do you know anything at all about how she died?"

"Nothing," Gabe admitted. "Not one of my few contacts down there knows a thing. Just that she was last living with this Ramos family on a farm. Surely they'll know what happened to her. Was it natural causes? An accident? Or…retribution against me."

"No one knew about you two," Mal said, wanting to take the look of abject pain off Gabe's face. "Only me."

"But after she got pregnant?" Gabe shook his head. "If I hadn't had to leave Gitmo and take down those pricks in Miami, everything would have been different."

"You were doing your job," Mal reminded him. "And you saved a lot of lives and stopped a lot of trouble by identifying Cuban spies."

"And made a lot of enemies." He raked his hand through his hair and looked away, misery in every pore on his face. "I need closure. I can't fucking *breathe* until I have closure."

"I'll find out what I can," Mal assured him. "But what about Chessie?"

"What about her?"

"She's smart, Gabe. She'll hear me ask questions. She might have a few of her own."

Gabe nodded, as if he'd already considered that. "Look, she knows there was a woman, obviously. And she knows I cared about her. She wouldn't wonder why you're trying to find out how she died."

"But what if I get classified information in the process?"

"I trust Chessie, but for God's sake, don't put her in harm's way. If anything happens to her, I'll kill you, and the rest of my family will kill me."

"Understood."

"And I mean *anything*, Mal. Half your job is to protect her, and the other half is to guide her around Cuba."

"What about getting the information you want?"

Gabe grinned and leaned back in his chair, putting his feet on the desk, a cocky son of a bitch again. "That's the third half."

But Mal leaned forward with one more question. "What are you going to do if you find out…if you don't like what I learn about Isa?"

Gabe immediately put his feet back down and leaned all the way over the desk to make his point. "If she didn't die peacefully and naturally, I will find out who is responsible for killing her and pluck out their eyes, break every bone in their body, and then stab them until they bleed out. What do you think I would do to anyone who even thinks about hurting someone I love?"

Mal swallowed against a dry throat. "Nothing less."

Chapter Seven

Half a million dollars?

She'd stripped down, fallen into bed, and spread her legs for a prison guard who'd gone to jail for embezzling half a freaking million dollars? A loser with forty-two postal address changes in thirty-eight years who still had some holes in his whereabouts?

This had to be the icing on a cake of bad choices in men.

"Damn it," she mumbled as she cruised through another database, unearthing one shocking piece of information after another. "You sure can look like one kind of person on paper and another in bed."

Why would Gabe trust this guy? Why would he trust her safety to him and the project of finding his most precious possession—a child? To be fair, Gabe was a fantastic judge of character, and he must know something that wasn't in these databases.

She brushed back some hair that fell over her face, vaguely realizing it had dried in the few hours since she'd showered and started researching her new "partner." As soon as Nino brought her clothes, she'd be marching over to Gabe's office for some answers.

Still wrapped in a fluffy Casa Blanca-supplied bathrobe,

she pushed the computer away and walked through the French doors to the pool deck that overlooked a glorious water view. Turquoise waves lapped at white sand, a stretch of beach dotted by the bright yellow umbrellas that were a signature of this high-end resort. The sound of gulls and the occasional song of a kid's laughter floated up from the sand, making her ache in a way she didn't understand.

No, she understood. Sometimes it seemed like her love life was one long series of bad choices, all of them denying her the chance for that sound to be *her* child. And instead of being melancholy, she needed to get mad.

Mad that Mal wasn't the one-night stand she'd hoped to have; now she had…feelings for him. She fisted her hand and banged the railing like she could punch the feelings away. She had to. He couldn't be more wrong for her.

She closed her eyes and blocked out the postcard view, replacing it with the stark black-and-white data that she'd discovered about Malcolm James Harris, thirty-eight years old, born in Houston, Texas.

High school dropout, arrested for a drunk and disorderly at eighteen, enlisted in the Marines, did two tours in Iraq and Afghanistan, then got out. More moves around the country in at least a dozen states—that's where the holes were—with three stints as a prison guard. Then he joined the Maryland Reserves, got sent to Guantanamo, spent a few more months with no real address, then was at Allenwood as a prisoner…charged with stealing half a million dollars in federal funds.

He wasn't a common thief; he was a big-time, showstopping thief.

And he'd never lay a hand on her again.

She closed the collar of the robe, as if she were physically blocking his access to her, and even that made her feel…sad. Mad. Frustrated.

Obviously, she'd never have sex with him again. Damn it.

That decision should suit her just fine—considering what she wanted in a man, and it sure as hell wasn't a world-class embezzler with a list of forty-two different postal addresses. But it somehow *didn't* suit her to think he was off-limits. Not primal her. Not Chessie who lost all control in a hotel with a stranger.

How could she forget how amazing that had been? How could she look at that face and not remember how his whiskers rubbed her thighs? How could she look at his mouth and not remember the taste of every kiss? How could she do this job for Gabe, pressed up next to Mal in an airplane, and not relive the way he owned every inch of her body and made her melt?

She jumped at a knock on the villa door. "Get a grip, Chess," she mumbled, pushing off the railing, mentally preparing to deal with her grandfather. Gabe might have told Nino about the child, but the "my partner is an embezzler" vault should stay closed for now.

He knocked again, harder.

"I'm coming, Nino. No need to beat down the door."

She waited for his typical response, a muttering in Italian or butchering of an English idiom, but there was nothing but silence from the other side of the door. Before she opened, she peeked through the peephole and sucked in a quiet breath. That was so not Nino.

Aw, *man.* This wasn't fair. Even distorted by the lens, Malcolm James Harris, transient thief, was all dark and smoldery. How was a woman expected *not* to fall into bed with him…hours after they met?

Because he stole half a million dollars, that's how. Imagine what he could do to a woman's heart.

"I have your bag from the airport," Mal said.

Well, she had wanted to talk to him alone, so this was as good a time as any. She tightened the robe again. She would have preferred to have real clothes on, though. And maybe a little makeup.

Not that she felt she needed to impress him, but she could use a dose of confidence in the face of his flawlessness.

Flawlessness? He was a thief with forty-two former addresses, one of them a prison cell.

"Let me in, Francesca."

The demand, spoken low and slow and without any doubt that she would let him in, did stupid things to her stomach. She opened the door, and he rolled the suitcase in, following close behind. Stepping back, she looked up at him, self-consciously pulling the robe tie.

"Are you going to blush every time you see me? 'Cause it's a dead giveaway."

She was blushing? She touched her face as if she could wipe away the heat. "I've been out by the pool."

Wordlessly, he nudged her into the hall toward the living area, carrying her suitcase for her. "We need to talk."

"I know," she said, a little ticked that he acted like it was his idea.

She dropped into one of the chairs, but he stayed standing, his torso blocking all the light from the patio. "You can sit down," she said.

He wore baggy shorts that showed strong, muscular calves with a dusting of dark hair. Sneakers that were at the very least a size twelve and a plain white T-shirt that showed off the result of hours spent at the gym. Or maybe he'd pulled hard labor in prison.

He loomed over her. Too close. Too big. Too good in bed *and how could she stand to not have that again, even just once?*

"You want to know if I told him, don't you?" he asked, obviously misreading her expression of horror at that last thought.

"What I want is for you to sit down. I know you didn't tell him since your teeth are intact, you bear no bullet holes, and your arms and legs are still attached."

He gave just enough of a smile to make her stomach do a somersault, and he did perch on the armrest of the plush sofa, taking away a little of his overpoweringness. A little. "Proof that our liaison is still a secret."

"Liaison?" She almost choked on the word. "That's a pretty fancy word for stupid."

His jaw opened just a little in reaction. "You think it was?"

This time she did choke. "Well, it wasn't smart."

"Yeah? And what makes you think that?"

"First clue? Your midnight escape."

"Okay, yes. Once you said your name and I put two and two together, I knew—"

"Gabe would beat your ass if he found out you seduced his sister."

"Not what I was going to say. And newsflash: I'm not scared of your brother."

She shot a dubious brow up.

"I'm not. That's not why I left."

"So did you leave because I didn't have a half million dollars you could steal?"

For the first time, a flicker crossed his dark eyes. Shame. Remorse. Maybe a little regret. Enough to almost make her want to take back the comment.

"That didn't take long," he said softly.

She shrugged. "It's what I do."

He gave her a direct look. "Would you like to know why I left, or would you rather share all the details of my life you've found online?"

She felt her own flash of remorse for digging into his private life, but pushed it aside. "Yes, I'd like to know why you left when you found out who I was."

"You said you were visiting your brother in Florida, so I figured I better get down here overnight, get my marching orders from Gabe, and get on the road before your flight landed. Save us both that awkward moment."

She fought a smile. "When you find out the stranger you slept with is your mission partner. Definitely awkward."

"So how do you want to play this?" he asked. "Our secret or not? It's your call, Chessie."

Chessie. So much for Francesca whispered in the heat of passion. She wished to hell that didn't disappoint her, but it did. "I'm afraid it's not our secret at all."

He just looked at her. "Who did you tell?"

"No one, but I have to show you something."

He looked surprised when she stood and walked to the bedroom door. She heard his footsteps behind her as she headed to the dresser, opened the top drawer, and picked up the cracked device she'd had in her jeans pocket. Holding it in her palm, she showed him.

"I found this on the bedrail in your hotel room when I was retrieving my clothes."

He looked at it and visibly paled beneath his tanned skin. "Fuck," he whispered.

"Yep. And with, it would seem, an audience."

He reached for it, but she shut her hand over his, trapping the bug between their palms. Electricity danced up her arm at the contact that felt both familiar and scary.

"You're going to leave, aren't you?"

"That's not what I'm thinking."

"But you are. I can tell by the look on your face you're planning your next move, which will be *out* and *far* and *fast*."

"How would you know that?"

She managed a wry smile. "Forty-two addresses in thirty-eight years. And those are the ones that are registered."

His gaze tapered. "That's some thorough background check you did."

"I'm nothing if not thorough," she told him, freeing her hand.

He took the bug and flipped it in his hand to see the other side. "You destroyed it?"

"Yeah, I, um, might have freaked a bit when I found it and realized our, um, *liaison* had been overheard by…someone." But who? Did he know?

"We have to tell Gabe about our hookup now," he said simply.

Hookup. She closed her eyes and pretended it didn't bother her.

"And he's going to pull us both from this assignment," he added.

"Why would he do that?"

"Because if someone is following me, it could be dangerous for you if we're together."

"Why the hell would someone be following you?"

He just stared at her, a look she knew so damn well from her brother. Need To Know. Need To Know. Always the freaking Need To Know and she didn't.

Irritation ricocheted through her. "I was in that room, too, Mal. I'm involved whether you like it or not."

"I know. I'm sorry." Sorry that he dragged her into this or sorry their *hookup* happened?

She had to let that go. It *was* a hookup. "Does that device have a tracking system in it?" she asked.

He turned it over and over in his hand. "I don't think so. It's pretty low-tech."

"That's what I thought," she said. "Maybe one of the housekeepers puts it in the rooms and gets off on people…liaising."

He didn't smile at the joke. "'Fraid not, Chessie. We have to tell Gabe and let him make the call."

"Do we, really?" Maybe Mal wasn't afraid of Gabe's wrath, but Chessie sure as hell wasn't prepared for his…disappointment. And wrath.

"Yes, we do. There's no room for argument, because this could change everything."

She blew out a breath, knowing deep inside that arguing was futile. "Let me get some clothes on, and I'll go with you. In fact, you should hang back and let me do the dirty work because I might be able to save your ass by taking most of the blame myself."

"Hell no."

"Excuse me?"

His jaw clenched as he reached for the collar of her robe, easing her closer. "You're not going to take any blame for what happened between us. You didn't come on any stronger than I did." His mouth was too close, his eyes too dark, and his touch too sure and strong.

"I could have stopped you at any point in time. I'll be sure to mention that to Gabe so you get extra bonus points."

"I don't need bonus points," he said.

"What do you need?"

He gripped the collar tighter, then let go, grazing her lower lip with a maddeningly slow touch. "More of you."

Speaking of *hell no.* But there she was, inching closer

like he was a magnet and she was a helpless piece of horny metal. "Sorry, it's called a *one*-night stand for a reason."

"He'll split us up," he said. "At the very least."

"I know," she said, staring at his gorgeous mouth.

He got closer. "Maybe was stupid, Francesca, but that was some damn good *liaising*."

"Really good," she whispered.

He lowered his head and put his mouth over hers, and it started all over again, just like last night. A low burn in her belly, a tight squeeze in her chest, and a crazy, lazy, dizzy sensation that made her head feel disconnected from the rest of her body. She let her eyes close and her hands grip his biceps, remembering how it felt when he laid her down and took ownership of her.

He ended the kiss long before she was ready. "I'll wait for you outside while you get dressed."

She managed a shaky breath. "I'll just be a second. Then we'll go to the hangman together." As she walked away, she glanced over her shoulder to see him staring at her. "What?"

"Gallows humor. I like that in a woman."

Great, just great. The embezzler with forty-two addresses and someone following him *liked* her. That was so not in her plan.

Chapter Eight

While Mal stood outside the villa waiting for Chessie, he examined the gadget in the sunlight. Pretty cheap quality, but effective enough if someone wanted to listen to him spill secrets to a lover. He knew who'd planted it, and it wasn't a fucking Marriott maid.

Drummand must have been laughing his ass off at him.

But who'd tipped the son of a bitch off? Someone at the airport? On that hotel shuttle? At the registration desk? All three? He should have been on his game and watching everyone, not just the woman he wanted naked and in the sack. He had a brain and should have used it to realize she was genuine sooner than he had, and then he should have realized someone else was on his tail.

But the only tail he'd been interested in was Chessie's—Gabe's baby sister. He didn't even do a standard check of the hotel room for bugs, which would have tipped him off that someone had followed him to Atlanta.

His only slim hope was that they didn't manage to track him here after all that maneuvering he did to lose them—which was probably how Chessie beat him here in the first place. And hopefully, they didn't know who she was.

Which was ridiculous. Drummand had plenty of

background on the former consultant, which likely included a dossier on every person in his family.

"Hey." Chessie stepped outside into the sunlight, dressed in faded jeans with holes in the knees and the boots he distinctly remembered dropping to the floor in the hotel room last night.

The memory fried his brain like he'd licked a finger and stuck it into the nearest socket.

"Yeah, this is a good idea," he mumbled as she closed the door behind her and slipped a bag over a bare shoulder. A loose, sleeveless top, practically see-through and cropped two inches above her jeans. The whole outfit showed way too much smooth, feminine skin that he knew tasted like sugar and sex. More fingers in sockets.

"You're staring," she said, an echo of the accusation she'd made a few moments after they'd first met.

You're gorgeous, he'd replied then. And she still was, but everything was different now. "You're…exposed."

She straightened her black-rimmed glasses, but that didn't hide her eye roll. "You've seen it all before."

That was the problem. That one time wasn't going to be enough.

"And what the hell do you mean 'this is a good idea'? Do you have even the slightest clue how my brother is going to react?"

"I'm afraid I do." He rubbed his jaw, anticipating the first blow as they headed toward the golf cart parked in the drive.

She paused and looked around, the Florida sunshine, still strong in early December, bathing everything—including her—in a warm glow. Taking a deep breath, she tipped her face to the sun and closed her eyes.

"What's frustrating is now I'm ready to go," she told him. "We have a plan, more or less, and a cause. A good cause. I think Gabe would be stupid to go all big-brother crazy and decide we need to be separated like a couple of teenagers who are too young to have sex."

He started to respond, then stopped. "You know we're combustible."

He could have sworn she shivered in the seventy-degree sunshine. "Combustible," she repeated on a whisper.

"We'd never make it through Cuba." Hell, they might not make it through this afternoon.

"Without a *liaise*?" she asked, the hint of a smile threatening, but he couldn't tell if it was for their dumb euphemism or just the idea of it.

"Look, I've been in prison for four years and—"

She held up a hand with a dry, sarcastic laugh. "I'm going to stop you right there. Because if you say that's why you hit on me—"

"Of course it's not why. I'm just explaining that I'm…that you're…"

She slipped her lower lip under her front teeth, regarding him from behind those glasses, which were somehow as sexy as if she stood in front of him buck naked. "Continue," she urged. "'Cause this really ought to be good."

How could he tell her that for the first half of their encounter he'd thought she was a spy and he was playing and testing and generally being a dick? And then, when he'd realized she wasn't, then he was just…

"Human," he muttered. "I'm only human."

"Oooh, *human*. Well, that's…a lovely compliment." She strode past him, a whiff of something spicy in her wake, and climbed into the passenger side of the golf cart. "Can't wait to hear you tell Gabe. 'Well, buddy, sorry I banged your sister, but extreme humanism made me do it.'"

Irritation clanged every nerve as he got behind the wheel.

"Extreme *attraction*, Chessie." He got right in her face. "Which I'm pretty damn sure went both ways."

She paled enough to confirm that it did, but recovered in a second, giving his shoulder a shove. "Move it, human. I'm sure he won't mess up your *attractive* face too much."

Chessie stayed pensive for a few moments as they drove, checking out the natural beauty as if she were drinking it in, but something told him she wasn't.

"You going to tell me why you think someone is following you?" she asked.

"No."

She gave a caustic laugh. "You sure you're not a spy, Mal? 'Cause you sure act like one."

He stayed silent, pulling the cart in front of McBain Security. "All that matters, Chessie, is that Gabe doesn't lose his shit so much over this bug and how you found it in my room—"

"Can't we say *you* found it in your room?"

He shook his head. "I'd have told him by now. I won't lie to him. It'd compromise the mission. What we can't do is let him try to go to Cuba himself."

She considered that, her frown deepening. "Why can't he? I mean, I know he can't say, but how do you know? Why are you..." Her voice trailed off, and her eyes cleared with comprehension. "Compromise the mission," she echoed. "Now that is not something you hear your run-of-the-mill prison guard say."

She was way too smart not to figure it out sooner or later. He just looked ahead and confirmed her guess with a quick close of his eyes.

"You're a spy."

"Not anymore," he said quietly.

She didn't move for a moment, except that her chest rose

and fell with a tight breath as this new information took hold. "I didn't get that from my research." She actually sounded a little disgusted with her failure.

"I think that's kind of the point of the job."

"Is that why someone is following you? Do you have classified information or...access to something? Why is it such a big deal that your room was bugged? And how'd they get a bug planted so fast in a hotel room that you didn't even reserve?"

"They're good. And that's a lot of questions you know I'm not going to answer."

"But we're on a mission together," she shot back. "We shouldn't be strangers."

"Didn't hurt us in that hotel room. In fact..."

She leaned closer when he didn't finish the thought, narrowing blue eyes at him. "If you say that was a big turn-on for you, Mr. I'm Only Human, I'm going to hit you harder than Gabe ever could. Answer my question. Why is someone following you?"

He exhaled, slowly. "I honestly don't know for sure. Anything I tell you would just be a guess."

"I'll take a guess."

He shook his head. "You know I can't do that."

She dropped back on the seat with a grunt of frustration. "Well, what about Gabe?"

"He won't tell you anything."

"But why can't he go to Cuba?"

He turned and gave her a *get real* look, which she accepted with a slight nod. The sister of a spy would be well trained to live with unanswered questions, and while he respected the fact that she knew when to stop asking, he also felt she was owed something. At least a reason for why they had to convince Gabe not to go to Cuba.

"I will tell you this," he said, reaching for her hand. "If he does go to Cuba, he will never come out alive. He made enemies. Deadly enemies."

She blinked at him, truly speechless, color washing over her fine cheeks. "Is he safe here?"

"As long as he never steps foot in Cuba, yes. But I swear to God, Chessie, there's a serious amount of money on his head, and if there's one thing crooked Cubans like, it's money."

She stared at him as that settled on her. "He trusts us enough to do this for him."

Mal nodded. "Though I can't say what he'll do once we find this child and prove he's Gabe's son." Because Gabe Rossi would risk life and limb to get his child. They both knew that.

"Then I know what we have to do," Chessie said, her voice calm. "We can tell him about the bug, and we can tell him how and why I found it. But then we have to convince him to handle the fact that we were together and let us go on this mission and find his son. One, two, three, that's what we'll do."

"Francesca, the planner," he whispered.

"That's me."

"I like it." He leaned closer, feeling the need to seal the deal with a kiss, but she edged back and gave her head a quick shake.

"Poppy," she said under her breath.

He frowned. "Excuse me?"

"The maid over there is Poppy. She works for Gabe. She's his eyes and ears around the resort, and I guarantee you she's taking everything in right now, including how you almost…" She slowed her speech and scowled. "Were you just so overwhelmed with being human that you were going to kiss me?"

He laughed. "Overwhelmed, yeah."

"Uh, excuse me." The woman's voice pulled them apart, and Mal turned to meet large, dark eyes under a furrowed brow. "Can I help…oh, Miss Chessie! I heard you were here. Didn't know that was you, and I have to check everyone out, you know."

"Hello, Poppy." Chessie climbed down from the cart and greeted the woman with an easy hug. "Nice to see you again. Have you met Malcolm Harris, Gabe's friend?"

She lifted a brow. "He has a friend other than Nino?"

Mal smiled. "The list is short." He shook her hand. "Hello, Poppy."

"Are you looking for Mr. Gabriel? Don't bother going in the office, he's not there."

Damn it, Mal didn't want to put this conversation off any longer. "Do you know where we can find him?"

"Yes, but…" A plump lower lip pushed out, and she tightened her mouth and looked from one to the other. "You're his sister, and you're his friend, right?"

"Right," they answered in unison.

"Well…" She glanced from side to side, as if she suspected they were being watched. "I don't know who else to tell because I tried to tell Nino, and all he does is tell me to mind my own business. Minding other people's business is my job now, doesn't he know that? Anyway, maybe you can help."

"What is it, Poppy?" Chessie asked, a note of impatience telling Mal she was as anxious as he was.

"It's Mr. Gabriel," the woman said on an exaggerated sigh. "I simply don't know what to do with him."

"What do you mean?" Chessie stepped closer, immediately more interested now.

"Well, I know I'm supposed to be watching other folks

around here and reporting back to him. That's my job, you see," she added to Mal, as if he hadn't picked that up yet.

"What about Gabe?" Chessie pressed.

"He just hasn't been himself since last time you were here, Miss Chessie. He's not taking any new business. He's always in the back of the house just slamming those iron bars around and doing so many of those push-up things it's a wonder he doesn't drop over dead."

They were both silent for a moment, unsure what this woman—a woman who obviously liked to know all—really *did* know about what was troubling Gabe.

"Well, he likes to work out," Mal said after a beat.

"He never sleeps," Poppy continued. "Never. His bed isn't touched when I go to the house to clean, and I've seen him at night when I'm leaving the office late or coming in to open." She pointed over her shoulder at one of the bungalows Gabe had told Mal was designated for the resort's housekeeping business. "Something's wrong with him."

"He has a lot on his mind," Chessie offered, as vague as Mal.

"He doesn't eat, not one decent meal. Not my good Jamaican food and not that thick spaghetti all dripping in cheese your grandfather insists on making. I cook good food, you know, with none of that—"

"Okay, Poppy." Chessie cut her off with a quick wave. "We're going to talk to Gabe right now, and I'll be sure he eats—"

"I've recycled far too many empty booze bottles from their trash."

Leave it to Gabe to teach the housekeeper how to be a good spy. Mal put a hand on Chessie's shoulder to guide her away. "Thanks for letting us know," he said.

"I'm sure he'll be fine," Chessie added.

The other woman shook her head. “Not fine, not at all. I hope you two can help him, because I’m worried he’s going to do something rash.”

“Rash?” Chessie stopped. “Like what?”

Poppy’s big brown eyes grew wide and scared. “I don’t know, but this change is so sudden. When I started working for him, he was, you know, funny and…happy. Now he’s…”

Grieving, Mal thought. “Thanks, Poppy,” he said quickly. “We’re here to help him, I promise.”

And that wasn’t a lie. If they found Gabe’s son, surely he’d climb out of his personal hellhole.

The maid gave a quick nod and pointed to the bungalow where Gabe and Nino lived. “Just go around the back and holler. He’ll have his ear things in and turned up to deafening, like he does when he beats the sweet stuffing out of that punching bag. You’d think that thing was made of the devil himself.”

“Thanks,” Chessie said with another quick hug of Poppy’s wide shoulders.

As they walked toward Gabe’s bungalow, she let out a deep sigh. “I don’t know what’s worse. Knowing my brother is in personal agony or not really understanding why.”

“I’ll tell you why,” Mal said. “He loved Isa.”

“Isa…” She said the nickname softly, her steps slowing.

“Your brother loved Isadora Winter like nothing I’ve ever seen before. Like nothing I thought…” *Could even be possible.*

She stopped completely then, taking that in. “I could tell when I found her name listed as deceased that he…he cared a lot.”

She didn’t need to know everything, but she needed to know this. “He *loved* her, Chessie. And he won’t admit it, or any weakness, but with Isa gone, he needs his son.”

Chessie nodded slowly, her expression in complete agreement with him. "First, we have to make sure the boy is his."

And find out what happened to Isadora. "And *we* have to do that," Mal said. "Or he'll risk his life trying to do it himself." He guided her down the narrow strip of grass that separated the bungalows.

They continued to the back of the house, coming around where a raised patio faced the expansive gardens of Casa Blanca. No sound came from the patio, and the heavy bag that had been jury-rigged to hang from a partial awning hung untouched.

Mal opened his mouth to call out Gabe's name, but a soft sound stopped him. Chessie heard it, too, looking up with a question in her eyes. It sounded like…sniffing.

They took a few more steps, cautious and uncertain, because who in their right mind would sneak up on Gabe Rossi?

They heard it again. The distinct sound of…oh *man.*

Chessie put her hand over her mouth to hold back any sound, and Mal just closed his eyes. Someone was crying—hard.

They both froze at the sound, so utterly foreign. It was easy to think of Gabe as invincible, emotionless, fierce to the bone. But he'd lost a woman he loved deeply, and now likely had a child he had very little hope of claiming as his.

And Mal was about to ice that cake with a frosting of bad news. *I slept with your sister, buddy.*

Chessie gave her head a quick shake, her eyes communicating that she was thinking the same thing. They couldn't do this. They couldn't make his life worse or more complicated. And, despite their best efforts, he'd insist on a change in the plan, and that would just take more time to find out what he needed to know.

Mal pulled Chessie back into the yard next to the house. "We can get in and out of Cuba fast and clean."

She nodded. "We'll find that boy, get the DNA, and be home in two days."

That may or may not be true, but he loved her optimism. They looked at each other, making a mutual, silent, absolutely correct decision. They weren't telling Gabe a thing.

Turning, they started to hustle back to the street, picking up speed just to get away from the stomach-wrenching sound of Gabe having a horrible private moment.

Just as they reached the front of the house, the full weight of a man pounced on Mal's back, smacking him to the ground with one smooth move and taking Chessie down with him.

Mal whipped around to meet a gaze that was hard as nails and mad as hell.

Chapter Nine

"Lila Wickham is here to see you, Mr. Drummand."

Roger Drummand stared at his assistant, hoping like hell the blood draining from his face wasn't visible to her. His assistant was no trained agent, of course, but she was sharper than the last one, which was never a good thing when you were hiding as much as he was.

He'd learned that the hard way...when Lila Wickham entered his organization.

"I'll be right with her," he said, shuffling the report he'd been reading. His gaze dropped to the picture of a young woman who shared eye and hair color with one of his most annoying, aggravating, and, damn it, talented former consultants. He couldn't tell if Francesca Rossi, who apparently had brilliant computer skills, also had her brother's aptitude in the field. But it was a safe bet annoying arrogance was embedded in their genes.

He flipped to the next shot, this one of this younger female Rossi toasting a brew at an airport bar, laughing, flirting, smiling at Malcolm Harris like the son of a bitch hung the moon. *Why*?

The report said they appeared to meet by accident, stayed in the same hotel after mass flight cancellations due to storms, and fucked their ever-loving brains out until Harris blew out in the middle of the night.

They'd lost him then. But the woman rented a car and headed south to Florida, where Roger happened to know Gabriel Rossi had moved to work for a private security firm. Or so he said.

"Roger." Lila closed the door behind her with a solid click, entered the office with an air of ownership, and took the guest chair, not waiting for an invitation.

"Ms. Wickham," he replied, purposely reminding her of her incredible lack of respect toward a CIA supervisor.

She angled her head and crossed her arms. "There was no money transferred to my account," she said, her British accent clipping each word. "Tuesday was your deadline."

He met her deep-brown gaze, enhanced by expertly applied makeup and a fringe of lashes so thick they had to be fake. A shocking contrast to her eyes, her hair was nearly platinum, always stick-straight and loose over her shoulders. The color accentuated olive-toned skin and angular, stark features. Her nose had a bump that would be a flaw on anyone else, but somehow gave her an air of a noble patrician, and her teeth were so white and perfect they reminded him of a toothpaste commercial.

He didn't consider her a beautiful woman, but certainly an arresting one. And a cold one. So icy a man's dick would turn into a Popsicle if it found its way inside her.

Cold and calculating, as she'd proven when she'd cornered him with her suspicions about his secret activities and private reports. That's when Lila Wickham went from low-level MI6 agent brought over from London to work on a joint task force to Roger Drummand's personal nightmare.

"I need some more time." He looked down at the files, hoping she'd take it as a dismissal, but of course he didn't call the shots with her. The balance of power had completely shifted to her when she uncovered what he'd so desperately tried to hide.

"Well, you don't have much. I've got an appointment with your father, and I think it's time to share some of my thoughts about a certain rogue program that never really died." She looked down and casually brushed one of her black-painted fingernails. "He'd be very interested in the idea of taking hardened, deadly terrorists and calling them 'ancillary agents' and placing them in key locations in the United States on the off chance they identify cells."

"If such a program existed," he said pointedly, banking on the fact that she, so far, hadn't shown him actual proof of his activities. "And if it worked, yes, my father and the entire agency would be quite happy to take the credit for stopping a terrorist attack on US soil."

She gave a chilling smile. "But if one of those terrorists-turned-spies were to, say, go missing and stop reporting and decide to walk through a mall or a packed stadium wearing a bomb, then the world, and William Drummand, would not be so proud of our, or your, secret program. Would they, Roger?"

"That's not going to happen." He hoped.

She inched forward. "Just in case it does, you will buy my silence."

Paying her one dime was tantamount to admitting he really did run this rogue program that no one knew about. He kicked back, purposely putting his shoes on the desk in a defiant act of swagger. "Going to see my old man, are you? Don't forget to genuflect."

She barely shrugged. "Well, you know his fascination with British intelligence. He's become rather fond of our visits." She gave a dry smile as if she knew how much it bothered him that she was invited to visit the elder Drummand, and not his own son. "He always asks about you. And I always tell him you're doing the most important work at the agency."

Fear, loathing, and disgust rolled around in his belly. He was doing nothing at the agency. What he was doing was far, far outside the auspices of the CIA, and it was very important work. Very important.

The fact that this bitch figured it out and threatened to expose the program made him want to kill her. But he didn't dare. Instead, she'd get what she wanted, which, like any soulless person, was money.

"I honestly don't have the amount you want."

She lifted a brow. "Then get it."

He swallowed hard. She had no weaknesses and a computer for a brain. A dangerous combination.

His gaze returned to the report on his desk. There was a good reason he kept track of Malcolm Harris. If that man decided to dig deep or go back to Cuba or have an in-depth conversation with his old pal Alana Cevallos, Roger's world could crumble.

But there was money…and if anyone could access it, it would be Malcolm Harris.

"Mr. Drummand?" she prodded.

He puffed out a breath and pushed the report to her. "Maybe you could help."

She looked disgusted. "That's not generally how this works."

"You want the money or not?" he shot back. "Find out where former agent Malcolm Harris is."

Her eyes flickered. "The embezzler from Gitmo? The one that earned you a juicy promotion after you discovered what he was doing?"

"The same." He gestured toward the report. "If you can find him for me, I might be able to get your money."

She scanned the page. "Who's the woman he was with before he disappeared?"

"Gabriel Rossi's sister, who continued on to the resort where Rossi works now."

She kept her eyes down, reading.

"You've heard of Rossi, right?" he asked. Lila may have come from MI6, but anyone who'd been around any international intelligence knew of Gabe Rossi, famed consultant and renowned bad boy highly regarded among the female agents.

She shook her head, already on the third page of the report. Speed-reader, of course. "Name means nothing to me, but I know about Mal Harris. Looks like he's quite adept at making himself unfollowable after his little tryst at the airport hotel."

"I had good people on him, too." He didn't know why he felt the need to defend himself to this little blackmailer. "My agent pulled some slick shit to get into the hotel room while Mal hung out in the lobby with the woman. I have good people."

"Not that good." She flipped the page. "They lost him."

"But not the girl, and the girl leads to her brother, and her brother…"

She lifted her gaze. "Her brother what?"

"Is a pain in the ass."

The faintest flicker of what might be humor hidden deep in the heart of a hardened woman passed over her expression. "Sure. I'll go to a lush resort on your dime, Roger. I'll see what I can find out." She leaned forward and speared him with a look. "And I'll be back in time to meet with your daddy. He's still big and strong, but that ninety-year-old heart might not endure a shock like finding out his son made the front page of *The New York Times* for his role in placing terrorists in our country and calling it a CIA program."

Nausea threatened. "You have no proof of that."

She closed the file. "You sure would blacken the Drummand name."

It was a bluff, wasn't it? Sweat stung under his armpits. How the hell had he gotten into this situation, and how was he going to get out? Mal…and the money.

She stood. "I'll call you from the beach."

Relief at the reprieve seeped through him. "Watch your step around Rossi," he warned, trying to sound much cooler than he felt. "He can smell an agent from a mile away."

Her mouth tipped up, as if the challenge turned her on. "He won't smell me."

Chessie rolled away, but Gabe kept Mal pinned to the ground. "I heard you," Gabe ground out the words through clenched teeth.

"Get off me!" Mal shoved hard, forcing Gabe to vault to his feet.

"You need to tell me and tell me now what the fuck is going on." Gabe turned his gaze—his awfully damned *dry-eyed* gaze—to Chessie, who scooted back more from the force of his look than any real fear.

"We were…working out the details of our cover story," she said.

Gabe pierced her with a look of distrust she'd known her whole life. For all his bravado and jokes and bad words and big heart, her brother didn't trust anyone. And for good reason, in this case.

"Who's following you?" he demanded.

Chessie almost laughed. "Damn, you're good."

"Good enough to hear you guys nattering up with the housekeeper and then whispering like a couple of teenage girls ten feet from where I was. And good enough to laugh my ass off at you two thinking I'm *crying* when I'm doing my last set of dead lifts." He jerked around to Mal, who was getting to his feet. "Good enough to know you're hiding something *very important* from me."

Chessie could have kicked herself. Of *course* he hadn't been crying. This was Gabe.

"Who the fuckity fuck is following you, Harris?" he demanded.

Mal stared at him, then reached into his pocket and pulled out the bug, turning it over in his palm. "I don't know, but Chessie found this."

Gabe took it, frowning. "Where was it, and why the hell weren't you going to tell me?" Gabe demanded.

Chessie took a shallow inhale, the sun beating down almost as furiously as Gabe's relentless fury. Which was only going to get worse. "It was in a hotel room in Atlanta."

"Whose?"

"Mine," Mal said.

"Then how did she…" He let out a breath. "Fuck."

Neither Mal nor Chessie spoke, letting Gabe's razor-sharp brain put the puzzle pieces together and come up with a picture of how he'd kill them both.

"I planned to help you find another way to handle your mission without involving Chessie," Mal finally said.

"Why?" Gabe asked. "Conflict of interest?"

Mal didn't respond for a second, and Chessie waited for

the expected answer. *I thought you'd kill me.* "I thought I'd somehow let you down. Even unknowingly. And I never want to do that."

Chessie's heart slipped a little, hearing it wasn't Gabe's wrath he was afraid of, but something that seemed more honorable.

Gabe turned away, no sign of any anguish in his expression, just that look of a raw, ingrained protective streak that had smothered Chessie for most of her life. And protected her, she admitted. But right now? It smothered. Right now, she wanted to breathe and not be watched or judged or saved from her own mistakes.

She took a step forward. "Gabe, listen to me."

"I don't want to hear a word you have to say."

"Well, you're going to anyway," she fired back, scooping up a heaping dose of righteous indignation. "I'm thirty years old, damn it, and a grown woman whether you like it or not." When he didn't reply, she forced herself into his averted gaze. "I met a guy I had no idea you knew. He was hot and nice and funny, and we were stranded in a hotel overnight."

Gabe blinked at her, stunned into uncharacteristic speechlessness.

"Look, we talked and had a beer and…" She glanced at Mal. "The attraction was mutual," she continued. "We ended up in his room. I went there on my own, to be honest. I liked him and he liked me and…" She stopped long enough to take a breath, barely aware that her pulse was slamming now, her chest tight, and that Mal had come to stand next to her. That silent support egged her on. "And guess what, Gabe? It was great. Best sex of my life."

Finally Gabe held up his hand. "TM-*fucking*-I, Chess."

"Well, I'm sorry, but you have to stop treating me like

I'm the teenager you left at home when you went off to save the world. This happened. Get over it. Nothing has changed because of it." Maybe she'd slipped off her Little Sister Pedestal, but that had to happen sometime. "And nothing will change because of it."

"Are you kidding?" Gabe thrust the listening device in her face. "*This* changes everything."

"Then it's a damn good thing she found it," Mal said.

"We didn't reveal anything," she added. "We've been over our conversation."

"Replayed the whole thing for old time's sake, did you?" Gabe snarled the question, his look far darker than any obscenity-laden diatribe he could fling at them. Instead, he turned to Mal. "What the hell were you thinking?"

Mal closed his eyes. "I thought she was…with the agency," he said.

He did? Chessie's heart stumbled at the admission, but Gabe's eyes sparked with raw fury. "And you threw her on her back and plowed her to make sure?"

Mal was in his face in a second. "Shut the fuck up."

Gabe brushed him off, his nostrils finally flaring with the anger Chessie expected. "You're defending her?"

"Hell yes, I am. She did nothing wrong, and I—"

"Took one for the team."

Mal grabbed Gabe's T-shirt collar so fast, Chessie sucked in a shocked breath. "Not another word, Rossi." He had Gabe by an inch in height and more trips to a real gym. "Not one more word about your sister and not one more idiotic middle-school comment about what we did."

Gabe stared at him, his laser-blue eyes slicing through Mal. "What kind of a bottom-feeder screws the woman he thinks might be following him?"

Good question. Chessie could feel herself backing away,

this news pressing hotter and harder than the sunshine. He'd thought she was a spy and—

"Shut the hell up." Mal's hand fisted and drew back, his arm nearly vibrating for a fight. "It wasn't like that."

"No? Then what was it—"

"Stop it!" Chessie got right in between them, fury and disbelief nearly blinding her. "Both of you, just stop it. It's done. We're...done." So, so done. "Let's figure out Plan B and get to Cuba, find your son, and get out fast. I'd like this whole thing to be over as soon as possible."

She could have sworn Mal flinched. Well, too bad. Her own puzzle pieces clicked together...comments finally making sense, subtleties in their exchange fitting into the big picture. The big *ugly* picture.

He'd thought she was one of the spies after him and he'd...*screwed* her. In every sense of the word.

"Even if you lost them before you left Atlanta, they could have followed Chessie when she left your room," Gabe said. "Shit, they could be on the property right now."

"They're not," Mal said.

"You don't know that, but just in case, why don't you knock on a few doors and see who you can bang some information out of?" Gabe stabbed his hand through his hair. "We'll accelerate the schedule. Change the flights. Send you through another country and get you to Cuba by tomorrow afternoon."

"Good thinking—"

Gabe glared at Mal, shutting him up. "I don't need your fucking approval, dickface. In fact, I don't need you at all. Pack up and head out. I'll figure something else out and—"

"Gabe." Mal's voice was low and harsh. "That'll take more time. Do you really want to spend even one more day wondering about this kid? You need me, man. And Chessie needs protection. I'll guard her with my life, I swear to God I will."

Gabe opened his mouth to spew some more venom, but nothing came out. The fire in his eyes didn't disappear, but his chest rose and fell with a slow breath.

Chessie fisted her hands, Mal's promise to protect hanging in the air, along with his determination to keep Gabe from going to Cuba. That alone was a point in his favor, along with his defense of her.

"Come on, Gabe," Mal continued. "Let me do this for you. Let me find the answers you have to have."

Chessie's heart warmed at the plea, which seemed genuine and was surely the right way to look at this.

And Gabe closed his eyes in silent resignation.

"You know it's the right thing to do," Mal finished.

Gabe inhaled and exhaled, fighting for control and common sense. "Here's what's going to happen," he said. "I'm going to put you on a plane to Cuba with my sister, and you're going to do what you have to do, keeping your paws to yourself, and then you can come back and kindly stay out of my life." He threw a look at Chessie. "Come with me. I need to talk to you."

Mal moved closer to her as Gabe walked away, but Chessie put her hand on his arm. "Let me hear what he has to say," she said. "Brother to sister."

"Chessie—"

"Please, I know what to say to him."

"You already said plenty."

"Maybe that's because I'm not a spy," she said dryly. "Even if I can pass for one." Without waiting for some lame-ass apology, she headed to the back patio, where she found Gabe still breathing hard, staring at the listening device.

"Look, Gabe, I know I let you down, but—"

He shook his head, stopping Chessie's speech before it started. "I acted like an asshole."

"Well. The first step *is* admitting it," she said in a teasing tone.

He puffed out a breath. "It just…surprised me. And, yes, you're right. You're a grown woman."

The statement stunned any argument out of her. "Thank you, but you don't have to worry about anything. The chances of it happening again are less than zero." At his doubtful look, she added, "Please. He put the moves on me because he thought I was a spy." The reality of it tightened her stomach into a ball of self-loathing. And Mal-loathing.

"I'm sure that's not the only reason, Chess. Plus, 'I went to his room' doesn't exactly sound like this was one-sided."

Shit, why had she told him so much? "It doesn't matter. Now I know why he turned on the charm. I'll avoid…him." On a mission to Cuba.

Gabe looked at her as if he was thinking the same thing.

"Look." He held up the broken device. "This is why you need to avoid Mal. He's got a target on his back, so he's not the guy you want."

"I'd already figured out he's a spy."

Both of Gabe's brows lifted. "You didn't find that out through some computer search."

"No, I didn't." She crossed her arms and stared him down. "Just used my God-given Rossi intuition."

He nodded slowly, impressed. "I knew you had the chops."

"So get off my case and let me do this job," she said. "Trust me."

"I do, but, listen, Chess, about Mal. About a *relationship* with Mal."

"There won't be one," she assured him.

"Good, because there are people who'd like to see him behind bars doing ten more years not behind a picket fence mowing the lawn and having backyard barbecues with the neighbors."

"That's what you think I want?" She tried to sound put off by the suggestion, even though…it wasn't far from the truth.

He lifted a brow. "You told me last time you were down here how much you want to have a family. How much you want to settle down and have a life and a home like the one we grew up in. So much you were willing to march down the aisle with douchetastic Matt. Did you think I wasn't listening?"

"I thought you weren't impressed by those mundane goals. I figured that's why you want me down here. So I can learn the business and go all badass like my siblings and cousins."

"The two aren't mutually exclusive," he said, leaning against the railing. "Look at Vivi. Badass and pregnant. Married to that stick in the mud Lang, who probably pulls out a rule book every time he takes a shit to make sure everything's coming out in the right order."

She bit back a smile. "I like Lang."

"As you should. He's the kind of guy who would be good for you, much as it pains me to admit it. But Mal? No. Not what you need, Chess."

Irritation squeezed her again, but she was more curious than angry at Gabe for making sweeping decisions about her life. "I know he's got a record and that he went to jail for a serious crime."

"Yeah, the crime of stupidity."

"Stealing money from the government is stupid," she agreed.

Gabe looked hard at her, opened his mouth, then shut it again. "Listen to me," he said. "He's never going to have a normal life. He's a risk."

"And yet you're willing to send me to a foreign country on a secret mission with him."

"He knows every inch of that island, and you won't be there long. I still think he's the best guy for the job."

Of all the bruising former military guys he knew, he had to pick one who turned Chessie's hormones into a sizzling pot of need. But she'd cool off...every time she thought about why he seduced her.

Gabe put his hand on her shoulder and gave a squeeze, "Don't fall for him, Chessie. You'd never have a normal life."

She snorted and wormed out of his touch. "No worries there, big brother."

And, really, she'd never meant anything more in her whole life.

Chapter Ten

Sunset washed Barefoot Bay in a mellow golden glow, dimmed by a rain shower that drenched the sands and bathed paradise in a dreary gloom. It suited Mal's mood just fine. Gabe and Nino had gone out, leaving Mal behind with the aroma of the older man's latest tomato-saucey creation wafting through the little bungalow.

Mal wasn't the least bit hungry.

He was tense, pissed, and itching to square things away with Chessie before they got on that flight to Cuba. But she'd disappeared and didn't answer her door when he'd knocked around dinnertime.

When the downpour let up to a misty drizzle, Mal decided to try again. From the cul-de-sac, he walked east through the small farmette that served the resort and along a deserted beach toward her villa, where he'd try one more time to set things straight.

He had to tell her that by the time she'd come to his hotel room, he knew she wasn't a spy. Would she believe him? Would she understand that he had to be suspicious of everyone?

The rain made his T-shirt stick to his chest and back, so he stripped it off and tossed it on the sand to let the mist wet his chest. It wasn't quite dark enough to take everything off and swim off his frustrations, but the sunset-tinted water looked inviting.

He got closer to the cluster of the villas where she was staying, smaller than many others on the property, but still luxurious and private. This grouping all backed up to the beach, so their pools had unobstructed water views, and guests could walk right out to the sand.

In the distance, a woman caught his attention, emerging from the water wearing a black bikini.

Not a woman. *The* woman.

Chessie twisted water from her hair, then scooped up a thigh-length white shirt and slipped into it, the cotton immediately clinging to her wet body. She bent again and grabbed a hat from the sand, perching it on her head, a red scarf around the brim floating down her back.

She stood still, apparently unaware of him, staring out to the water and the lone orange ball about to disappear below the horizon.

Even a football field away, Mal felt a primal response to Francesca Rossi, and it wasn't just the normal reaction of a man who'd spent four years celibate in prison. This was a deeper hunger. A craving for…*more*.

Maybe it was better if she believed the worst about him. Better if she thought him a thief who'd tricked her into sex. Because if she felt anything like he did, if she wanted another night in bed as much as he wanted it, then they weren't going to get from Havana to Caibarién without pulling over and giving in.

She glanced in his general direction, but he noticed she didn't have her glasses on, so she likely didn't see him. Or she was just ignoring him—a very distinct possibility.

She walked along the water's edge in the other direction,

her bare feet kicking up wet sand. The hat protected her from the drizzle, but the light rain only made the shirt completely transparent, which made him more anxious to…peel it off her.

She stopped after about twenty feet, letting the gulf water swirl around her ankles. She seemed not only oblivious to the rain, but kind of enjoying it. As if the outdoor shower were washing away crappy thoughts, ones he put there because of his broken ability to trust anyone.

He approached her soundlessly from behind, trying to think of an opening line that would make her laugh or take down her guard. Maybe something that would—

"I know you're back there."

He stopped, fighting a smile.

"Do you really think you can sneak up on me?" she asked, still not turning around. "I was raised in a family of bodyguards, cops, FBI agents, and investigators."

"And one particularly cagey spook."

"Definitely made for interesting dinner conversation with a table full of tough talkers, that's for sure."

"I bet you talked some of the toughest."

She snorted softly. "I was the overprotected baby, as you surely figured out during our lovely exchange with my brother."

He came closer, but stayed behind her. "And how do you feel about that?"

"The exchange with Gabe or life at the bottom of the Rossi food chain?"

He'd meant their conversation, but both topics interested him. Hell, everything about her interested him. "Let's start with how you feel about your unfortunate birth order in your family of overachieving world-savers?"

"Funny." She gave a soft laugh, toeing the sand and water. "I was just asking myself the same question."

When she didn't elaborate, he waited, staring at her back and the lines of neat muscles curving down to her ass, all revealed through the wet shirt.

Yeah. Gonna be a tough few days in Cuba together.

"So," he prompted when her silence lasted too long. "What's your answer?"

She sighed. "Being the youngest of five siblings, plus two just-as-protective older cousins who were raised with us, is my lot in life, I guess. I will be forever viewed and treated by them as the baby. That pisses me off. Gabe pissed me off."

"Hey, he's your brother and he cares about you. Anyway, let's talk about who you're *really* pissed at right now."

She slid a glance over her shoulder, just enough that he could see a bemused expression under that hat rim. "There are no words."

As he suspected.

"Did you come to apologize?" she asked, finally turning to face him.

"Define apologize," he replied, slipping into one of his favorite ways to deflect a conversation he didn't really want to have.

"Usually it starts with 'I'm sorry' and ends with 'I owe you one.'"

He took a step closer, tempted to lift the hat so he could see her face without shadows. "Well, I'm not sorry," he finally said.

Her mouth opened so far it was almost comical.

"Let me rephrase. I'm not sorry that you had the 'best sex of your life.'"

She dropped her head back with a disgusted grunt. "I knew my little rally cry for independence was going to bite me in the ass."

"For the record—"

She held up a hand to stop him. "If you say that was the best sex of *your* life, I swear to God, I'll hit you."

"Why?"

"Because you had an agenda, Mal Harris," she ground out. "How good could it have been when it wasn't anything but…but…a *job* to you? An exploratory mission? Or, worse, a little vendetta?" Each word exploded in his gut.

"It wasn't any of those things," he insisted, earning a sharp bark of disbelief. "I swear, Chessie, once I knew for sure—"

"You never really knew," she said, marching away to walk along the water. "Not until I told you my name."

"I knew before that," he insisted, following her. "When we were in the hotel lobby, there was something in your eyes. Something real. Innocent, even."

She snorted. "Please. There was nothing innocent about that encounter. We were eyeing condoms like little kids in a candy store."

"Okay, innocent is the wrong word," he allowed. "But, when we were in that store, I knew. I knew that I had let my inability to trust anyone get in the way, and I knew right then that you were exactly who you said you were, and I…" He reached for her, turning her around to face him. "I wanted to be with you more than…more than…" He swallowed the admission, only because he didn't want to sound desperate. "Anything."

She rolled her eyes. "Nice speech. Did they teach you that at Langley?"

He bit back a curse, shaking his head. He deserved this. "If you hadn't come to my room, I'd have probably knocked on every damn door in the Marriott till I found you."

"And then our room wouldn't have been bugged," she said wryly.

"And you might not hate me."

"I don't..." She stopped herself, her gaze dropping over his bare chest, then she shifted her attention to the water. "Jeez," she muttered.

"Jeez, what?"

"It's just my luck to have my very first field job with the same person I had my very first *hookup* with."

The confession surprised him only a little. "I could tell," he said.

She scowled at him. "I wasn't a virgin, Mal. I've had sex before, but not with a perfect stranger I was pretty sure I'd never see again. No, not part of my life plan. Never was, anyway. And never will be again." She shook her head vehemently. "And this whole thing is proof that shit goes down the drain when I go off plan."

"Look, the first thing I can tell you, field rookie, is that plans are nothing but contingent out there in the real world."

She sliced him with a challenge in her eyes. "Sex with me was a *contingency* plan?"

He leaned closer. "Sex with you was *amazing*," he said, his voice a little husky. "And if you want an apology, I'll give you this: I'm not sorry it happened, but I'm sorry if you feel I duped you."

She searched his face for a long time. "Huh, look at that. You do know how to define an apology."

He managed a smile. "Do you know how to accept one?"

"Maybe." Her eyes narrowed with the next question. "Would you have hit on me if you weren't being hounded by God knows who?"

"I don't know."

Her shoulders sank a little. "Gee, thanks."

"I mean, I don't know how else to live, so I'm going to

assume everyone is out for me. Once I trust someone, Francesca…" He tipped her chin to lift her face toward his.

"You can *liaise*?"

"Frequently." He took a chance and inched closer.

"No." She shook off his touch. "Can't do that. Stop flirting with me." She backed away some more, pointing at him. "And quit calling me Francesca."

"I can't call you by your name? Why not?"

"The way you say it is entirely and unfairly sexy."

Really. He'd have to hide that away in his arsenal of things he might need later. "Well, I never want to be sexy, that's for sure."

"And no more inside jokes and almost kisses, and please, *please*, put a shirt on for the rest of your life."

Her humor gave him a little hope, and relief. "Are we good, then?"

"Define good," she fired back, just enough of a smile in her eyes that he knew she was yanking his chain.

"I'd define it as—what was the phrase again?—'the best sex—'"

She slammed her hand over his mouth. "Do not push your luck, Malcolm Harris."

He kissed her palm and watched her eyes flutter the tiniest bit. So, he pressed his hand over hers and kissed again. And once more, because even kissing the inside of her hand was pretty much the best thing his mouth had done for hours.

She didn't move her hand. "And yet you continue to push your luck."

He turned her hand and threaded their fingers, keeping her knuckles close to his lips. "I don't know how to stop doing any of those things you want me to stop doing," he admitted. "I know you probably are thinking 'never again,' and I don't blame you for one second, and I have no idea what kind of promises you made to Gabe, but—"

"No promises," she whispered, holding his gaze, the connection as fiery and real as it had been in the hotel room. "I haven't made any promises."

"Good." He kissed her knuckle. "'Cause contingency planning means anything can happen, Francesca."

"Contingency plans and liaisons. Can't you call it what it is? *Sex*."

"It could be," he agreed, leaning in to capture her mouth. She let go of his hand and placed it on his cheek, letting him pull her rain-dampened body into his chest.

And she felt every single bit as real and soft and sweet and warm as last night. Their mouths just fit so perfectly, her tongue against his teeth, his lips over hers. Everything just fit and felt so damn good.

"What the hell are we doing?" she murmured into his mouth.

"Kissing." He nibbled her lower lip. "I think it's a standard part of any apology."

She smiled into the next kiss, less tentative, but still not fully *happy* about the direction her little walk in the rain had taken, he could tell. "Don't forget the 'I owe you one' part."

He kissed her again. "I owe you one."

"One what?"

"One more kiss. One more…" He lifted his head. "One more night."

She closed her eyes and sighed, her resignation practically palpable. "What the hell *is* it about you?"

"Francesca." He pulled her even closer. "I know you've never had a one-night stand or hookup or fling or whatever the hell you want to call it, but have you ever just had sex for fun? No strings. No promises. No commitments. No expectations or hopes?"

"Yeah, last night."

"We could do that again," he whispered. And again and again and again. "For fun."

"It was fun," she agreed begrudgingly. "All that rolling around and laughing. That was pretty much textbook fun."

"Went way past fun," he said.

"Well into ridiculous. And I…" Her eyes narrowed in mock anger. "I wanted to do it again."

"I'm sorry I left." He slipped his hand around her neck, tunneling under the hat. "For a whole bunch of reasons, I'm sorry I left."

Her expression changed, the spark of anger disappearing from her eyes. "Now that, Mal Harris, was a genuine apology."

He punctuated it with another salty, slow kiss. "We are going to be alone for a few days," he reminded her. "So…there's always another chance."

She let out a slow, low exhale. "Mmm. Road-trip sex?"

"*Fun* road-trip sex."

She eyed him, still on the brink of going either way. Any second she would nod or throw herself back and tell him to drop dead. "We'd need…rules."

A zing of something like hope fired through him, a sensation so utterly foreign he couldn't even grab it before it was gone again. "Rules? Like a few mission regs?"

"Yes." She lifted her hand to start ticking them off, one finger at a time. "No unnecessary physical contact, just, you know, the deed. No flirting. No intimate conversations. No kissing at unexpected moments or holding hands in the car or whispering promises in the dark. And…" She was on her other hand now and getting closer. "For the love of God, Malcolm Harris, do *not* make me like you."

"What if I like you?"

"Absolutely not, no." She shook her head. "You cannot like me. And this only happens on foreign soil. The minute we land back here, it's over."

"I can live with those regs."

She tipped her head a bit, as if he'd agreed too quickly. "Am I missing something?"

"You sure about the foreign-soil part?" He dragged his thumb down to circle the sweet spot in the hollow of her throat. "Because tonight…"

"Foreign soil only," she finally said. "And that thing you're doing with your finger on my…that?" She pointed to where he touched her, and moved her finger in an accusatory circle. "Against the unnecessary-physical-contact rule."

He wanted to tell her it was very necessary, but didn't want to push his luck. "How about this?" He stepped back and held out his hand for a shake. "We have a deal?"

She took his hand. "Sex with no strings, no commitments, no messy explanations, no feelings, no emotions, and no…hope."

He nodded and shook again. "Hopeless sex. Got it. Deal."

"Deal."

She stepped away. "On foreign soil."

"In foreign beds."

"No hope."

He nodded. "Utterly hopeless."

"Okay, then. Good night, Mal."

"Good night, Fran—"

She held her finger up in his face. "It's Chessie. Just Chessie."

For now. "G'night, Chessie."

Satisfied, she gave a little nod and glided across the sand with a little too much speed, her red scarf flouncing like a flag of victory in the wind.

"Francesca," he said softly.

"I heard that," she called back.

Damn it. He'd already broken a rule. He liked her.

Chapter Eleven

"Cuba." Chessie leaned over and looked out the fogged-up window of the plane, peering down to the island below. "Land of the world's coolest cars."

Mal gave a dry laugh. "If you like vintage clunkers made before 1959."

"I love them." She sat back from the window, aware, as she had been throughout the flights they'd taken to get here, the pressure of a sizable arm and thigh as he adjusted his body for comfort in the tight coach seating. They'd fallen into an easy rhythm of conversation, reading, quiet, and more talk during the long day that started at dawn.

And always, the undercurrent of…sex. A joke, a touch, a tease, a look. And at every turn, Mal reminded her of the deal, keeping the power turned up on the electricity between them. As much as she rolled her eyes and tried to spar with him, she was definitely up for some of that *hopeless* sex on her first mission in the field.

"Computers and cars," he mused. "Not to sound sexist, but those aren't typical hobbies for a woman."

She shot him a look. "You're kidding, right?"

"I said I didn't mean it in a sexist way," he insisted. "It's actually kind of hot."

She looked skyward as if to ask, *Why me, Lord*? Then, "Computers aren't a hobby for me, Mal, they're my job."

"It's unusual, is all I'm saying."

She thought about it, but couldn't remember a time when technology or engines didn't interest her much more than dolls and dresses. "I guess it was the overload of testosterone around me. Someone was always working on a car in the driveway."

"You have a sister, though, don't you?" he asked.

"One, Nicki, the shrink. And my cousin Vivi, who, along with her twin brother, Zach, were raised with us after their mother died in Italy."

"Plus three brothers. Damn, that's a lotta kids," he mused.

"Well, we had three parents, if you count Nino, who lived with us since I was a baby. But, yes, a great big Italian family with noisy dinners and heated arguments and hands…" She glanced at her own, making a gesture. "Hands flying. What about you?"

He shrugged. "No."

"No?" She laughed lightly. "No, you won't tell me, or no, you didn't have a big family growing up?"

"No big family, no noisy dinners, not much of anything, really."

She felt a frown tug at her brow, trying to gauge if that was sadness or resignation or something a little darker in his eyes. Anger, maybe. Something not pleasant.

She couldn't even think of a situation where there was *not much of anything*. But then she remembered all those addresses, all the way back to birth. "What about your childhood? How did you grow up?"

"On my own, mostly. My dad was"—he shook his head—"gone by the time I could speak. And my mom is a big dreamer but not much of a doer. Unless by doing you mean recreational drugs, which were her pastime of choice. We spent a lot of years moving around."

She knew that, of course, but felt an ache for him. "It can't be easy to be a single mom."

"No, it's not," he agreed with a little more vehemence than she expected. "It's probably the hardest thing in the world, but my mother made it about twenty times tougher than necessary." He shifted in his seat again, and something told her it wasn't physical discomfort bothering him now. "And I'm calling foul on the regs, Francesca. Wasn't there something about intimate discussions?"

"Talking about your family and growing up isn't intimate."

He looked away, pretending to be more interested in the empty aisle of the plane.

"Unless it is," she added.

He gave another shrug, and a face that tried to say he didn't really care. Which made Chessie want to know more.

"So what's your relationship with your mother like now?" she asked.

"Define relationship."

She laughed. "That's your answer whenever you hate a subject."

He gave her a look that was both impressed and surprised. "And I thought your sister was the shrink."

"Don't need to be Freud to figure out when you want to turn the conversation away from something. 'Define *evasion*, Francesca,'" she mocked.

She expected a playful response, but got a clouded, intense look instead. "I'm not evading anything, Chessie.

There's nothing to share about my family. I didn't grow up like you and Gabe did."

"Sorry. I didn't mean to upset you."

"I'm not upset. It's just…never mind." He turned away again just as the sound system crackled with an announcement from the flight crew, telling them they'd be landing in Havana in a few minutes and reviewing the customs instructions for the third time since they got on the flight. It didn't sound any different from any other country, Chessie had noticed.

When the announcement switched to Spanish, he pulled a file from the seat pocket that he'd been reading earlier. "Let's go over Gabe's dossier one more time."

When he opened the folder, Chessie skimmed the "schedule" her brother had laid out for them. A rental car was reserved at the airport for their drive to Caibarién, where they were staying at a place called Mar Brisas.

"Let me guess," she mused. "That translates to Sea Breezes?"

"Or shitty hostel with very little running water and dirty windows."

"Mmmm," she said. "Sounds dreamy." But it could be when *hopeless sex* was happening. She tried to force herself to concentrate on the agenda.

"We'll start with the Ramos farm, of course," he said, pointing to words he was obviously having no problem reading. "Of course, there are no guarantees little Gabriel will be there."

"It makes me crazy how hard it is to get information on people in Cuba," she mused, finally focused on the document. "It's like a big black hole in cyberspace."

"It's a big black hole on Earth, too."

"I read somewhere that less than five percent of people in

Cuba have access to the Internet," she said, still astounded by the statistic. "And then I read there are Cubans on Facebook. So which is it?"

"Depends on where you are. In Havana, you'll get Internet and Facebook. Out in the country? There could be nothing."

"That ought to be illegal."

He laughed. "It's called Communism, and it is illegal to us."

"I know, but now that relations are better, maybe more of them will get Internet. Why wouldn't they want it?"

"Castro doesn't want his people to see what they're missing. You think he wants them downloading reality TV from America and thinking there's an actual government like they see on reruns of *The West Wing*? His whole regime would topple."

She got that, but still. "This whole job would be so much easier if we could get birth notifications online."

"You can't get DNA online," he said. "You still need the child in person to do that."

She turned to look out the window, thinking about the moment she'd see that child in person and how emotional and wonderful it would be. "I wonder if he looks like Gabe," she mused.

Mal started to answer, then seemed to catch himself.

"What?" she asked. "What were you going to say?"

He just gave his head a quick shake.

"Can't you even tell me what she was like? I mean, she was the mother of my nephew. Maybe."

"No maybe about it," he said softly. "The chances of Isadora being with someone other than Gabe after they met are somewhere between zero and zero."

"Really?" She leaned closer, so fascinated by this woman

who elicited such an emotional response from Gabe. "And it went both ways?"

He laughed. "Yes. If anything, he was more nuts about her."

Chessie tried to grasp that, and failed. "I've seen a lot of girls lose their minds and hearts, and other parts, over Gabe, but not ever the other way around. How long were they together?"

"I don't know, honestly. They were already a secret couple when I met Gabe and were still together when I left."

"Secret?"

"No one knew, only me and only because Gabe and I were close."

That, too, was surprising. Gabe must really trust this man. "How did you meet him?" she asked.

"I met him at Guantanamo," he said simply.

"I know that, but how did you two get to be such good and trusting friends? Gabe doesn't let a lot of people into his private circle."

"We had an unusual assignment," he explained in a soft whisper meant only for her ears. "Gabe was there to butter up the detainees and make them fall in love with the US, and I was there as a guard to watch them. We developed very different relationships with detainees, then we had to share what we learned. Plus, I was undercover to them, and he wasn't."

She considered that, and gave into a thought that had plagued her for a long time. "Please tell me he didn't torture any prisoners."

Mal's laugh surprised her. "Detainees, and no. Quite the contrary. He made friends with them."

"So they would tell him secrets," she guessed.

"Essentially. And so they'd consider switching sides." He

folded up the paper. “It doesn’t matter, Chessie. The program he worked on is long closed. And we’re not going to Guantanamo, we’re going to Caibarién.”

“What about Isadora? Was she a spy, too?”

He smiled at her relentlessness. “Yes. Isa was CIA. A translator and language expert. She must have spoken ten or twelve different languages. Farsi, Arabic, Persian, Kurdish, Chinese, Japanese, and every Romance language you can imagine. Perfect dialect, just an incredible talent. And they worked side by side, day and night, Gabe and Isa.”

Isa…who could have been her sister.

The importance of what they were doing hit again, and Chessie vowed to put her fantasies about *hopeless sex* out of her mind for a while. Right now, she was here on a mission of hope. Hope for her brother, and for this child of a woman she’d never know but somehow knew she would have loved.

She couldn’t forget that.

Chapter Twelve

So far, so good.

But then, Mal knew that Gabe would have covered every base with the documentation to get into the country. Posing as Mitchell Walker, executive producer and owner of Green River Productions, Mal sailed through customs, and from his vantage point, it looked like Chessie, aka Elizabeth Brandt, had done the same.

He'd briefed her on how to act with the Cuban officials—humble, innocent, and warm—and prepared her for the questions she'd be asked. Leaning against a wall in the tight hallway, he checked his watch against the next flight's departure time, looking up when a man approached him.

"Got the time?" he asked, as American as Mal.

Mal told him, and the man blew out a sigh. "Damn, I'm late." He glanced around the short, enclosed area, and Mal could have sworn his gaze lingered on Chessie, who was putting away her paperwork and just about finished at her counter. "Can I get a favor?" the man asked.

Mal's internal alarm went off, of course. He looked at the guy in silent response, taking in his thinning hair, a paunch, inexpensive clothes. Yet he had the money to travel to Cuba.

The man fumbled to get something out of his pocket, and

Mal instantly stiffened. But he pulled out a phone and brought it to his face, tapping a button. The sound of a camera clicked.

Instinctively, Mal held up a hand. "Hey—"

"Sorry," he said quickly. "New phone and I'm not sure how to work it. Can you take a picture of me with that in the background?" He pointed over his shoulder at a large "Welcome to Cuba" sign above a row of customs officials. "You know, for my Instagram account? Proof that I was actually in *Coo-bah.*" He used a crappy Spanish pronunciation.

Mal started to say no, but then realized by taking the phone, he could delete the picture the asshole had just taken. "Sure." He took the device and touched the camera icon on the screen, but no picture of him appeared. He scrolled, but it was like the guy hadn't just snapped a shot.

Maybe Mal was just being paranoid, as usual.

"Here, I'll show you," the guy said, reaching for the phone.

"I got it," Mal told him, holding it up to take a picture with the sign.

The man stood still and then pointed up to the sign over his shoulder, like a tourist. Mal snapped it.

"Thanks," the guy said, extending his hand to get the phone back.

But Mal didn't give it up. "Let's check it," he suggested, but the guy snagged the phone immediately.

"Nah, I'm late. I'm sure you got it. Thanks!" He took off just as Chessie came up, shouldering her bag.

"All set?" she asked.

He tamped down the bad taste the guy had left, and nodded. "How about you?"

"A little hassle checking the laptop because I had to register it."

"You're not going to be able to use it anyway," he reminded her.

"Not true. You told me I can tap into Canadian servers, and if there is a way, I will do it." She added a grin and adjusted her glasses. "Anyway, I'd sooner go naked than travel without a laptop."

Which would be fine, but distracting as hell.

As they walked out of customs through a bright, modern terminal, Chessie leaned closer. "No issues with the docs?"

He shot her a warning look. "Not a word. Elizabeth."

"Got it. Mitch."

Another man made quick eye contact with Mal as he passed, setting off the old familiar warnings again. Everyone was suspect, damn it. *Everyone*.

A few minutes later, after a stop to exchange American dollars for enough CUCs to pay for everything they'd need, they had rented a Kia—much to Chessie's vocal dismay, because she really wanted a 1959 sea-foam green Chevy convertible with gull wings. Before taking off, they stopped at a café across the street from the rental place to grab a bite for dinner.

Food would be scarce on the drive down to Caibarién, and they were both starved. Across from him, Chessie sipped a steaming espresso, menu in hand, but her attention was on the colorful, noisy surroundings.

Of course, Mal was paying more attention to the patrons and passersby than the food listing.

"Why didn't I take Spanish?" Chessie flipped a page of the menu, then closed it and put her elbows on the table. "Nino said when in doubt, get plantains and beans. Or a *medianoche*. Can never go wrong."

A couple sat down at another table, out of hearing distance, but when the woman threw Mal a long look, he turned away, barely acknowledging what Chessie had said.

"Eyeing the blonde at the next table?" she teased.

"Was she blond?" He winked, keeping things lighter than he actually felt. "Didn't notice."

"Yes, you did."

"Only because she's a potential threat."

Chessie started to slide her glasses down from her hair to her eyes to get a good look, but Mal stopped her with a light hand on her arm. "Don't."

"Do you really think I would be that obvious?" She didn't look, but instead put her glasses on the table to look hard at him. Which was so direct and intense, it might have been better for her to look at the other woman. "Can't you do something, anything at all, to put a stop to it? I mean, you paid your dues, right?"

Without her glasses, he could really see the concern in her expression, the caring about his welfare that made her eyes endlessly blue. Had anyone ever really looked at him that way? He'd spent a lifetime keeping people at an arm's distance, and this would be a dumb time to stop that practice.

"That's not a question someone who wants to keep things *hopeless* should ask," he said.

Chided, she looked down, her long lashes brushing against her cheekbones. He loved the way that looked. Probably because it reminded him of when he'd been buried inside her and she'd closed her eyes, lost to pleasure, her mouth open as she took ragged breaths and moaned for more.

"Mal?" she asked.

He shook the fog off. "Mitch," he reminded her quietly.

"See what I mean?" She picked up her espresso and blew on it. "I'm so not cut out for this kind of work."

"You're doing fine," he assured her, glancing to the side. And that damn woman staring at him again. He had to change the subject. "What are you ordering?"

"Look," she said, leaning closer and keeping her voice at barely a whisper. "I know you are always watching your back, and I get that. But that chick over there? She's—"

"Looking at me."

"Because you're *hot*. I don't blame her."

He started to argue, but laughed instead. "You just like me."

"As if I would break a rule like that." She gave a sly grin and pushed back from the table. "Order me plantains, and I'll split a rice and beans with you. Be right back."

"Where are you going?"

She lifted both brows. "Bathroom. Is that okay?"

"Be careful. And fast."

"Promise." She scooped up her handbag and glasses, then threaded through the tables, avoiding a route that would have taken her near the staring woman.

The server came to the table, blocking Mal's view of the blonde. He ordered in Spanish, handed back the menus, then, when the server stepped away, the woman was gone. To the bathroom, of course.

He fought the urge to pop up and head over there, protective and worried. It was the absolute wrong thing to do. Chessie was smart and on the alert. If the woman followed her, she'd never engage. Would she? She *was* an untrained rookie.

A minute passed, two. The man the blonde left behind was studying his menu, oblivious to everything around him. Another two minutes, and the woman came out of the bathroom, walking toward her table slowly, her attention riveted on Mal. Something about her clothes and stature said

Euro to him, maybe northern Italian, but definitely not American.

Her eyebrow flicked, and the hint of a smile tipped up one side of her lips. Was she trying to communicate something? She'd talked to Chessie? She'd warned Chessie?

She'd *hurt* Chessie?

Shit, where *was* Chessie? Each passing second ticked his heart rate higher, making him wonder who the hell thought this was a good idea. Cuba was crawling with CIA. It was their damned second home.

He shot up and headed toward the hallway in the back where the bathrooms were.

As he came around the corner, the men's room door opened, nearly hitting him in the face. "Oh, hi," a man said as he stepped out.

It was the camera guy.

Son of a *bitch*.

The other man gave a funny look and brushed by, reminding Mal that he was doing exactly the wrong thing by doing anything at all. Battling the urge to yank the women's room door open—the very dumbest thing he could possibly do—he waited a few seconds until it creaked slowly, and Chessie stepped out.

"What are you doing here?" she asked.

He grabbed her arm. "What took so long?"

She pointed her index fingers to her face. "Sue me for a touch-up on the blush and mascara, bro. I've been traveling all day."

He nudged her back into the restaurant, his gaze landing on the blonde's table. The now empty table. "Why did they leave?" he asked under his breath.

"I heard her on the phone in the bathroom. Heavy German accent, but she spoke English. They stopped for coffee and were meeting friends at a hotel in Havana. They've been here for ten days, on holiday, and she's bored with her husband." She grinned. "How's that for field work?"

"Impressive." But what was the camera guy doing there? "Who was she talking to, do you know?"

"Gosh, I'm not that good. Yet." She sat down, and then she shifted slightly to follow Mal's gaze out to the street.

"That's her," she said.

"Talking to the guy who 'accidentally' took my picture at the airport."

"Shit," she whispered.

"No kidding."

"What do we do?" she asked.

Mal reached over and touched her hand. "Everything I say. Got it?"

Silent, serious, she nodded.

"We're going to get up very casually, walk to our car," he told her. "We're going to drive it around Havana and watch for a tail. When we're sure we don't have one, we're returning the Kia and then buying something else they have on the lot, for cash. Then we're driving out of town, and no one is going to follow us."

He could have sworn she paled.

"And we're not going to talk in either car until I give the all clear. Not a word in any language. Got it?"

"Yes."

Chessie did exactly as she was told, silent during the whole process of driving and exchanging the car, until she climbed into the passenger seat of the new car.

"You can talk now," he said, confident no one could have bugged this baby.

"You mean complain."

"About what?"

She tapped the torn leather of the bench seat. "A 1959 lime-green Ford Prefect?"

"Is that good or bad?" Mal turned the ignition, and the engine choked before starting. Then he tested the gas, which didn't do a whole lot.

"It hurts my very soul. So close to cool, but so very far away."

"Cool wasn't on my list of criteria," he said, turning to scan the area and make sure they weren't followed.

"I was picturing a souped-up Fairlane 500 convertible with an ass-kicking V-8. Not the little engine that could*not*." As if offended, or warning her to shut up, that engine sputtered, and she shot Mal a look.

"I think it was an inspired choice," he said, giving the skinny wooden steering wheel an affectionate squeeze. "We'll fly under the radar in this."

"There is that," she agreed. A bright pink Impala, '58 or '59, cruised by. "I could fly anywhere in that," she said, longingly eyeing the wing flare in the back. "Anywhere."

He ignored her, continuing a thorough scan of every car and pedestrian within twenty feet as he drove.

"Do you really think they were following us?" she asked.

"I think there was a good chance of it."

"It might have been a coincidence."

He fired a look at her.

"Hey, we met by coincidence."

"We were both traveling to the same place to meet with the same person, and Atlanta is a major hub." He turned again and eyed the guy behind them in a Peugeot. "Not a coincidence."

She opened a map Gabe had supplied—which was a good thing since the rental car guy had actually laughed when Mal asked for one, suggesting they pick up a hitchhiker for help getting where they were going—and studied it quietly, then looked up at the road they were on.

"I'm not sure this is the fastest way to Caibarién," she said.

"There are three ways to go," he told her. "Safe and fast, slow and treacherous, or uncertain and possibly deadly."

She laughed a little. "I hope you've completely ruled out door number three."

"Yes, so we'll take slow and treacherous."

"And what exactly is wrong with safe and fast? I like safe and fast. It's how I drive, how I work, and how I live."

"Question for you, rookie: *Why* do you think I'm taking the slow and treacherous route?"

"Because it has the least likelihood of us being followed."

He grinned at her. "Give an A to the pretty girl in the front row."

"Pretty, my ass."

"Your ass is pretty, too."

She looked skyward. "So how slow and treacherous is this route that guarantees we won't be followed?"

"First, no guarantees. Second, it'll add a few more hours to the drive, so it'll be quite dark when we go over the roads that are the most likely to wash out in a rainstorm. But, big picture, we'll be safer, I promise. And when I see somewhere to grab food, we will, but we'll eat in the car."

"Okay." She leaned her head back and gave a sigh. "What else can you teach me about being a spy?"

"Why do you want to know?"

She closed her eyes. "You know, in case we get into trouble. More trouble. Anyway…" She reached over and put a hand on his arm. "Your voice is sexy."

He couldn't help smiling. "No one's ever told me that before."

"Then no one was listening to you."

He just smiled, wishing they could take the fastest route, because the sooner they could start hopeless sex, the better.

Chapter Thirteen

Gabe put his fork down and glowered across the table. "Do I have basil hanging out of my mouth or something?"

Nino instantly looked down at his plate. "There's no basil in this, Gabriel."

"Then do you want to tell me why you have been scrutinizing me for this whole meal like I'm a research monkey under observation?"

Nino just shook his head and stabbed at the chicken. "I'm worried she's right."

"Who?"

"Poppy."

Gabe resumed eating. "This again. You and that woman have to work it out, old man, because she's a natural spook and isn't going anywhere."

"She's all under my business, Gabriel."

He smiled at this latest malapropism. "You mean up in your business. 'Cause if she's under your business, you've been holding out on me, you dirty dog."

Nino ignored the tease. "She's always looking for trouble."

"Makes her a good spy. People think she's sharing inside info, and they do the same."

"She thinks she knows everything."

Gabe grunted, already sick of a conversation that hadn't really started. "Oh, for crap's sake, if this is about some Jamaican-Italian kitchen showdown between you two, I'm going to—"

"She's not right about food," Nino insisted, underscoring that with a bite of chicken pointed directly at Gabe. "She actually thought she knew a better way to make *pollo Romano* than this. I said to her, 'It's called *Romano*, woman.' Like Rome. Not *pollo* Kingston."

"Look at you, knowing your capitals of foreign countries."

Nino harrumphed and straightened the dish towel that hung from his collar. In Gabe's entire life, including *La Vigilia* on Christmas Eve, he'd never seen Nino use a napkin. He wore his *mopina* and never got a spot of sauce on his shirt.

"So what's the problem?" Gabe asked, spinning through the possibilities like the pasta on his fork despite his shitty appetite. It pained Nino when he didn't eat with gusto. "She doesn't know where Chessie and Mal went, or why. We don't have a client on site at the moment, and I haven't asked her to do anything but take the fresh flowers out of our bathroom because they're too fucking happy in the morning."

"That's what she's right about," Nino said, nothing but seriousness in his deep-brown eyes.

The flowers? "They're pink, for crying out loud. On the bathroom counter where two guys live. Is that necessary?"

"She's right about…" Nino swallowed hard like a chicken bone was caught in his throat. "You and the happy… You're not happy."

"Damn right I'm not happy about the flowers."

"No, Gabriel. You're not happy about anything."

He snorted softly and picked up the juice glass of homemade wine that Nino had brought from his stash in Boston. "Dude." He downed the wine. "Shit's real, and you know it."

"Shit, as you say, is always real with you," Nino countered. "But I suspect this whole child thing in Cuba is affecting you more than you realize."

Oh man. Really? He started to reply, but nothing came. No quip, curse, or comment. What could he say? He never lied to Nino. By omission, of course. Gabe lied by omission by breathing. But flat-out lie? Not to Nino.

"She thinks you're experiencing..." His bushy brows furrowed as he tried to think of something. "Situational depression."

"What the holy fuck is that?"

"She showed me a book about it, and, I have to say, you have some of the symptoms, and I—"

He pushed back, practically knocking over the chair. "You know what I have, Nino? Situational anger. Seriously royal pissed-offedness that I am fucking helpless to get my own kid. And you know what else frosts my situational ass? The only woman I ever loved is dead. I think you know how that feels."

This time Nino couldn't even swallow. His eyes filled up as he stood. "You're damn right I do. It feels like...like..." He fisted his ham hocks and punched his barrel chest. "This is broken and bleeding red-hot misery."

"Go easy," Gabe warned. "You crack that feeble chest, where the hell would I be without you?" He scooped up his plate, more for something to do than a favor for the cook. "And tell that woman to stick her nose in the business I pay her to stick her nose in, which isn't mine."

"You don't think you're depressed?"

He couldn't even conjure the words to deny that moronic question hotly enough. "I don't know what that shit is, Nino. I'm…I'm impotent."

"Oh dear, that's—"

"Not *literally*." Though he couldn't remember the last time being with a chick was anything but a physical release. Maybe…five years. Since he'd last seen Isadora.

He yanked the dishwasher door open with so much force it was a wonder the thing didn't go flying. "I mean I can't do anything. Do you know what it's like to have to send my pal and my little sister to do the job I should be doing? It sucks balls, I tell you. But if I get killed, then that kid won't have a mother *or* a father. I can't do that to him." He turned to Nino, knowing his own expression was probably as pained as his grandfather's. "So, excuse the fuck out of me if I don't want to look at pink flowers when I drag my sorry ass out of bed to face another day in this shithole that I moved to so I could be closer to her before I knew she was…" Dead. Dead. *Dead*. "Gone."

Nino blinked. And, damn it, a tear almost fell out of his watery eyes. "This child could give you a new life."

"Christ knows I could use one." He stuck his fingers in his hair and dragged hard, but that didn't pull the misery out. "I'm going out."

"Like, for the night? Maybe that's a good idea, grandson. Stop into that Toasted Pelican and meet a lady. You need—"

"I don't need a lady."

"Somebody to just get your mind off things."

"A substitute," he muttered. "Which is what every woman will be from now until the day I close up shop and head to hell."

He marched out the back door, ignoring the call of

his makeshift gym, his shirtless body, and bare feet. He ran.

He ran through the stupid gardens with too many pink flowers—especially those things that looked like lilies and smelled like hot nights in Cuba. Hibiscus. Isadora used to put them in her hair.

Crushing the memory, he headed to the resort road and down to the beach with too many bright umbrellas and, of course, a picture-perfect sunset that could make the most miserable person happy.

But not him. He didn't know what the hell situational depression was or meant or how it felt or how long it would last. But he sure as hell didn't like the darkness of his soul and didn't need to give it a name other than loss. Frustration. Agony.

Love.

God, he'd loved her so hard. He turned away from the umbrellas and the happy resort people, heading to where the sand was far less populated. He jogged in the soft stuff because it was a challenge, ignoring the stabs of stones and broken shells on the bottoms of his feet. He heard his own breath and felt his blood pump and waited for some chemical release in his brain that would numb the pain.

He passed a couple walking hand in hand, throwing some mental shade at them for being so lucky. A father and daughter picking seashells. He turned away so he didn't stare at them.

There was no one else for another hundred feet, except a woman in a long black beach cover-up, walking slowly, bending to pick up shells. She stood and looked out at the sunset, brushing some blond hair off her face and…

Gabe slowed his momentum ever so slightly. That gesture. That move.

Damn it, would he go through life seeing her in every woman…but not seeing her at all?

She walked to the water's edge, her shoulders squared, but her gait was long and even and…familiar. *Come on, Rossi! You gotta stop.*

She glanced to her side as he approached on a run, doing the slightest double take, then looking away. His spy training kicked in as he summed her up and figured out her life in one half-second glance.

Thirties, a little too skinny, probably one of the bridesmaids for the weddings they were always having at this place. Pretty enough, too proud to accept the nose job her father offered when she was fifteen.

He ran closer, and she stole the slightest look, one so sly a less-well-trained spy wouldn't have noticed it, but she was checking him out. Comparing him to the best man her sister was trying to set her up with, no doubt.

She did that thing with her hair again, but this time it wasn't so much like Isa, who used to finger her thick brown curls endlessly. She continued toward the water, and he could see now that he was wrong about her walk, too. She had a nearly invisible hitch in her step.

Just as he reached her, she slowed, as if to avoid getting any closer to him. But he smelled it…just the barest, slightest, spiciest hint of Chanel No. 5.

He almost howled. It took everything in him not to scream in her face. *Only Isadora can wear that!* It was her perfume, her scent, her siren call to Gabe.

He closed his eyes and ran harder, sucking in the salt air to get rid of the scent of a woman he would never, ever forget. This wasn't fucking depression. This was grief, and it had him by the balls and the heart and the soul, and it wouldn't let go.

Chessie was on the T, desperate to get off at the next stop. She was stuck on the last car on the train as it rolled under Boston, the ancient tracks jostling her and sending her tumbling three steps back for every one she made forward. It felt like she was clawing her way uphill, bumping into people, trying to swim through the crowd and get to the exit. But every few seconds, the train would clatter and bounce to a near stop…except out the window, the Green Line stops were whizzing by like they were going a hundred and fifty miles an hour.

Copley. The Pru. Brigham Circle. *Stop*! "I have to…get off."

"I might be able to help."

"Gabe needs—" Her head slammed against a window. "Owww."

"Sorry. Potholes. This is why we call it slow and treacherous."

On the train tracks? Wait. Chessie fought to open her eyes, but nothing in her vision made sense. "I was…" Dreaming. "Why is it so dark?" So, so dark.

"It's night. Has been for a long time."

She squinted into the near blackness, able to make out the hood, and the man next to her, lit by the dim, yellow dash lights.

"You talk in your sleep, did you know that? Said you need to get off."

She frowned at him, a memory pulling. "Did you actually make a sex joke to a person talking in her sleep?"

His grin was sly and slow. "I didn't really think you heard."

She tried to look around, but, damn, it was dark. "Where are we?"

"Here." He held out her glasses. "We're miles from any civilization that would have working electricity. Just some farms out here and whoa"—he jerked the car to the left into the other lane—"and the occasional discarded oven door. We narrowly missed a refrigerator a few miles back, so someone mustn't have tied down their traveling kitchen too well."

She shook her head and squinted again, frustration rising. "Why don't you have the headlights on?" she demanded. "And do not tell me it's some spook safety thing and you don't want to risk getting attention."

They clunked into a pothole so deep she could hear the road practically crack the axle. Somehow he managed to drive them out of it. The old beast didn't have too many of those left in her.

"I have nothing against headlights," he said. "It's just that…" He clicked a switch on the dash. Twice. And one more time to make his point. "They must be optional on this model."

"They don't work." She dropped her head back, expecting to hit the headrest…but there was no headrest.

"Moon's strong enough for me."

She peered up at the half-moon, neatly sliced as if Nino's chef knife had cut it in two. It shed just enough light to show gathering clouds. And definitely not enough to—

"Hang on," he said, reaching over to hold her arm with his right hand while he whipped around a turn she had never seen.

As they made it around the corner, the moon cast light over a wide body of water. It was too dark to make out what it was, but they were able to see waves caused by the wind.

"I don't remember seeing a river on the map," Chessie said.

"I took a little detour because I actually know this road, and, believe me, very few others do."

"And you're driving from memory in the dark with no headlights?"

He shot her a smile. "Found that farm stand before you crashed, didn't I?"

"Reminds me I'm starving." She twisted to grab the bag they put on the backseat, her empty stomach screaming for attention. She pulled out a peach and dropped it back, hungry for something more substantial. But the bananas were hard and, she guessed, green, and the sweet bell peppers were not the least bit appealing. "Was kind of hoping for a *medianoche*."

He gave a dry laugh at the fantasy of a Cuban sandwich. "We'll find one in Caibarién. Tomorrow. Eat a pepper."

She made a face at the suggestion, which turned into a big smile when her fingers hit something hard at the bottom of the bag, then closed around a bottle. "Hot damn, Mal Harris. You bought booze from that guy?"

"While you were in the bathroom."

Bathroom? "And we use that term generously when referring to the horse stall with a hole."

"Welcome to rural Cuba."

She pulled the bottle out, immediately recognizing the snap cork that Nino had used for the homemade wine she grew up drinking. "Mama's milk," she cooed, holding the bottle up to the dim dash lights, but it was tinted brown, hiding the color of the wine. "I like it dark, thick, sweet, and tasting like the earth and sweet plump grapes."

"Really." He slid her a look she couldn't quite read. "And here I took you for an Amstel Light girl."

"When the situation calls for beer, I am." She pushed the

bar of the swing-top cork, which opened with a satisfying pop. "I don't suppose that farmer had plastic cups."

"Put on your big-girl panties, Francesca, and take a swig. See how you like the…what did you call it?"

"Mama's milk. I was raised on homemade wine." She lifted the bottle to her mouth, the fragrance far sweeter and a little stronger than what she expected, but she tipped the bottle and took a good, long—

"Pffff!" She managed not to spit it out, but swallowing the bitter, disgusting stuff wasn't easy.

"This isn't"—she choked as her throat burned like someone had stuck a sparkler in her mouth—"wine."

He was laughing, damn him. "They don't grow grapes in Cuba, at least not out here. There are some imported plants that service the few wineries on the island, but that, my friend, is—"

"Rum." She smacked her lips noisily as the burn wore off and left her numb. "God, I hate that shit."

"Sorry. It was this or nothing. I thought we might need a drink." He held out his right hand. "In fact, I do."

"While you're driving with no headlights inches from rushing water?" She turned to hold the bottle far away. "Not on your life. Not on *mine*."

"Give it to me, Francesca."

She puffed a breath. "I love when you go all alpha on me."

He didn't move his hand, waiting, driving around the next turn—that she hadn't even seen, thank you very much—with one hand.

"Oh, what the hell. Apparently I've proven I can't say no to you." She handed him the bottle.

After drinking a decent gulp, he gave it back. "You can say no any time, by the way."

"Oh, I won't."

That made him smile. "Good. Can I have a pepper now?"

She complied, handing him a whole red pepper that she brushed on her shirt to clean. He ate it like an apple and drove like a boss. And Chessie took another sip of the rum, letting the tiniest little buzz hum through her as her eyes finally adjusted and she was able to see the road. Sort of.

"Thought you hated rum," he remarked.

"It's growing on me." But she corked the bottle after the next sip.

"Don't let it grow too much, that stuff can knock you on your ass."

It hadn't, but she could feel the first sensations of heavy arms and a lovely relaxation in her neck. "Are we almost there yet?" she asked with the pretend whine of a child.

"Maybe…five more hours."

"All this to avoid people we don't even know were following us."

He didn't reply, but a distant rumble of thunder echoed, making Chessie lean forward to check out the sky. Thick with clouds now, there were no stars, and the half-moon was just about obliterated.

"Are you going to stop if it rains?"

"Depends how hard it pours."

"Do the windshield wipers work?"

He reached to the dash and felt around, but she already spotted the dial. "It's here." She twisted it and…nothing. Tried again, nothing. "How many pesos did you part with for this beauty, again?"

"You can't put a price on freedom, honey. Ask any Cuban you meet on this trip." He took a slow curve up a slight rise in the road, then down again. The car still bumped and rolled over potholes, and every once in a while they slid through mud and the tires shmooshed in the slush.

And then the heavens opened up and mocked them completely.

"Son of a bitch," Mal muttered as he slowed when visibility dropped to zero.

"We should just stop until it clears. Maybe until morning."

He considered that, inching along and leaning forward with a frown. "Not out in the open."

They hadn't seen another car since she woke up, and she seriously doubted they would, but she knew better than to argue with a spy. "Maybe we can find a secluded place in the trees."

"I don't want to get stuck in mud. Hang on." Fully concentrating, he eased them through a small lake. "If we can get to higher ground, we can see lights coming in either direction."

"And then what will we do? Drive in the opposite direction so they don't see us?"

"No, we'll get out and hide, and anyone who finds this will think it's an abandoned car."

"That they will steal."

"We'll take our bags," he said with the confidence of a man who clearly thrived on these kinds of situations. "They're right there in the backseat, easy to grab if we have to run. And there is no higher ground, I'm afraid, so here we are."

"The fun never stops."

He threw her a heart-stopping smile and pulled off the road. "Baby, it hasn't even started yet."

And her stomach dropped down and fell right through the creaky floorboards.

Chapter Fourteen

Mal didn't think anyone had followed them after leaving Havana, but he would have bet good money there'd been a tail in the airport.

So as much as he started to relax, eating green bananas and listening to the rain on the roof, he paced himself carefully on the Cuban firewater, barely taking the occasional sip.

But Chessie was enjoying the booze, and he was enjoying watching her drink it. She held the bottle high, which, with adjusted night vision, he could see was respectfully, but not shockingly, dented.

"This could make a rum drinker out of me," she said. Looking past the bottle, he could make out her features in the dark car. She'd abandoned her glasses, and he could see her eyes were brighter than they'd been, her smile looser, her hair tousled from the long day.

Goddamn beautiful is what she was.

"Why do you have that look on your face?" she asked.

"What look?" Longing? Lust? Or just garden-variety admiration? He was too tired to hide any of it.

Plus, they had that deal…though he'd prefer a proper bed and a totally sober lover.

"That look," she said. "Like you really don't want to tell me what you're thinking, but you're going to have to tell me, and I'm not going to like it." She took a quick breath and leaned forward to see through the rain-washed windows. "Did you see someone? A light? Do we have to run?" She nodded, as though trying to psych herself up. "It's okay. I'm ready. I've been planning this. First, I'll take my stuff from the back. One bag because I already put my purse into the suitcase. I'll swing that over my back—so glad Gabe told me not to bring a roller—and then I'll—"

"Stop." He put his fingers over her lips. "Stop planning."

"That's like asking me to stop breathing."

"Then stop doing it out loud." He brushed her lower lip with his finger, lingering there a second longer than necessary. "I think we're safe enough to try and get some sleep. You can, anyway." He finally let his hand fall in the large open space between them on the ancient Ford's bench seat.

"You sleep," she said. "I had a nap, so I'll be on guard."

"I think you've had too much rum to be on guard."

"I have not!" she denied hotly, holding the bottle up to eyeball the contents. "We're splitting this. You've had just as much."

"I outweigh you by sixty pounds at least." He took the rum from her hand and tipped his head toward the backseat. "Go get some rest. You'll need it tomorrow."

She didn't move. "You want me back there, don't you?"

"There's space to stretch a little, and you can use your bag for a pillow." He thumbed in the direction of the back. "Go."

With a sigh that held a mix of frustration and resignation, and proof she really *couldn't* say no to him, Chessie knelt on the bench seat. She lifted her leg over the seat back and hoisted herself the rest of the way. Automatically, he reached to give her a boost, his hand closing over her buttocks. He almost sucked in a breath at how firm and sweet her curves felt to grip.

He could have sworn she lingered just a moment too long before pushing herself to the backseat. She landed softly and stretched out, resting her head on their two soft-sided bags behind the passenger seat. She'd had plenty of rum. She'd sleep and that was good.

Because ten more minutes in the front seat of this Ford and—

She suddenly popped up, inches from his face. "I'm not going to be able to sleep."

"Just try."

"I cannot possibly sleep without first going to the bathroom. I don't think I ever have in my whole life."

"Not in the plan, huh?"

She flicked her finger at the arm he'd draped over the top of the seat as he leaned into the door. "Don't knock plans. If we'd had better ones, we might not be sitting in a downpour with no headlights, no windshield wipers, no food, no bathroom, and no hope."

"We have hope. And a flashlight if you want to use the ladies' tree."

She squished up her nose, as if considering the pros and cons of the rainy, dark non-facilities. "I'll wait until the rain slows down, but I honestly can't sleep. I'd rather talk."

"I talked you right to sleep on the way down here. Anyway, don't you have rules about that?"

Even in the dark, he could see a flicker in her blue eyes. "We've already butchered the 'no intimate conversation rule,' and since you just copped a feel of my ass, there goes the 'no unnecessary contact rule' down the drain. And you insist on calling me Francesca, despite the fact that I specifically asked you not to."

"You like it when I call you Francesca. You told me so."

"It puts me off-balance."

He smiled at her. "That's the rum."

"Yeah?" She took the bottle and helped herself to one more swallow, as if to say she wanted to be off-balance. "So…" She pushed a lock of dark hair out of her eyes, but it fell right back and partially covered her brow. "Talk to me, Malcolm Harris."

"You may have underestimated the potency of the local rum."

"*Pah.*" She blew the hair, but it fluttered over her eye again. "Maybe. I am starting to like you, and I told you not to make me do that."

"Which of my grand gestures won you over? The going off route, buying a car you hate, or waiting until we were in a rainstorm in the dark to discover the windshield wipers don't work?"

She gave a slightly loopy sideways grin, suddenly looking a little like Gabe when he was in a playful mood. "The rum."

He leaned a little closer, the cracked leather seat back making an effective barrier between their bodies, but it was low enough to get face-to-face and mouth-to-mouth.

"You're a little tipsy, Francesca," he whispered.

"Not really…but we could play a drinking game."

He laughed. "That won't help things."

"Might even them out and get you tipsy, too. Here's the game," she said. "Every time you say something that makes me like you, I'll take a drink. And vice versa. And we'll just…talk."

"Or pass out."

She reached for the bottle. “Okay, that was funny. Cute. Drink-worthy. Gimme.”

He watched her take a tiny sip, barely enough to wet her lips.

“So tell me about Door-Matt,” he said.

And she choked on that baby sip. “What?”

“I want to hear about this guy who broke your heart.”

“Mood killer,” she sang lightly.

Exactly. Because if one of them didn’t kill the mood, they were not going to make it to the hotel to start on their hopeless sex.

His approach worked, since she slid away from him to lean against one of the bags, essentially as far from him as she could get in this car. She stretched out her legs, dropped her head back, and closed her eyes.

And everything in Mal that made him a man ached to crawl over the seat and stretch right on top of her.

“He didn’t break my heart,” she finally said. “He just didn’t like my plan.”

“Which was?”

She tipped her head, as if to remember just what that plan had been. “Date for two years, get engaged, buy a house, get married, pop out a few kids, have noisy Sunday barbecues and sleepy Christmas mornings, bicker over meaningless things because what really matters is the two of us and we are solid until we get old and gray.”

He stared at her, trying like hell to process that, but failing miserably. “*That’s* your plan?”

She eyed him. “Too 1950s for your taste?”

“Not if you like your life the way you like your cars.” But that wasn’t what got to him. He couldn’t figure out what it was, but it wasn’t the old-fashionedness of her dreams. It was…the impossibility of them.

"Exactly how I like things," she said, unaware that her statement had caused him any turmoil. "Classic, simple, pure, and maybe a little out of sync with the rest of the world. Yeah, I do." She nodded as if she were only thinking about that for the first time. "I really do."

"It's not out of sync with the world, Chessie, since people live those lives all the time, but the whole picket fence thing is really out of sync with what I know about your family."

"You're only considering the family that craves danger and excitement. It's also the family that is full of love and security and happiness. And lots of spaghetti. I want that, too. God, I would kill for Nino's spaghetti carbonara right now. *Kill.*"

"You want permanence and security." Nothing he could ever give a woman, not the way he lived.

"And carbonara." She lifted her head, eyeing him as if his tone had just sunk in. "What? Is my plan too sweet and innocent for you?" she asked, scrutinizing his expression.

"Too far from…reality," he said. His reality. He couldn't even imagine a childhood like that.

"Reality is what you make it, big boy."

"And it wasn't the reality of this Matt character? He didn't want the kids, fence, and Christmas dinners?"

"He checked off some boxes," she said after a long pause.

"Loaded, hung, and…dreamy-looking?"

She snorted a laugh. "Yeah, a regular swoonfest."

"Hey, I'm trying to speak 1950s to you so you'll like me."

Her lips curled up slowly as she shook her head and reached over the seat for the bottle leaning next to him. "You had me at dreamy." She took the rum, leaned forward to take a sip, then handed it back to him. "Are you playing?"

"I already like you," he admitted, taking the bottle back. "And one of us has to stay sober."

"I'm sober," she assured him. "And for the record, dreamy wasn't one of the boxes he checked."

Back to Matt.

"He was grounded, you know?"

Actually, Mal didn't have a clue what grounded was, so he just listened to her talk.

"Good family, stable lifestyle, respectable job."

If those were her boxes, he sure as hell came up empty. "And the Christmas mornings?" Mal did a shitty job of keeping the bitter out of his voice.

"Don't knock Christmas. It's big in my family. Well," She laughed lightly. "I guess Christmas is big in every family, but—"

"No, it's not."

She looked up at him, frowning. "Assuming you celebrate it. Maybe you did Hanukkah or some other winter festivity."

"Nothing."

She sat up again, looking hard at him. "Nothing?" Pure disbelief in her voice. "No tree, no gifts, no big dinner?"

"Not that I recall." He gave her a hopeful look. "Does a shitty childhood make you want to drink? I'll take sympathy points."

She leaned all the way forward, putting her hand on his arm, which still rested on the seat back. "It makes me sad for you. I love Christmas."

"I hate it."

She looked at him for a long time, her face not far from his, her fingers warm on his arm. "Have you ever had one? A real Christmas?"

Never. But she didn't need to know that much about him. "Once," he lied.

"Aww." Her eyes glistened, and she inched closer. "Tell

me about it. I have a feeling it's going to make me drink."

"I can't," he said, feigning a little heartache. "Hurts too much to remember."

"Oh, really?" She gave his arm a solid squeeze. "Please tell me."

He faked a sad sigh. "Okay. It was two years ago. At Allenwood. They had a tree, and we got rubber turkey instead of mystery meat and sleigh bells instead of the lights-out alarm." He could feel his lips curling in a wry smile. "Santa came sliding down the guard tower when we were all tucked in."

She rolled her eyes. "You son of a bitch." She grabbed the bottle from him. "Stop it."

"I thought you only drink when I say something you like."

"You did. Made a joke." She didn't actually drink, holding it even though he kept his hand on it, too. Her other hand was still possessively around his forearm. So, basically everywhere they could be touching with a fifty-year-old cracked leather seat back between them, they were. "You can definitely stop making me like you now," she said softly.

"And you could stop touching me."

She gave him a very slow, very sexy, slightly looped smile…and didn't let go.

He slipped his hand under her hair, grazing her jaw, curling around the narrow column of her neck. "For the record, Francesca, I really wanted to wait for a bed before we had our hopeless sex."

She inched closer. "What could be more hopeless than the backseat of a car? I think it's perfect."

"I think you're perfect," he admitted on a gruff whisper.

He watched her eyes drift closed as his mouth hovered

over hers. He could feel her breath, her pulse, her soft skin, and, finally, her lips.

She tasted like rum, only sweeter and warmer. And despite his best efforts to stay sober, Mal was instantly intoxicated.

Chapter Fifteen

God, she was tipsy. Spinning. Lightheaded. Kicked-in-the-ass high on...him. It wasn't the rum, though that might have made Chessie a little chatty and given her a slight push closer to him. No, it was the feel of his lips. The touch of his hand. The slip-slide play of his tongue against hers as he kissed her like a man appreciating fine wine and not bad rum.

"You okay?" he whispered as he pulled away enough for them to look at each other.

"Yeah." Except her eyes weren't open, and her whole body was tingling. "Better than okay."

She felt him laugh against the next kiss, a rumble that made her want to reach over this stupid bench seat and flatten her hands against his chest so she could feel that laughter vibrate against his gorgeous pecs.

"Here." He took the bottle as if he knew she was about to drop it, stuffed the top to close it, and set it on the floorboard. That gave her just enough time to think about what they were doing. And wait for a litany of *stop, be smart, don't do this* to sing in her head.

But the only thing she heard was the thumping beat of hot

blood pulsing through her body, which sounded a lot more like *yes* than *no*.

When he turned back to her, his expression was serious and…exactly like it was in the hotel room the other night. His jaw set, his gaze unrelenting, his breath remarkably steady for a man who had to be on the edge of the same sensations that had a hold on her.

Wasn't he? Didn't he want to touch and kiss and undress as much as she did?

"I know what you're thinking," he said, running his finger along her lower lip as if it fascinated him.

"Do you?" 'Cause if so, it was game over.

"This isn't part of your plan."

"No," she agreed with a laugh. "The car, the rain, the lights, the wipers, the water, the detour, the whole damn trip is off plan. And making out with you in a 1959 Ford Prefect? In another league of off the plan."

"Sometimes…" He trailed his finger down her throat, into the hollow of her neck, down another inch, where the back of the seat forced him to stop. "You have to go with the flow."

"Ah, yes, contingency sex."

"Exactly." His finger slid up her throat again, and he spread his whole hand against her cheek and jaw, holding her face so that she had to look at him. He threaded her hair, twisting strands and sliding through them.

He pulled her closer and kissed her again, angling his head, owning her mouth, tracing her teeth with his tongue. Each second of the kiss brought them closer, leaning up, fighting the barrier that was the only thing keeping them apart.

The windows, closed against the rain, were completely fogged, blocking out the world they couldn't see anyway.

She tilted her head and let him pepper kisses on her throat while her hands grasped his arms and squeezed the hard curves of his biceps. Up to his neck, fingers into his hair, her legs trembling already, and her breasts aching with the need to be touched.

Thankfully, he seemed to read her mind, climbing easily over the barrier, barely breaking the kiss.

She laughed into his neck. "We didn't make it twenty-four hours."

"Not the first time either." He slid lower, getting his mouth into the vee of her T-shirt and his hand underneath it with little effort. He stroked over the satin of her bra, her senses exploding with pleasure as his body pressed against hers, hard and hot.

A whimper escaped as she pressed against his erection, and sparks shot through her as he dragged her top over her head. "I've never…" *Felt anything like this.*

"Never what?" He snapped off her bra with ease and slid the straps off her. "Never did it in the back of a Ford Prefect?"

"Any car."

He smiled and kissed her, tossing her bra into the front seat. "First stranger sex. First car sex. First hopeless sex. I like being your first for things."

"You just like sex."

"Mmmm." He lowered his head to take one of her breasts into his mouth, but that just meant she couldn't think at all. Instead, she clutched his head, holding it against her, guiding him from one sweet spot to the another.

They rocked their hips, already thrumming with the same rhythm and need, his hard-on rubbing exactly where she needed and wanted it. She rolled over the ridge again, the contact like electricity, sparking and twisting.

The muscles between her legs clutched, and she broke the kiss to try to get her breath as an orgasm started firing through her, throbbing and unstoppable, his hands all over her while he let her ride him until she felt like the whole world was…rolling away.

"What the fuck?" Mal shot up, stealing his body and making Chessie cry out in abject frustration. "What's going on?"

"Um…if I have to explain it to you—"

He vaulted over the front seat and opened the door to the sound of the steady rain hitting the car…the car that was *floating.*

"Flash flood!" He turned the key, and the engine screamed…but didn't turn over. Of course not, Chessie thought. If water had gotten into the fuel line, this car would never start.

"Damn it!" He revved again. Nothing. "Get up here, Chessie. I'll get out and push."

She scrambled to the driver's seat, vaguely aware she had no top on, taking his place as he jumped outside into a calf-high mud lake.

"Keep trying to turn it over," he ordered, then disappeared into the darkness. She turned the key again, tapping her foot on the sticky, useless accelerator while she patted around the front seat and found her glasses.

This car would never…

Move. It *moved.* She squinted into the rearview, but the glass was still fogged up.

Furious at the weather, the car, the situation, she rolled her window down a few inches, ignoring the rain that came in, desperate for a clear look.

"Try it again!" he called.

She twisted the key and worked the gas pedal, feeling the

whole vehicle moving, but not because the flooded engine was on. And then the rear window finally cleared enough for her to see a sight she'd never forget.

Mal, drenched in rain and mud, his shirt sticking to every impressive muscle, his body lit red by the rear lights. He clenched his jaw and stretched his arms and pushed the damn Prefect through the water.

Like some kind of god.

Desire and admiration ripped through her, punching her in the gut and the heart just as he rolled them out of the rushing water. On drier land, the engine sputtered, shuddered, and finally caught, and Mal yanked the driver's door open.

Wordlessly, she slid to the side like the whole thing was choreographed, giving him the driver's seat. He pressed the gas, and they shot forward, spitting rooster tails on either side of the car.

"We're not stopping again until we get there," he announced.

Chessie clutched the seat, wishing like hell the old beast had a seat belt she could drag over her bare breasts. "And you wonder why I don't want to work in the field."

"Like I said, gotta go with the flow. Or flood, as the case may be."

An utterly unfamiliar sensation thrummed through her, as strong as the sexual desire that had just rocked her, and every bit as thrilling. She didn't dare admit it, she couldn't. It was so off plan.

She liked the rush of this job. A lot. And, holy shit, she liked Mal Harris more than any man she'd ever met.

Roger Drummand leaned against the stiff leather sofa outside his father's office, tapping his shoes on polished oak floors and glancing out the colonial-style panes to see the bare trees of early December in Georgetown.

Why the hell had he been summoned here? It couldn't be good. It couldn't be. If that bitch outed him...

From behind the closed door, he couldn't hear Bill Drummand's voice, of course. He was a spy through and through, using only a soft voice and a few well-placed words. He elicited information more than he gave it, and although long retired from his work at the agency, he was, at ninety-one, still interested in everything that went on there.

But why had he called in one of his least favorite supervisors for a meeting? It wasn't like they had a warm father-son relationship. It wasn't like they had any relationship at all. Ever. After all, if Roger hadn't been born, Donna Lee Drummand would likely have survived the appendicitis that she developed when he was only four days old. And if given a choice between the two, Bill would have picked Donna Lee over Roger in a heartbeat.

The old sting still hit, though he was used to the fact that he'd never pleased Big Bill. But if his operation succeeded? Well, he'd please him then, all right.

The door opened, and a beautiful young woman in a black suit stepped out, an electronic tablet in one hand. Bill didn't remarry after his young wife died fifty-five years earlier, but rumor had it that from that day on he lived like the original James Bond and fucked every gorgeous woman he could get his hands on. Still? Shit, who knew? Anything was possible with the old bastard.

She gave Roger a warm smile.

"Mr. Drummand can see you now."

Yeah, the way all sons want to be greeted by their father's assistant. "Thanks." He stood and entered the ultimate man cave, a library stacked with rich leathery first editions, a desk that matched the importance of the man behind it, and a view of Georgetown that gave the town house its three-million-dollar price tag.

Maybe he should ask his father for Lila's blackmail money since the man commanded hundreds of thousands for a speech and still gave them frequently.

"Hello, Bill." He knew better than to call him Dad or Father. From childhood, he'd been instructed to use his first name. It was a wonder he didn't have to call him Mr. Drummand.

"Roger, have a seat."

He didn't get up to come around the mountain of mahogany to hug his son, of course. His body was still strong, if smaller, and even his face, though wrinkled, maintained its handsome structure. Roger hadn't inherited that. None of his father's "presence," in fact.

"Did Ashley offer you coffee?"

"No, thanks. I'm fine."

Smoky eyes narrowed. "Are you."

It was not a question. "Last time I checked. Why?"

He folded his arms and leaned forward to put his elbows on the desk. "I've heard something, Roger, and I feel it's only fair to go directly to the accused source to find out the truth."

Son of a bitch, she told him. She didn't wait for the money, she didn't go to Florida, she fucking told him. Shame and fear heated his whole body. He would deny everything. The one thing he was positive of was that Lila Wickham was working on conjecture, not fact. That made her a good spy, but not a great blackmailer.

"What would that be, sir?"

"I've heard you're spending agency money and time and personnel to track the man you discovered embezzling from Guantanamo Bay."

A modest amount of relief cooled his gut. "The money was never recovered, and I feel certain he knows where it is. If I catch him accessing it, not only do we have him red-handed again, but we could return five hundred thousand to the US government and put that thief back in prison where he belongs." And where he could do the least amount of damage to Roger if he ever talked to the wrong people. "I think that's the right thing to do."

His father nodded slowly, never one to argue about what's right. Doing the work of the government was what was right; his unwavering loyalty to the cause was what kept Bill Drummand alive.

"You need to stop."

"Why? You don't think he'll lead me to the money?"

"I don't care, and neither should you. It's not a priority any longer and successful agents look forward not backward. You know how I feel about rear view mirrors."

Fighter pilots don't use them.

He'd heard the words in every speech. "The government is short a half a million dollars, sir."

"The government has enough money, Roger." His glare shut down the argument far more effectively than the words. "Enough to pay for an agency chief of staff position opening in a month, and I want you to have it."

Roger's jaw almost dropped. Oh, he'd enjoyed his share of nepotism in his career—his last name opened plenty of doors within the CIA. But his father had never actually gotten him a top-level job. "That would be wonderful, sir."

Bill's steely eyes narrowed. "There will be, of course, the usual process to vet you and an in-depth investigation of all your current projects."

Shit. "Of course."

"But there will be nothing untoward," he said confidently. "You are my son."

Roger blinked. Had he ever, in fifty-five years, heard Bill say that with any amount of pride? He couldn't remember, but just the hint of it actually tightened Roger's throat. His father's approval was all he ever wanted, and all he never had. Until now.

"I am indeed you son, sir." He cleared his throat and willed himself not to get emotional. Bill hated emotions.

"You'll have to be approved by the director himself, but we're golfing next week." In other words, Bill had that approval in the bag. The golf bag.

"I'm happy to meet with the director myself."

His father laughed, enough to show he didn't think that meeting would amount to a pile of shit. "I'll handle it."

Then Bill stood, meeting over. "You'll do a good job, Roger. Don't waste money. Don't waste time going after things that are already done. Don't forget that the United States of America pays your salary and your job is to keep it safe, not rich, so prioritize. Prioritize."

Bill's favorite word. "I certainly will, sir."

Bill nodded and gave a slight gesture of dismissal toward the door. Without so much as a handshake, Roger turned and left, his shoes echoing in the wide, high entryway and out the door into the chill of Washington, DC.

If he didn't pay Lila Wickham, he could lose this opportunity. He'd lose the chance to gain his father's approval. He had to pay her. And, irony of ironies, she was the one in Florida trying to get a lead on Mal.

He dialed a number he knew by heart and listened to half a ring before it was picked up.

"What?" Lila Wickham's bitchy English accent jarred him, even though he was expecting it.

"Why haven't you checked in?" he demanded.

"Too busy having sex with the pool boy while I get a European facial. What do you want?"

"An update."

"I could make shit up, Roger. Would that make you happy?"

He closed his eyes. "It would help."

"I think you're forgetting who's calling the shots now."

"Have you found Mal Harris?"

"I have not."

"Gabe Rossi?"

Nothing for a millisecond, then, "I wouldn't know him if he walked into me, so I couldn't tell you. But I'll keep digging around. Meanwhile, you better find some other way to get that money, Mr. Drummand. Your father's assistant just texted me to confirm our meeting."

Roger drew in a slow breath, wishing he had an answer. As he exhaled, his other phone buzzed. He pulled it out to read a text of his own.

Harris is in Cuba with a woman. See picture. Report on locations attached.

He instantly recognized Francesca Rossi, the hacker from the family of do-gooders. Of course he knew why Mal was taking her there. Of *course*.

He almost told Lila what had just come in, but thought better of it. She didn't need to know he had a backup plan, and the longer she stayed out of his way, the better. "Keep looking," he said. "I'll be in touch."

He hung up before she replied, already knowing what he had to do.

He had to beat Mal Harris at his own game. He had to get back to Cuba before little Miss Happy Fingers could dig into the wrong information. He had to get that money, pay off Lila, and eliminate any evidence of his secret program to place former terrorists in the US to uncover new cells. Then he'd take his new job and do his name and father proud.

He texted the spy who'd sent him the information, knowing his words would go into an official file.

This project is closed and Harris is no longer a person of interest. You may close the reports and stop following him.

He sent the same instructions to two other agents, then skimmed the report on Mal's whereabouts in Cuba. A documentary producer, huh?

Roger knew how to get the money, and he knew Mal Harris's weaknesses. And if the bastard and his hacker pal died in the process…well, that would be Cuba's problem. The US wouldn't blink if "Mitchell Walker" and "Elizabeth Brandt" disappeared in Cuba. As far as the US was concerned, they didn't even exist.

He turned around and glanced at the multimillion-dollar row house and thought of the powerful man inside. He had to be worthy of being his son. He had to be. No matter who died in the process.

Chapter Sixteen

Mar Brisas was even worse than Mal had feared.

The hostel had a shower in the hall that offered a dribble of water, a used bar of soap that smelled a lot like a goat, and a towel the size of a napkin. But at least he could wash off the mud and clear his head after a long drive to Caibarién.

Maybe Mother Nature had been sending a message with her flash flood: *Bad idea, Mal. This woman deserves better than hopeless sex.*

How did his nice little arrangement manage to get a handle like that anyway? She'd called it hopeless sex…but she seemed pretty hopeful to get it. And he was starting to entertain something that felt a lot like hope, too. Like hope there could be more time with her after this assignment was over. Which didn't make any sense.

Except now he didn't just like her or have the hots for her, he *admired* her.

Plenty of experienced intelligence agents couldn't have handled the mess they'd gotten into last night. But an untrained civilian? Any effects of the rum had instantly disappeared, and she'd silently dressed and helped him navigate the dark drive, working as a dependable partner in every way.

She hadn't complained when they pulled up to a "hotel" in a town that was little more than a decrepit village famous for crabs that walked around on the streets narrowly avoiding being crushed by the horses and carriages that were as common as old rust-bucket cars.

Yes, he admired her. That wasn't the same as—

"No mas! Basta!"

Mal squinted into the lukewarm, slightly yellowish water that he was being ordered to stop using. If it even was water. But he shut off the spigot and dried.

He stepped into jeans, the only thing he'd grabbed from his duffel bag when he left Chessie in their basement room down the hall. He didn't want to leave her alone for long, anyway. It wasn't safe. And it wasn't…what he wanted.

Shaking the thought along with his wet hair, he headed back, slowing when he noticed the door was slightly ajar. Had he left it that way? Inching it open, he peered into the room lit by only a hint of the morning sun coming through one jalousie window near the ceiling.

The bed was empty. Damn it, that was exactly where he wanted her. *Now.*

He spun around, wondering if there was another room that she'd taken. She hadn't even blinked when the owner told Mal they had only one available room. Another bathroom? She'd taken a shower first, right after they'd arrived, and warned him that the only bathroom had lousy water and the owner timed the showers.

Mal took two steps to the bed, since the room was not much bigger than the undersized double bed, spying her soft-sided bag, but not her purse. There was no closet, no other door.

Why would she leave? A slow burn of worry slid up his chest, overpowering anything like disappointment or frustration. Maybe he shouldn't have left her alone even for five minutes. He snagged his satellite phone from the dresser and bolted, slamming the door behind him.

He marched back down the tiny hallway, up the stairs to the bathroom he'd just left—still empty—and past two other rooms to the front entrance. No one was at the desk where they'd found the owner.

He stepped through the doorway onto a planked walkway under a wooden awning supported by rotted, peeling posts. This part of town was little more than a street of wooden structures, most painted in the same hue of blue or yellow, if they were painted at all.

A few locals peppered the area, but where the hell was she?

Looking up and down the street, a low-grade anger and worry bubbled in his chest, making him fight the urge to call out her name. Where would she—

A trill of laughter and the squeal of a delighted child pulled his attention to a run-down grassy area next to the hostel. Instantly, he saw Chessie standing in the midst of about ten children who circled her like they were dancing around the maypole.

She held her hand high in the air, laughing with them, and then turning to see Mal. "I stepped outside with my satellite phone, and they all appeared like magic."

Relief punched, surprisingly intense. She certainly hadn't gone far, she wasn't lost, and she was only trying to get better reception on the sat phone like Gabe had instructed. So why had her momentary disappearance bothered him so much?

He didn't know, but he strode across the planked walkway, irritated and annoyed that he'd lost her for even one second.

But Chessie beamed at him, apparently proud of her Pied Piper skills, then did a quick once-over of his bare chest.

"You forgot to tell me you were leaving," he said, purposely letting her know he was angry.

"You were in the shower, Mal, and I couldn't get a signal in—"

"*Señora! Teléfono! Señora*!" one of the kids yelled, jumping up high enough to touch the phone.

She reacted instantly, whirring out of reach and tossing the device to Mal, who snatched it in midair. The kids cheered and clapped like they were watching a sport.

Chessie beamed. "Some of them speak English," she told him.

"I do!" one of the taller boys, likely nearing his teens, said.

"Me do, too!" a girl added, then put her finger to her mouth. "*Pero*…no tell."

They weren't supposed to brag about it, Mal surmised. A few of them came to him, still anxious to see the phone. "*Estados Unidos*?" one asked. "*Abuelo*! *Abuelo*!"

He wanted to call his grandfather in the US. Mal sighed and shook his head, looking at Chessie.

"No, darling, sorry," she said, coming to Mal's aid and his side, putting a hand on the young boy's head. "But if you help us, maybe we can help you?"

He looked confused and glanced to Mal for an explanation, who turned to Chessie to see where she was going with this.

"If they help us find the family we're looking for," she said, "maybe we can let them make one call. It's like a gift, like the other stuff we brought to give to kids."

Candy and books, not time on a satellite phone. But it made sense because that phone call might be the one thing they wanted the most.

"Tell them what we're doing," she urged. "About the TV show, just to get them talking."

He gathered them around him in his best Spanish, taking out his phone to show they had two and getting a huge cheer for that. Chessie observed and moved from kid to kid, a casual touch on the shoulder, a genuine smile. She was as comfortable around them as if they were her own family. Yet another thing that was attractive to him, a man who automatically put a wall between himself and strangers.

Trying to follow her lead—how was that for a role switch?—he explained that they were here to talk to children and families about how things might change in their world.

That got a lot of blank stares for this killer documentary idea. *Thanks, Gabe.*

Chessie stepped in for an assist, crouching down to get eye level with the two kids who spoke passable English. "We have to talk to families, too. Like the Ramos family. Do you know them?"

His eyes widened, and he stared right at Chessie. "No."

It didn't take training in intelligence gathering to know that the little potential informant was lying.

"Are you sure?" Chessie prodded. "This is a small town, and we would like to go to their house."

"It's a farm," the girl said.

"Caralita." The boy took a step back, reaching for his sister's hand to pull her away. "*Vamonos.*"

Mal and Chessie shared a silent glance, a lot of questions and observations zinging between them with the ease of two agents who'd worked a long time together. With the tiniest nod, she managed to tell him she'd handle the English-speakers, and he should be with the others.

He didn't argue, letting her take a few steps with the two

kids, engaging them with questions and chances to look at the phone.

He kept talking to the ones around him, finally relenting and letting them play with the phone, while he kept one eye on Chessie. After a minute the kids stopped walking away and talked to her. The little girl more than the boy, Mal noticed. Chessie listened, got down on the ground, and started digging things out of her purse.

Gum. Candy. A toy. All the while, they talked. Mal mentioned the Ramos family to his group, but had no reaction whatsoever, just kid-lust for the phone. So he finally let one attempt a call, but it didn't go through.

He lost a few fans then, but Chessie stood and gave hugs to both her kids. And waved the others over, passing out candy to all of them while Mal just watched and, damn it, *admired* her some more.

That was unexpected.

The kids scurried off, dancing, laughing, chomping on colorful candy like they'd been given the keys to the kingdom. Chessie came closer to Mal and placed one hand flat on his chest.

"All this gorgeous male pulchritude on display, and I got what we needed with a few bags of Skittles." She grinned up at him. "The Ramos farm is a few miles east of here. On a dirt road past a big orange tree."

"That's...good. But not too specific."

"Put a shirt on, big guy. We can find it." She started walking ahead of him, back to the hotel, but he grabbed her arm and stopped her, spinning her around.

"Are you mad I left?" she asked. "Because I only stepped onto the street and... What? Why are you looking at me like that?"

"I don't know. I don't fucking know." Without thinking

too much about it, he leaned into her mouth and kissed. Not long, not hot, not wet and sexy, but a good kiss nonetheless.

When he backed away, she lowered her glasses to get a better look. "Was that a reward for my top-notch field skills?"

"It was just a kiss 'cause I wanted one."

"Oh." She bit her lower lip. "Well. That's…interesting. But here's the deal. As much as I want to go back in there and, you know, get hopeless, I need to tell you something."

He frowned, waiting, catching the serious tone.

"There's something strange about the Ramos farm. They didn't want to tell me, but I got the feeling it's not a normal farm. The little girl, Caralita? She whispered a word in my ear, and I think it might be a password."

"A password?" Now she was going overboard. "What did she say?"

"*Maestra*. Like 'maestro' with an a."

"Teacher," he translated. "Maybe not a password, but a clue."

"A clue?"

"About where we're going." Taking her hand, he guided her back to the hotel. "Gabe made a good choice for this team."

She gave his hand a squeeze, and he knew the feeling was mutual. Hopeless, he reminded himself, but mutual.

"Tell me more about what they said about this farm," Mal said as he drove them through the roughest roads they'd come across yet.

"It was what they didn't say," Chessie recalled. "They

were evasive, especially the older one. I thought maybe they figured we were with the government."

"They're taught from a young age to be extremely careful who they talk to, but generally that means men in uniform," Mal said. "Tourists and visitors, especially in these parts, are so rare that they are more likely to open up."

"These two had been to the farm," she said. "The little girl was pretty specific about the orange tree. Like a giant orange umbrella, she told me. Turn right on the road just after it."

"A royal Poinciana," Mal said. "They're all over Cuba. They call them flame trees."

"Hopefully, we don't take a wrong tree turn."

He threw her a smile, certainly not the first since they'd arrived in this town. His obvious approval of her field skills? Or…his obvious approval of her. It wasn't smart that she wanted both, but she did. *Remember, Chess…forty-two addresses in thirty-eight years. One a prison.*

"I think it could be a culture school," he mused, pulling her back to the mission at hand.

"What is that?"

"Other than illegal? All over Cuba, in private homes and in rural areas, the people try to teach their children the ways of the country before Castro, so customs, culture, and truth don't die with each generation. If they get caught running something like that, the adults on the property would go to prison for life. The children?" He gave a deep, long sigh as the car rumbled down the road.

That wasn't a sigh of exhaustion, Chessie mused. It was a sigh of pain. "What happens to the children?" she asked.

"You don't want to know."

She inched closer. "I do."

"They get overlooked, ignored, wasted, lost, and,

ultimately, indoctrinated into a system that shows no mercy and gives no hope." He threw her a look. "Take it from me, that's no way to live."

His voice was low and dark and honest. "And you know that because of those forty-two addresses in thirty-eight years?"

"What happened to me was different, but yeah," he said. "These kids who have a whole political system to fight."

"But the result is the same, a life of constant upheaval and uncertainty."

He nodded. "Makes for a good spy."

"But you're not a spy anymore."

He tossed her a quick look, a warning in his dark eyes. "Don't we have a rule against intimate revelations about our past?"

She sighed. "I can't help wanting to know about you," she admitted. "I mean, that's how people get to be good partners in the field, right?" And in life, she added silently.

"You're good," he said. "Very good." The compliment warmed her, but then he nodded and pointed ahead. "There's a huge Poinciana and a dirt road. I think we've found the farm."

The tree, true to its nickname, flamed bright orange with blooms twenty feet in the air.

"Wow, that's a pretty tree. Like a great big explosion of hope." She put her hand on her chest, feeling it. "And I hope my nephew is at the end of this road."

"Yeah," he said, narrowing his eyes as he turned onto the road. "But let's lose the documentary cover on this call."

"What?" She whipped around to face him. "How can we do that? We don't have another cover. Who do we say we are or why we're here?"

He put a hand on her arm. "Contingency, Francesca. They'll never let us bring cameras in here if this place is what I think it is. We're...teachers. Just like the little girl said. American teachers doing research or looking for a chance to help them. They should respond to that. We'll offer cash. And gifts. And..."

"Hope," she supplied.

"That's your department."

The Prefect sputtered over the rocky path—there was no way it could be technically called a road—taking them through more lush foliage. Luscious, sweet scents of pineapple and mango floated through the open window, hanging on still, tropical air.

They followed the dirt road until it turned and ended at a cluster of four or five structures, a mix of wood and stucco, surrounded by a few goats, at least ten chickens, and one mangy-looking dog.

As Mal drove closer to the buildings, Chessie checked her bag again. She'd brought money, of course, and candy. Some children's books in Spanish, pens and pencils, a few bars of soap and shampoo, and hair brushes. All gifts that she hoped would gain her access and the trust of the whole Ramos family.

"Whoa."

Chessie looked up at the note in Mal's voice, following his gaze to see four men—well, three teenagers and a grown man—emerge from what looked like a barn, standing side by side like a human wall. The man held a rifle pointed directly at the car.

"Whoa is right," Chessie murmured, shifting in her seat. "Quite the welcoming committee."

The older man made no effort to lower his rifle when Mal brought the car to a stop about forty feet away. "Stay here until I call to you," he said, opening the door. "Keys are in the ignition if you have to take off."

If she had to take off? She felt her eyes pop, but he reached over and touched her cheek in a lightning-flash move of reassurance. "If I point my finger straight in the air, that's your signal. Don't question it, just leave."

"O-okay." Although, deep inside, she doubted she'd have the nerve to just leave him here. So she watched him get out of the car and prayed she wouldn't have to make that choice.

Her throat went dry and her fingers curled around the cracked leather edge of the front seat, her heart beating fast. The windows were open, but the only sounds she heard were the distant cry of a child and the bleat of a goat.

Mal held his hands up, moved slowly, and spoke in Spanish.

She didn't understand the words, but she understood body language. Mal's open and friendly. The men? Not so much.

The fight-or-flight flutters collided in her, leaving chills in their wake and a sudden itching to grab her computer and find a solution.

But there was no database that could get them out of this. Just words, gifts, actions, and hope. No wonder Gabe hadn't wanted her to come here and do this alone.

The man with the rifle spoke the most, unintelligible Spanish. Mal replied, his voice low and steady. She picked up very few words, but did hear *maestra*. Teacher. And he pointed to Chessie, making all eyes zero in on her.

Rifle Man came closer to Mal and said something under his breath. Mal replied. And Rifle Man's entire body language changed as he put a hand on Mal's back and both of them started walking toward her.

"You can get out now, Elizabeth," Mal said, reminding her that they should use their fake names. "And bring your computer. And the bag of gifts."

Chessie gathered what she needed, and suddenly the passenger door was opened for her by one of the boys, who grabbed everything she had in her hands and started running.

"Hey!" she called, looking to Mal for help, but he just shook his head hard.

"Let it go," he said.

Let it go? "But my computer and my—"

"Good faith," he said quietly. "We're showing good faith."

She got out of the car slowly, automatically holding out her hands to show how empty they were. And full of *good faith*.

Rifle Man fired off some Spanish.

One of the teenage boys came around and started patting down Mal for a weapon. He didn't move, but held his hands out, allowing them to inspect him.

Mal nodded to her. "Let them do the same to you," he ordered.

She did, extending her hands, letting him pat lightly over her waist, hips, and legs, and the man with the rifle signaled to the other boy and shouted an order. The kid—who couldn't have been fourteen and was grossly underweight—gestured for them to follow him.

Surrounded by Rifle Man and his boys, Chessie and Mal were taken to the back of the building, then toward another barn-like structure. Chessie's blood thumped wildly as she looked at Mal, but he didn't give away anything. Not fear, not worry, not a plan for what to do if these people were taking them into the barn to shoot them.

She didn't speak, but gave him a pleading look and got nothing but a nearly imperceptible headshake in response. Basically, *just shut up and do what they want you to do*. Like she had a choice at this point.

She followed the youngest boy, who stopped at a huge padlock on the barn door. He turned to their leader, Rifle Man, who gave a gruff order.

The boy disappeared around the back, and they all stood in the merciless sun for five minutes until he returned with a key, which he slipped into the lock.

Rifle Man stepped up to the door and glowered at Mal, speaking in hushed Spanish.

Mal replied in Spanish, then he glanced at Chessie. "I've just promised on the lives of our own families that we will never reveal what we're about to see. Tell him the same thing."

She blinked, then looked at Rifle Man. "I promise," she whispered.

"In Spanish," Mal urged. "Say '*le prometo.*'"

She repeated the words exactly as they sounded.

Finally, the man ripped off the padlock and slowly opened the barn doors.

Excerpt, it was no barn. It was a massive warehouse full of desks, chalkboards, maps, and at least twenty children ranging in age from toddler to teen.

"*Esta es la Escuela Ramos*," the man announced with pride.

"The Ramos School," Mal translated.

Chessie took a breath and let her gaze slide over all the little faces full of surprise and curiosity. Was one of these her nephew? Her throat tightened with hope so tangible she could taste it.

Chapter Seventeen

It didn't take long for Chessie to figure out where she wanted to go in the little schoolhouse. There were several small "sections" that were loosely divided into age groupings. The older kids in the back, the midsize ones along the sides, and up front, the very youngest.

Chessie gravitated to these kids, maybe age five and under, scanning their little faces, looking for any sign, anything at all, that she might be staring at her brother's son. There wasn't a blue eye in the bunch, so that ruled out her most obvious clue. The little Cuban faces were a sea of beautiful and expressive dark eyes, delicate but deeply tanned features, and constantly moving mouths that smiled easily and laughed heartily, despite the fact that they were in hiding, obviously hungry, and living on the hairy edge of real poverty.

Nestor Ramos, their rifle-carrying host, relaxed more with each passing moment, obviously deciding that some prayer had been answered as he walked from one side of the warehouse to the other, observing the guests carefully.

The lessons were in full swing within an hour or two. Reading from new books. Writing with colored pens. Even some math, counting out wrapped candies to learn addition and subtraction.

Chessie tucked herself in a corner with the toddler-age little ones, a boy and a girl on her lap, introducing them to *Winnie the Pooh*, with pages in both English and Spanish.

She divided her attention between the book and the precious little faces, who beamed heartfelt, gap-toothed smiles as she stumbled through the Spanish, their slender fingers wrapped around her arms as if to keep her there.

Every time she looked up to scan the room and drink in what was going on, her gaze fell on Mal, who was on his knees in front of a few teenage boys, getting a purely marvelous reaction while he used Chessie's laptop to show them a video game, which apparently held universal appeal for boys in any country, under any political regime.

"*Otra vez! Otra vez*!" one of the children on her lap cried, pulling Chessie's attention back to her own circle of students. She didn't have to know Spanish to understand the plea of a child who wanted a story read a second—well, a fourth time. And she didn't mind, except this wasn't getting her any closer to finding the child she'd come here for.

"I have an idea!" she said brightly, lifting the two from her lap and waving over several others. "Let's play the…" How could she find out which child was Gabriel? What did she know about him other than his name and… "The birthday name game!"

They all stared at her, utterly confused.

"*Cumpleaños*," a woman behind her said. "*Un juego de su cumpleaños*."

Chessie turned around to find a pair of warm, dark eyes on her. The young woman looked to be about twenty, as thin and ragged as everyone else, with an infant wrapped in a carrier hanging from her neck. "A birthday game?" the woman asked. "That's what I told them."

"Yes, *si*," Chessie said. "I could use the help. I'm…" Not

Chessie, she remembered before her real name slipped out. "Elizabeth. And you?"

"Rosalia." She took the hand Chessie offered. "Rosalia Ramos."

"*Señor* Ramos is your father?" Chessie guessed.

She nodded. "*Si. Papa.* And..." She pointed to the original line of teenage boys who'd greeted them, now engrossed in Mal's video game. "My...brothers."

All of them? And practically the same age?

But she was grateful to find someone who could help her identify the children. "And who is this little angel?" Chessie gave the infant a gentle touch on thick black curls.

"Miguel." She smiled and lifted him a little higher. "My son."

"He's precious." Chessie stroked the curls again and turned to the half-dozen young ones who'd gathered round. "So here's what I'd like to do. I'd like to know all of their names and their birthdays so we can learn months and days," Chessie said, speaking slowly and hoping the idea worked. "Do they know their birthdays?"

Rosalia's smile wavered. "Maybe. Mostly. Birthdays mean presents."

"And I'm going to give presents," Chessie assured her, reaching for her bag and the little container of chewing gum she'd brought.

Chessie sat on the floor and helped Rosalia gather eight children around her in a semicircle, listening to the other woman explain the game in rapid-fire Spanish. There was some squirming and giggling, some jockeying for a position closer to Chessie, but finally they settled and stared at her.

"I want each one to tell me their name and their birthday." Was one of these children Gabriel, born in the right year? Would they know the year they were born? They might know their age.

She glanced up and caught Mal looking at her, and she held his gaze. Her heart ratcheted up as the eye contact lasted long enough for her to get his silent message of approval. And they shared a smile that was as sweet as the candy she'd been giving away all day.

Rosalia pointed to the first child, a little girl with a heartbreakingly beautiful face, and gave the instructions in Spanish.

The girl's eyes opened, and she held up four fingers. "*Cuatro.*"

"She's four," Rosalia supplied. "And your name?" she urged the child. "*Y su nombre?*"

Not that it mattered, Chessie thought. She wasn't Gabe's son, so she'd just move—

"Gabriella."

Chessie startled. "Did she say…Gabriella?"

"We call her Gabrielita."

Chessie's heart clutched. "What's her last name?"

"Ramos," Rosalia said quickly.

"She's your sister or cousin?"

Rosalia shook her head and leaned closer to whisper so softly no one but Chessie could hear. "She doesn't have a last name yet."

An orphan? And Chessie's heart stopped just before it cracked into a million pieces.

Could the database have been wrong about the gender of the child? Could she have misread it? Was *Gabriel* really *Gabriella*?

She searched the child's arresting face and big brown eyes, more the color of Mal's than Gabe's. "Gabrielita?"

The little girl suddenly shot up and lunged toward

Chessie, wrapping eager, hungry arms around Chessie's neck and squeezing all the love out of her heart.

Oh dear God in heaven, *was this her niece*?

Working for calm, she inched the little body back. "When is your birthday, Gabrielita?"

Rosalia leaned closer again. "We don't know her birthday, really."

Of course not. She was an orphan. Because her mother was dead, and her father was…waiting in Barefoot Bay. She tried to tamp down hope, but failed.

"Could it be in the summer?" Chessie asked, a little too anxiously.

Rosalia shrugged and touched the head of the boy next to her. "Let's give the others a turn," she said.

So Chessie had to back off and continue the game. There was no Gabriel among the rest, and only two who knew their birthdays, and those were in winter months.

If the child was here, like Gabe believed, wouldn't he—or she—have to be among this group?

"Is anyone missing today?" Chessie asked the woman next to her as she liberally handed out sticks of gum to eager little kids.

Rosalia smiled and shook her head. "They never miss. School is like heaven to all of these kids. It is joy and happy." Her expression grew sad. "We cannot lose what my father has worked so hard to have for the farmers and families of Caibarién."

"Is there a chance of that?"

"Always a chance. The government will close us down if they discover we are teaching. The government must own the schools. And tell us what to teach."

"But isn't that changing?" Chessie asked, automatically reaching out as Gabrielita scrambled higher on Chessie's lap.

Rosalia gave a sigh. "Cuba might let more tourists and businesses in," she said. "But that will not change our government. The only thing that will ever change that is education for our youngest citizens." She sounded like she was reciting something she'd heard someone—likely her father—say many times. "It is our hope that when the Western culture infiltrates, children like this one…" She patted her baby's head. "Like my little Miguel…will seek the truth, and justice, and fight the oppression."

"Many people think that will happen," Chessie told her.

"Only if we educate them," Rosalia said. "Schools like this…" She made a sweeping gesture with her free hand. "They are the most important, and secretive, places in all of Cuba."

Was that why little Gabriel Winter had been here? If his mother was American…but his mother had died and the child might be considered an orphan.

The little girl squirmed on Chessie's lap and looked up with adoring eyes. "Mamá?" she whispered.

For a second, Chessie could barely breathe. She kissed Gabriella's head, closing her eyes to memorize her sweet scent, suddenly overwhelmed by an emotion that felt awfully like love. And protection. And, yeah, love.

But she'd hadn't come here looking for a girl, and she couldn't let one wide-eyed orphan with a similar name derail her from her real mission.

"Rosalia," Chessie said softly. "Was there ever a boy at this school named Gabriel? He would be the same age, around four."

The other woman looked up from her baby, meeting Chessie's eyes, frowning, but not answering. Maybe she didn't understand.

"It would have been in the last few years, maybe recently."

Chessie knew there was a note of desperation in her voice, but this was the only lead they had, the only address.

The database she'd seen hadn't listed a date that the mother had passed away, Chessie thought. It could have been anytime in the last four years. She could have died in childbirth, which might explain why she'd been silent all these years.

For a long moment, Rosalia was still, so, so still, it was as though she'd been frozen. "I will ask my father." She stood quickly, walking away, leaving Chessie with her arms around Gabrielita.

If there was no boy named Gabriel, then…

"Let me brush your pretty hair," Chessie whispered.

Gabriella just looked up and gave a warm smile. "Mamá?"

Chessie's heart folded over itself, leaving her speechless. "I have a nice hairbrush I can use."

Getting one of the brushes she'd brought for this express purpose, Chessie ran the rough bristles through Gabriella's curls, easily picking up a dozen strands that could be tested for DNA. After a few moments, she surreptitiously dropped the brush back into her handbag. As she did, she looked up and found *Señor* Ramos looking down at her.

"Come," he ordered, surprising her with English and gesturing for her to get up and follow him.

Chessie stood, easing the child to the ground, but Gabriella was having none of it. She wrapped her arms around Chessie's leg and squeezed.

"I'll be back," she promised the little girl, but Gabrielita just clung tighter.

Señor Ramos bent over and spoke softly, putting a gentle hand on the girl's shoulder. After a moment, she let go of Chessie, but still gazed up lovingly.

Chessie smiled and patted her back with a silent promise to return, then glanced around for Mal. "My friend?" she asked, not seeing him in the schoolhouse barn.

He muttered something in Spanish and pointed outside, then made a gesture that she interpreted as bouncing a basketball. She hadn't even realized he'd left.

Chessie followed the man outside, around the back to another structure, much smaller, wooden, unpainted. He opened the door and gestured for her to go through a crooked opening into a dimly lit room with a bed, a cardboard dresser, and a toilet and sink. The floor was broken concrete, and the windows were open.

He faced her, a frown pulling thick black brows together. "Why are you here?"

His accented but perfect English threw her, almost as much as the accusation in his voice. Damn it. She shouldn't have gone with him. Mal was outside, and she was…on her own. "I'm a teacher, like—"

"Who are you looking for?"

Chessie felt the blood drain from her face, realizing how vulnerable she was. Not that she thought this man would hurt her, but they were here on a lie. A lie that…might be keeping her from truth.

But she'd already asked Rosalia about a four-year-old boy named Gabriel, and she wasn't going to leave the farm without knowing for certain if he'd been here.

"A child named Gabriel, about four years old. His mother is dead. I have reason to believe he was brought here."

Very slowly, *Señor* Ramos shook his head, nothing but honesty in his eyes. "No one named Gabriel."

She closed her eyes as the finality of that hit. Maybe the child she was looking for was a girl. Maybe that little—

"I would like to give you something, *señorita*," he said,

holding up a hand to make her stay where she was. Wordlessly, he crossed the room to the simple cardboard dresser, opened the top drawer, and pulled out a chain, like a heavy necklace or…no, it was a rosary.

"For you," he said, handing her the rosary. "*Para darte las gracias*. To thank you."

To thank her? Chessie looked at the thick beading and the heavy silver cross at the end, decorated by a gorgeous red stone.

"The sacred heart," *Señor* Ramos said. "*El Sagrado Corazón*."

"It's beautiful," she whispered. And valuable. Very, very valuable. "But, no. You should keep this for the children."

He just held it closer to her.

"Or sell it for the school?" she suggested, rubbing her fingers together to indicate the money this piece could buy. "You could buy supplies and books and food."

"It might help you," he said.

Meaning she could pray with it? Or—

He leaned closer, making Chessie think he was going to kiss her cheek. Instead, he whispered in her ear, "Seek him at the *municipal*. Go there. Today."

The word was soft, the Spanish accent heavy, and she wasn't sure she'd heard him correctly. Something about the municipal?

"What are you doing in here?" At the sound of Mal's voice, she turned to find him standing in the doorway.

"We're talking," she replied, stepping back to realize *Señor* Ramos had closed the rosary in her hand.

Mal looked from one to the other and asked Ramos a quick question in Spanish. Surprising her, the man answered in Spanish, then gestured around the room as if to say he was showing Chessie around.

And not revealing that he spoke perfect English, had just given away a valuable necklace, and had whispered a possible lead in her ear.

"I think we can go now," Mal said.

Yes. To the *municipal*, which sounded like the English word 'municipal' —so it might be the community's government, and a place of public records. Definitely a lead.

The other man nodded and added something in Spanish, walking out and leaving the two of them alone in the tiny room.

"What did he say?" Chessie asked.

"He said, 'I hope you find what you're looking for.'" Mal walked out ahead of her, leaving Chessie to consider that as she tucked the rosary in her pocket.

"So do I," she whispered. "So do I."

Chapter Eighteen

"Just don't get your hopes up, Chessie."

"You've said that three times," she replied.

"I'm being realistic, is all."

But she still seemed as enthused about the idea of storming the municipal offices as when they left the Ramos's farm. Now they were already seeing the hideous apartment buildings of Caibarién, and she hadn't backed off. "The *municipal* isn't going to be like your local post office, willing to help," Mal reminded her.

"Do you have a better idea? Where else can we go but the building in this area that houses exactly the kind of paperwork we want? Where the guy who we think owned the place where Gabriel was last seen *sent* us?"

So many caveats in there, he lost count but added a few more. "The building that is *supposed* to house it, if they'll let us in, if they're open and not fishing."

She grunted and smacked the leather of the front seat. "Why are you so pessimistic?"

"Because I've lived in Cuba before. Ramos probably has a friend who works at the *municipal*, and he knows we're prepared to grease every palm that's extended to us."

"Pessimistic, bitter, *and* cynical."

He threw her a look. "Well, you didn't want to like me."

She made a face that looked an awful like…it was too late for that. "And maybe Ramos was trying to tell me that there was a recording error and the boy we're looking for is a girl," she continued. "I should have asked him."

"No, you shouldn't have. In fact, you shouldn't have told Ramos the real reason we were there," he said. "First rule of being in the field: stick to your cover story, no matter what."

"If we never accomplish our mission, what good is the story?"

He understood that question and had grappled with it himself in the field, but she didn't have the experience to know when to trust someone.

"We don't want anyone on our tail, Chessie," he explained. "It's one thing to try to find a kid anonymously and get some DNA for Gabe. It's another to get on the wrong radar and put you in any danger. If I so much as smell something that could hurt you, we're gone. Out. Back to Barefoot Bay." He didn't mean to sound quite so vehement, but that's the way he felt.

"Got it." She let out a sigh as if to acknowledge her mistake in judgment. "It was just those kids…they all seemed to need something so much."

"Yes, they do. And if there's one thing you, an obvious nurturer, needs to know is that you can't save them all." He understood that longing, though. "Even if they get under our skin," he added. Because wasn't that what got him in the mess that was his life, his record, and his lost career?

"I know," she said, but he doubted she did. "Like Gabrielita. Such a precious little thing, Mal."

He heard the hitch of pain and sympathy in her voice. "Careful, Francesca," he said, purposely using the name he called her when he really wanted her attention.

"She could be related to me." She reached into her purse, picking up the hairbrush she'd already stripped of potential DNA-producing hair, which was now tucked safely into a sealed plastic bag. "Although she didn't look like Gabe. Did she look like Isadora?"

He thought about the child in question and remembered Isadora's near perfect beauty, with caramel-and-chocolate-colored curls and haunting green eyes. "Not really."

"I know!" She snapped her fingers. "Maybe there's information about Isadora in the municipal office."

"Highly unlikely. She was a translator for the CIA and an American citizen. And you *cannot* go in there and start dropping the names of agents."

"I won't," she promised him. "And I didn't say their names to Ramos, you know. I never mentioned Gabe or Isadora. I never said a last name."

"No, but just cool your enthusiasm. I realize it's motivated by boundless hope and big family love, but be chill."

"I am chill." She turned to him, her gaze scrutinizing. "You jealous of that stuff, Mal? Of my boundless hope and big family love?"

He tapped the brakes as a crab crossed the street in front of them, the sight comical, but Mal couldn't laugh. Instead, he imagined what it would sound like if he drove over that crab and cracked the shell. It would sound a lot like that question she'd just asked breaking the protective barrier he'd spent years building, just like that free-range crustacean. And killing the poor guy.

"Define jealous."

She just laughed at that, totally on to him now. "You know you don't have to go through your whole life clinging to pessimism and changing addresses."

Actually, he did. Something hot and tight squeezed his chest, making him incredibly uncomfortable and actually glad to see the offices of the *municipal* down the street. "Speaking of addresses, we're almost there."

She took the bait and shifted her attention to the road. "All I need to do is call that Canadian number I have to get the server for Internet access. I've already figured it out and have a plan."

Of course she did. "You do know there are no computer files in this office, right? Maybe in Havana, maybe at the national level. But in a municipality with a population of about six thousand? The best you'll find is yellowed, handwritten papers, which were probably filled out by someone drunk or on the take. Or both. And you don't even know what you're looking for."

She gave a soft laugh. "Bitter, cynical, and pessimistic is back."

"Okay, just for fun, let's say you find a birth record for Gabriel," he said, rumbling toward a parking space. "Or even a record of Isadora's death. What would you do with that information?"

She turned her whole body to look at him as if he'd grown another head. "That is a *trail*, Mal," she told him. "When you're trying to find someone, you follow the trail. The municipal office is the only lead I have. Unless…" She patted her jeans pocket.

"Unless what?"

"Maybe this is part of our trail." He glanced over as she revealed a long, beaded necklace-type thing with a bright red stone on a cross. No, not a necklace. A rosary. He peered at it, taking his eyes from the road to really give it a good look.

"I've seen that before." The rosaries were around Cuba, of course, on the black market in the country that was supposed to be atheist but housed a good number of Catholics. But something about that one…and then he remembered.

"Gabe gave one that looked a lot like that to Isadora."

"Really?" She practically jumped out of her skin. "Then it is a clue!"

"Or he was giving you a gift, and it just looks like the one your brother bought on the street. I don't think they're that uncommon, just kept out of sight for the most part."

"You were there when he bought it? You recognize it?"

"I remember the day because Gabe said it was to make up for the fact that he swore so fucking much."

"Sounds like Gabe," she mused.

"Isa hated his language. She might have been Catholic, and she liked rosaries, I think. I don't remember." He fingered the beads. "I could never be sure this is the same one. But…" He stared at the red stone. There had been something unusual about it, but he couldn't recall what it was.

"Why *else* would Ramos give it to me?"

"Good question." He let go and looked at her. "And if you're right, it gives some credibility to Ramos's direction that we go to the *municipal*. Like he wants us to find this child."

"Thank you," she said, flouncing back on her seat in satisfaction.

"But with a…plan."

She grinned. "You keep this up and I'm going to kiss you, Mal Harris."

"I hope so."

"And hope, too?" She leaned across the space and pecked his mouth. "I've created a monster."

"Just don't waltz in, all American and demanding and

shit, and slap money in their hands until they open the file room."

"Honey catches flies," she agreed.

"And money."

"Okay, I'll be sweet, you be generous, and together, we are unstoppable."

He looked at her for a long moment, swamped by her optimism and hope and plans and warmth. And before he opened the door, he had to kiss her. And she kissed him right back.

Unstoppable, indeed.

Gabe looked up at the tap on his office door, fighting the urge to cringe at the sight of Poppy's bright smile, worn faithfully by the housekeeper-turned-spy he'd hired to keep an eye on things at the resort.

"Popcorn," he said with his own smile, tempering the impact of a nickname she didn't love. "Come to make sure I haven't committed *hara-kiri*?"

Her smile faltered as she sauntered in uninvited, crossing her arms with her *Ima tell you what's what* face that Gabe had grown to know preceded a lecture he likely didn't want to hear.

"Nino had no right sharin' that information with you, Mr. Gabriel."

"Look, I know we've only been at this gig a few months, but you should know one thing by now: My grandfather tells me everything, Poppy. You tell him, you're essentially telling me." He gestured toward the chair. "Now sit down and let me assure you that I am not, in any way, depressed, sleep-deprived, or alcoholic. Just not a fan of pink flowers."

She took the chair and angled her head, openly assessing him. "I'm proud of you, Mr. Gabriel."

"For not needing a shrink?"

"For saying all that without dropping one F, B, S, H, or D bomb on me."

"Don't push your luck, woman." He threw a glance at the swear jar on the bookshelf, overflowing since she might not be doing much to clean up his act, but she was definitely Hoovering his wallet. "But let's get this straight. I'm not unhappy."

She lifted two black caterpillar eyebrows, dubious of his pronouncement. "You're not happy."

How the hell did he respond to that? "Not everyone goes around belting out *Amazing Grace* and slinging joyful Bible quotes around like you do. But I'm okay, really."

She looked like she was not buying what he was selling.

"Look," he said. "I've had some shit happen."

She pointed to the jar.

Damn it. He stood and opened his wallet, stuffing a five in, which was more than *shit* cost on the Poppy Price List. "I got credit now. Listen to me." He came around the desk to lean on it and tower over her to make his point. But she looked directly up at him, a woman who didn't fear a towering man. And he loved that about her.

"What do you want to say?" she demanded.

"That I appreciate your concern for my well-being." He did, too, and the realization made him reach out and take her hand. "A lot. But not long ago I found out that someone I cared about…"

Died.

"Passed," he said.

"Lucky girl."

He frowned at her. “How is she lucky? And how did you know it was a she, anyway?”

Poppy beamed. “She because of the look of love on your face. Lucky because she’s with the Lord, assuming she was saved. Was she saved?”

Not by him. And that was at the bottom of what hurt the most. “She collected rosaries,” he offered.

“Then she’s with the angels, including the one you’re named after.” She grinned. “He is a mighty angel.”

Not mighty enough, he thought glumly. “Okay, but I want you to know there’s nothing wrong with me except a little garden-variety…mourning.” Even that sounded a little weak to his ears. But what else could he call this torture he felt over losing Isa forever?

Poppy grabbed his hand in both of hers, her palms rough from housework, her grasp strong with conviction. “Mr. Gabriel, you know what you need, right?”

He braced for a conversion speech and an invitation to her church. Or maybe the name of a shrink who she knew happened to be staying at the resort.

“Young man, you need a little hair of the dog.”

“A drink? I thought you were counting my empties in the trash.”

“No, a little something of what your body is missing. A woman.”

“What?” He barked a laugh. “Is this St. Popsicle of the Blessed Virginity suggesting I drown my sorrows in sex?”

“Not *that*, Mr. Gabriel!” She looked horrified. “Just, you know, the nice company of a pretty lady.”

The only nice company he’d be interested in would have to be flat on her back. He wasn’t in the mood to chat up a woman for fun.

"Mr. Gabriel, you need love."

And he *really* wasn't in the mood for that.

He stared at her for a minute, wondering just how open he should be, something he rarely was. But this once, he didn't feel like hiding the truth from this large, loving woman who always had his best interests at heart.

"I had love," he finally said. "And it sucked."

She twisted her head from side to side, tsking like a metronome.

"What?" he asked. "Is 'suck' on your list of bad words?"

"Child, you know what sucks?" She stood, practically pulling him closer. "The fact that you are holed up here on this island in this office with your ornery old grandfather and a nosy, fat black lady for companionship."

He narrowed his eyes. "You're not fat."

She hooted. "Just like you're not handsome, which you know you are."

"Popcorn, if I could fall in love again, it would be with you."

She gave him a gentle push away. "Shut your lying mouth, child. You ain't looking hard enough. You should scour this resort and find yourself a sweet woman."

He had a sweet woman, he wanted to scream. "I'm not here to find company," he said instead.

"I know, I know. You're here to hide folks who need hiding, change names, and create new lives. Why can't you do that for yourself?"

Good fucking question. "I don't need to hide, change my name, or make a new life, Pops. I just need to help other people do that." He put his hands on her shoulders, forcing himself to stop oversharing. "And you are a great assistance in that regard. Do you need a raise?"

She *pfft* out a breath. "I need you to be joyful, is what. So spread your gorgeous self around the hungry female population of this place."

"Think I could do every bridesmaid on the resort?"

"I don't mean *do*, I mean *date*."

Gabe shook his head. "I just told you why I'm not interested."

"God doesn't want you to be alone, Mr. Gabriel. And all I'm talking about is a harmless dinner date. How about that pretty lady staying in Rockrose this week? She's all alone."

Rockrose? The northernmost villa? Gabe thought back to the blonde he'd seen on the beach, checking him out. She wasn't exactly hot, more of an ice queen, but something about her…no. Every woman was going to remind him of Isadora just so he could discover how grossly they fell short. "Sorry, she's not my type."

"Well, she'd like to be." Poppy gave a smug little smile as she picked up some papers on his desk and made a show of straightening them. "That is, if I'm any good at reading human nature, and I do believe my ability to do just that is why you pay me so handsomely to find out everything that's being said by guests and staff here at Casa Blanca."

That was true; Poppy was the original busybody, but her style worked and worked well.

"So how do you know about this woman?" he asked.

"Jus' doing my job. Getting people to talk, which, in this lady's case, was quite easy. She must have seen you on the beach and wanted to know if you worked here or were staying here."

"And you told her…"

"Nothing!" Her eyes popped wide. "Mr. Gabriel, I know better than that."

"But my name came up?"

"No, no. She described you, all casual and chatty, you

know, but I could see through that. And then she asked if I knew you. Showed me some pictures of the beach she took that you just *happened* to be in."

What? A four alarm fire rang in his head. She had pictures of him?

"Of course, I said I wasn't sure who she meant," Poppy continued. "But the words she used were not from a woman who was casually noticing a man. Words like…handsome. And fine."

"Really." He had to know more about this woman, and not because she thought he was fine. "Rockrose, you say."

"That little one-bedroom villa all the way at the end of the beach."

"I know which one it is. Good work, Pop-Tart." He stood and gave her a peck on the cheek before heading to the door.

Outside, he stole a golf cart from housekeeping and cut through the garden and down the resort path, making it to the edge of the Casa Blanca property in under ten minutes. Like many of the expensive villas, Rockrose was surrounded by thick foliage, set back to allow it to have privacy and a water view.

He approached the villa slowly, not completely sure what he'd say to the woman, but experience told him he'd figure it out when he had to. She was hunting him, and he wanted to know why.

At the villa, all was quiet, with no sign of life, no beach towels hanging over the deck, no sounds of activity.

He walked up to the front door and did the obvious, simple thing: He knocked. And as he did, he realized the door wasn't latched. It pushed open at his tap, leading into the living area.

"Hello," he called out. "Resort security."

Nothing. The living room looked untouched, as if the

maids had been there and the guest had long gone. He stepped into the kitchen area, finding it the same.

"Resort security. Is anyone here?"

Silence. The bedroom looked just as cleaned out as the rest, with no clothes in the closet, no personal items around. He pulled out his cell and dialed the front desk as he continued his inspection.

"Hey, it's Gabe Rossi with McBain Security here," he said. "I need to know the name of the guest currently staying in Rockrose."

The Casa Blanca employee didn't hesitate. "Ms. Wickham," she said. "But she checked out about an hour ago."

"First name?"

"I'm sorry, she just went by her last name. Veddy proper British," she added with a fake accent.

"British? Okay, thanks." He walked into the bathroom and stopped cold, closing his eyes as the scent almost knocked him over.

Damn it! God damn it, why did he come over here?

He dropped down on the closed toilet and let his head fall in his hands as the Chanel No. 5 slayed him. Son of a bitch, why did this woman have to wear *that* perfume? Why did he have to follow a dead end for no reason and get bombarded with memories of hot, long, sweet kisses and tropical nights on the beaches of Cuba? Why did he have to drown in this heartache and choke on his pain?

He didn't know why. But he sat there for a good two hours and let the memories, and the lingering perfume, crush him.

Chapter Nineteen

Chessie followed Mal into the hostel bedroom, hoping the dark basement room and lower temperature would cool her down and assuage her bitter disappointment.

"How can a municipal office just close in the middle of the day and week?" she asked.

"You can't really be surprised by now."

"I'm not," she replied. "Just so damn frustrated. Should I try Gabe again? It's not like him not to answer the phone."

"Don't. You need to go outside to get a signal." He put his hand on her shoulder and guided her into the room, his touch so warm and secure and comforting. "There's nothing to tell him yet, Chessie. Get some rest. We haven't slept for well over a day."

She couldn't argue with that. Exhaustion pressed on her heart, along with the events of the day. She sat on the bed for exactly three seconds, then fell back on a flat pillow and closed her eyes, asleep before she took her next breath.

When she woke, the room was still and shadowed, that dusky kind of dark when the world was slipping from evening to night. Through her lashes she spied Mal sitting on the edge of the bed, bare-chested again, wearing jeans with the top button undone.

It wasn't too dark to notice *that*, she thought wryly. Not too dark to appreciate the cuts and dips of his muscular body, the way a lock of hair fell over his forehead, or how the shadows formed in the hollows of his unshaven jaw. Not too dark to admire the strength in shoulders that rose and fell in one of those sighs that sounded like it came from his soul, not his lungs.

Something clicked between his fingers.

The rosary. She inched up, and instantly he turned to her, sensing she was awake.

"I wish I could remember..." His voice was raspy, as if he hadn't spoken in hours or...something was choking him.

She sat up very slowly. "Ten Hail Marys and a few Glory Bes, I think."

"I mean, what was so special about this rosary? There was something that Isadora said. She collected them, I think."

Chessie filed that totally surprising fact about Gabe's lover in her head and reached for Mal. "Did you sleep?"

"Not like you. I admit I checked for breathing a few times."

She smiled. "I was really tired."

He let the rosary fall into her bag on the floor and turned his full attention to her. "I tried to call Gabe but couldn't get through. I showered and got you some food." He angled his head to the dresser and a brown paper bag. "*Medianoches*, like the lady requested."

"You're the best." Without thinking, she reached out and stroked the side of his head, her fingers sliding through his hair, the dim light catching one of the few silver threads. She half expected him to move out of her touch, but he did just the opposite, leaning into her hand.

"How'd you get gray hair?" she asked. "You're not even forty."

"Prison," he answered simply.

"So you were all dark-haired before you did time?"

He didn't answer.

"Will you tell me why you went to prison?" She stroked his hair again, feeling intimate and calm and very close at that moment.

"A crime."

She leaned back on the pillow, staying close to him. "I just refuse to believe you're a common thief."

"Nothing common about half a million dollars," he said wryly.

"Mal. Tell me the truth."

He stayed silent for a long time, but finally turned to her, taking her hand in his. "Someone needed help for her family."

She wasn't at all surprised to hear that, but maybe a bit taken aback by the sharp sense of relief it sent through her. She hadn't realized how *much* she didn't want him to be anything less than…noble.

"So it was some Robin Hood action? Stole from the government to help the poor?" Noble, but still wrong.

"Something like that." He rolled down on the bed, turning flat on his back. "I hate what you think of me."

The admission twisted something deep inside of her. He *cared* what she thought of him?

"You hate that I think you went to prison for stealing something to help out a family? Yeah, you're horrible."

He smiled, his eyes closed, his expression serene. She reclined next to him, on her side so she could keep looking at him. And touching him, stroking his hard muscles and the soft black hair on his bare chest with her fingertips.

"Tell me something, Mal," she whispered. "Tell me a secret."

"Define secret."

"Oh no you don't." She tapped his pec. "Talk to me."

He turned just enough to regard her through half-shuttered eyes. "I've never had a family." His confession, whispered in the dark and coming up from that same place in his soul that had him sighing, made a little rip in her heart. "And you were right about me being jealous of yours. I can't get that question out of my head."

"Oh, I'm sorry I hit a sore spot. I didn't mean to, really."

He ran a knuckle over her cheek. "I know. You just care. You're a caring woman. It's really…attractive."

"And here I just thought you liked my smart mouth and busy fingers." She realized what she'd said and laughed. "I mean, my sass and computer talents."

"I like them all," he said, leaning closer to her. "I like the hell out of you and your sweet mouth and soft spot for kids you just met."

She smiled. "I would take Gabrielita and raise her and love her in a"—she patted his chest—"heartbeat."

He turned a little, stroking her hair, the intimacy so natural and organic, she didn't question any of it. "They can't all be that lucky."

"You weren't, were you? Did you go to foster homes, or what?"

"I was in a few, but my mother always pulled her act together enough to get me back."

"So she did love you," Chessie said.

"Love isn't enough." He twirled a strand of her hair through his fingers. "You have to sacrifice for kids. You have to be willing to put them first. You have to recognize the responsibility that they are."

Chessie felt her jaw loosen. That was *exactly* how she felt, but her strong beliefs stemmed from living in a family that did just that, and wanting to replicate that. His background might be different, but the end result—the way he thought—was the same.

"You look so surprised," he said.

"You constantly surprise me."

He didn't answer, but pulled her all the way into him, guiding her head to rest on his chest. While he stroked her hair, she listened to the sound of his steady, strong heartbeat and each slow intake of breath. She could feel his muscles under her cheek and had a perfect view of his chest and abs and the dusting of hair running right into the unbuttoned jeans.

Slowly, lightly, she rubbed a circle over his heart, more tender this time. "There's some good stuff in here, Mal Harris."

"I'm not that good, Francesca." He shifted his body, lining them up more, closer to her mouth, close enough to feel his breath. "Nothing I'm thinking about is good right now." He pressed his lips to hers. "In fact, it's…*hopeless*."

She smiled into the kiss. "It's like we have our own secret password."

"Yeah. Except it's no secret…" He slid farther on top of her, an enormous erection pressing against her stomach.

But it was *hopeless*. Trying to remember that and not think of this as anything except the casual, meaningless, impossible-to-resist fling in the field that it was, Chessie tunneled her fingers into his hair and tightened her grip on his head.

She kissed with all she had, opening her mouth and

arching her back and sliding one leg over his to offer herself.

His hand worked under her T-shirt, burning her skin at the first touch, making her whimper with need as he cupped her breast and circled her nipple.

It was a lie, she realized with a start. She'd never be able to have sex with him and not hope for…something. Even if it was just that they would have more time together.

But she kissed him anyway and decided that just made them even. He didn't tell her everything last time they had sex, like the fact that he suspected she was a spy.

And she wasn't telling him everything now, like the fact that she suspected she really cared for him and what was about to happen was exactly the polar opposite of hopeless sex.

Mal rolled over to get more of her. More of her mouth and tongue against his and more of her sweet body in his hands. Except more wouldn't be enough. He wanted it *all*.

Chessie moaned with invitation and affection, easing him on top of her, letting their bodies mold in the most natural way. He kissed her again and again. Each time she tasted a little different. Sometimes sweet, sometimes peppery, sometimes a flavor he'd never experienced.

And still he wanted more.

Against her, his erection grew even harder, straining his zipper, already throbbing for release. That's all this was, right? A release for both of them. A way to shake off the day's work and the challenges of this trip and this country and this life. A way to be…partners.

So he took it. Took all of it and all of her.

He had her top off in seconds, and then her bra. He groaned at the sight and feel of her breasts, nipples budded and dark with color. He suckled, pulling her into his mouth and earning a gasp of pleasure as she rocked her hips.

"You like that," he murmured, happy that he could make her feel so good.

"Define like."

He laughed and headed south, working on her jeans as she was unzipping his. She slipped her hand in and closed her fingers around his shaft, sending a shock through his system.

"And you like that," she teased with kisses on his chest, each one making him fall a little harder for her.

She pushed his jeans down and used both hands to stroke him, temporarily paralyzing his efforts to get her undressed. He couldn't think about anything but the heat of her hands, the way she worked his cock, up and down, around the tip.

Release threatened way too soon.

"Don't," he muttered, trying to pull out of her hand. "Wait."

"I can't." She ignored him, stroking harder. "I won't wait."

He almost laughed at her determination, but other sensations got in the way. Heat and blood and an ache that started low in his back and deep in his balls.

"You made me come in the car," she said, pushing him onto his back.

"That was different. I don't want to be done…yet." He bit the last word, fighting the urge to just give in and let her stroke and…oh, kiss him. Down his stomach, her tongue flicking, her hands caressing…her mouth on him.

"Francesca." He dug his fingers into her hair, holding her head, guiding her…just for a second. A few seconds. A minute. He rocked into her kisses and let her suck lightly, then harder. "Stop it."

He pushed her head away, so close to coming he could barely see her through eyes he had to squeeze shut.

"Condom," he muttered, reaching toward a nightstand like one would magically appear.

"In my bag." They both said it at exactly the same second.

He laughed softly, rolling to grab whatever bag was closest. "We both brought them."

"Talk about hopeful."

He grabbed the box and tossed it on the bed. "Don't talk at all," he ordered.

She held his gaze, long and hot, and he could read everything in her expression, as clear as if she said the words. *This isn't hopeless.* He should have known.

He should have known because he felt the same way. Damn it.

Kneeling over her, silent, he tore the box, grabbed a packet, and started to slide it over his engorged dick, refusing to look at her while he did, hating that his hands didn't feel steady.

But then she reached out and touched him, taking over, rolling the condom down.

"C'mere," she said huskily, drawing him down. As he got on top of her, she wrapped her legs around his hips and met his gaze. "I can't wait anymore."

He closed his eyes and found his way into her, arching enough to watch her face as he entered her body, holding back before he plunged in. Pleasure swamped him, silencing everything. She was hot, tight perfection. Beautiful and willing and warm and wet.

And he was so lost he couldn't have remembered his name if he'd had to.

This didn't need a label, but it had one. And it sure as hell wasn't "hopeless."

Not when she murmured sexy words and scraped her nails over his back. Not when she bowed her back and invited him deeper inside her. And when she bit her lip and cried out and a climax clawed at his conscience and crushed his senses…it was full of hope.

Fucking overloaded with hope.

He silenced that by listening to the sultry sounds of her orgasm. She moaned and whimpered and fought for control, losing it as completely as he did until they both collapsed in a heap of satisfaction and, damn it, hope.

It was Chessie's secret power, and he was drowning in it. And all he wanted in the whole world was more.

And more and more.

"We're not done yet," he whispered huskily in her ear.

"We have all night," she agreed.

But that wasn't what he meant. Not what he meant at all.

Chapter Twenty

The *municipal* finally opened mid-morning the next day, along with the palms of the three people who showed up for work. Mal greased them liberally, making slow progress until they were finally allowed into a file library.

He hadn't been kidding about the paper.

Chessie turned slowly, blinking at boxes upon boxes, file cabinets, and loose papers piled on the floor. She felt a slow burn of frustration roll through her—the first time she'd felt anything other than satisfaction since they'd fallen asleep together, woke up in the middle of the night for another round, and repeated it all at dawn.

That whole no-strings thing? It sure felt like it was getting a little stringy. But she couldn't think about it today, not now that she'd gotten what she wanted most: access to real information.

Sort of real. Sort of information. Regardless, she threw herself into the process of finding a trail that would lead to a four-year-old boy who would call her Aunt Chessie.

The man who'd brought them into the room pointed to a stack of cheap cardboard file boxes stuffed with blue, pink, green, and goldenrod papers. "*Registros de nacimiento. Diez años.*"

"The last decade of recorded births," Mal explained as the man left the room without a good-bye.

"Are you kidding me?" Chessie dropped on to one of two chairs next to a folding card table. "We have to go through every one to find a birth record for a child named Gabriel Winter?"

"We know the year."

"It'll take a year." She pulled out a bunch of the tissue-thin papers from a crate. "Crap, it's all in Spanish." Chessie fingered one of the bright orange sheets, transported back to her childhood when she'd tag along with Mom and she'd file papers in Dad's law office. These were carbon copies, right out of another century. She hadn't known they even made that stuff anymore.

She dropped the pages on the card table and started to read.

"Did you bring that rosary?" Mal asked.

"Prayer isn't going to make this go any faster." She gestured toward her bag. "It's where you put it last night."

He dragged it out. "I was thinking about something in the middle of the night."

She gave him a look. "A rosary?"

"A message. I'm wondering if Ramos really wanted to give you a message."

Chessie looked up, blinking at him. "Really?"

"There's no other explanation."

A message? Was everything always code words and secret messages with spies? She searched his face, feeling her heart ratchet up. "Okay, but until you figure that out, we dig for the needle in this haystack. Maybe when you reach Gabe, we can find out."

Gabe had called back, but this time they'd missed his call and the message was garbled.

"In the meantime, I have an idea that you would call ridiculously hopeful," she said.

"Hey, bring it. I'm starting to become a believer in you."

She grinned at him. "Mal Harris, that's the nicest thing you've ever said to me."

He lifted a brow, the look a sexy reminder of all the nice things he'd said last night.

"In the last ten minutes," she added, pulling out her laptop. "I think I can get on the Internet in here."

"Possibly, but how is that going to help us go through these files?" he asked.

"See these?" She tapped the brightly colored papers on the desk with one hand and clicked to bring the screen to life with the other. "They're copies. Pink, blue, green, and, my personal favorite, goldenrod."

He looked at her like she'd slipped off her rocker, but she grinned back and touched the track pad.

"You know what that means, Mal?"

"I think I'm about to find out."

"It means that somewhere there's an original, which is white. Always white. You know what I don't see? White paper, not anywhere in this room." The screen hummed to life, and she waited to get Internet access through the Canadian server she'd lined up earlier that morning on the satellite phone. "The whites went somewhere. Most likely Havana. Didn't you say everything funnels up to the national level in this country?"

"The national *Communist* level," he said, lowering his voice as if there were a possibility they were being spied on. Of course Mal would think that.

"Communists keep files of births," she replied.

"They do," he agreed. "They just don't put them in Excel spreadsheets or hackable databases."

"They might." No Internet. Chessie took a breath. "You obviously do not know my database-hacking skills, my personal level of determination to get shit done, and the burning desire I have to walk into my brother's office and tell him he has a reason to live again."

After a moment of staring at the damn spinning circle, she looked up to find his eyes boring a hole through her. "What?" she asked.

"I believe in you." He sounded nothing less than stunned by the realization. His voice was low and genuine. A lot like he sounded in the throes—and aftermath—of sex.

"Well, thanks."

"No, I'm serious. You're impressive. You don't quit, do you?"

"Not when I want Internet," she said, going for light because the look on his face was anything but.

"Not when you love someone."

She felt her jaw loosen in amazement and some blood rush to her face. "You're right, I don't," she agreed. "Why do I get the feeling that surprises you?"

He shook his head as if he couldn't, or wouldn't, answer the question, pretending to be overly involved in a few of the papers in front of him.

"Mal?" Chessie prodded. "Who quit on you?"

"Everyone I ever knew," he answered.

"As I said, you must be hanging out with the wrong people."

He finally looked up, hurt around the edges of his eyes. "Must be."

The computer flashed and stole her attention, the screen turning white with the home page of the Canadian website she wanted. "And I must be"—she grinned at him—"a miracle worker. I just got Internet."

He leaned closer. "Really? Now what?"

She started clicking, slowly working her way through backdoors and secret places that were like a second home to her. "This could take a while."

He shuffled papers. "So could this."

"Then let's see who finds something first, okay?" She tapped a key and found a little wormhole of information, but that place required a password. So she moved on to the next corner of the Internet maze.

"I found a pile of papers from 2011," he said.

"Well, I found the SQL server injections that I need to crack any database in any secure environment," she replied.

They both worked in silenced for a while.

"Aha," Mal said. "I found four babies named Gabriel, but their parents are noted and not names I recognize."

"Good," she said, a tad condescendingly. "But I found a Metasploit command prompt. Time to play guess the password."

He put his papers down and leaned closer. "How the hell are you going to do that?"

"I have my ways, master spy. I have my ways."

They returned to silence as she battled configurations, threads, and password combinations, and he pulled more papers. And sure enough, the config emerged, and she landed the rhosts, and about two hours and sixty thousand fluttering word combinations later, she had sysadmin privileges.

"Woo-hoo," she said, pushing back.

"You have a password."

"Not yet. But soon."

"I have seventeen Gabriels in 2011. Six in the summer."

"Parents?"

"All wrong."

"Keep working," she ordered. "By the way, what's the

winner get? I'd like to think about it while I grab the hashes here."

He rolled his eyes at her tech talk. "The winner gets…anything he—"

"Or *she*—"

"Wants."

"Anything?" She smiled and tapped faster. "Motivation is a marvelous thing."

"So are you."

By three thirty in the afternoon, Mal had a pile of papers listing boys born in 2011 in this municipality named Gabriel—none with the right last name, but some vague enough to merit researching. Several addresses were near enough to drive to today, and Mal actually considered starting the search.

But Chessie had been telling him for the past two hours that she was close. At least, he thought that's what she was saying. Mostly she mumbled to herself in computer-speak.

He'd paid the *empleado del municipal* a handsome sum to leave them alone, but he had a feeling even that much cash wasn't going to buy them enough time. And he doubted they'd get back in tomorrow. That guy would likely take the day off and spend his two months' free wages.

"How close are you, Bill Gates?" he asked.

"So close." She hadn't broke concentration, except for the three times she'd lost her Internet connection and sounded a lot more like a different Rossi when her language got colorful. But she never stopped trying.

When he'd stop to look over her shoulder at the screen, it

was nothing but a sea of binary numbers, white on black, flickering and flashing, moving. Mal's findings weren't great, but they were immediate. And tangible. And the day was getting late.

"How much—"

She held one finger up to stop him. "*Portonueve*."

"What?"

"Come here and read this." She reached for his hand, pulling him around to point to a word on the screen. "That's the password that's going to open many, many file drawers in cyberspace for me," she said excitedly.

"Really? That's great."

"But this is where it starts to get a little iffy."

"Starts?" She'd been at this for five hours.

She gave his arm a poke. "Be positive, honey. *Pos-i-tive.* Translate for me. *Portonueve* means…"

"It means door nine. Or ninth door. Does that help?"

She blew out a slow breath and typed. "Maybe. There's a code in there that should be found in every password. *Porto* is door?"

"And *nueve* is nine."

"Let's try changing the number. Count from one to ten in Spanish and spell."

He did, and she typed, but every time, access was denied. "Damn it," she muttered on the last one. "Let's flip it. What's the word for window?"

"*Ventana*."

She typed it. "Nope. How else can you get into a house or building?"

"Chimney?"

She laughed. "Okay. What's the Spanish word for it?"

"Uh…*chimenea*, I think." He spelled it, and she typed as he spoke. *No access.*

"Damn it," he muttered.

"No, no, don't panic," she said, typing again. "Did you see that little string of numbers that flashed under it?"

"No."

She clicked on a line of code, highlighting it. "You're on to something with the chimney, Santa Claus. Tell me those numbers again."

"*Uno, dos, tre*s…"

Her fingers flew, and suddenly, the whole screen flickered, turned black, turned white—

"Oh no," he said.

"You are such a pessimist, Mal Harris!" She held her fingers off the keyboard and stared at the screen, and suddenly, line after line after line started appearing, as if someone else were typing. "And a genius," she added. "We are in the official government database listing every birth in the country of—"

"*Perdóname.*" A woman they hadn't yet met walked in, pointing to a clock on the wall. "*Estamos cerado. Se tenien que ir.*"

"She says they're closing," Mal explained.

"It's not even four o'clock!" Chessie exclaimed.

Yes, too early to close in the States, but not too early to siphon money off the Americans who really shouldn't even be in the room. Mal reached into his pocket, aware that, at the table, Chessie slowly inched her screen down low enough to hide what she was doing but not turn off the laptop.

The woman's expression softened almost immediately when the cash was flashed. Glancing at the door, as if she might get caught, her dark features melted. "*No, no…*" In other words: *How much can I get?*

Nothing had changed since he'd been in Cuba last,

despite the fact that more flights arrived and an American flag now flew over an embassy. He handed her a wad of bills, and she let out a sigh and murmured an apology.

Mal nodded and gestured for her to leave, but the woman's gaze drifted over the stacks of papers to the computer, and then she gasped.

Busted for the laptop, no doubt. That'd cost Mal twenty more.

But her eyes weren't on the computer. They were on the rosary, on the table where Chessie had left it.

"El Sagrado Corazón." She pointed to the beads. "Please to touch it?"

"Of course," Chessie said, picking up the rosary to hand to her.

The woman took it with loving care, caressing the beads that clearly meant something to her and pressing the cross to her heart for a moment. "*Donde consiguiste esto*?"

Mal wasn't about to tell her where he got it, or who its real owner was. "*Fue un regalo.* A gift." He shot Chessie a look that he hoped she'd understand meant *don't offer this as payment.*

She didn't say a word, though, keeping one hand on her computer and looking far more nervous about losing her laptop than the rosary.

The woman held the string of beads in the air, letting the cross turn on its beaded chain. Then she took it to the window and held it up, the red jewel at eye level. "Ahh," she said, pointing to the heart. "*Está grabado.*"

"What did she say?" Chessie asked.

Mal stepped closer. "It's engraved?" And *then* he remembered what was special about these crosses. They had the owner's name and usually a prayer engraved inside. Had it been engraved when Gabe bought it?

The woman nodded as she held the cross still, letting the light filter through the stone, where there must be tiny words.

"*Un bebé*," the woman said.

"A baby?" Mal stepped closer, but Chessie was faster, inching next to the woman, who handed her the rosary.

But the woman had lost interest in the rosary, tapping the money in her hand as she brushed by Mal. She mumbled an offering of ten more minutes and then left the room, closing the door behind her.

"Oh my God, Mal," Chessie whispered, peering at the stone with the window light behind it. "It is a message! You're right." She turned to him, surprising him with eyes wet with tears. She handed it to him, her hands—her whole body—shaking. "Read it."

He took the chain and held the cross to the light, the center made up of a round red jewel about half an inch in diameter. Mal squinted at the tiny letters, each word punching his gut.

Gabriel Rafael Winter 29 Junio 2011

"Chessie." His voice was thick in his throat. "We found him."

"We haven't found him yet." She was already at the computer, fingers flying, typing so hard and fast it was a wonder she didn't break the keyboard. "But I have a name and a birthdate and a beautiful, working password of *chimneyeight*—thank you very much—that just opened up a world of possibilities."

He stood behind her, putting both hands on her shoulders just to feel the vibrations humming through her body. The buzz of determination and relentless optimism and…hope. The woman was damn near overflowing with the one thing he hadn't even thought existed.

"Got it!" She practically jumped out of her seat. "I found him, Mal! I found him! Look." She pointed to a line of text, and he read it out loud.

"*Gabriel Rafael Winter, nació el vente y nueve de junio, en el año dos mil once, a Isadora Winter*." He squeezed her shoulders and translated. "Born June 29, 2011, to Isadora Winter."

"Oh my God, look, Mal." She pointed to a word on the screen. *Adoptado*. "Does that mean what I think it means?"

"Yes," he replied. "He's been adopted."

She put her hand to her mouth. "Someone adopted my nephew? How can Gabe ever get him back, Mal? How?"

"I don't know. But first we have to find him."

Chapter Twenty-One

By the time they neared their hostel, they had a plan, which Chessie clung to as tightly as the rosary that had been engraved for her nephew. Ramos was the person who'd given Chessie the rosary, and surely he'd known what he was doing when he handed her that information.

Mal didn't one hundred percent agree with that, but he was willing to go back to see Ramos in the morning on the off chance he'd tell them who'd adopted the child. But he was sure that *Señor* Ramos helped local orphans, which most likely also included getting them out of the country, which would explain his secrecy, and he wasn't likely to easily spill the name of the family who had Gabriel.

She put the rosary in her bag and took Mal's hand as they walked into the dark and dingy building they currently called home. They headed downstairs to the basement and down the hall, but Mal stopped short five feet from the door.

"What's the matter?" she asked.

He pointed to the scruffy thatched mat in front of the door. "I left that corner over the threshold so it would only move if someone's been in the room."

"Housekeeping?"

Even as she said the word, she knew how ridiculous it was. They hadn't seen anyone who looked anything like a maid since they got to this dump. He turned, surprising her, suddenly pulling her into a tight, deep embrace.

"Mal, I—"

His mouth came down hard on hers, a breath-stealing kiss so unexpected she grunted and tried to pull back, but he was having none of it, pushing her against the wall and devouring her mouth.

"Listen to me," he murmured into the kiss. "Don't talk, just listen."

She nodded, her heart suddenly pounding for more reasons than just the pressure of his body against hers.

He pinned her to the wall, kissed her neck and finally worked his mouth to her ear. "If nothing's missing, then we have to find what they left behind," he whispered. "Most likely audio, because I'd spot a camera."

The room was bugged?

"Work with me, Chess," he said. "We're going to use sex as our cover. Just follow my lead."

She nodded.

"Act like you like this," he breathed into her ear.

She *did* like it. She just didn't like…someone watching or listening to just how much she liked it.

"Please," he insisted, the word sounding like a plea for sex, but she knew it wasn't. "You get on the bed while I look for a *condom*."

But he didn't mean condom. Not for one second, and she knew that. He squeezed tighter, silently telling her what to do.

"A condom. I like that plan." She slid her hands up his arms, squeezing his muscles, closing around his neck to tell him she would give him a hundred percent on this. "And you know how I like a good *plan*."

He pulled back long enough to wash her with a look of gratitude. And a little challenge. This was a test, and she was going to pass.

He kissed her again and went to the other ear to whisper more instructions. "Every word, every action has to be believable."

She nodded.

"And it's all about sex."

Only it wasn't. It was all about finding a bug.

"You distract on the bed. Talk to me, seduce me, do what you have to while I search for it."

"And then?" She dragged out the words and stroked his head as if begging for sex talk and not a plan.

"Contingency, Francesca."

In other words, go with the flow.

"I like that," she said, purposely coy.

"And then we'll get out of here," he murmured. "Just follow my lead."

She answered with the openmouthed kiss of a desperate, horny, sex-charged woman, not a determined, deceptive, mission-focused agent.

But that's what she was now.

She dragged her hands down his chest, vaguely aware that his heart hammered like hers. "Whatever you say…" She tried to sound sexy and provocative, but still get her clear message across that he could trust her. "I'll do."

His eyes grew smoky, and his mouth almost tipped in a smile. "In the room, Francesca. *Now*."

She damn near melted from anticipation and the way the demand turned her on.

That was no good. This had to be an *act*. A really good act.

She let him walk her to their door, holding him tight,

kissing his shoulder, caressing his back like any lover would while he found the key and opened the door, then banged it hard and dead-bolted it.

"Are we—"

"Shut up," he insisted, punctuating that with a kiss so hard he slammed her right against the wall.

He cupped her breasts and pushed into her, pretty damn hard for a man who was acting, glancing over to the wall behind the bed before backing away. But she could see his eyes were open, searching everywhere he could while kissing her and turning her around.

At her ear, he breathed, "Make a lot of noise. I need it for cover. Don't ever stop talking."

Make noise. What the hell should she say?

"Talk sexy to me, Francesca." He guided her to the bed and pushed her on it. "Tell me what you're going to do to me, baby. I'll get a raincoat."

Talk sexy. Make a lot of noise. Of course, she was speechless and frozen like a statue.

Some freaking spy she made.

Leaving her on the bed, he backed against a wall and was slyly scanning the room, probably on the off chance there was a camera. Abandoning that, he threw her a look that said everything. *Do it, Chessie. Play the part. Be a spy. Be my partner.*

And all she wanted in the whole world was to prove herself to him. And, maybe, to herself.

Kneeling on the lumpy mattress, she fingered the bottom of her T-shirt. "I can't wait for you to strip me," she said, inching the shirt up provocatively.

"Oh yeah. I'm going to strip you." But he was digging through his duffel bag, feeling around, carefully pulling out clothes and shaking them.

"Oh yeah, hurry up, baby." *Hurry up, baby*? She was going down as the worst dirty-talker ever. What the hell would Gabe do? Gabe would go all-in and fry his partner's ears.

"I want you to fuck me, hard."

Mal whipped his head up, eyes wide at the words. She saw his mouth slacken ever so slightly. His eyes flickered with encouragement, and then he went back to work.

Okay, dirty talk. Dirty talk. "I…I…want you…" Hopefully, whoever was listening or watching didn't speak English.

Unless they were CIA.

Oh *God*. What if Gabe saw this? Well, he'd say she was doing her job in the field. That she came from a family of badasses and…deserved to bear the Rossi name.

"I want your mouth all over me. Licking. Sucking." She closed her eyes, slowly pulled her top off so she could finger her nipples over her bra. "Everywhere, Mal. Right here."

Mal finished that suitcase and moved to hers, glancing up at her. "I intend to. And you won't be able to walk when I'm done." Impatience edged his voice, and she suspected it wasn't because he was desperate for sex. Where was the bug?

"I don't want you to be done…I want you to be inside me all night." The words were coarse and crude and not what she liked, except…her hands dragged down to her jeans, playing with the snap. "I want you inside me. Your big cock. Hurry!"

His head shot up with a look that said he was doing his damn best.

She unzipped her jeans, making it slow and noisy and as stripper-y as she could. "You know what it's going to feel like, Mal. Heaven."

"Hot and wet and tight, woman."

It didn't sound like him. He'd never talk like that to her. Which helped remind her that this wasn't real—anything either of them said or did was for the benefit of whoever might be listening or watching.

She pushed her jeans open and slid her hand inside her panties. Well, the words were working on her, at least. She touched herself and moaned noisily with her head back.

From under her lashes, she saw him look, his eyes flashing for a moment, then he gave her an all-business, nearly imperceptible nod. "Nice."

The move or her spy work? "I'll show you nice. Get over here."

"Yeah, baby. Show me," he said, pressed against a wall and carefully digging through the other suitcase. "And *tell* me," he insisted. "Tell me how you feel."

In other words, make more noise and cover for him.

"I feel…" At her long pause, he looked again, the message in his eyes clear. "I feel sexy when I'm with you. It makes me want you so bad, Mal. I've always wanted you."

He switched to the last bag, not even looking at her as he searched. *Okay, here we go.*

"From the moment I saw you…" She caressed her womanhood, half proud of herself, half furious with her body's response to something that was supposed to be fake. He finished searching her suitcase, tossing it aside and starting on the window casing and vent. "I wanted you—to kiss me, to taste me, to fill me up until I scream for more."

That got his attention. He glanced over his shoulder, his brows slightly raised. "Yeah, baby." His voice sounded gruff. "I want that, too."

"Then find that condom, honey." *Because I can't keep*

talking like a rejected page from Penthouse Forum for much longer. And I might come.

"I'm still looking for what I need," he said. "But you're making me hot, baby."

"I'm hot, too." Oh man. *Lame, Chess.*

He threw her a quick smile. "That's good." He gave up on the window and moved to the only other piece of furniture in the room, a cheap dresser. He opened the top drawer. "Maybe they're in here," he said.

"Hurry up, Mal. I'm not sure how much longer I can wait." She touched her hard nipple, scraping the lace of her bra.

What a weak-ass she was. No decent spy would actually get turned on by this. Mal was all business, that's for sure.

He turned to give her another look, pausing in his search to stare at her. His eyes darkened. His jaw locked. His chest rose and fell with one tight breath. "Keep going," he said, his voice more than a little rough.

Or maybe not.

She pushed the jeans over her hips and shimmied out of them just to make more noise, moaning the whole time, leaving her thong on. "My panties are wet, Mal." He didn't even look, working his own way down to the lower drawer. Of course he didn't look, because a real spy would use a more effective P-word than panties. "Mal, my pu—"

Suddenly, his fist shot in the air with a thumbs-up, then he beckoned her closer. "C'mere, baby," he said. "Come over here and see…what I got for your wet panties."

She scooted off the bed and stepped closer to see. Under a yellowed, crispy piece of tissue lining the bottom of the drawer, there was a tiny disc she recognized immediately.

"Sound only," he mouthed without making a noise.

"Oooh," she cooed. "That's…huge." Then she held her hands out as if to ask, *Now what?*

"Let's use one right now," he said, pushing her back to the bed. But there was no condom, and there was no way he meant they were really going to do this. She let him fall on her, knowing he had a plan and she had to trust it.

He kissed her—noisily—and added a satisfied moan. She did, too, and not just for the benefit of their listening audience. His hands were kneading her breasts.

"We're going to fuck, baby," he said, still using a nickname and a word that sounded so wrong to her ears…so it couldn't have been for her ears.

She inched him back with another question in her eyes. They were?

"All night long. We're not going to stop until these boxes of condoms are empty and used up and so are we." He winked at her, silently telling her that it was going to be okay, the cheesy talk was all part of the game.

Damn it, she liked his game as much as she liked him.

She responded with a kiss, making it as loud as his, moaning, groaning…faking it until she wasn't anymore. And neither was he. His hard-on was massive, nearly bursting out of his jeans.

"Just like that," he said, grinding against her. "Let me have you just like that."

She gasped at the pressure. "Oh!" He knew she'd come like this. He'd made her come like this in the car. She gripped his shoulders and cursed her body for turning into a pool of hot, achy liquid.

But he was into it, too. As much as she was. Not inside her, but the rough denim of his jeans over his erection grinding against her wet silk panties was taking them both closer to reality.

"Make it sound good, Francesca," he whispered in her ear. "Make it real."

"It *is* real," she hissed in his ear.

For a moment, he stilled, then pushed against her. "Yeah." He dragged his hand down her body, between them, cupping her with his palm. "So real," he murmured.

He pressed the heel of his hand right on her sweetest spot, making her let out a little cry.

"Inside," she demanded. "Inside me."

"Perfect, baby. Perfect." She didn't know if he meant her acting—which wasn't acting—or her body's response to him, but it didn't matter. She was confused and excited and trying to stay in the moment but desperately, wickedly gone.

"Like that?" he asked, one finger inching into her. "Or more?"

Blood rushed so hard, her body lost it at the touch, the danger, the illicit, fake sex that wasn't fake. Anyone listening would assume they were copulating like crazy and she…oh God, she wanted to.

Desire crackled through her. "More," she whispered. "Oh my God, Mal, more."

He obliged with two fingers, and it took everything in her not to reach down and grab him and tell him what she really wanted.

"Like that, baby?"

Fire shot through her, an orgasm so close she almost wept. She lost control. Just lost it. She stuck her hand between them, sliding into his pants, clutching his erection as if she could drag it right into her and ride it for hours.

"Oh." He grunted and moaned and rubbed her harder, circling and stroking and torturing her. She did the same, squeezing and pumping and pulling an orgasm out of him.

"Mal…I have to…"

"Come with me, Francesca. Come. *Now.*"

She fell into the climax, still clutching him, still stroking, still dying for his entire manhood to fill her up, and as she rocked with one and another and another physical quake of pleasure, he lost it, too, coming as hard as she did.

Very slowly, still fighting for breath, he forced himself up. "Don't move," he mouthed.

As if that were possible.

"I gotta hit the head," he said, moving around and making way more noise than necessary. "Don't you get out of this bed, woman." But he gestured for her to do exactly that, then put one finger on his lips to remind her to move silently.

Without making a sound, she managed to get one foot on the ground. Damn, her legs were shaking. Couldn't they have two minutes of postcoital rest?

Apparently not. Mal was already lifting their two bags, his muscles straining as he picked them up off the ground without making a sound.

Put clothes on, he mouthed.

She nodded, glancing around for what she'd been wearing before. Too noisy to get back into jeans. She tiptoed to the dresser, spying a beach cover-up in the open drawer. That would work.

She gestured to it so he knew what she was doing and lifted the cotton dress, letting it go over her head soundlessly, falling to her thighs.

He pointed to her bare feet. *No shoes*, he mouthed. She nodded, then he indicated the bed, and instantly, she understood. She sat on the bed and rubbed her hands all over the sheets, moaning like a woman completely satisfied.

"Hurry back, sweetheart," she said, patting the pillow. "There's more where that came from."

He angled his head toward the door, using the suitcases to tell her to go first. She tiptoed by him, snagging her handbag.

"I'll be back," he said pointedly in the direction of the listening device. "You just stay right there and wait for me."

He nodded to the door, and she snapped the dead bolt. The minute they were in the hall, she closed the door tight.

"Run," he ordered in a hushed whisper. "Straight to the car. Run!"

She flew down the hall and up the stairs, saying a thankful prayer that there was no one around. She darted outside, turned left, and bolted to the Prefect, yanking the door open. He was right on her tail, tossing the bags in the back, then starting the engine.

Which sputtered.

"Holy fuck, not now," he growled. "Come on, girl. Come on." He sounded very much like he had in bed, cajoling an orgasm out of her. His jeans still hung open, his T-shirt stuck to his body with sweat from their pseudosex.

Finally, the Prefect engine hummed to life, and Mal threw it into drive and shot down the alley, flying through the streets of Caibarién like a hunted, wanted man.

Which, she had to remember, he was.

Chapter Twenty-Two

Mal took a roundabout, convoluted, mangled trip over deserted roads, through wooded areas, and deep into the farmland of Cuba and lost anyone who might be on their tail. Yet, he was barely fifteen minutes from town and making his way to Ramos's farm.

Except for helping him navigate the winding, unpaved roads without benefit of headlights, Chessie had been quiet, even when she found out where they were going. Was she upset about the bug in the room and what they did to escape? Brimming with questions she knew he couldn't answer? Or, as he was, fighting the feeling of slipping closer to someone who was wrong on so many levels?

Still silent, she reached over the seat and dug into her bag, producing a pair of sneakers. After she put them on, she resituated herself against the passenger door, far away from him.

Too far away. Mal lifted his hand along the bench seat, letting his fingers graze her bare shoulder. His need to touch her—constantly—was more intense than ever. Real sex, fake sex, hopeless sex—whatever the hell they called it—had done nothing to satisfy his craving for her. It only made things worse.

"C'mere," he said, giving her bra strap a little tug. "There has to be some advantage to no seat belts and no console. Sit next to me, Francesca."

Before she moved, she shot him a look. "I know what you're doing when you say my name like that."

"Addressing you?"

"You want to get intimate."

"While driving without headlights? I think we've had enough adventurous sex for one evening." Although, he always wanted more.

She scooted over and dropped her head on his shoulder. "There are other kinds of intimacy," she said.

Like a sweet girl laying her head on his shoulder as if she depended on him for security and happiness and love and a whole host of other things a guy like Mal couldn't supply.

"For example," she continued. "Sharing the *truth* with a person." She sat up straight and looked at him, but Mal kept his concentration on the dark road ahead. "Truth with a person who just proved she's up to field snuff."

He gave her a squeeze. "You were amazing. I'd brag to your brother about what a great spy you'd make, but I like my balls and don't want him to cut them off."

"Gabe of all people would know you do what you have to, right?"

"True," he agreed. "And, Francesca Rossi, don't listen to the voice inside your head telling you that you don't have what it takes to do what your siblings and cousins do. You're rock solid."

He could practically feel her smile. "Then tell me the whole Robin Hood story because you know you can trust me."

He didn't answer, but turned onto another side road, glancing in the rearview, confident they hadn't been followed.

"Then I'll just ask questions and figure it out on my own," she said, impatience adding an edge to her tone.

After watching her in action at the *municipal*, he didn't doubt that she had the intelligence and determination to do just that.

"But you have to make me a promise," she said.

Whatever it was, he already knew he'd say yes, just like he knew she was going to get the whole story out of him one way or another.

"That you'll tell me when I'm right or wrong. Like twenty questions."

"Okay," he agreed, because he knew she'd start the process with or without his consent. "Log on and start hacking my brain."

She shifted as if she needed to settle and get comfortable. "Okay, you stole five hundred thousand dollars from a government account that funded certain activities at Guantanamo Bay when you were a guard there, except you were not a guard, you were an undercover spy for the CIA. And you stole that money to help someone in trouble, right?"

He stayed perfectly still, then he shook his head.

"Oh, really? Something in that statement wasn't right?" She turned to him. "You stole five hundred thousand…"

He swallowed. Hard.

"You didn't steal five hundred thousand dollars?"

He let out a slow, low sigh, and she put both hands on his thigh and squeezed. "You stole more?"

"No."

"Less?"

"No."

"Ohhh." She had that nice, satisfied tone in her voice, like when she tore down a firewall with her flying fingers.

"You *didn't* steal the money. Someone else did, and you took the blame."

He ripped his gaze from the road to give her a look. "You sure you didn't train to be a spy, or is interrogating a genetic gift in your family?"

She gave a dry laugh. "Okay and, wow, *okay*." She dragged out the last word with the sound of appreciation in her voice.

"What does that mean?"

"It means my lover isn't a thief."

Something in the vicinity of his chest felt like it cracked a little. Her lover? Not a thief? As true as both those statements might be, he didn't dare hope. "Tell that to the US government."

"Someone should." She turned in her seat to face him again. "And your name would be cleared."

"If only it were that easy." If Alana got arrested for the crime, there was no telling what would happen to the kids. Maria was twelve now, so she'd be shipped off to some heinous place near Havana. Jorge would be ten, so he'd go to military training. And Solana had been two the last time he'd seen her, and she was just a little heartbreaker.

"The money was never recovered," he added, mostly for the reaction he knew he'd get.

As expected, she gasped. "So where is it?"

"Beats me. But they think I know, so I'm on a watch list just to be sure I don't suddenly buy an Aston Martin."

"Nice car choice," she said. "But if we found the money, couldn't you be cleared then?"

He couldn't help giving her a squeeze. "Your optimism is charming. Downright adorable."

"Don't be condescending."

"I'm not. It really is charming. It's…infectious."

"Okay, then tell me the whole story, Mal, if you're so damn infected by me. Don't make me guess anymore."

He was infected by her. *Affected* by her. Ready to open up in a way he'd never done before, and he hadn't known her a week.

He slowed the car, almost stopping at a pitch-black section of forest and farm, not far from that Poinciana tree now. But he had enough time to tell her the truth, and deep inside, he knew he owed that much to her.

"I didn't steal the money. A woman named Alana Cevallos did, or someone close to her."

"How did she do it?"

"I'm not entirely sure. She worked as a high-level admin at Gitmo, a secretary to my boss and a liaison with the local community, since she's Cuban. She and I became friends while I was there, and she came to me in a panic because she claimed she had found an enormous sum of money in an offshore account her husband had opened before he was taken away."

"Taken away?" she asked.

"By the government. And now he's dead."

"What? Why?"

"There doesn't have to be a reason, Chessie. Suspected of being a dissident, most likely. And with Alana having the quite unusual job of working as an administrative assistant for a US operation? Government made a move on him." About a month after baby Solana was born, the bastards.

"And she just found the money?"

Mal shrugged. "My guess is she didn't want to implicate her husband any further, since he was already a prisoner of the government. Anyway, she said she didn't take it, but…"

"But you think she did."

Did he? There was no other explanation, no matter how

much he wanted to believe her innocent. "Probably at the urging of her husband, but he didn't have access to those funds at Guantanamo, and she did. So it's moot. They did it."

She looked out into the darkness of the night, thinking. "Why did she go to you?"

"Like I said, we were friends."

Chessie inched back and dropped her glasses so she could look over them, the question in her eyes obvious. "A married woman, Mal?" she asked.

He laughed softly at the implication, which couldn't be further from the truth. "Alana is in her forties with three kids, Chess. When shit at Gitmo got ugly—and, man, it could get ugly there—you need an escape. Gabe had Isa, and they used to go off, but I didn't have that many people who knew I wasn't really a guard. Alana did, because she worked for our boss. So sometimes I went to her house for dinner, and I liked it there."

"What did you like about it?"

He suspected she was still sniffing around to see if he'd had a romantic relationship with Alana, which he had not. "I liked her kids a lot. And there was a lot of good feels in that house, even with the father being gone. She kept it solid for those kids." He shook his head, just thinking about what would have happened if she'd been arrested for embezzling US funds. A Cuban citizen who had all kinds of special clearance to work at Gitmo? "I hated to see that end for those kids."

"So, what did you do?"

"She did it, actually. She created an account in my name that only I could access and put the money in there so the trail would lead to me."

"But she didn't put the money in there?" Chessie asked, confused. "I mean, you said they never found it."

"It disappeared."

She dropped back on the seat. "The answer is in the computer," she said.

"There is no answer, Chessie. Who knows what her husband had arranged before he died? Someone got that money, maybe used it for other dissidents to fight the Cuban government, or who knows? Doesn't matter. I took the blame for her."

"It matters to clear your name," she insisted.

"It might clear mine, but it would damage hers forever. So what good would my four years in prison have been? She'd be dragged off, and no one would ever see her again, and I couldn't…" He struggled for the words, his throat thick, an old fear resurfacing, as it did any time he thought about going through this and trying to clear his name without implicating Alana. "I couldn't do that to those kids."

After a moment, he realized Chessie was staring at him, hard. He turned, ready to defend his decision. He'd certainly had this fight with her brother often enough.

But she'd pushed her glasses back, and he saw a tear slide down her face.

"Chessie, don't cry," he said, lifting his hand to wipe it away. But she grasped his hand and pressed it to her lips. "I can't change this to save myself, and I won't let those kids' lives get lost just so I can find mine."

She dropped her head back and closed her eyes. "So, do you think we can scare up Internet access out here?"

"Doubtful, why?"

"I want to find that money."

He actually laughed at that wild level of optimism. "Sorry, but that's not why we're in Cuba. Gabriel Rafael Winter, remember?"

"How could I forget? But I still want to find that money."

"Talk about hopeless."

"I don't believe in hopelessness," she said. "I believe that somewhere in the deepest, darkest corner of cyberspace, there's a way to clear your name, and if I can find it, then maybe you can do something good with that name."

Like give it to you. He closed his eyes and pulled her closer, the only way to keep himself from voicing that stupid, hopeless thought out loud.

Chapter Twenty-Three

The Prefect bumped over the dirt as they followed the rocky road after the Poinciana tree, and Chessie kept expecting some kind of light at the end of the road.

But it couldn't have been darker at the Ramos farm.

"It looks so deserted at night," Chessie said.

"Come on, let's walk the rest of the way." Mal tucked the car behind a small grouping of trees, getting out and reaching his hand to help Chessie slide out the driver's side. "Let's try the barn," Mal said, guiding her forward.

They walked slowly, getting their footing on rocks and dirt, using Mal's small flashlight to reach the back barn used as a school. Mal put his hand on the massive door and jiggled, which opened instantly and easily.

Once inside, Chessie gasped softly at the sight of…nothing. Absolutely no sign that there had been a school—the books, tables, boards, and chairs were gone. Just some hay strewn around the dirt floor.

Mal kept walking, scanning the empty area, while Chessie mentally clicked through the options. Did Ramos break the school every night? Had the government come and shut it down? Were they all in hiding?

And what happened to Gabrielita? The very question made her heart ache.

"Let's try the little house," she said, and Mal agreed, heading back outside and around the barn to the small structure. "Where is everyone?"

The sound of a rifle being cocked echoed, and Mal instantly whipped Chessie around and pushed her to the ground to protect her.

"Everyone is right here." Nestor Ramos's thick accent was barely audible over Chessie's thumping heart.

Slowly, Mal straightened, positioning himself in front of Chessie, keeping the light down so he didn't blind Ramos. "*Señor* Ramos. It's us. The teachers."

He snorted. "I know you are not teachers."

"Where is everything?" Mal asked. "The school? The books?"

"What school? There is no school here." There was just enough sarcasm in his voice to make Chessie wonder if he was jerking them around, or really going to deny what they'd seen there. "There are no books. This is a farm."

Chessie pushed to a stand. Screw sarcasm and denial. They knew the truth. "Where are the kids?"

"My children are sleeping. My boys are placed around this farm to kill you if they have to."

Chessie put her hand over her mouth, stunned at this turn and his…authority. He didn't speak like a rural farmer. His accent couldn't hide intelligence and…training.

Mal took a non-threatening step closer. "I came to warn you that someone might know we were here today. We wanted you to be prepared, but I see you already are."

Ramos just stared, his rifle still leveled at Mal's chest. For each achingly long second that passed, Chessie's breath got tighter and her heart pounded harder.

And no one said a word.

The older man let out a long, slow sigh. "A man came here today," he said in halting English. "American. That's twice in two days. That smells very bad to us."

"What did he want?" Mal asked.

Ramos let out a dry laugh. "He wanted you."

Chessie felt the world sway a little under her.

Ramos's eyes shifted to her, and even in the ambient light she could see them soften just a little. "Both of you. He didn't see the school. He didn't get beyond the tree. I made sure of that. But he was like you…CIA."

She just blinked at that, and Mal stepped closer. "Did you get his name?"

Ramos laughed softly. "He didn't leave his card. But I know. I know you. I…know about you."

Why? How? She actually took a breath to ask the questions, but Mal gave the slightest signal, and she closed her mouth.

"*Señor* Ramos, please. We're seeking a boy who was here on this farm," Mal said. "We don't want to hurt you. Or report you. Or bring any attention to your school. We are looking for Gabriel Rafael Winter, who was born on June 29 in 2011. You gave us the rosary with his name and that date engraved on it."

Even in the dark, Chessie could sense the information hit the man hard. "I gave it to her," he said, nodding toward Chessie. "As a gift. I know of no such child."

He was lying. She clenched her fists as Mal leaned closer. "He was adopted," he said. "Did you aid in that adoption?"

He shook his head very slowly.

"But you do that, don't you?" Chessie asked. "You take in orphans, and you find them homes?" It sure explained how the baby could be here last, and then be listed as adopted. And how Ramos could have so many of "his own" kids the same age.

His attention shifted back to her, his night vision obviously good enough to allow him to take a long, hard scrutiny of her face, and once again, his expression changed from threatening to curious and, maybe, a little trusting.

"Otherwise..." He leaned closer to lower his voice. "They would be owned by the government and lost forever."

His honesty gave her the nerve to move on instinct rather than rules. "*Señor* Ramos," she said softly. "This child is my nephew, my brother's son. Please." Damn it, her voice cracked. "Do you have any record of where he might have gone?"

"I don't know," he said. But it wasn't a cold refusal to answer. It was a genuine admission that he didn't have all the facts. Then he angled his head toward the little cottage. "Come."

He opened the door, and they followed him into a dark room. After a moment, he switched on a small lamp that cast a golden glow over the room, which looked the same as yesterday except for the addition of a tiny cot in the corner, where a little body stirred when the light came on.

A young girl sat up and blinked sleepily. And Chessie had to fight the urge not to scoop Gabrielita up in her arms.

The little girl wiped her eyes and yawned, her attention landing on Chessie, a smile brightening her little face.

"Hello, Gabrielita," Chessie said, taking a few steps and kneeling down next to the cot. "Sorry to wake you."

The child obviously didn't understand, but held out both arms, and Chessie lost the battle, scooping the tiny body into her arms and settling on the dirty floor to hold her. Gabrielita looked up at Ramos as if she expected to be reprimanded for the move, but Ramos smiled.

"Is it okay for you?" he asked Chessie.

She nodded and stroked the girl's hair, holding her closer. "It's fine. It's perfect." Her gaze shifted to Mal, who looked exactly as he had when he'd warned her earlier...*you can't save them all.*

Well, she could hold this one and love her for a few minutes.

Ramos sat on the edge of the bed and dropped his head in his hands, threading his fingers through his hair. Chessie held her breath, praying and hoping and trying not to squeeze the little girl too tight.

"His mother hid here, and we helped her."

Chessie almost fainted with relief. "Hid? From who?" she asked.

Ramos shrugged. "I do not ask questions when that much money is offered," he said, his expression unapologetic. "She gave us enough money to buy many books and desks. Everything came from her."

"What was her name?" Mal asked.

The man's eyes narrowed as he peered at his visitors. "I am not ever supposed to say."

"But the boy"—Chessie leaned closer—"is family."

Ramos gave the shakiest smile. "I can see that."

She sucked in a soft breath, the words stirring her. Her nephew looked like her? The baby had blue eyes like hers? Of course, she and Gabe were the only blue-eyed Rossis. She couldn't stop the smile pulling at her lips.

"We called him Rafael."

"Oh." Chessie couldn't help the little sound that escaped and the tears that welled up. "Rafael."

Mal leaned forward and put a hand on the man's arm. "Do you know where he is?"

He looked from one to the other. "I know who took him when his mother…"

"She died," Chessie said. "We know that."

"Can you tell us how?" Mal asked. "It would be a great comfort to the child's father to know."

Ramos turned, his eyes growing cold. "She died in a car accident, hit by a truck. It was very tragic, and the baby was less than a few months old."

"Oh my God," Chessie whispered. "How sad."

He nodded in agreement. "During her pregnancy, she'd been teaching the children, and we were all devastated."

Emotions swamped Chessie at the news, along with some relief. She could give Gabe closure. He needed that.

"Why was she here?" Mal asked, apparently not satisfied with that closure. "Why would she choose this place to hide?"

Even in the dim light, Chessie saw the flash of something in the man's dark eyes that disappeared just as fast. "A friend sent her here. And that friend"—he puffed out a breath—"adopted the baby."

Chessie's heart swelled, hope overtaking the ache. "Please, please, *Señor* Ramos. I'm not going to take the child or upset him if he is in a happy home, you have my word. But…I want to meet him. I want to arrange for him to meet his father." She blinked and didn't care that a tear trickled and slipped under her glasses. "I beg you with all my heart and soul to tell me the name of the family who adopted him."

He took a deep breath and let it out. "It is why I gave you the rosary," he admitted. "I knew what she would want."

"Isadora?" Chessie whispered. "The child's mother?"

He nodded. "She was very special. Very beautiful. In here." He tapped his chest. "Like you."

Chessie leaned forward, her arms wrapped tightly around a sleepy child, her heart flat-out on full display. "Please," she whispered.

"Her name is Alana Cevallos."

Alana Cevallos? Chessie dropped right back again, shocked. She closed her eyes to take it in and opened them to see Mal looking just as shocked. No, worried.

"*Señor* Ramos," he said, getting closer to the man. "This visitor you had. CIA. Thinning hair. Blue eyes? Marks on his face?" He touched his cheeks. "'Bout this tall?"

Ramos nodded. "And he knew Alana's name. Asked if she was with you."

Mal muttered a soft curse and turned to Chessie. "It's Roger Drummand, the guy who's after me. We have to go to her tonight. Now. Before he does."

"Okay." Chessie lifted the little sleeping girl back onto her makeshift bed.

Gabrielita moaned, and her eyes fluttered open. "Mamá," she whispered, holding her arms out. "Mamá."

"Shhh," Chessie patted her back.

"Her mama is gone," Ramos said. "And her father, too."

"Your daughter told me," Chessie said.

"If the government finds her here, they will take her. This is why…" He held out his hands. "I do this."

"God bless you for it," Chessie murmured.

"We have to leave now," Mal said. "We have very little time to drive to the town where she lives. It will take hours, maybe all night on back roads."

"Your vehicle is…" Ramos shook his head. "*No bueno*."

"No kidding," Chessie said. "Do you have a better one we can borrow?"

"Something that can get us there fast," Mal added.

Ramos considered that for a moment, then gestured for them to follow him.

He rushed them back to their car, where they got their bags, then hustled them through the darkness, walking a good seven or eight minutes without saying a word.

Finally, they came to a large stand-alone garage, and as Ramos worked the lock on the oversize pull-up door, Chessie stepped closer to him.

"*Señor* Ramos," she said, keeping her voice low. "Can we offer you some money for this?"

He shook his head, his eyes flashing negative. "No, no. This is for Rafael." He smiled at Chessie and touched her cheek. "He is your blood."

Impulsively, she hugged him. "Kiss Gabrielita for me. Tell her I will be back."

He gave a sad smile, probably because she might not be able to keep that promise, and yanked open the garage door. Inside, he flipped a switch that cast a harsh yellow light over the whole area. "Can you fly, *señor*?" Ramos asked Mal.

Chessie stared at the propeller biplane crop duster not a whole lot bigger than the Prefect.

"Well enough," Mal replied.

Chessie let the words echo in her head as she walked into the homemade hangar without hesitation. When she reached the plane, she realized it was even older than she'd thought, and her seat would be tiny, in front of the controls, which consisted of a joystick that looked older than Nino. No roof, no windows, no helmet, just frayed seat belts and some ancient dials behind filthy, cracked glass.

When she looked over her shoulder at Mal, she caught Ramos handing him a pistol and waited for an expected wave of worry or even fear over this latest turn of events on her rookie mission. This was not in the plan.

But no worry or fear came. Screw plans. She was nothing but ready now.

Chapter Twenty-Four

Alana Cevallos locked the last file drawer, put her computer to sleep, and turned off the lights of the tiny office in Guantanamo Bay, as she had every weeknight for almost ten years.

She went through her checklist once again, forcing herself to think only in English, no matter how exhausted the long day had left her. After a decade of working in high-level administration at the American owned and operated prison that had, over its lifetime, gone from a tent shelter for Haitians to the home for the most dangerous prisoners, she spoke perfect English, but often slipped into her native Spanish when she was tired.

And after an eleven-hour day, much of it spent staring at spreadsheets, she was bone tired. At least there hadn't been any crises on the home front.

She checked her phone again to see if there were any new messages from her mother, but things had been quiet for the last few hours. Mamá, who'd finally mastered the art of texting and used the phone that the US government provided all of the local Gitmo employees, would have texted if anything were happening with her children.

But, at twelve, Maria was as much in charge as her

abuela when it came to watching out for the littler ones. Alana had weathered the worst storms in their younger years and kept this position as a secretary to the director, one of the best jobs in the entire country. For the first time in many years, Alana felt something very few Cubans ever experienced: security.

Of course, the prison would close eventually. At least, that's what the rumors were. There were only about a hundred detainees left, and most guests were attorneys trying to work out the details of their release.

The president of the United States had sworn that Guantanamo Bay had outlived its usefulness, but now with everything changing in Cuba, who knew?

What she did know was that she had a little bit of money, healthy children, a helpful mother, and a home that had been in her family for several generations. She was a widow now and had accepted that.

She said a silent prayer of gratitude to the Holy Mother, who had put true angels in her life when she needed them the most. Still smiling and humming a quiet tune, she stepped into the darkened hallway, ready to make the forty-minute drive to her home in the village of El Salvador. She would stop and—

A hand slapped over her mouth, and a man pulled her backward, stealing her breath and sanity. *Ay Dios mio!* Her worst fear. A detainee had escaped, and she was a hostage.

"Nice to see you again, Alana."

For a moment, she couldn't even process the English words, let alone the voice. But then it hit her with vicious clarity.

Roger Drummand.

"Aren't you happy to see your old boss?"

Fear and shock vibrated through her as she tried to hold

perfectly still and think. Should she try to kick him? Scream? Get to an alarm?

But she just grew weaker as he dragged her back toward her office.

She didn't wonder how he got in; the former CIA supervisor still had top clearances at the prison, and he'd been there now and again in the past few years. But never when no one else was around.

"Let's get back to your desk," he said. "And I don't think you want to make any noise or even think about that alarm, because I have your kids."

She froze again. What did he want? "*Qué quieres*?"

"No Spanish, Alana. Remember how much I hate it." He jabbed her back with something hard and cold. Of course he had a gun. "Get the keys and open the office."

She tried to swallow, but her throat was dry. Her hands were exactly the opposite, vibrating with terror as she dug in her bag for the office keys. When she pulled them out, he yanked them away with his free hand, keeping the gun firmly in the middle of her back.

"Where are my children? My mother?" she managed to ask.

"Detained. By the government."

She let out a soft moan. Those were the last words she'd heard about her husband until she'd gotten word he had died *in service of his country*. "Why?"

"To get you to cooperate." He got the door unlocked and shoved her inside. "Remember your old friend, Malcolm Harris? Did you know he is in Cuba?"

Mal. Why was he here? What did he want?

"He's dragging around a computer hacker, which tells me he wants something, and you can get to it before he does." He added some pressure. "Something I know you can do."

For a moment, she couldn't think, in any language, but then clarity came. The account...would be empty. "No, *señor*. I can't do that."

He pushed her into the chair and banged the back of the pistol against her shoulder. "Don't fucking lie to me, Alana. You know exactly where that money is, and I've done you a big favor by staying away."

He'd done himself a favor, more like. He'd kept his distance from the crime scene and she'd counted on him never coming back.

"But now I need some cash," he continued. "So now it's time to move it, safely and silently, to where it belonged in the first place: my account."

She looked up at him, narrowing her eyes. "You stole the money, Mr. Drummand. Or did you forget that you made it look like I did it with my husband? My husband...who was taken away and killed not long after."

"It's good that you know the consequences of bad behavior in this country."

Except Guantanamo Bay was not Cuba. It was the United States of America, and Roger Drummand was a dirty, deadly thief who had the power to ruin her life and harm her children.

He gave her a hard push. "Turn your computer on and get ready to transfer the funds. I have a brand new account ready to take them."

She'd never thought he'd take this chance. Never. Once Mal had gone to prison for the crime Roger Drummand had committed and tried to blame on Alana, she'd hoped to be done with this man.

"Hurry!" he ordered.

Ice crystallized in her veins. She couldn't transfer funds that weren't there. And what would he do to her children and her mother when he found out what she had done with that money?

Buying time, she did as she was told, her fingers shaking over the keyboard.

"You know the bank," he said when the screen lit up. "And you have the right fingerprint. Do it."

She logged into the bank site. Waited. Heard him breathing. Knew what was about to happen.

"Mr. Drummand…"

The screen flashed for the request of a fingerprint and password. If she did that, he'd know she'd already moved the money. And then he'd kill her…

"There. Fingerprint." He gave her arm a shove. "Now."

She did, pressing her index finger on the scanner, getting the immediate prompt for the password. "Now the password. Now!"

Dear Holy Mother, help me. She slowly typed in the ten digits and letters that were burned in her brain, closing her eyes when the screen flashed to show the amount available.

"Ten dollars?" he shouted in her ear. "Where the fuck is the rest of it?" He smacked her head with the gun, sending shock waves ringing through her.

She couldn't answer. She couldn't tell him.

But he leaned close to the screen and used his free hand to click to the last transaction. "Money transferred to another account? Whose? Where is that money, bitch? And I know it was you because you and I are the only people who knew where it was. You had no right to take my money!"

"You had no right to take my husband." He'd arranged for Jorge's death as sure as he'd pulled the trigger on a pistol.

"Well, you're going to join him right now."

She squeezed her eyes shut and stopped breathing,

bracing for the pain, needing and wanting to live so badly. "I didn't take it," she whispered. "I moved it to another account."

"Whose?" His hand slipped around her throat and squeezed. "Where is the goddamn money, Alana?"

She couldn't breathe. He pressed so hard on her windpipe, all the air was cut off.

"Do you really want to die?" he demanded. "Because I will kill you if you don't tell me where it is."

She tried to choke in air but couldn't, blinking as her vision darkened. But if he killed her, he'd never get the money.

"You die and your kids go to the government," he rasped in her ear. "Is that what you want, Alana? Is it?"

Or maybe he would. Maybe he was just mad enough, and desperate enough, to kill her. "Mal," she managed to say.

He loosened his grip. "What?"

"I put it in an account that only Malcolm Harris can access."

He loosened his grip as if he needed to really think about that. "So it will look like he really did steal the money?"

No, so he could have it. But she didn't argue.

"That was brilliant," he said. "Get it."

She slowly shook her head. "You need his fingerprint and his password to take money out. I don't know them."

His eyes flashed as he grabbed a handful of hair and wrenched her head backward, shooting pain down her spine. "You're lying."

"No, I'm not."

He twisted her hair and jabbed the gun harder. "Then this is what we're going to do, Alana. You're going to bring him here to me. Tonight."

"I can't get him here. He's not allowed on the base." She

was thrashing for excuses now, trying to get time to think.

He gave a sharp laugh. "Alana, I'm surprised at your lack of creativity. When you worked for me, I thought you were one of the smartest people around Gitmo. You'll think of something."

She closed her eyes. The last person in the world she should betray was Mal Harris. And yet…her family. Her children. Her mother. Her whole world…they could be gone so easily. That was how a Cuban lived, even one who worked at Guantanamo. They lived on the edge of death.

He finally released her, pulling out a cell phone, and she knew one phone call could be way more fatal than one bullet.

"I'll arrange for your kids and the old lady to be taken to Havana. Could be years before you see them again. If ever."

Her babies. Her mother. Or Mal. Who needed her more? Once again, she chose family over a friend. "I'll bring him here."

He gave a dry smile. "I'll wait in my old office. It'll be just like old times, won't it?"

Dead reckoning. That lovely sounding concept, according to Mal, was their navigation technique. It amounted to knowing the direction, estimating the approximate miles, and hoping for fair winds.

That did not sound like a *flight plan* to Chessie.

Still, there was a seat belt, which Chessie had both hands wrapped around to pull it tighter against the turbulence that tossed the little plane as they cruised over miles of farmland.

As far as speed, the crop duster, which looked and felt like it was built before Chessie was born, was a big step up from the Prefect they left at the farm. But it was not on the ground, which was a strike against it. And it was in the hands of a man who, she was starting to believe, really had never flown an actual plane in his life. Maybe in a video game. Maybe in some kind of simulated training.

But she was in his hands now, and all she could do was hope for the best.

Wind sang through the open-air cockpit, which was about the size of the seat of a VW Bug. The *back*seat. Mal sat behind her maneuvering the stick with his right hand, a rusty throttle in his left. Chessie had stuffed herself into the tiny seat in front of him, her loose beach cover-up a pathetic fashion choice for night flying.

Ramos had given them a lightning-fast lesson on the dials while they'd donned helmets and climbed in. Air speed, altitude, oil pressure, and horizon position, which in this plane were visible to both pilot and passenger, all looked to be functioning fine and giving a good read. Fuel? Every time they hit an air pocket, that dial dropped to empty, then popped back up again.

This was flying by the seat of your pants, on a wing and a prayer, and every other cliché she could think of to keep her mind occupied. When she ran out, she thought about the whole situation of the money and the child, the woman and the secret school that arranged adoptions…and tried like hell to make sense of it all.

Mal hadn't stolen money to help a woman; he'd covered for her. Somewhere in that fact lay the answer to his life's problem: clearing his name without ruining hers. Could something be done with the money? The accounts?

Chessie itched to get on a computer and dig around, but

first, she had to find Gabe's child. And they were flying to the woman who'd adopted him, so that meant they were closer to little Gabriel Rafael.

Surely the woman whose life Mal had essentially saved would be on their side.

"Hang on!" Mal hollered, and Chessie did, clutching her seat and squeezing as they soared over some unexpectedly high trees.

She glanced over her shoulder to look at him, but her hair whipped over her face. She couldn't see far anyway, since she'd taken off her glasses for the ride. When she pushed it away, she caught sight of him concentrating on the dials and sticks, his whole being into the job of flying.

Don't fall for him, Chessie. You'd never have a normal life.

Gabe's warning howled in her head, louder than the wind.

Who wanted a normal life when you could have a life of adventure and fun with Malcolm Harris? But couldn't a girl have other fantasies? Less sweet and innocent and more hot and wild? What if she were willing to give up those girlhood dreams and…follow him? Stay with him? Fall in love with him?

The plane dipped low and sharp, stealing her breath and sending her stomach on the same ride.

"Sorry," he said. "My bad."

Not really. He didn't have a bad bone in his body. Certainly not his heart, which was in the right place, or they wouldn't be in this plane, but…the spies, the danger, the looking over his shoulder?

"Hang in there, Francesca."

"I'm trying," she said dryly.

"I promise we won't crash and burn."

Really? Could he promise that? Because her heart was flipping around in her chest like this crappy little plane.

"It's not far now."

She lifted her head and peered into the darkness. "How can you tell?"

"Instinct. Just listening to my gut."

She turned again to throw her next question into the wind. "What's your gut tell you about me?"

"That you are the best..." He hesitated and the plane dipped. She filled in the blank during the silence. The best partner? The best lover? The best thing that ever happened to him? The best –

"Not good. Fuck, this is not good."

She squinted at the fuel dial, the needle hovering over empty.

"It does that," she said. "It'll jump back."

"It's not jumping back, Chessie. Damn it." He worked the stick and the throttle, backing off the acceleration, probably to save fuel. "I can see the lights of El Sal, maybe five or six miles away. We're close enough to put her down soon," he said. "I'll find an open field. Hopefully before we run out of fuel."

Hopefully.

This from the man who didn't believe in hope. But she trusted him. She had to right now.

"Landing, Chessie," he yelled. "Hang on."

She turned to face the front and slammed her hands on the leather panel in front of her as the plane dipped and dove, tilting from one side to another. She hated this. It was wild and scary and out of control. She *hated* it.

And when she entertained stupid, crazy thoughts about life with a guy who was just like that, she had to remember how much she—

The nose of the plane tilted straight down, making her cry out in terror.

She heard him swear again. "I got it." But it didn't feel like he had it. He pulled back on the stick, and the plane straightened out, but they were definitely headed down. Fast. Really damn fast.

"Whoa!" she cried out, balling her fists and pressing them to her cheeks. "Mal!"

But he didn't answer, battling the plane and the low winds that buffeted them up and down and to both sides. The treetops were close—way too close—but he shoved the throttle all the way forward, and the engine sputtered and choked, then the whine of the propeller changed pitch, as if it were slowing down.

She opened her eyes, squinting into the wind to see where they were headed. The tree line. They had to get over that tree line and pray there was a field beyond it.

If not…

The engine sounds deepened and slowed, and the plane dropped a little more. They were not going to make it. They were going to hit the trees and flip this plane and crash and burn.

"No, Mal, no! We're not going to make it!"

"Oh yes we *are*." She could hear him battle the stick, yanking it from side to side, fighting the tilt of the plane as he tried to work the dying machine over the trees.

They weren't going to make it. They were going down fast. Chessie closed her eyes and tried to say her mental good-byes, working to conjure up images of her parents, her brothers and sister, Nino and…

Mal.

Behind her, he swore mightily, losing the fight to gravity as the propeller snapped the top of the trees.

It was him she'd miss. The chance with him. The possibility of him. Damn it, she'd just found him, and now they were—

"Got it, you son of a bitch!" He glided over the last of the tree line, powered by wind and momentum and…hope.

The ground rushed toward them, the shadows of the field below flying by, coming up, meeting them…with a thud and bump. Her teeth cracked together, and her bones felt like they'd slammed into each other. They rocked and tipped and bounced over the ground and finally came to a stop.

Chessie didn't let out the breath she'd been holding until Mal grabbed her shoulders and turned her around.

"Hell, yeah, Francesca. We made it."

She shuddered out a sigh and reached for his face, closing her hands on his cheeks as relief and affection and joy ricocheted through her body with the same force as the landing.

"We could make it, you know." The words tumbled out of her mouth, fueled by adrenaline and the brush with death. "We could beat all the odds." She pulled him close and kissed him without even trying to hide how she felt about him.

She couldn't let go. Couldn't stop kissing and touching and giving in to the words that bubbled up like a pent-up volcanic eruption. "We're so good together, Mal. We're special. We're a team. I never met anyone like you. I want you to—"

His hand pressed on her mouth, sweaty and strong and silencing. "Stop," he said gruffly.

She blinked at him, and he slowly dropped his hand. "I don't want to stop," she whispered. "I want to tell you how I feel."

He gave a sharp shake of his head. "You're just…it's just…near death."

"Yeah," she agreed. "Nothing like a brush with mortality to make you realize how you feel about someone."

He just stared at her, silent. His eyes looked longing, but a frown creased his forehead, and his jaw was set in a way that told her he was working hard not to say a word.

"Mal…" She was still catching her breath from the rough landing, and her voice cracked. "Can you really look me in the eyes and tell me this…this…thing we feel is absolutely and truly hopeless?"

She counted her heartbeats, thumping so hard they echoed from her chest to her brain, waiting for his answer.

"Can you?" she whispered as hope slipped away with each passing second.

"Yes. Let's go. We have a long walk."

He climbed out of the cockpit, and she sat perfectly still for a long moment, letting the sadness and pain hit her heart. They did crash and burn, after all.

Chapter Twenty-Five

Of course it was hopeless. Irrevocably hopeless. The truth of that slammed at Mal's heart and head with the same intensity his feet slammed against the muddy field they crossed on the long, mosquito-infested, two-mile walk to the outskirts of El Sal.

Neither one of them spoke, since a bug flew into Chessie's mouth the minute she'd opened it. So they trudged along in silence, with her confession hanging in the air as thick as the Cuban humidity, making them both sweaty and uncomfortable.

We could make it, you know. We could beat all the odds. We're so good together, Mal.

Could they? Did he dare even think that he could—

A bug bit his neck, and he slapped at it a little too hard.

Of course not.

"Why are you so opposed to happiness?" she asked, obviously willing to risk swallowing a mosquito to psychoanalyze him. "And if you say 'define happiness,' you'll eat my fist instead of a bug."

He fought a smile because…because shit. She made him smile. And that was the fucking problem. "I'm not opposed to happiness."

"Oh, it's just me you're opposed to?"

He closed his eyes and slowed down, kicking a little mud in frustration. "I'm not *opposed* to you, Chessie."

"But you don't want to take a chance on anyone who might make you happy."

He looked skyward, wishing like hell they could talk about the blanket of stars and how they looked pink and how the whole Milky Way was visible out here. But no, they had to talk about his *happiness*.

"I wasn't born into it, like you were."

"And this is, what, Medieval England, and you can't change your stature in life? People have shitty childhoods and grow up to let go of that and make a better one for their kids."

"*Kids*?" The word popped out before he could manage to just think and not say it.

"I don't mean *ours*," she said, and he could hear the disappointment in her voice. Or was that in his own head? "I'm speaking…hypothetically. Ew. Pfffft." She turned away and spit. "Gross."

Spitting out a bug or the idea of kids with him?

"Why don't you try?" she asked. "Why don't you try to find happiness?"

"How do you know I haven't?" he fired back.

"But you do know that my brother has a business helping people who are in precisely the situation you're in, right?"

"I know what Gabe does."

"Then why not use his services? Why not have him get you a new ID and a new life? Disappear if you have to. Get away from this Roger Drummand guy who has it out for you. Start over and…and…"

He waited, half dreading, half aching to hear what she'd say next.

"Find someone," she finished.

I found someone. I'm walking next to her. I'm half in love with her.

Holy, holy hell. He was in trouble. "It's not that simple," he said. "Gabe helps people hide from bad guys. I'm hiding from the good guys."

She blew out a frustrated breath. "Yeah, well, they don't sound so good to me."

"They aren't all good."

"*Could* you ever have a normal life? You know, not look over your shoulder? Not be on the CIA shit list? Could you ever…"

He stopped walking for a second and turned to her. The need to set her straight welled up in him. "Logistically? Technically? Physically? Yeah, there is probably a way for me to live a little less on the edge of doom, and maybe Drummand will outgrow his hate-on for me, and maybe I could find a place where I'm someone else, doing something else, even though I'd really rather just be me doing what I was trained to do."

It was her turn to stare at him, mouth closed, but eyes wide as she waited for what he had to say.

"But I can't just…love someone."

Her mouth opened, dropped into an O of disbelief. He closed it for her, touching her chin and making sure she didn't eat any more bugs.

"You want to know why?"

She nodded, her eyes just a little bit damp, which scared him and touched him and kind of amazed him. Did she really care that much?

"I can't really tell you why. I just know that I'm not meant for that. Every time I've given a person a chance, they screwed me over. Starting with my mother, who spent my childhood screwing me over, and a couple other women here and there, and even Alana…"

"So you *were* romantically attached to her," she said.

"No." He shook his head. "I swear, we were friends, but even that friendship, she used me, and then…" He turned, looking toward the distant lights of the town of El Salvador. "She had to have kept the money. She was the only person who knew where it was in the first place. And that's made my life even shittier."

"While we're there, why don't you ask her about it?"

He shrugged. "She'll just deny it. And what am I going to do? Implicate her? I served my time, and I saved her kids."

She reached for his arm. "And that amazes me," she said. "So why don't you save yourself?"

And ruin her life? "I wouldn't even know how to settle down, Chessie. I know what your plan is, and I'm not the man for you. I'll always have a record. I'll always be an embezzler. That's not what you want, is it? A guy who's done time at Allenwood?"

Her eyes flashed hot in the moonlight. "Can't I be the one to decide that? Can't I know whether or not that bothers me?"

"It has to bother you," he insisted. "In your perfect family of law-abiding, crime-fighting, good-doing heroes, you want to drag an ex-con who did time for stealing half a million from the US government to Christmas dinner?"

When she didn't answer, he nodded, hard, and gave her a nudge to keep walking. "I didn't think so."

"But I know the truth! You didn't do it. You took the blame to help her." She marched next to him, her white high-top sneakers caked in mud and splashing more with each angry step. "It's so damn unfair!"

"I've accepted the unfairness of it."

"Not that! I could fix that. I could prove you're innocent, and you know what? It wouldn't matter."

"It would matter. It would mean I spent four years of my life in vain. She still has kids. They'd still be taken from her."

"Oh please." Disgust darkened her voice. "You could be cleared of everything and free to have lunch with the freaking president of the United States, and you'd come up with some bogus reason why you're all wrong for me, because, you know what, Mal?"

He had a feeling she was about to tell him.

"You're *afraid* of love. You're *terrified* of the real thing. You don't think you're worthy of it, so you build some kind of wall and move every four months and do undercover work that keeps you from being real, because you're just so damn scared of someone leaving you or hurting you."

He just closed his eyes and huffed out a breath. "I'm not having this fight here. We have to—"

"Find that kid and get home," she finished. "I can't get away from you fast enough."

The announcement smacked him, so far from what he was feeling and how she looked. "That's the adrenaline dump talking," he said.

"It's my *heart* talking," she shot back, walking so fast now he had to work to keep up with her. "My bruised and lonely and really stupid heart that picks the wrong guy over and over again. Like I can fix him or something and make him…not quit."

"Not quit?" The indictment stabbed like a steely knife.

"Yeah. You know my plan? My silly, 1950s innocent life plan? It requires a man who doesn't give up when the going gets tough."

"Is that what you think I am?" he asked, his gut burning. "A quitter?"

"You're giving up on your life and happiness before you even have it, so yeah. And I don't like that. I don't like you."

Somehow, they'd gone from *we can make this work* to...*I don't like you.*

"Which is exactly the rule we set, remember?" he reminded her.

"I remember. Like it was yesterday. Come to think of it, it practically was. Come on, let's move it. I want to find my nephew and get home."

Her shoulders hunched, her head down, her hair falling in her face, Chessie walked on like a prisoner who had...no hope.

Taking that from her was his worst crime. He was innocent of embezzlement. But he was one hundred percent guilty of stealing all the light, hope, and heart from Francesca Rossi.

And he hated himself even more for that.

The tension between them stretched like a steel wire that could snap at any second.

Chessie stayed perfectly silent, focused on the plan of the moment: find that child. She could be on a plane tomorrow morning.

Her little hopeless interlude end in failure, but the mission would not.

She peered into the blackness, following the beam of Mal's flashlight.

Alana Cevallos lived in a small house tucked into dense woods at the end of a dirt road. Mal scanned the place with the small light that highlighted a well-kept front yard and a recently painted home that had a welcoming feel, except for the utter blackness of everything.

"This whole freaking island is dark," Chessie said. "It's like the land of blackness."

"True enough," he agreed.

"Wouldn't there be a light on somewhere? It's only nine or ten o'clock."

Mal didn't answer, his eyes narrowing as he looked around. "Yeah, I've been here this late before, and she had working electricity, and there'd been plenty of activity in the house."

Working electricity, which Chessie now knew was not always the case in rural Cuba. Did Alana Cevallos have some special deal? Or…a lot of money? Money that was "never recovered"?

"I want you to wait out here, over there." Mal aimed the light to a clearing about fifty feet from the house. "I don't know what I'm going to find when I get there."

"I have a better idea," she said. "If this somebody who's following you is in there and I knock on the door, he won't know me. I'll say I'm lost or my car broke down or something. If he's not, I'll tell her that I'm with you."

He cut her with a look. "Not a better idea. A really dumb idea. Whoever it is knows we're together. You're going to stay hidden. With this." He held out the gun to her, barrel down. "You know how to use it?"

"In my family? That comes before riding a bike, but you need it. I'll stay out of sight, I swear."

He moved suddenly, turning toward the road, and a second later, Chessie saw a beam of headlights and heard the hum of an engine. A sizable engine, possibly a truck.

"Someone's turning in." Mal gave her a solid nudge to the side, making her take the gun. "Hide in the bushes back there. Stay there until I tell you."

"Mal, I—"

"Holy shit," he murmured, staring at the double headlights turning into the drive. "That's a Gitmo van. Go." He gave her a gentle push. "Hide and stay out of sight, no matter what you see or hear."

She didn't hesitate, darting away before she got caught in the lights. She practically dove into a thicket of bushes, not caring that they scratched as she found a place where she wouldn't be seen. She squinted through the darkness at Mal's shadow, watching him hang just outside the beam of light as the van approached and stopped. The door popped open, and Chessie instantly raised the gun, ready to shoot to defend Mal.

But the woman who climbed out of the driver's seat didn't look like she'd hurt anyone. Small, wiry, with enough wear on her forty-some-year-old face that it was clear she'd been through plenty of hell but had landed on her feet.

"Alana," Mal said, making no move toward her. "Where are the kids? What are you doing in a detainee van?"

"Malcolm." Alana didn't exactly exclaim his name, more like exhale it in sheer frustration. She muttered something in Spanish. Then, "My car was taken away by the government. They are still watching me, Mal." She spoke accented English, crossing her arms and shrinking back in a little as he approached her. "Sorry. I'm sorry."

Chessie didn't know the woman, and she had to remember she wasn't speaking her native language, but she didn't sound sorry.

"Where are the kids?" he repeated, more edge in his voice.

"My mother has them because I had to work late." She sounded scared. Tentative. Mal moved one step closer, cautiously, it seemed, as if he sensed the same thing.

Of course! The little boy. She probably guessed that's why he was here and felt protective about him. Chessie wanted to just come forward and tell her story, explain who she was and see the child. But she'd promised Mal she wouldn't, so she hung back and listened.

"I need some information, Alana. And I need it now."

"I…I…can't do this." She looked from one side to another, her voice cracking. At the sound, Chessie's heart did the same thing. *She's not going to give him up.*

"I'm not asking you to do anything."

"But he is," she hissed in a whisper.

"Who?"

Chessie cursed the sudden uptick of her heart and the pulse in her ears. She wanted to hear this.

Alana walked toward the house, muttering. "It's not enough that you went to prison," Chessie caught her saying. "Not enough that you protected me when I needed it the most."

Mal turned and signaled to Chessie to stay, then followed. "Alana, I understand you adopted an orphan."

Alana slowed, glancing back at Mal with a strange look. Guilt? Surprise? Chessie couldn't tell from this distance.

"Isadora Winter's child?" he prompted.

She let out a long, slow sigh. "He is over there now, in the field." She pointed to the bushes, not far from where Chessie stood, then pivoted and walked into the house.

Mal froze for one second, then he asked, "What?" as if he couldn't believe what he'd just heard.

"Come in here. I'll tell you." And he stepped inside, the door closing behind him.

Chessie looked at the wide-open area free of bushes or shrubs about twenty feet away. No structure, no place for a child. What was…in that field?

Deep inside her, somewhere dark and shadowy and sad, Chessie knew. But she walked there anyway, slowly, with the pistol at the ready.

Once there, she could barely make out anything in the dim light, just about eight or nine large rocks, evenly spaced, slightly off the ground.

Oh no, they weren't rocks…they were grave markers.

"No." The word slipped out of her mouth as she rushed closer, all thought of staying hidden forgotten as the very real possibility of what *in the field* meant slammed her heart.

No, it couldn't be. It *couldn't* be.

"No!" She practically flung herself on the first stone, flattening her hand on the name and moaning in relief.

Jorge Mario Cevallos 14 octubre 1967—3 abril 2009

Her husband? A brother? It didn't matter. It wasn't him.

She leapt to the next stone and squinted at the name.

Roberto Jesus Cevallos 21 agosto, 1943—15 diciembre 1993

Older, maybe that was Alana's father. There were only six more stones. Six more.

She moved a little more slowly to the next one.

Elia Maria Cevallos 14 junio 1945—29 marzo 1995

A tendril of hope wrapped around her heart as she crawled on her knees to the next one. She had to have misunderstood. He couldn't be…

She just stared at the words carved into the stone as another set of chills tumbled over her. Her breath caught as she tried to inhale, her heart beating too wildly for her to get any air.

Gabriel Rafael Rossi Winter Cevallos 29 junio 2011—7 febrero 2013

Rossi. She stared at the added middle name, one that

wasn't in the municipal records. One that eliminated any need for testing. One that shattered her heart.

It wouldn't compute. It just wouldn't process. He was *dead*?

"No," she whispered, shaking her head, fighting tears that did not want to be held back. Her nephew had been born and died before she ever had a chance to hold him. She tried to get to her feet, wanted to run to Mal, to tell him and be comforted.

But nothing could comfort her now. Nothing. He was dead. How…*how* could she ever tell Gabe?

She pushed herself flat on the ground and dropped the pistol so she could cradle the little stone in her arms and cry.

It was the closest she'd ever come to holding this lost member of her family.

Chapter Twenty-Six

Mal knew what was *in the field*. The family graveyard where a few generations of Cevallos members were buried. He stared at Alana, waiting for more, refusing to accept what she was telling him.

"I'm sorry you came all this way to find him, Mal," Alana said again. "And I'm sorry you have to break the news to Gabe."

Not to mention Gabe's sister, who was outside, in the dark, about to have her heart ripped out of her chest.

Alana crossed her arms, still tense and flustered, it seemed, at the sight of him. Usually a pretty cool cucumber and brimming with nurturing empathy, this Alana looked like she was wired for sound and ready to pop.

Something was definitely up.

Mal stole a glance toward a front window, but saw nothing in the shadows. He trusted Chessie to stay put, but not for long. First, he had to get more information for her. And for Gabe. He couldn't leave Alana's tonight without everything he'd come to Cuba to get…except for the child.

He obviously wasn't leaving with DNA samples.

"What happened?" he asked.

"He got ill. Very ill." She looked from one side to

another, as if expecting someone to jump out at any second. "A high fever and…would you like to see a picture of him?"

"Yes." Gabe would like that. That would help, wouldn't it? At least it was something rather than nothing.

"It's in my room." She started to turn, then gave him another look. "I'm really sorry," she added. "I wish it didn't have to be this way. I hope you believe me."

Why wouldn't he? Something in her voice didn't sound right. He angled his head, looking hard at this woman he'd once known so well and cared about. But he couldn't forget…she had stolen a lot of money. Money that disappeared. She couldn't be all good.

"How did you get the boy, anyway?"

"Nestor Ramos is my friend," she said.

"Who runs the school."

"And he gets children to the States, you know. Or into good Cuban homes."

"So she was trying to get the child to the US?"

"Of course! But then Isadora…" She shook her head. "It was a terrible accident, Mal. So young."

"And you took her son." Which made sense. She loved children, and he recalled Alana and Isadora were friends. "What about…the father?"

He wasn't sure if she knew about Isadora and Gabe. Their relationship had been a secret, but if she and Isa were friends.

"She never told me who the father was," she said. "So, yes, I adopted Rafael and…" She stepped away. "I'll go get the picture."

While he waited, he leaned out to check outside, scanning what he could see of the property for any movement. "How old was he when he died?"

For a long moment, she didn't answer, and Mal stood

straight, cocking his ear toward her bedroom door, waiting for the answer. "Alana?"

"Not yet two," she finally said.

"What kind of illness did he have?"

Again, he waited a good thirty seconds for the answer. Then he heard a click. A familiar click. A click that sounded like…

The sound of a safety being thumbed. What the hell?

He bolted toward her door, but something caught his eye outside. A movement, someone walking. Chessie? Of course, she'd come to check on him, but if Alana had a—

"You're coming with me to Gitmo."

He whipped around to stare at a SIG P229, a CIA-issued weapon he'd seen all over the prison.

"I need you to come with me," she said again, her hand shaking ever so slightly.

Mal stayed very still, thinking through his options. She didn't seem to know Chessie was outside, but that didn't help him if she came bursting in here and Alana shot her.

He could jump her and get the gun, but she seemed nervous enough to shoot. He had to relax her. Talk her down.

"Not to sound like a cliché or anything, but after all I've done for you, Alana? This isn't a very nice thank-you."

She swallowed hard. "I'm not very nice."

"Then you've changed." Maybe Drummand had beat him here, after all. "What happened in the past five years?" Or five hours?

"I need you to do something for me."

"I think I've proven I have a difficult time saying no when you're in a bind."

"Go with me to Gitmo." She nodded to the door. "You

can hide in the back of the van, and I'll get you in. No one will stop me."

Hide in the detainee hot box? Hell no. He'd shoved enough terrorists in that space to know it was airless and small and not happening tonight.

"I'm not going anywhere until you tell me why you're doing this."

"For my kids," she whispered, her voice cracking.

He scowled at her, shaking his head. "What the hell is going on, Alana?"

"You have to come with me to Guantanamo, Mal. It's the only way I'll ever see them again. Please come with me."

"Why?" he demanded.

"Because Roger Drummand is going to kill my kids if you don't help me move the five hundred thousand dollars that's in an account that only you can access back into his."

Nothing about that made sense. "That I can access?"

"The money isn't lost, Mal. I was waiting until you got out of prison to tell you where it was and how to get it. Remember they installed that biometric scanner at the prison? I had your fingerprint on file and used it. No one can ever get that money but you. Especially Drummand. He can never get it back into his account."

"*Back* into his?" But as soon as he asked the question, the answer was obvious. "He stole the money."

She sighed, visibly pained. "He did and made it look like I did it to save his ass. And you saved mine."

"And by default, his." He practically choked the words as rage rocked his whole body. "Why didn't you tell me, Alana? I didn't go to prison for him, damn it."

"No, but I would have gone if you hadn't." She blinked back tears in her dark eyes.

"And you put the money into an account in my name?"

"He didn't want to touch it because he knew there'd be an investigation, so when you helped me, I decided to move it. I thought, well, they think you stole it anyway, so if they ever found the money, it would not make any difference. And if they didn't, then you could do what you want with it. Return it, if I know you. Or use it to build a new life." Her eyes shuttered in agony and guilt. "I owe you so much."

But not half a million dollars that belonged to the US government.

"He knows about the account now," Alana said. "And he wants the money, which is why he wanted me to get you here."

"Sorry. I'm not going to help either one of you."

She lifted the gun and aimed it right at his heart. "You know I'll do anything for my kids."

"Alana, give me the gun."

She stared him down. "Do as I ask."

"Give me the gun."

She took one slow breath, her nostrils quivering, and lifted the pistol higher. Mal lunged just as the shot went off.

Chessie jerked up at the sound of a gunshot, pushing herself up from the ground with Mal's name on her lips.

"He's too much trouble." A man grabbed her from behind, wrenching her hair and snapping her whole body into his chest. "But you'll do."

In the house, she could hear a woman screaming. Someone had been shot. Mal!

Chessie's whimper turned into a holler for help, but the

hard stab of a pistol in her side silenced her as the man dragged her away from the field.

She tried to look over her shoulder to the house, but he had her twisted in the other direction, her feet stumbling to keep up with him.

"Stop it!" She jerked her arm, risking a shot to pivot again. She opened her mouth to call out, but he whacked her head with the side of the pistol.

"Move it, or you'll both be in that graveyard."

She squinted into the blurry darkness, realizing her glasses had fallen off when she'd been crying. Her glasses…were with the gun Mal gave her.

A rookie mistake. A wave of fury and frustration rolled over her, momentarily blocking out any chance to reason. But she had to think. Think, think, *think*!

He threw her forward and shoved the gun in her back. "Faster or you're dead. And no one will ever find you out here, Francesca. Your country can hardly come looking for a documentary producer who doesn't exist."

He knew her name? And her cover?

"Who are you?" She took a chance on another look at him, getting a quick, unclear glimpse of thin, light hair and narrowed eyes. "What do you want with me?"

"Just your brain and fingers." He shoved her toward a dark compact car hidden near the end of the drive, yanking the driver's door. "Get in and drive."

She didn't move.

He pushed her into the seat and slammed the door, pointing the gun at her head while he hustled around to the passenger side. Damn it, why was she just sitting there while Mal was shot? She feared a bullet?

Mal could be dead!

She smashed her hand on the ignition, feeling for keys.

None. As he reached the passenger side, she grabbed for the door handle, but he was in and pointing the gun at her before she could escape.

At least now she could see him. See his beady eyes and pock-marked face. So this was the son of a bitch trailing Mal.

She couldn't show fear. Hadn't she learned that from everyone in her family? What good were all those damn family dinners if she hadn't picked up a single tip on What To Do When Kidnapped in the Field?

"Where to, Rog?" she asked, purposely cocky.

He flinched a little, then glared at her. "I guess I shouldn't be surprised."

"By what?"

"That Gabriel Rossi's sister would be a pain in the ass, too."

"It's a family curse."

He lifted the gun to her temple, any trace of amusement gone from his scarred face. "Drive where I tell you, or I'll kill you. It's very simple."

"If I drive without my glasses, I might kill us both."

"I'll tell you where to go. Drive."

She twisted the key hanging from the ignition and switched on the headlights—at least this Hyundai had them—and then she squeezed the steering wheel with raw determination.

She could do this. She could get out of this. She had no idea how, but damn it, she would.

Chapter Twenty-Seven

Alana kept screaming like she'd fired a bullet right into Mal's heart. Fortunately, he'd knocked the gun from her hand before she had. But the bullet had taken a bite out of his shoulder, sending white-hot waves of pain to his brain.

"Shut up," Mal ordered, grabbing the weapon when she dropped it. "We're going outside."

"To the prison, Mal, please! I am so sorry I shot you, but—"

He yanked her toward the door, half expecting it to fly open any second. There was no way Chessie would stay put after hearing a gunshot, and he wouldn't want her to. Trained or not, instinct would kick in, and she'd be here in…

Why wasn't she here? He'd expect her to ignore his orders now. "You have a computer here, Alana?"

"No. At work."

"Then we'll drive to the plane and get the one we left there. Chessie can fix this." If she didn't hate him too much.

"She is a nurse?"

"Better." He kept a good grip on Alana as he opened the door. Drummand had stolen the money! And if they could trace the original stolen funds, they could prove that.

Chessie could prove that. So where the hell was she?

And then he knew. She'd gone to the field. She'd heard Alana say where he was and…damn it. He wasn't there to comfort her. Giving up on dragging Alana, he jogged toward the bushes where he'd left her.

"Chessie?" he called, the pain in his body suddenly numbed by concern. "Are you out here?"

He rounded the bushes and peered into the darkness of the tiny family graveyard that he'd often visited with the Cevallos kids. But she wasn't there.

"Chessie?" He pulled the small flashlight from his pocket, shining the beam on the half-dozen little stones, catching a reflection of glass on the ground.

His heart dropped as he walked closer, turning the light to illuminate the names and dates of members of Alana's family.

And then he found the glass. No, *glasses*. And next to that, the pistol he'd given her. They rested against a stone that read *Gabriel Rafael Rossi Winter Cevallos 29 junio 2011—7 febrero 2013.*

He scooped up the glasses and gun, his worst fears realized. "Someone took her. He took her."

"It was Drummand," Alana said, running toward him. "He probably followed me here. He wants you. He wants the money, Mal. He's desperate."

He just stared at her, putting it all together. He pointed the pistol at the detainee van. "Let's go. I'll hide in the hot box, and you drive like your life depends on it, Alana, because it does."

"I will, I will, Mal." She reached for him, tears streaking her face. "I am scared for my children. And you helped me once."

"Don't let those morons at the gate stop you." He swung

open the back door and climbed into the tiny box where they stashed detainees when they'd moved them around the prison. He folded himself in half to fit.

His arm stung like hell, but what hurt the most was his heart. He wasn't going to quit until he found her, saved her, and told her she was right about everything. He held on to her glasses in one hand, the gun in the other, and closed his eyes.

In the dark, dank box, bleeding and sweating and clunking along the rutted road, all Mal could think about was hope.

Define hope, his brain screamed.

Hope was Francesca Rossi at his side. Hope was happiness, and they were all intertwined. He just had to keep himself—and her—alive long enough to share that.

She needed a plan.

Well, she needed her glasses more than anything, but as Chessie drove the little car down a deserted road for what felt like forever, she was certain she could ignore her pounding headache if she had a plan of attack.

Only, she had nothing but a gun in her side and a blur in her line of vision.

"So you know my brother," she said conversationally, hoping to distract him.

"He worked for me."

Really. "Yeah, I heard you were a dick."

"You heard right. Shut up and drive."

After that, he was dead silent, except for his heavy breathing, dividing his attention between her and the road, speaking only to warn her of an oncoming truck, which even a blind woman could see.

She stole another look at the man next to her, a hundred questions bouncing around in her head. She might not escape, but she could ferret out some information that could help her when they got to wherever they were going. *If* she didn't accidentally drive them into a tree before then.

"So why do you hate Mal so much? He really is a nice guy, you know."

He slammed her with a dirty look. "Is your whole fucking family like this?"

"Way worse. My cousin Zach? A one-eyed monster."

After a minute, he shifted in his seat. "I don't hate him."

She snorted. "You want him in jail or dead. You send people after him to bug his hotel rooms. You have him looking over his shoulder every minute so he can't live a normal life." She fired a look at him. "Sounds hateful."

"Watch the road."

"I can't *see* the road."

"Pothole ahead."

"Welcome to rural Cuba," she said, the echo of Mal's words and dry attitude making her chest pang with how much she wanted to see him again.

She avoided the deep rut at the last second, seeing little more than a dark spot in the headlight beam. What would happen if the little car fell into one of those holes? That might work as a plan. At least it would delay things and require help.

Or he'd shoot her and run.

"Mal has something I want," he said. "And with your help, I'm going to get it."

Something he wanted. She thought about that like a line of unfinished code, filling in the ones and zeros for an answer. Which, honestly, wasn't that hard to figure out. "Money."

She felt him look hard at her, but he didn't answer. Instead, he gestured toward the road. "Watch out for that one!"

She drove straight toward the massive pothole, gritting her teeth for the impact, but Drummand swung the wheel at the last minute and they missed. Shit.

He jabbed her side with the gun. "Don't fuck with me, Francesca. I have no qualms about killing you in Alana Cevallos's car on the side of the road. Nothing would happen to me, and she'd suffer the consequences."

And her kids would be orphans—the very thing Mal gave up four years of his life to avoid.

She glanced in the rearview when something flashed, catching the headlights of another vehicle behind them. Maybe she could intentionally have an accident?

"Where are you taking me?" she demanded.

"A place we call Gitmo."

She was going to Guantanamo Bay? "Why?"

"So you can do what you do, Francesca. Hack into a computer and move some funds back to where they belong."

The car—no, a truck—was catching up, going at least ten miles an hour faster, but she couldn't see well enough to really judge how close it was. Maybe if she went really slowly, he'd pass, and she could swing out and cause a collision.

Her side of the car would take the worst of that hit. Still, it was something. She lifted her foot off the accelerator very slowly, praying Drummand wouldn't notice. A little more. The truck gained on them.

She didn't dare hit the brakes—he'd know exactly what she was doing. She had to distract him.

"What funds? Move them from where?"

"My funds. Mal Harris's account."

She was off the gas completely now. "What?"

"It would be better if he did it with his fingerprint, his password, but that won't prevent you from getting my money, will it?"

"*Your* money? It belongs to the government." Maybe if the truck hit them from behind… She had to keep Drummand thinking about something else. "And, as I understand it, that money was never found. It can't be in Mal's account. Wouldn't it have been recovered then?"

"Oh, we found it," he said, a certain smugness in his voice. "Alana did her good deed and tried to pay him back for covering for me, but—hey!"

She hit the brakes as the truck behind them barreled closer. She braced for impact or the shot, whichever came first, but somehow the driver behind her veered sharply to the left and missed them. Drummand grabbed the wheel again, jerking it to the right and making her wrestle for control. The back spun one way, then the other, rolling into a gully off the road while the truck disappeared ahead of them.

"Damn it!" he screamed when they came to a stop, a good four feet lower than where they'd been. "What the fuck are you trying to prove?"

She blinked at him, the impact of the near miss hitting her brain almost as hard as his words. The ones spoken *before* the accident.

"Covering for *you*?" she asked in a hushed whisper. "*Alana* didn't steal the money?"

"Of course not. She came in handy when I needed your hero Mal to take the blame. And now I need everyone to stop fucking around so I can get the money and fork it over to someone who's threatening to ruin my life." He looked around, carefully keeping the gun on her. "Now what the hell are we going to do?"

So he was being blackmailed. And he was desperate.

And then…her head cleared. Cleared and made way for a plan. Finally.

He wanted her to get into this bank account he thought was Mal's and move the money. And until she did, he wouldn't kill her. Even better, once she found the account…she might be able to clear Mal's name.

That was a good plan. A great plan. Now she had to act, and she'd better nail the part.

Slowly she turned to him and lifted a brow. "I'll drive if you push."

"How stupid do you think I am?"

He only had to be stupid enough to let her hack bank accounts that could possible prove *he* was the embezzler, not Mal. And Mal could have his life back.

"Listen to me." She cocked her head, channeling her inner badass, which, up until this week, she didn't even know she had. "Let's make a deal, Rog."

Silent, he eyed her suspiciously.

"You need my services, pretty bad, as I understand it."

His beady eyes narrowed even more, but he stayed quiet.

"And I need money. Let's say…" How much would be enough to get him to say yes and trust her? "Ten thousand." Before he could argue, she put her hand on his arm, hating the touch, but praying it could work. "Ten thousand transferred to my bank account, the rest to yours."

Very slowly, he shook his head. "I don't believe you. You're fucking his lights out."

Lovely. She gave a light laugh that was pure hope and great acting. "Rog." She gave a put-upon sigh. "Do you really think I'm working for nothing? You really think I'm traipsing all over Cuba and spreading my legs every time he snaps his fingers because I need a good time?"

He just stared at her, definitely off-balance with this.

"That guy has been hiding cash for years. My brother told me all about it, and the day Mal Harris was out of prison, I went for him. You think we were in that airport together by accident? I knew he was coming to see my brother, and I zeroed right in on that poor deprived horn dog and played him like a fiddle."

Okay, a little heavy on the clichés, but as his suspicious look morphed into admiration, Chessie powered on to close the deal.

"But now?" She *pffft* a disgusted breath. "Who needs him? We could be a good team."

She stared at him, waiting. It felt like those suspended seconds when she'd type in a password and pray that it would work. When he didn't respond, she tried one more time, tipping her head toward the back of the car. "You want to drive or push?"

"I'll drive. You can't get far on foot."

"I'm going as far as the money, honey." She reached for the door handle and opened it gingerly, half expecting to be shot. But he let her get out. She checked out the ground, which, thankfully, wasn't muddy. She could push this car for Mal, couldn't she?

She walked to the back of the car and watched Drummand maneuver his body into the driver's seat. As she did, another vehicle came roaring toward them, easily doing ninety.

She looked up as it passed, and when she got a glimpse of the white van, her heart dropped as hard as the car had into the ditch. That was the van Alana Cevallos had driven to her house. The detainee van. It was headed back to Guantanamo.

Mal was in that van. Alive and looking for her. She had to believe that.

She put her hands on the hatchback of the little Hyundai and gave a nod to Drummand, her new partner in crime. He revved the engine, and she pushed so hard her brain almost popped out.

Mal was on his way to Gitmo. He could die doing that—and he'd be doing it for her. She could do this for him. She would do anything for him.

Chapter Twenty-Eight

The wound in Mal's shoulder had him drifting in and out of reality. Images of Drummand and Chessie darkened his mind. A flash of a gravestone made things worse. His arm burned and his head throbbed with each crevice and rut the van clunked over.

And then he could smell Gitmo. At least, he recognized the scent of oily chicken and burned pizza, telling him they were on the two-mile avenue lined with fast-food joints that led to the main entrance.

He could remember the road clearly. They were probably passing the Navy Lodge Hotel with that pit of a bar called Windjammer. Or Cockjammer. Gabe used to call it that because of the distinct lack of women inside. Then the Navy Exchange. Walmart for sailors.

It was like Little America in the heart of Cuba, flanked by guard towers manned by some of the best snipers in the business. Not American snipers—Castro's snipers, making sure none of the locals made it over the "border" and got into Gitmo safely.

The van slowed, he figured because they approached the main shack, an aluminum deal that used to be armed with rotating National Guardsmen armed with M16s and a few nine-millimeter pistols. Was it still? And would they search the van or let it through? Back in the day, they'd have searched.

But now, Gitmo was essentially a holding tank. And he had to hope they didn't care about a secretary coming back to her office.

Sweat trickled down his temples and stung his eyes. It had to be a hundred degrees, even at night, in his hot box, but it wasn't the heat or the pain of a bullet graze that had Mal sweating.

He was a convicted embezzler who, anyone who worked here believed, had siphoned off half a million dollars from the US government. Shoot on sight? Maybe not, but they'd throw his ass in a cell for trespassing a place he had no clearance to be.

But Mal didn't care. He had to find Chessie.

If that asshole hurt her, if he so much as touched a hair on her head… Mal squeezed her glasses, still clutched in his hand, as the van came to a stop. He had to give them to her and hold her again. He had to do whatever was necessary to save her and…keep her.

Maybe he would let Gabe make up a new life for him. But she'd need one, too. And they'd have to live far from her family, and she would never do that.

Not even for him.

Maybe for him.

Had he lost his mind?

Though surrounded by metal, he could hear the exchange between Alana and the guard. A gruff, unfriendly man asking typical questions even though he had to know her. And Alana answering, light and quick, lying like a pro he knew she was. Not CIA, but damn good…unless her kids were in physical danger. Then she crumbled.

Finally, the van moved, and he closed his eyes, remembering the layout of the employee parking lot. She drove north, toward the admin offices. Camp Delta was off to the east, nearly empty now. He knew every cell in the place.

Camp No was just outside the northern perimeter, but still on American soil. In there was the CIA facility commonly known as Penny Lane, where so much torture had taken place. And beyond that, in the darkest, farthest corner of the deepest secret in Gitmo, was the small group of cells he had guarded in his undercover role, where Gabe had lured terrorists to the other side, and where Roger Drummand had called the shots.

The van came to a halt, sudden and sharp, jerking his shoulder right into the iron wall that surrounded him. He sucked in a breath and touched the dried blood stuck to the wound. He was probably covered in blood, which made him hope to hell no one was around when he tried to get into wherever the hell she was taking him.

Hurry, Alana.

As if she'd read his mind, the back door of the van lifted up with a squeak, and she opened the hot box.

"I came around to the far side of admin," she said. "No one is here, and I can get in the back door."

He urged her toward the building. "Come on. I'm a blood-covered sitting duck out here. Where will he go?"

"My office."

"And he'll take Chessie there, because he probably knows damned well she has the ability to hack into a bank account."

"She doesn't have your fingerprint or password."

"She doesn't need either one." They entered a dimly lit hall, a good fifty feet of offices away from the admin headquarters where Alana worked.

At the door of a kitchenette he gave her a nudge inside. "You're staying here," he told her, starting off.

"Mal! Wait!" She ripped a corner of a paper towel hanging on the wall and grabbed a pen from a cup on the counter. "The original account. Drummand's account. If you ever get into it..." She scribbled something on the paper towel and shoved it into his hand. "Here's the password."

He took the paper, then checked to make sure the SIG's safety was off and stuck the Glock from Ramos in the back of his jeans.

"Don't leave this room," he said as he left and headed down the hall, stopping at the door with Alana's name on it. He pressed his ear and listened, hearing nothing. No keys clicking. No talking. No nothing.

Very slowly, he turned the lock and opened the door, his weapon poised to fire.

The room was empty. A tidy office, an empty desk with a computer. He walked around to the screen, tapped a mouse to flicker it to life, picking up the last screen where she must have left it in a hurry.

Place finger on scanner to enter account.

His account? Of course, she'd gotten this far with Drummand and stopped because they needed his fingerprint.

Slowly, he touched his index finger to the small scanner next to the mouse.

Balance $523,694.58

Holy shit.

Could he do something with that money now? Move it? Transfer it to the government? Prove it came from Drummand? With this password Alana gave him, he might be able to.

He slid the tiny corner of paper towel under the edge of the keyboard and—

Suddenly he heard the sound of boots pounding on the linoleum. Guard boots. Instantly, he cleared the screen, just before the door flew open, and Mal was face-to-face with three M16s.

Son of a bitch.

"Drop your weapon," one of the guards demanded.

"And get away from the computer," another man yelled from behind.

No, not another man. Roger Drummand.

Mal slowly lowered his weapon as his gaze met the blue-eyed slits of his nemesis. Where was Chessie? What the hell did he do with her?

"In here, Francesca." Drummand turned, but not before he sent a smug look to Mal, who was already surrounded by the sergeant on patrol and two other men.

"Francesca…" The word slipped out, a little desperate, a lot relieved.

The SOP shifted his attention to Chessie as she came in from the hall a second later, dirt on her face and the beach cover-up, her hair a wild mess, her eyes…hard. Cold. Focused.

"This is my technical assistant," Drummand said to the SOP. "We need some privacy to see what damage this thief has done to the computer system." He nudged Chessie to the computer.

And she practically flounced to the keyboard without so much as a glance to Mal.

"This man needs to be put in a cell," Drummand said. "Immediately."

"Should we take him to Delta?" the SOP asked. "Or medical?"

"Take him to the north block," Drummand said. "First floor."

Camp No. As in *no one knows where it is*, and it would be completely deserted. At least he wasn't going to the third floor for a waterboarding date.

"Yes, sir."

Drummand put a possessive hand on Chessie's shoulder, guiding her into the seat in front of the now darkened computer screen. "Francesca, can you please find that missing file now?"

"Of course," she said, settling into the seat with her fingers on the keyboard.

She turned to glance over her shoulder. "I can find anything." For one millisecond, her eyes grazed Mal, telling him nothing.

Except that she was so damn good in the field, even he might buy this act.

He realized he still held her glasses in his left hand. Reaching out, he offered them to her. "You'll need these. So you can see clearly."

"I can see perfectly." She took them, but their hands brushed in the exchange. At the electric touch, her gaze flicked to his, a millisecond of eye contact, long enough for her to communicate that she had a plan.

But a plan wasn't going to keep her alive. He squirmed as the guards surrounded him and grabbed his arms, preventing him from scooping her up and getting her out of here. Instead, he was led away like a dirty prisoner, powerless to protect the only woman he ever…oh, hell, why fight it? The only woman he ever loved.

Blood. Caked to his T-shirt sleeve. Splattered all over his

chest and stomach. Dripping down his arm and smeared on his face.

Chessie's stomach turned as she remembered how defeated Mal looked, and her heart stuttered with fear at how much blood he'd lost and where they could be taking him to lose even more.

She wanted to scream and throw her arms around him, but this was a mission and she had to play her role or they both would die.

She had to clear his name. Had to.

She picked up her glasses as though his smeared fingerprints were their only connection. She didn't need them to see what she was about to do, but if she had to make a quick getaway, she sure did.

First, she had to find the proof—or create it—that Roger Drummand committed the crime that put Mal in jail, and get that proof into the hands of someone who could, and would, do something about it. Then Mal could be free…for her.

Holy crap, that was a lofty plan and impossible goal under these circumstances. But it had to be done, by her fingertips, on this computer. She had the power now, and she had to use it.

She touched the screen, and while it flickered to life, glanced around the neat office, her gaze falling on a picture of a family. Four kids and a mother. She recognized Alana Cevallos as the woman she'd been spying on in the bushes. Those must be her children. But there were four. Mal had told her Alana had three kids.

One of them must be Gabe's son.

She reached for the photo and brought it closer to look at the smallest child in the photo.

"Oh my God," she whispered. He was a carbon copy of his father. The same blue eyes, the same black hair, the very same mischievous smile and teasing tilt to his head, even though he was maybe a year or fifteen months in this photo.

But now he was dead.

She set the picture down, remembering the pain that the last hour's adventure had numbed. She had to fight through that, and think.

Think, Chessie, think. This is what you do.

But she also made fake deals with criminals and pushed cars out of ditches and jumped on crop dusters and sneaked out of rooms half naked.

They'd been through so much…only to discover little Gabriel Rafael was dead. This mission couldn't be a complete failure. She had to clear Mal's name and kick Drummand's sorry ass to jail in the process. She *had* to.

"What are you waiting for?" Drummand demanded, coming up behind her.

To be alone. "Where's Alana?"

"Never mind. Start working."

"No, not never mind," Chessie shot back. "Mal was in her office, on her computer. She might be hiding because there are men with guns everywhere, but what's to stop her from getting in our way?"

"The fact that I locked her in a janitor's closet."

"Oh, that. Is she okay?"

"What do you care?"

Think, Chessie. "But what if someone comes in here? Anyone. Those guards. What if she makes noise or gets out? Check on her," Chessie demanded. "Make sure no one is in the hall. We don't need a witness, Rog."

He took a slow breath, rattling his nostrils, before he finally turned to step outside. "I'll watch. You work."

He'd have to come around the desk to see what she was

actually typing, but she still wanted him out of the room.

"You can do this, can't you?" he asked when she hesitated.

"Not with you in the room instead of watching out for witnesses."

"You think I'm leaving?"

"Oh, for crying out loud." She flicked her fingers in the air, wishing she could actually hit his face. "You are not dealing with a rookie, Rog."

He shook his head. "A family curse, all right. Hurry up. We don't have much time."

"I'm not putting my fingers on this computer with that door open," she said. "Close it and stand outside. Knock if someone's coming."

At his hesitation, she threw her chair back and her hands in the air. "Fuck it, Rog. Find your own damn money."

The bluff worked. He walked out and closed the door. Chessie brought the screen to life again and started to dig through the bank website.

Bank IP address. Wait and scan. Credits transferred to that IP. Wait and move that information to a file. Find the ACCNO number. Get out of one page and to the next. Save logs. Move them. Delete logs. IP scan.

The door popped open, and she gasped.

"Do you have it yet?" Drummand demanded.

She just glared at him until the bastard backed away. God, this would be fun if her life wasn't on the line. And Mal's.

Refusing to give in to the little squeeze of anxiety that thought caused, she focused on the screen, determined to prove the man outside the door was the mastermind of this whole half-million-dollar embezzlement.

Her fingers were shaky, but with each new keystroke, each fallen firewall, and each file logged and copied and moved, she felt closer.

Finally, she found her way to the original account, where the money had first accrued. Dropped in over a two-year period, taken from government accounts using what she was certain were bogus invoices that got lost in the bureaucracy.

Invoices submitted by a company—a shell company, no doubt.

Her gaze moved to the picture a few inches away, focusing on little Gabriel Rafael Rossi Winter. Finally, the screen flashed, and a new name and account appeared.

Roger Drummand, Primary Account Holder. Please enter password.

The door popped open, and Drummand marched around the desk, staring at the screen. Then the pistol smacked the side of her head, hard. Then again, twice as hard, knocking her right off the chair. She couldn't help grabbing the side of her head now as waves of pain ricocheted around her brain.

"What are you doing?" he demanded.

She looked up at him, vaguely aware that blood trickled from her mouth. "Moving money into your account."

"No, you're not." He yanked her up from the floor and tapped the screen to life. "Where is it? Where is the money?"

Tucked away in a temporary account she'd just made. But first she needed to get into his original account and get a screenshot of the embezzlement proof. She wouldn't quit until she had it. He pushed her further aside, the gun still on her as he tapped the back arrow and landed on the temporary account. "What's the password?" he demanded.

She shook her head.

He stuck the gun in her face. "One second to tell me the password or you die."

"You won't kill me here," she said, seizing a lot of bluster she didn't actually feel. "You won't pull the trigger and kill an innocent American citizen in an office in this place."

"You're right. I won't kill you here." He shoved her to the door. "We have other ways of getting information here at Guantanamo Bay."

She closed her eyes and stumbled to the door knowing exactly what *ways* he meant.

Chapter Twenty-Nine

As two guards escorted him through a series of covered, outdoor pathways through various buildings, Mal forced himself to remember every little thing he knew about this place.

"This way," one of the guards said, the first and only thing out of the young Marine's mouth.

The north end had been like a second home to Mal. That's where they'd worked, where they'd tried to convince terrorists to be double agents.

And then Gabe's voice came back to him.

There's a Beretta Nano stashed in that cubbyhole.

But was it still there? If he could get into the Country Club...he could get out of it, too.

Memories flooded as they turned the corner and headed toward that hall. But there were six holding cells where prisoners waited their turn to go to the Country Club, and the guard slowed enough that Mal knew they were putting him in one of them.

"Have a little mercy, Private Mullins," Mal said to the closest guard. "Gimme the last room on the left."

"That's not a cell."

"There's a real bed in it. You and I both know I could be

here a long time."

"This one, right here." The other man, an Army National Guardsman whose badge said Harcourt, pulled out a key to one of the holding cells.

Mal eyed him. "California or Texas Guard, Corporal?" he asked.

The man ignored him and unlocked the door.

"I was with Maryland Reserves," Mal said. At least that had been his cover when the CIA sent him here.

The guard turned to him. "You're a fucking thief, Harris. Not a soldier. This is where you belong for what you did."

But the other guard, Mullins, moved closer, obviously intrigued. "You're the embezzler?" Mullins asked. "I've heard about you."

"I did my time in a cell for that crime," he said.

The guardsman looked disgusted and backed away. "I'm going to do the paperwork. Lock him in here." He gave the key to Mullins. "And don't leave this hall, Private."

When his footsteps faded, Mullins nodded toward the open door, a wretched stench already wafting out. The cell was less than six by six, with a wooden box the only thing to sit on.

"C'mon, Private," Mal said. "That key works in the last room, and you know as well as I do Corporal Harcourt is going to sit in his office and jack off until he's off duty. He left you with the shit job."

Mullins sniffed and turned his head, the ancient smells of a room where men were held for days with no bathroom still offensive. "No way," Mullins said. "I'm not going to stand out here and suck in that shit."

Mal's spark of hope turned into a full-blown bonfire.

Mullins let him into the Country Club and gave a dry laugh when he looked inside. "Bed's gone, Mr. Harris," he noted, tapping a hideous overhead light. Air conditioning likely hadn't been run since the project closed, leaving a different kind of fetid, moldy stench.

The bed was, indeed, long gone. All that was left in the room were two beat-up leather sofas, a table, and benches along the wall, with wooden tops that lifted for storage.

Storage for secret notes exchanged by an agent and a translator. Storage for porn they gave to the detainees. And, God willing, storage for a Beretta Nano.

"I'll be fine. Thanks." Mal went in, pretending not to be in any rush.

"I'll be out here," Mullins said. "Pound on the door if you need to piss."

He left Mal alone, the thick metal door blocking out any sound of the private's footsteps. Which meant he couldn't hear Mal, either. Not that what he was hoping to do would make any sound.

Without hesitation, Mal walked to the wood slats that covered the benches, going to the spot at the end where he remembered Gabe leaving or retrieving notes for his lover.

Mal put his hand on the last wooden slat and tried to lift it. Nailed shut. Damn it. He yanked again, and again, ignoring the pain in his arm, determined to tear the wood off.

His fingers bled as he worked, sweat streaming and heart pounding, but he finally cracked a slat open enough that he was able to stick his hand in the hole and get a little more leverage. He couldn't get his right arm all the way down without excruciating pain, so he tried his left, biting his lip with the effort.

It had to be there. Had to be. Finally, he bent over and stuck his arm deep in the hidey-hole they'd made, and his fingers grazed…paper.

Not the pistol they'd put there.

He tugged at the slip of paper and pulled it out with two fingers, swearing under his breath. There was something written on the tiny page, probably "suck it, dickhead, I took your gun" in Arabic.

But the words were in English, in a woman's handwriting.

Gabriel, my angel…

He closed his eyes. Guess Gabe missed one. He stuffed it in his pocket, more determined than ever to get home and hand that letter to Gabe.

He shoved his right hand into the hole again, grunting as the jagged wood stabbed his wounded arm and drew more blood. Just as he was about to give up, he heard the lock of his door unlatch—

And his fingers touched the barrel of the gun.

He pushed all the way in and managed to grab the gun, tugging it out and getting it behind his back just as the private walked in.

He stared at Mal and the broken wood.

"We hid porn in there," Mal said coolly. "Figured I might as well pass the time."

Mullins gave him a strange look, but he didn't make any effort to go for his own weapon.

"I'm getting coffee," he said. "You want some?"

Such a nice kid. But probably not nice enough to help him, so Mal would have to make his night duty hell.

"Listen, Private Mullins." Mal walked closer, the pistol in his right hand behind him, but he covered by holding the other hand over his bullet wound. "I really need to see medical."

"I can't take you—"

Mal whipped the gun around and slammed the barrel against the kid's neck, instantly getting his arm and twisting it. He fought, but Mal had adrenaline and determination and years of experience in this kid's shoes on his side. Mal flipped him around in a flash.

"Drop your firearm, or I shoot," Mal said into his ear.

Private Mullins complied immediately.

"Arms out."

Holding the gun steady on Mullins's neck, Mal reached in and took his com device. "Where's your phone?"

"Don't have one."

Liar. They all had them.

"Boots off," Mal ordered, backing away but not taking his aim or eye off the guard.

He obeyed again, and an iPhone fell to the ground.

"Give it to me."

Mullins didn't move. "You won't kill me. I heard about you. You're legend around here."

"Don't push me, kid. Give me the phone."

Mullins dropped slowly, got the phone, and Mal tossed it out the open door. He ripped the keys from Mullins's other hand and didn't wait for one second to let the young guard remember his training.

He closed and locked the door and ran toward the back entrance that only employees knew existed, but just as he stepped outside, he saw a light flicker on and off from the third floor. No one should be up there. Not anymore. That was all over.

No one should be in those hideous, heinous rooms where men had been reduced to animals and treated worse.

The light went out, nearly as fast as he thought it had come on. Was it Mal's imagination? Who could be up there?

The pain in his arm stabbed, like a reminder of the pain that could be inflicted in those rooms. But it wasn't his problem anymore…his problem, the one that mattered most to him, was Chessie.

The light flickered again, and suddenly he knew exactly who could be up there.

Chapter Thirty

It was so cold. Bitter, freezing cold. Not like anything she'd ever felt, even in the worst winter in Boston.

Chained to an iron chair in the dark, Chessie felt a fine mist of icy water fall over her, making her teeth chatter and her bones feel like they could break like icicles.

She barely remembered getting here, with Drummand's gun in her back while he whisked her through what felt like the back alleys of this hellacious prison.

Every inch reeked of death and misery, making Chessie want to hold her breath and force images of torture out of her head. That's what they'd done in this room.

What he was doing to her now.

Starting with the brutal, frigid mist that caused a different kind of pain than she'd ever felt before. The kind that made you want to give up. The kind that made you want to tell anyone whatever it was they wanted to hear just to get relief.

It was pitch dark, impossible to see, except for when it was as bright as looking into the sun, the light right in her eyes, blinding and painful, then it would go black again.

It was the not knowing when it would happen that created the first level of torture. The actual misery wasn't as bad as the anticipation.

"So what exactly were you doing on that computer, Ms. Rossi?"

Drummand's voice kept coming from a different place in the room. He was circling her, and with no light it was impossible to be sure where he'd be next. Behind her. Next to her. Close to her ear.

"M-m-moving money."

"Where?"

She jerked back when the words came at her an inch from her face, and the barrel of that pistol stabbed in her chest.

"T-t-to…your…a-a-account."

She screamed when the light came on, like fire pointed at her eyes, then it was gone, and all she could see was the burning white spot against the black.

"Francesca." He breathed her name into her other ear, the syllables that sounded so poetic when Mal whispered them merely offending her now. "Tell me the password for that account."

And never clear Mal's name? She bit her lip hard, refusing to even think about the simple password she'd just made up.

She'd been so close. She almost proved he'd stolen it, but she'd been one freaking keystroke away when he caught her. One more keystroke, and she would have cleared Mal's name.

Now she'd probably die in this place, and Mal…what would happen to him?

"We can go back there now. Just tell me the password and this"—the blinding light burst like an explosion in her eyes—"will be over."

"I w-w-will if you clear Mal."

He laughed in her face. "Making deals, kiddo? Of course. You've got a pair like your cocky-ass brother." She heard him step away, maybe back to the light, maybe somewhere else.

"The password, Francesca." He flashed the light on and off, on and off, on and off, like a strobe. And then the mist turned into a drenching of freezing misery from above that made her choke and squirm and want to die.

"Tell me the goddamned password!"

She opened her mouth, but it filled with water.

Another light flashed, and something crashed, making her scream again and get another mouthful of water. A gun fired. A man yelled.

Choking, gasping for breath, she tried to see through the downfall of water that poured from some hole in the ceiling. But the water was rushing so loud she couldn't hear what it was or see anything.

Another shot and lights came on. Soft lights. Warm lights. And the water stopped.

"Chessie, oh my God, Chessie." Mal nearly sobbed the word as he fell to his knees in front of her.

"Mal." She fought for breath and sagged forward, the relief of life and air and protection and *him* washing over her with more force than the submersion she'd just experienced.

She looked past him at Drummand, who rolled on the floor, howling in pain, blood oozing from his leg and arm. "Is he…did you…"

"He'll live, unfortunately."

"Then we have to do something. Can you free me? Can you get me back to that computer?"

To his credit, he didn't argue or question her. Just produced a key and went to work unlocking the first cuff.

"Hurry, Mal. Before they come after you."

"I don't care," he said, twisting the lock the way his

broken voice twisted her heart. "I only care about you. That's it. That's all that matters. You."

He released her other hand and immediately she reached for him, throwing her arms around him and pulling him close. He was so warm and so big and so strong and so safe.

Then she pushed him back. "We have to go!" Shaking and fighting shock, she tried to get out of the chair but her legs were wobbly.

"No! Please!" Drummand called out, his hand extended for assistance.

"We'll get help to you," Mal said gruffly, gently helping Chessie up.

"Kill me! Please, please, kill me." He lay helpless, bleeding, and crying. "I'm begging you."

"We'll send help," Mal told him. "Come with me, Chessie."

"No, they'll keep me alive," he sniveled. "I need to die. I have to die. I…can't…face him."

"You should have thought of that before you stole money and laid a hand on her." Still cradling her with one arm, Mal guided Chessie to the door, but she caught one more sight of the pathetic man on the ground.

"I can't face him!" he cried again. "Please, I beg you, one more shot. Right here." He slammed his hand over his heart.

"You want to die so bad?" Mal kicked a gun closer to him, but still out of his reach. "Do your own dirty work, coward."

Without waiting, they charged into the hall and toward the stairs just as they heard one more howl and the loud pop of a gunshot.

Chessie froze for one second, but Mal urged her on, making it to the stairs as an alarm rang somewhere in the distance.

He ignored it. "This way. Back way. Can you run?"

Chessie shoved her wet hair out of her face and nodded, ignoring the freezing cold of her soaked cover-up, her shaking legs, and the blurry world since, once again, her glasses were history. "I can do whatever I have to, Mal. Just get me to that computer."

Footsteps pounded around the next corner, and she fought the urge to gasp, letting Mal pull her against the wall, then into an alcove, silencing her with a look.

Four foot soldiers passed through the opening, headed straight to the building they'd just left. They kept marching without stopping. Relief almost strangled her as they stayed hidden, waited a few heartbeats, then took off again, staying close to buildings, in the shadows.

She recognized the outside of the administration building Drummand had forced her to enter, but Mal kept them well in the back, coming to another back entrance, where he produced keys he must have gotten from Alana.

"Alana!" Chessie remembered. "He put her in a closet."

"We'll get her."

"This first," Chessie said, pushing past him when he unlocked the door and she recognized the hallway.

Fueled by adrenaline, she got ahead of him just as one more alarm screamed and she swore every light in Guantanamo Bay exploded as the search for them must have hit DEFCON 1.

They reached Alana's office, and Chessie practically threw herself at the desk, stabbing at the keyboard, her heart pounding so hard it almost drowned out the alarms.

"How can I get his password in time?" she cried.

Mal lifted the keyboard and pulled out a slip of paper. "Try this."

"Really?" She tapped the string of letters and numbers

with shaking fingers, instantly getting access. "Damn, Mal. You're good."

"We're good."

She wanted to smile at that but she was too busy with this goldmine of incrimination she'd uncovered. She called up the saved files, one after another, and finally found the ones she wanted most: the fake invoices, the offshore account, the money. Roger Drummand's fingerprints were all over his crime.

Outside, thumping footsteps of what had to be an entire regiment of soldiers shook the building they were in, along with shouting and more screaming alarms.

"Hurry, Chess."

Five more keystrokes to move these files. Four. Three.

A gunshot echoed, and the door behind them exploded open, but Chessie touched one key and then—

"Don't move!"

Mal threw himself in front of Chessie, blocking her like a human shield.

"Hands up!"

"You're under arrest!"

"Don't touch her," Mal insisted, still blocking her from the soldiers. "Do not hurt her. She's innocent."

And so are you. Chessie reached around Mal and smashed the last key with a satisfying stab, then lifted her gaze to face more weaponry than she'd ever seen in her life. Mal stood his ground, but one of the soldiers burst forward to grab him.

"Too late, Harris."

No, it wasn't. "Don't lose hope," he whispered to her. "We got this."

"We sure do," she said.

He searched her face, his expression slowly changing

from dread and uncertainty to a slow, warm grin. "You did it." Not a question, she noticed.

"Not bad for a rookie, huh?"

He inched closer, the noise of the soldiers, alarms, and the world that seemed lined up against them fading into the background as he held her gaze.

"Francesca," he whispered. "I love you."

The words stunned her. Maybe they were spoken in the craziness of the moment, but they sounded so completely right. She resisted the urge to say them back, knowing she'd have time. Maybe a lifetime.

Chapter Thirty-One

Sleep faded easily, pulling Chessie from a dream about the Ramos School. A little girl ran around her in circles, laughing and calling Chessie *Mamá*.

She inhaled without opening her eyes, not smelling guava *pastelitos* and bitter espresso, but the sweet air of Barefoot Bay and the masculine scent of her lover still on the sheets. She automatically reached for him, hitting a pillow and empty space.

Blinking into the soft pink glow of dawn, she lifted her head to see Mal silhouetted against the morning sky, standing at the patio rail facing the bay, a cup of coffee in his hand. She took a minute to appreciate the physique she never tired of, his broad shoulders that seemed tailor-made for leaning on, and the way his boxer shorts hung low on narrow hips.

He dragged his hand through his hair, and although she couldn't hear it, she imagined the sigh that lifted and dropped those mighty shoulders. Without hesitation, she rolled out of bed and glanced down at her naked body. Tempting as it was to go to him this way, he was facing the open beach. She pulled open a dresser drawer, snagged the first T-shirt her fingers touched, and slipped it over her head.

It fell to her thighs, covering her enough to pad barefoot to her lover and see what made him sigh.

"I hate when you disappear from my bed," she said, coming up behind him to wrap her arms around his waist and lay her cheek against his strong, warm back.

"I hate disappearing from your bed." He turned enough to bring her around and press a kiss against her forehead. "Coffee?"

He offered her his cup, and she took a big sip. "Poor man's tooth-brushing technique," she joked.

He reached down and kissed her mouth, tasting just as creamy as the morning blend. "Works for me." He leaned back and flicked the shoulder of the T-shirt. "Is this a joke?"

"No, I…" She glanced down and saw what she'd chosen.

Allenwood Federal Correctional Institution

"It has sentimental value," she teased. "Your first gift to me."

"We did have an auspicious beginning." He placed his hand on the words, conveniently located directly over her breast. "And an adventurous middle."

They looked at each other for a long moment, and Chessie broke the silence to say what she suspected they both were thinking. "But what about the end?"

He slid his hand up to tuck it behind her neck and thread his fingers through her hair. "We're doing a good job of dragging that part out, Francesca."

"A week in paradise after what we've been through?" The CIA had kept them in Cuba for what had seemed like an interminable time, long enough for everything to get straightened out. Reports were filed. Investigations launched. Criminal records cleared.

Chessie had been able to make one trip to the school, but it was still a farm with Nestor Ramos saying he was keeping it closed indefinitely. And, of course, Gabe had to be told the sad news about his son, and the fact that they couldn't be here to share his pain had been devastating.

"Anyway." She gave him a poke in the belly. "Christmas is in two days, pal. Nino's pulling out all the stops for your first one."

She had arranged a grand Christmas Eve on the sands of Barefoot Bay. Nino hoped it would cheer up Gabe, and Chessie wanted to roll all thirty-eight Christmases Mal hadn't celebrated into one.

"So, I wouldn't call it dragging anything," she said.

"I can't stay on this island forever," he said on a sigh, making her wonder if that's what he'd been thinking about earlier.

"It would be time for address number forty-three," she said, hating the burn of sadness just saying that brought to her chest. "So the big question is, where is that mailbox going to be?"

"I still can't wrap my head around the fact that I'm free to go anywhere."

"I imagine it's pretty exciting," she agreed. "You could stay here and work for McBain Security."

He lifted a shoulder. "I might if Gabe were staying."

She closed her eyes at the mention of Gabe. So far, he hadn't moved on. He hadn't done much of anything, to be fair, but work out and hide. He'd turned down three new clients, and Uncle Nino was starting to make noise about going back to Boston.

And speaking of Boston. "We, could, um, use you at the Guardian Angelinos?"

"Which sounds like a very cool place to work, but…" He shook his head, his lack of enthusiasm for any of her near-miss plans obvious. "I'm not in the private security business, you know? I'm a spy, and I don't know how to turn that into a life now that it's over."

"I understand. Hell, I empathize. I can't tell you how many times I've thought about that mission we were on and…" She made a face and gave voice to something that had played at the edges of her brain for weeks. "Is it crazy that I kind of want to work for the CIA, too?"

"Not crazy at all. You'd be fantastic, and they'd be lucky to get you."

But she didn't want anyone to *get* her but him. "You could take over Gabe's undercover business if he leaves." It wasn't exactly what she wanted him to do, but maybe they needed a compromise to get this plan off the ground.

Mal gave her a steady look. "Let's stop dancing around this, Chessie. I can go where you go. And I want to. So we can…"

She looked up at him, half aware she was holding her breath. "Plan," she finally said, giving voice to her thoughts.

He fought a smile. "You would like a plan."

Well, of course she would. She shrugged both shoulders as if to say she refused to apologize for who she was. "Half the fun of a plan is making it," she said.

"Is it? Then let's make one. Together."

She wasn't at all sure what he meant, but she felt her arms automatically tighten around his waist. "I imagine it would be filled with contingencies."

"If by contingencies, you mean sex, then, yeah. Loaded with them."

"I actually don't mean sex," she said softly. "I mean…making love."

"It is." He leaned closer and pressed his forehead to hers. "It is making love. Every single time."

The words warmed her, but they still weren't exactly

what she wanted to hear. She knew how she felt about him, but they hadn't been together that long.

She bit her lip. Once he'd said he'd loved her, but that could easily have been a thoughtless burst of appreciation for a masterful hacking job. Since then, he'd shown her, but never said the words.

"So the question isn't where that address number forty-three is," he continued, "but whose name is on my mailbox."

"Malcolm Harris?"

He gave her a look like she should know damn well what he wanted it to say. "I want to feel settled, Chessie."

Okay, enough of this. She narrowed her eyes and wound up her best shot. "*Define* settled."

He laughed softly and pulled her closer. "I can, actually, define settled." He kissed her hair. "It starts with *will you* and ends with *yes*."

"Mal." His name caught in her throat. "Are you…was that…did you—"

"Malcolm! Malcolm Harris!"

They both spun around at the sound of a man's voice from the beach, a punch of frustration nearly knocking her over. Who would interrupt this? He was about to get down on—

"Mr. Drummand?" Shock made Mal's voice waver. "William Drummand?"

What? Chessie stared at the old man who made his way across the sand to approach their private patio. Despite the shock of white hair, narrow shoulders, and ever-so-slight stoop to his shoulders, he moved with surprising grace and determination.

"I was told I'd find you here," the man said, adjusting wire-framed glasses and making Chessie realize just how very little she had on. "I'd like to talk to you. Now."

Chessie inched back, gauging Mal's reaction to a man who was, as he'd told her, a legendary spy…and the father of a man who'd taken his own life after begging them to do it.

"May I come into your villa?" he finally asked, the note of humility surprising Chessie.

She longed to tell him to go away, that he'd just ruined the biggest moment of her life, but Mal nodded slowly. "Yes," he said simply. "You can talk to both of us. We're a team."

A near-naked team. "We should put clothes on," Chessie whispered.

"Come around to the front door," Mal instructed, walking inside with Chessie, where they stood in the bedroom, staring at each other.

"What are you going to say to him?" she asked.

"That his timing sucks." He took her hand and pulled it to his mouth, kissing her knuckles. "We're not done with that conversation, Francesca, but let's hear what he has to say."

She'd rather hear what Mal had to say, but instead she dressed and braced for a meeting with a legend who had every right to hate her.

Mal opened the door to Bill Drummand with absolutely no idea what was about to happen, but he met the other man's level gaze and extended his hand to shake.

"Mr. Drummand." He stepped aside and ushered him into the villa. "It's an honor to meet you."

Drummand gave a wry smile. "I'm not sure if I'd call it an honor to meet you, young man, but some things have to be done in person. May I?" He gestured toward the living room, then headed there without waiting for Mal to answer.

Chessie sat on the sofa, dressed and looking as tense as he felt. Still, she rose and shook their guest's hand, managing a smile at what had to be an incredibly awkward moment.

"Can I get you a cup of coffee?" she asked.

"Absolutely not." Bill sat on the edge of a chair and folded his arms, nodding to silently order Mal to sit across from him.

He wore authority like some men breathed, despite the fact that he had to be past ninety. Mal took the sofa, and Chessie's hand, guiding her right next to him.

"I'm here on a simple mission," Bill said. "And that is to offer you a job with the Central Intelligence Agency."

Mal blinked at the curve ball that almost hit him in the head. "Excuse me? I thought you wanted to talk about your son."

The other man closed his eyes and seemed to pale slightly. "Roger is dead," he said. "And he has no one but himself to blame."

Talk about stating the obvious.

Chessie leaned forward. "Mr. Drummand, I—"

He quieted her with a raised hand. "Nothing he did surprised me. And you have no apologies to make. My son was not a source of pride for me, nor for the intelligence agency I represent. In fact, you've saved us a lot of trouble, harm, and embarrassment." He shook his head slowly. "All to say that Roger's transgressions go even beyond the financial discrepancies that you uncovered in Cuba."

Mal almost snorted. Financial discrepancies?

"And his decisions cost you four years of your life," Bill added, taking the wind out of Mal's indignation. "We are prepared to compensate you for your lost income and offer you any position for which you'd qualify at the agency." He braced his elbows on his knees, peering hard at Mal. "Just a simple yes or no, son. We want you back."

And Mal's brain ticked with many, many responses, none of which was simple.

He glanced at Chessie, who couldn't begin to hide the glow in her eyes. She knew what he wanted—and he wanted this. But that wasn't all he wanted. He wanted a plan. And he wanted her.

He gave her hand a squeeze, and, like always, a thousand words were communicated with just a look. They were such a good team.

"I have a few stipulations," he said.

Bill inhaled and exhaled slowly. "Name them."

"For one thing, I want my criminal record completely erased from every file known to man."

"Done."

Mal nodded. "I want Alana Cevallos fully cleared of any wrongdoing and her children given security and supervision in case the Cuban government goes after her."

"The entire family is one hundred percent protected."

"I want the same protection for Nestor Ramos, along with a generous stipend from the United States government in full support of his education and adoption operation down there, which will now work secretly under the auspices of the CIA until his program is legal."

Chessie's hand tightened ever so slightly.

"We can certainly do that."

Mal swallowed as the next requirement formed in his head. It was so obvious, and suddenly he wanted this so much. "And I would like the government to arrange and expedite the adoption of a young girl in his home named Gabriella."

Chessie's nails dug into his palm now.

"And I want to claim her and adopt her...as ours," he finished with a warm look at a very happy Chessie.

"Mal," she whispered, tears springing. "Thank you."

"We can easily arrange that," Bill said. "I hope that's all."

"It's not." Mal leaned forward. "I would like Francesca Rossi to be given an interview and the opportunity to apply for employment at the CIA and to have that employment be contingent on basing her wherever I am as my partner."

She tried to stay perfectly still, probably to match his command of the conversation, but he could feel Chessie's whole body shiver at that last one. And it gave Mal so much satisfaction, he could have hooted.

Bill Drummand looked at her. "You certainly proved yourself in Cuba, Ms. Rossi. I would welcome you into the agency, assuming you pass all the entrance tests. And you may stay with your...partner. And your adopted daughter."

She beamed. "I'd like that," she said, smiling at Mal. "Any other tricks up your sleeve?"

Bill chuckled and slapped his knees. "I hope not."

"Nope, we're good," Mal said, standing to end the meeting. "I appreciate the fact that you came here yourself."

Bill pushed himself to a slow stand, the move showing his advanced age. "I wanted to meet you both in person," he said. "You've made quite a name for yourselves at the agency."

"We're just getting started," Mal assured him, sliding an easy arm around Chessie as they walked him to the door to say good-bye. As the door latched behind him, he turned to Chessie, whose eyes were bright and smile was even brighter.

"I don't know what to say." She put her hand over her mouth.

"How about I love you?" He pulled her into his chest and held her like he wanted to hold her for the rest of his life. "Because I love you, Francesca Rossi. I love you, and the amazing life we're going to have together, forever. How's that for a plan?"

"That's a great plan." She pulled back, tears streaming now. "And I love you, Mal. Oh, I love you so much."

He kissed her mouth, tasting salty tears and sweet joy.

"Can you finish what you were saying outside?" she asked. "You know, the thing that starts with *will you* and ends with *yes*?"

He laughed and took a step back, dropping to his knee right there in the hallway of their villa. He was surprised at how fast his heart beat and how much he wanted this moment to be perfect.

"Francesca Rossi, I love your spirit and your optimism and your relentless determination. I love the way you make me laugh and refuse to quit anything until you have what you want. I love your fearlessness in the field, your passion in bed, and your fiery spark in life. Will you marry me?"

Very slowly, she knelt down to meet him, pushing her glasses up like she did when she really wanted to stare him down. "Malcolm Harris, I love your strength and courage and heart of pure gold. I love the way you fight to the death for the people you love. I love that you always do what's right, you always go with the flow, and you turn my whole body to helpless mush every time you touch me. Will *you* marry *me*?"

He couldn't speak, so he just kissed her until they rolled to the floor, fell into each other, and both said yes.

Epilogue

Christmas Eve on the beach. It was the stupidest, kitschiest, lame-ass-iest thing he'd ever seen.

Gabe crossed the sand toward the long tables and flickering candles and six billion white lights strung like they were trying to re-create the whole damn Milky Way over Barefoot Bay. The scene was flanked by not one but two giant fake Christmas trees draped in sparkly seashells and topped with trumpet-blowing angel mermaids. Of course, cheery holiday beach tunes were pumped in over the sound system used by wedding parties that frequented the beach.

The pungent aroma of garlic and pesto for a dinner he'd grown up with for Christmas Eve mixed with the sea air instead of cinnamon and firewood. The incongruity of scents he associated with snowy nights in Boston hit his heart like a sour note.

This wasn't tradition, but Nino had killed himself to make it so. Not to mention that half the Rossi family might never speak to Gabe and Chessie again for keeping their cook away on his big night. But Nino had convinced them to stay put in Boston, a move that Gabe knew was for his benefit, and he appreciated the privacy during these dark days.

But tonight wasn't dark enough.

There had to be at least forty people at Nino's traditional Italian Feast of the Seven Fishes with a surfside twist.

With each day of mourning his soul-ripping loss, Gabe felt his chest turn more into any icy dungeon to house his broken heart, and his reason for doing anything simply faded away.

But he'd promised Nino he'd come to the party, mingle with some of the resort guests, staff members, and their families. A play area had been roped off for kids, all of them vibrating with Christmas Eve anticipation, none of them caring that there wasn't a chimney in sight.

"Mr. Gabriel!" Poppy, dressed in a crisp white housekeeping uniform topped with a ridiculous-looking Santa cap, rushed over to him, barefoot like everyone else on the sand. "So good to see you out and about, Mr. Gabriel! Merry Christmas, sir."

She reached out and gave him a squeeze, which he returned with far less enthusiasm. "Merry…*ahem*…Christmas."

She sucked in a furious breath. "That would have cost you a thousand dollars."

"I bet this Italian Christmas is killing you," he teased.

"We worked it out, Nino and me, just like you said we should." She gestured toward the rows of tables. "Tonight is all about his fish. Pasta with fish, salad with fish, rolled-up crepes with fish. Enough fish to empty the ocean. And tomorrow?" She grinned, her smile bright and white against espresso skin. "A Jamaican Christmas, mon! Curry goat, stewed oxtail, and spicy rum, and fruitcake."

"I might have to take Nino's side in the Jamaican-Italian War."

"You haven't tasted my goat."

"Oh, the places I could go with that."

Poppy came closer, sliding her arm under his. "I know you've got a heavy weight on your heart, Mr. Gabriel."

She didn't know what it was, though. No one did. Just the vault, which now consisted of Nino, Chessie, and Mal. Everyone else just thought he was Gabe the Grinch.

"But I have some good news." She added a happy squeeze. "Remember that pretty lady who was staying in Rockrose a little while back? The one who kept asking me about you and took a picture?"

The one who left a trail of heartbreak with her perfume? "I remember."

"She's here, Mr. Gabriel! She's checked back into Rockrose." Poppy beamed with her news. "Would you like to sit next to her at dinner?"

"No."

Poppy's face registered disappointment, but brightened again. "Then you can sit with Mr. Malcolm and Miss Chessie. Have you seen the engagement ring he gave her today?"

"I have not, but I'm sure I'll be blinded by the light."

"They are happy, Mr. Gabriel."

Good for fucking them. "I know. It seems I have a freakish matchmaking ability at this new enterprise."

"For everyone but yourself," she said dryly. "Would you rather I put you next to some of those fancy-pants billionaires? Mr. Nathaniel Ivory and his fiancée, and, of course, my boss, Mrs. Mandy Nicholas and Mr. Zeke. All everyone is talking about is the minor league baseball team they're building to come to Barefoot Bay next year. The Barefoot Bay Bucks. Have you heard?"

"I'm trying really hard, Pop-Tart. But I simply cannot dig up a single shit to give about that."

She let out a put-upon sigh. "I'm going to give you a Christmas Eve pass on that language and tell you this, Mr. Gabriel. You can't steal my joy by wallowing in your sour sad. You have to shake off whatever is eating at your soul and move on. You hear me?"

"I hear you." *But I'm not listening.*

With a quick peck on her cheek, he made his way across the sand and found Chessie and Mal, by way of the bar.

Chessie immediately latched on to Gabe, but he grabbed her left hand.

"Lemme see the rock."

She fluttered her finger, bearing a sizable diamond. Gabe looked over at Mal. "So you took the CIA payout and spent it all on my sister?"

"Not all. We still need a honeymoon."

"In Langley, I hear." Gabe reached over and put his hand on Mal's shoulder, letting go of everything except gratitude to his sister and friend who risked their lives for him. "I'm happy for you. Happy for you both."

"Gabe." Chessie reached for him. "I want you to be happy, too."

"Well, it's never going to happen, Chess, so…" A wave of something strong hit him, the sense of…being watched. Instinctively, he looked up and smacked right into the direct gaze of the blonde.

Her eyes were dark and intense, mysterious, and a shocking contrast to the stick-straight platinum hair that spilled over her shoulders. And there was something about the way she tipped her head in silent acknowledgment. Something challenging. Something tempting. Something that said she defied the odds and mocked her critics.

Not beautiful, maybe not even conventionally pretty, but…

No, damn it. No.

Gabe closed his eyes and put his drink down on the table with enough force to splash some scotch. "Fuck this. I'm not in the mood for Christmas Eve. Give my regards to Nino."

"Gabe—"

But he marched over the sand, making good time, but not good enough. Mal's hand landed on his arm.

"I don't want to—"

"Gabe, I have something from Isadora."

Something else? That rosary with his son's name engraved on it wasn't painful enough? But when he looked down and saw a familiar pale blue slip of paper, his heart slipped sideways.

"I found it in the Country Club when I nabbed that gun. I haven't read it, but I know it's from Isadora to you. I didn't know if I should give it to you or—"

Gabe grabbed it, tore it from Mal's fingers like it was a bone and he was a starving dog. "It's mine," he said.

"I know, I know, but I didn't want to make things worse until you—"

"Leave me alone. Just…leave me alone." Gabe started to walk away, then glanced down at the paper, the fake starlight highlighting the words.

Gabriel, my angel.

Every cell in his body ached to devour her words, but he turned to Mal, whose face reflected the pain in Gabe's chest.

"Hey, man. Thanks," Gabe said, mustering up a smile. "Thanks for what you did in Cuba. And thanks for loving my sister. And thanks for…knowing how important this is." He held up the paper and took a few steps in retreat. "Merry Christmas."

Mal nodded, and Gabe walked slowly away from the

party, as far along the beach as he could go but still have ambient light from the fake stars. Sitting on the cool sand, he opened the note with surprisingly steady hands and brought it to his nose first, the familiar peppery scent transporting him to another beach, another time, another life.

Gabriel, my angel.

He closed his eyes for a moment, not at all sure he could take this. But he had to take it. He had to read one last message from the only women he'd ever love.

I don't know for certain if you'll ever get this letter, but it is the only way I can communicate with you now.

Now? He stared at the words, then looked up to the moon-washed bay, hearing her distinct voice, always soft and sexy no matter which of the ten or twelve languages she spoke fluently rolled off her lips. She could say *I love you* so many different ways, but he'd never gotten tired of hearing it. Although, her natural, flat, Midwestern-toned English was his favorite.

He forced himself to look down and continue, not wanting this last shred of a connection with Isadora to be over too soon.

You will be told that I'm dead. I am not.

And in that instant, the world stopped spinning. And he stopped breathing. Blinking and taking a shaky inhale, he continued to read.

You will be told our son died when he was less than two years old. He did not. I am under deep cover and so is he. I promise you will understand when I explain it to you.

Someday, when I can see you again.

What? He forced himself not to howl. *She was still alive?* And their son? They had proof of her death! And a grave marker of a child. What the hell did this mean?

Vaguely aware that his body was strung as taut as a wire,

he shook his arms and cleared his head before reading on.

Gabriel, wait for me. Promise me you will wait for me. It might be years, but the very moment I am free, I will find you, I will come to you, and I will tell you everything. But I give you my word, on our love, that I am not dead. And neither is Rafe, who is a carbon copy of you in every way.

Rafe. Deep inside his gut, everything hardened. And froze. And made him sick. Was this real? A joke? Ancient history or…a reason to live?

No matter what, my darling angel Gabriel, wait for me. I will come to you as soon as I can. When that day comes, you may not question me. You may not doubt me. And you may not recognize me.

Isadora

The sound of a cleared throat yanked him back to reality and spiked his blood pressure. He turned to see the blonde making her way across the beach, a look of determination on sharp, angular features, her defined jaw lifted as if to say she dared him to send her away.

Ballsy bitch.

But it was Christmas Eve, so rather than be a prick, he just looked down at the letter and hoped she had the brains and class to see he wasn't in the market for a quickie.

"Gabriel."

Son of a bitch, she knew his name. He slammed the letter on the sand as two bare feet with bright red toes planted themselves next to him. "Look, lady, I—"

"Like the angel."

That wasn't an English accent. That was…natural, flat, and Midwestern.

His blood turned to ice and drained from his head into a cold pool of disbelief in his gut. He was hearing things again. She didn't even remotely resemble Isadora. She was taller, leaner, *colder*. Blond-haired and brown-eyed, no chestnut curls and grass-green eyes.

Gabe looked up, completely off-balance and almost unable to breathe again, but when he did, another whiff of her fragrance tortured him. "Do I know you?" he asked.

She just gave him a Mona Lisa smile that said everything…and nothing.

He started to push up, but she held out her hand to stop him, opened it, and dropped a hotel card key in his lap.

Without a word, she walked away.

He sat there in stunned, speechless silence until his gaze dropped to the letter on his lap.

When that day comes, you may not question me. You may not doubt me. And you may not recognize me.

What did she mean by that? He couldn't acknowledge her…or he literally couldn't recognize her?

How the hell was he supposed to know her then? He stood, peering into the darkness to see the blonde's shadow disappear in the direction of the villa called Rockrose.

Everything spun out of control, making his head light with hope that she lived…and fear that his imagination was working overtime.

Who was she? A shameless stranger who wanted his body? Or the woman he loved?

Maybe she could be both.

Watch for Gabriel Rossi's unforgettable love story…

Barefoot with a Bad Boy

Coming in early 2016!

Books Set in Barefoot Bay

The Barefoot Bay Billionaires
Secrets on the Sand
Seduction on the Sand
Scandal on the Sand

The Barefoot Bay Brides
Barefoot in White
Barefoot in Lace
Barefoot in Pearls

Barefoot Bay Undercover
Barefoot Bound (prequel)
Barefoot with a Bodyguard
Barefoot with a Stranger
Barefoot with a Bad Boy (Gabe's book!)

The Original Barefoot Bay Quartet
Barefoot in the Sand
Barefoot in the Rain
Barefoot in the Sun
Barefoot by the Sea

About the Author

Roxanne St. Claire is a *New York Times* and *USA Today* bestselling author of more than forty novels of suspense and romance, including many popular series and stand-alone books. Her entire backlist, including excerpts and buy links, can be found at www.roxannestclaire.com.

In addition to being a six-time nominee and one-time winner of the prestigious Romance Writers of America RITA Award, Roxanne's novels have won the National Reader's Choice Award for best romantic suspense three times and the Borders Top Pick in Romance, as well as the Daphne du Maurier Award, the HOLT Medallion, the Maggie, Booksellers Best, Book Buyers Best, the Award of Excellence, and many others. Her books have been translated into dozens of languages and are routinely included as a Doubleday/Rhapsody Book Club Selection of the Month.

Roxanne lives in Florida with her family and can be reached via her website, www.roxannestclaire.com, her Facebook Reader page, www.facebook.com/roxannestclaire, and Twitter at www.twitter.com/roxannestclaire.

AUG. 2016.

CPSIA information can be obtained
at www.ICGtesting.com
Printed in the USA
LVOW12s0923170716
496666LV00007B/548/P